the retribution of mara dyer

ALSO BY MICHELLE HODKIN

The Unbecoming of Mara Dyer

The Evolution of Mara Dyer

VOLUME 3 OF THE mara dyer TRILOGY

the retribution of mara dyer

MICHELLE HODKIN

SIMON & SCHUSTER BFYR

NEW YORK LONDON TORONTO SYDNEY NEW DELHI

SIMON & SCHUSTER BFYR
An imprint of Simon & Schuster Children's Publishing Division
1230 Avenue of the Americas, New York, New York 10020

Also available in a SIMON & SCHUSTER BFYR hardcover edition
Book design by Lucy Ruth Cummins
The text for this book is set in Caslon.
Manufactured in the United States of America
First SIMON & SCHUSTER BFYR paperback edition November 2015
8 10 9
The Library of Congress has cataloged the hardcover edition as follows:
Hodkin, Michelle.
The retribution of Mara Dyer / Michelle Hodkin.
pages cm
Sequel to: The evolution of Mara Dyer.
Summary: "Loyalties are betrayed, guilt and innocence tangle, and fate and chance collide in this shocking conclusion to Mara Dyer's story"—Provided by publisher.
ISBN 978-1-4424-8423-8 (hc)
[1. Supernatural—Fiction. 2. Love—Fiction. 3. Murder—Fiction. 4. Psychiatric hospitals—Fiction.] I. Title.
PZ7.H66493Ret 2014
[Fic]—dc23
2014017679
ISBN 978-1-4424-8424-5 (pbk)
ISBN 978-1-4424-8425-2 (eBook)

For the bad girls, and the boys who love them

"What is done out of love always takes place beyond good and evil."

—Friedrich Nietzsche, *Beyond Good and Evil*

1

THE EXAMINATION OF MARA DYER WAS TAKEN ON [redacted] at the Horizons Residential Treatment Center for Behavioral Health. 31821 No Name Island, Florida. Video transcript time: 2:13 p.m.

Examination by: Dr. Deborah Kells

Also present: Mr. [redacted]

KELLS: Hello, Mara. My name is Deborah Kells, and this is Mr. ____. We're here because your family says that you have agreed to residential treatment at the Horizons Residential Treatment Center for Behavioral Health on No Name Island,

Florida, just off No Name Key. Is that correct?

[Silence]

KELLS: How much Amytal did you give her?

MR. ____: Forty ccs.

KELLS: Anemosyne?

MR. ____: One hundred micrograms.

KELLS: And the midazolam?

MR. ____: Fifty milligrams. Same as the others. She won't remember any of this.

KELLS: God, she's like a zombie. Mara, Mara—are you awake? Do you understand me?

MARA: . . . Yes.

KELLS: Great. Thank you. Is it correct that you agreed to being treated here?

MARA: Yes.

KELLS: Thank you. Now, if at anytime you don't understand what I'm asking you, just let me know and I'll try to make it clearer, okay?

MARA: Okay.

KELLS: Now, you'll notice that there's a video camera in the room here with us. We want to record this just so we have a record. Is that okay with you?

MARA: Yes.

KELLS: Excellent. Okay, Mara. Let's start with the basics. What is your full name?

MARA: Mara Amitra Dyer.

KELLS: And how old are you?

MARA: Seventeen.

KELLS: Where were you born?

MARA: Laurelton.

KELLS: Where is that?

MARA: Outside Providence.

KELLS: Rhode Island?

MARA: Yes.

KELLS: Thank you. Can you tell me a little about why you're here?

[Silence]

KELLS: She's struggling with the open-ended questions. Can we counteract the Anemosyne?

MR. ____: She might not be as cooperative.

KELLS: Well, she's not exactly cooperative now, is she?

MR. ____: I'll have to do it intravenously—

KELLS: Obviously. Just—

MARA: I hurt people.

MR. ____: Do you still want me to adjust—

KELLS: No, let's see where she goes. Mara, who did you hurt?

MARA: My teacher.

KELLS: What was her name?

MARA: Morales.

MR. ____: Her file says that her teacher, Christina Morales, died of anaphylactic shock in reaction to fire ant bites on [date redacted].

KELLS: Let me see.

MARA: Also a . . . a man. He hurt a dog. I—I—

KELLS: It's okay. Take your time. Just tell us what you remember.

MARA: Rachel.

MR. ____: Rachel Watson, deceased, died Wednesday [date redacted] in Laurelton. Remains discovered at six a.m. with those of—

MARA: Claire.

MR. ____: Claire Lowe, yes, as well as her brother, Jude Lowe—

Mara: Noah.

MR. ____: Noah Shaw? I don't—

KELLS: Quiet.

MR. ____: Sorry—whoa. Did you see that? She just—

KELLS: What else is she on?

MR. ____: The hundred milligrams of Zyprexa, as prescribed prior to intake. It shouldn't interfere.

MARA: [speech unclear]

KELLS: What did she say?

MR. ____: I don't know. Jesus, look—

KELLS: Is she on anything else?

MR. ____: I don't—

KELLS: Is she on anything else?

MR. ____: No. No.

KELLS: Does she have a history of epilepsy?

MR. ____: I don't think so.

KELLS: Well, do you think or do you know?

MR. ____: No— Jesus Christ. Is that a seizure? Is she seizing?

KELLS: Turn off the camera.

MARA: [speech unclear]

KELLS: What did you say, Mara?

MR. ____: I'm going to call—

KELLS: Don't call anyone. Turn off the camera. What, Mara?

MARA: [speech unclear]

MR. ____: Did she just say our names? Did she just say—

KELLS: TURN OFF THE CAMERA.

MR. ____: Oh, God—

[End video examination, 2:21 p.m.]

2

THE FIRST FACE I SAW WHEN I OPENED MY EYES WAS my own.

The wall in front of the iron bed was mirrored. So were the walls to my right and left—there were five mirrors, or six maybe. I smelled nothing, heard nothing, saw nothing but me.

During the past several months, I hadn't spent much time looking in mirrors, for reasons. Now that I was forced to, I couldn't quite believe that the girl I was seeing was me. My dark, thick hair was parted in the middle, and it hung limp and dull over thin shoulders. My lips were almost the same color as my skin—that is to say, white. There were angles to my face that I'd never noticed before. Or maybe they hadn't existed before. I was looking at a ghost, a shell, a stranger. If my parents saw me, they would never know who I was.

But they never did see me. That was part of the problem. That was why I was here.

"Yeah, we look like shit," said a voice.

Said *my* voice.

But I hadn't spoken. My lips hadn't moved.

I bolted upright, looking at my infinite reflections. They stared back, looking panicked and wary at once.

"Up here."

The voice was above me. I craned my neck—the ceiling was mirrored too. I saw my reflection in it, but this one, this reflection, was smiling at me. Even though I wasn't smiling.

So. I'd finally lost it.

"Not yet," my reflection said, looking amused. "But you're close."

"What—what is this?" A hallucination?

"Not a hallucination," my reflection said. "Guess again."

I dropped my gaze for a moment, glancing around the room. Every other reflection turned when I did. God, I hoped I was dreaming.

I looked back up at the reflection above me. The girl in the mirror—me, I guess—tilted her head slightly to the left. "Not quite. You're in that kind-of-unconscious-kind-of-not space. Which should make you feel better about your sanity."

Marginally.

"Also, you should know that there are sensors monitoring our pulse and heartbeat, so it would be better for both of us if you'd lie back down."

I swung my head, looking for the monitors, but didn't see any. I listened to the girl anyway.

"Thanks," she said. "That Wayne guy comes in and examines us whenever our heart rate spikes, and he really creeps us out."

I shook my head, the papery pillowcase crinkling with the movement. "Don't say 'us.' That creeps *me* out."

"Sorry, but it *is* us. I'm you," my reflection said, arching an eyebrow. "I'm not exactly your biggest fan either, you know."

I've had weird dreams. I've had weird hallucinations. But weird didn't even begin to touch this, whatever this was. "So, what are you? My . . . my subconscious or something?"

"You can't talk to your subconscious. That's stupid. It's more like—I'm the part of you that's aware even when you don't know you're aware. She's been giving us a lot of drugs—a *lot* of drugs—and it's dulled our—sorry, *your*—awareness in some ways and heightened it in others."

"'She' being . . . ?"

"Dr. Kells."

The machine beside me beeped loudly as my heart rate spiked. I closed my eyes, and an image of Dr. Kells rose in the blackness, looming above me, so close that I could see tiny cracks in her thick layers of lipstick. I opened my eyes to make her go away, and saw myself instead.

"How long have I been here?" I asked out loud.

"Thirteen days," the girl in the mirror answered.

Thirteen days. That was how long I'd been a prisoner in my own body, answering questions I didn't want to answer and doing things I didn't want to do. Every thought and memory was fuzzy, as if they were smothered in cotton; me, locked in what looked like a child's bedroom, drawing picture after picture of what used to be my face. Me, extending my arm obediently while Wayne, Kells's assistant in therapeutic torture, drew my blood. And me, the first day I woke up here, held captive by drugs and forced to listen to words that would change my life.

"You've been a participant in a blind study, Mara."

An experiment.

"The reason you've been selected for this study is because you have a condition."

Because I'm different.

"Your condition has caused pain to the people you love."

I've killed them.

"We tried very hard to save all of your friends. . . . We just couldn't get to Noah Shaw."

But I did not kill Noah. I could not have killed him.

"Where are they?" I asked my reflection. She seemed confused, then looked at the mirror on my right. Just a normal mirror, I thought, but then the glass went dark.

An image of a girl, or something that had once been a girl, materialized out of the blackness. She was kneeling on carpet, her black hair falling over her bare shoulders as she leaned over something I couldn't see. Her skin glowed bronze, and shadows flickered over her face. She was blurred and indistinct, as if someone had spilled a glass of water over a painting of her and the colors had started to run. And then the girl lifted her chin and looked directly at me.

It was Rachel.

"It's just a game, Mara." Her voice was scratchy. Distorted. When she opened her mouth again, the only sound that came out was static. Her smile was just a smear of white.

"What's wrong with her?" I whispered, looking at Rachel's flickering image in the glass.

"Nothing's wrong with her. I mean, aside from the fact that she's dead. But there *is* something wrong with your memory of her. That's what you're seeing—your memory."

"Why does she look like—" I didn't even know how to describe it. "Like that?"

"The flickering? I think it's the candles. The three of us lit them before taking out the Ouija board. Don't tell me you've forgotten that?"

"No, I mean she's—she's—distorted." Rachel's arms moved in front of her, but her hands were dipped in shadow and I couldn't see what she was doing. Then she lifted one of them to her nose. Her arm ended at her wrist.

The girl in the mirror shrugged. "I don't know. Not all of your memories are like this. Look left."

I did, expecting the new mirror I was staring at to go dark too. It didn't—not at first. I watched my reflection as the ends of my hair bled from dark brown to red, until it was red to the roots. My face filled out and rounded, and the eyes that stared back at me from the glass were Claire's.

Claire sat up, and her image split off, separated from mine. She walked out of the white surgical gown I wore, and black threads wove around her pale, freckled body, until she was clothed in the dark jeans and puffy coat she'd been wearing the night we went to the asylum. The bright light in the mirrored room flickered and went out. Roots cracked the concrete floor beneath my bed. They grew into trees that scratched the sky.

Claire looked over her shoulder at me. "Oh my God. She's freaking out already."

When Claire spoke, her voice was normal. She wasn't blurry, and she didn't flicker or warp. She was whole.

"I don't know what it means either," the reflection above me said. "Jude is the same."

My mouth went dry at the sound of his name. I glanced up and followed her gaze to the mirrored wall to my right; Jude appeared in it. I saw him standing in the center of a manicured Zen garden, with huddled, hunched people arranged around him like rocks. Jamie and Stella were among them. He held

Stella by her shining black hair. I could see the veins in his hands, the pores in his skin. Every feature, every detail of him was clear. Sharp. I felt a flare of rage.

"Don't," my reflection said. "You'll wake us up."

"So what?" I said. "I don't want to see this." I never wanted to see him again. But when I looked again, there was a different image of him in the mirror. He was pushed against a bare white wall, a hand gripping his throat. The hand belonged to me.

I looked back up at the ceiling and the girl in it. I didn't want to remember Horizons, or what had happened to me since. I looked down at my wrists, at my ankles. No restraints. "Just tell me how to get out."

"They don't need restraints to keep us chained up," she said. "The drugs do that for them. They make us compliant. Willing. But they're changing us too, I think. I don't know how yet, but it has to mean something, that your memory of Rachel is broken but your memories of Claire and Jude aren't."

"What about my brothers? My parents?" *And Noah*, I thought but didn't say.

As I spoke, images of each of them filled the mirrors around me. Joseph was wearing a suit with a pocket square, rolling his eyes at someone. Daniel was laughing in his car, making a face at me from behind the wheel. The image of my mother showed her sitting on her bed, laptop on her lap, her face drawn and worried. My father was sitting up in his hospital bed, eating a contraband slice of pizza. And Noah—

Noah's eyes were closed, but he was breathing. Sleeping. One of his hands was curled in a loose fist by his face, and his T-shirt, the one with the holes in it, was twisted, exposing a sliver of skin above his boxers. This was how he looked the morning after I told him what was wrong with me. After we figured out what was wrong with us.

I couldn't stop looking at them—the people I loved, laughing and talking and living behind silvered panes of glass. But as I did, I realized something wasn't right. I looked closely at Noah. He was sleeping, not moving, which made it easier for me to finally see. His edges were faded. Blurred. I glanced back at the images of my parents, my brothers. Their edges were soft too.

"We're losing them, I think," the girl said. "I don't know why, but I think Kells does, and I think she's doing it on purpose."

I was only half-listening. I couldn't stop staring at the mirrors.

"I'm never going to see them again, am I." It wasn't a question.

"My sources say no."

"You know," I said to her, "you're kind of an asshole."

"Well, that would explain why we're so popular. Speaking of, Jamie and Stella are here too. In case you were curious."

"Have you seen them?"

She shook her head. "But Wayne mentioned 'Roth' once, and 'Benicia' twice, to Kells. And he talked about them in the present tense."

I swelled with relief. My throat tightened and ached and I felt like I might cry, but no tears came. "What about Noah?" I blurted out the question before I could think about whether I really wanted the answer.

The girl knew. "Kells mentioned him once."

But my question had gone unanswered. And now I had to know. "Tell me what she said."

"She said—"The girl didn't finish her sentence. Something hissed and clicked behind me, and she went still.

"What?" I asked. "What did she say?"

She didn't answer. When she spoke again, her voice shook. "They're here," the girl said, and then she was gone.

3

UNTIL THAT MOMENT I HADN'T BEEN SURE IF I was awake or hallucinating. But now the sounds I heard seemed very real. Too real. The click of high heels on the linoleum floor. The rush of air as a door opened somewhere behind my head. I glanced at myself in the ceiling. Opened my mouth. My reflection did the same thing.

So I was alone now, definitely. I might not have been sure what was real and what wasn't, but I knew that I didn't want Kells to know I was awake. I squeezed my eyes shut.

"Good morning, Mara," Dr. Kells said crisply. "Open your eyes."

And they opened, just like that. I saw Dr. Kells standing beside my bed and reflected in front of me hundreds of times in the small, mirrored room. Wayne was beside her, large and puffy and sloppy, where she was slim and polished and neat.

"Have you been awake long?" she asked me.

My head shook from side to side. Somehow, I don't know how, it didn't feel like I was the one who shook it.

"Your heart rate spiked not long ago. Did you have a bad dream?"

As if I weren't *living* a bad dream. She looked genuinely concerned, and I'm not sure I'd ever wanted to hit someone as much in my entire life.

The urge was sharp and violent and I enjoyed it while it lasted. Which wasn't very long. Because as soon as I felt it, it thinned. Vanished, leaving me cold and hollowed out.

"Tell me how you're feeling," Kells said.

I did. It didn't matter that I didn't want to. I didn't have a choice.

"I want to run some tests on you. Is that all right?"

No. "Yes," I said.

She took out a composition notebook. My handwriting was on the front of it, my name. It was my journal, the one I was supposed to write my fears in, at Horizons. From days ago. Or weeks, if what my reflection had said was true.

"You remember this, don't you, Mara?"

"Yes."

"Excellent," she said, and smiled genuinely. She was pleased that I remembered, which made me wonder what I might have forgotten.

"We're going to work on your fears together today. G1821—the genetic condition that's harming you, remember?—causes your ability to flare. Different factors switch it on. But at the same time, it switches *off* a different part of you." She paused, studying my face. "It removes the barrier between your conscious thought and your unconscious thought. So to help get you better, Mara, I want to be sure I can prescribe you the accurate dosage of medication, the variant of Amytal you're being given—Anemosyne, we call it. And in order to see if it's working, we're going to trigger the fears you recorded in this journal. Sort of like exposure therapy, combined with drug therapy. Okay?"

Fuck you. "Okay."

Wayne opened a case he'd been carrying and laid out the contents on a small tray next to the bed. I turned my head to the side and watched, but then wished that I hadn't. Scalpels, syringes, and needles of different sizes gleamed against the black fabric.

"We are going to measure your response to your fear of needles today," she said, and on cue Wayne lifted a plastic-capped cylinder. He pinched the cap between his fingers and twisted it. The seal broke with a loud *snick*. He fitted the needle onto a large syringe.

"You've certainly seen plenty of these, considering your

time in hospitals, and judging from your records, your instinct is to fight back when touched nonconsensually by medical professionals," she said, raising her penciled brows a fraction. "You punched a nurse on your first hospital stay in Providence after the asylum incident, in response to being touched and forcibly held." She looked down at a small notepad. "And then you hit the nurse at the psychiatric unit in the hospital when you were admitted after you attempted suicide."

At that moment two images competed for space in my mind. The first one was sharp and clear, of me standing alone on a dock and taking the shining blade of a box cutter to my pale wrists. In the other image, blurred and soft, the outline of Jude stood behind me, whispering into my ear, threatening me and my family until the box cutter bit deep into my skin.

My mind clamped down on the second image, the one with Jude. I hadn't tried to kill myself. Jude had just tried to make it look like I had. And Kells, somehow, was trying to make me forget it.

Wayne bent down then and withdrew something from below the bed, beyond my range of vision. He stood up, holding a complicated-looking system of leather and metal restraints. Shackles, really. Still no fear.

But then Kells said, "Just relax."

Her words echoed in my mind, in someone else's voice.

Just relax.

There was a little flip in my chest, and the monitor beside

my bed beeped. I didn't understand. Was it the words? A bead of sweat rolled down Wayne's forehead. He wiped it away with his sleeved forearm, then moved his thick fingers to the crook of my elbow. My mind flinched and my muscles went tense.

Wayne seemed to feel it. "Are you sure—are you sure she's stable?" He was nervous. Good.

Kells looked at my arm. "Mara, I want your body, your arms, and your hands to go limp."

As soon as the words left her mouth, they did. I looked at myself in the ceiling mirror. My expression was slack.

"When you see something you're afraid of, your mind tells your body to react. It tells your kidneys to release adrenaline, which makes your heart rate increase, and your pulse, and your rate of breathing. This is to prepare you to run away from, or to fight, the thing you're afraid of, regardless of whether that fear is rational. In your case fear triggers your anomaly. So what we're doing is making sure that the medicine we've developed to help you is doing what it's supposed to, which is to separate your mental reactions from your physical reactions. The main goal, of course, is total aversion—blocking the pathway that transforms your . . ." She rubbed a thumb over her bottom lip as she searched for words. "Negative thoughts," she finally said, "into action. Anemosyne doesn't *prevent* your thoughts, but it prevents the physical consequences of them, rendering you as harmless as a non-carrier. Now turn her," she said to Wayne.

Wayne swallowed, his jowls trembling with the movement as he took me by the shoulders and began to turn me over. At some point an attachment had been fitted to the bed that allowed me to lie on my stomach without craning my neck to either side. I stared at the floor, grateful that it too wasn't mirrored. At least I wouldn't have to watch.

My ankles were strapped down. He positioned each arm so that it hung over the side, then shackled my wrists together, like I was hugging the bed.

"Show her the syringe," Dr. Kells said to him.

Wayne moved the needle in front of my eyes, letting me see it from every angle. My heartbeat sped up, and with it, the monitor.

"Should her heart be beating like that?" Wayne asked nervously.

"Just a reflex," Kells explained. "Her body is still capable of responding to reflexes, but her emotions, her fear, can't trigger her ability regardless of what she thinks," she said matter-of-factly. "Consciously or subconsciously."

Wayne lifted the back of the white hospital gown they'd dressed me in. I didn't want him touching me, but I couldn't do anything about it.

Then something scraped, slid toward me on the floor. A mirror. It showed me my face, which was white and bloodless, and in the ceiling mirror I saw my exposed back. I looked thin. Unhealthy.

I didn't want to see whatever it was they were going to do to me, and that I *could* do something about. I squeezed my eyes shut.

"Open your eyes," Dr. Kells said, and I did. I had to, and I hated it.

She angled the mirror, and I watched as Wayne took a cotton ball from the metal stand beside the bed and drenched it in iodine. I flinched when he rubbed it on my back.

He noticed. "What does that mean?"

"Just a reflex," Kells said, her voice thin. Exasperated. "To the cold," she said to him. Then to me, "If I were to hit your knee with a hammer, Mara, it would jerk. It's just your response to fear that we're trying to dull. If we're successful, you'll be able to live a normal, productive life unhindered by your irrational fears, and without having to worry that you will unintentionally will consequences that could be disastrous for the people you love and others."

I vaguely remembered that I used to care about that.

"We're going to extract some of your spinal fluid first," Kells said, and Wayne positioned the needle closer to my skin. "This will only hurt a little."

Every movement from that moment on was processed in slow motion. The needle as Wayne allowed it to hover just millimeters from my skin. The feel of cold steel piercing my skin, first a pinch; then, as it went deeper, a sting, an ache, a burn, and I wanted to thrash but I didn't move, couldn't move.

Kells told me to watch my face in the mirror, and I did. It was still blank. A mask of skin hiding every feeling. My mind screamed but my mouth stayed shut.

There was pressure as the syringe sucked fluid from my spine. "You're doing very well," Kells said, her voice toneless. "Isn't this better, Mara? There's nothing to be afraid of. It's just a needle and it's only pain. Pain is just a feeling, and feelings aren't real."

After what felt like hours Wayne withdrew the needle, and the pressure stopped but the pain didn't. Something cold and wet trickled slowly down my skin before Wayne pressed a piece of gauze to absorb it. My breath was deep and even. I didn't gasp, I didn't throw up. I'd thought those were reflexes. Guess not.

Wayne cleaned up my back, unshackled my wrists, unbuckled the straps from my ankles, and then gently, in a way that made my mind sick, turned me over onto my back.

"I know that wasn't pleasant for you, Mara," Kells said. "But despite your internal discomfort, it was a very successful test. What the drug is allowing you to do right now is separate your mental reactions from your physical reactions. The side effect, though, is also quite exciting." She didn't sound excited at all.

"I'm sure you wanted to react during that procedure. I'm sure you wanted to scream and probably cry. But thanks to the drug, your physical reflexes will remain intact, but they're divorced from your emotions. In other words, with Anemosyne, if someone chops onions near you, or if an eyelash is stuck in your eye, you'll still tear in response to stimuli. Your eyes will try to flush out the irritant. But you'll no longer cry because of fear, or because of sadness or frustration. It severs that connection to prevent you from losing control." She hovered over me. "I know it's a strange sensation for you now, but you'll adapt. And the benefit to you, and others, will be enormous. Once we settle on the appropriate dosage for you, we'll need to boost your infusions only every few months. You'll eventually be able to go home to your family, come to therapy with me, and have the normal life that you wanted, as this drug keeps working." She reached out to smooth my hair in what I supposed was meant to be a maternal gesture, and I felt the urge to bite her.

"We're going to give you another drug now so that you won't even remember today's unpleasantness. Won't that be nice?" A smile snaked across her lips, but then her eyebrows pinched together. "Wayne, what's the current room temperature?"

Wayne moved over to the left, pressing a spot on the mirrored wall with his thumb. Numbers appeared in the glass. Fancy.

"Seventy degrees."

Kells pressed the back of her hand to my forehead. "She's hot. And sweating." She wiped her hand on the blanket.

"Is that . . . normal?"

"It's atypical," Kells said. "She hasn't reacted this way to any of the previous tests."

Previous tests? How many had there been?

Kells withdrew a penlight from her pocket and said to me, "Don't squint."

I didn't squint. She shined the light into my eyes; I wanted to close them but couldn't.

"Her pupils are dilated. I don't understand. The procedure's over." Her voice wavered just slightly. "Wayne, the Amylethe, please?"

He withdrew something from the black case. Another needle. But he must have been sweating too, because he fumbled with it. It fell to the floor and rolled.

"Christ," Kells muttered under her breath.

"Sorry, sorry." He reached for a new syringe but stopped when the monitor by the bed beeped.

Kells looked over at it. "Her blood pressure's falling. She's having some kind of reaction. Could you be any slower?"

I'd never heard her sound anything less than completely composed. But looking at her now, her body was tense. The tendons in her neck were corded. I was probably imagining it, but I could practically smell her fear.

She was terrified. Of me? For me? I didn't know, but I liked it.

Wayne clenched his jaw shut and unscrewed the cap on

the syringe. He reached for my arm and stabbed my shoulder with the needle.

My vision swam, and my head went thick. "Take her to the examination room," was the last thing I heard before I blacked out.

4

BEFORE

India, Unknown Province

THE DAY AUNTIE DIED, OUR NEIGHBORS WATCHED warily as we walked from the village bearing her body. The air was as dead as she was; the river sickness had taken her just days after Uncle had brought me home. Auntie had been the only reason they'd tolerated him, in his different clothes, always blue, with his different words and different looks. She'd been special, Uncle had told me. When she would assist at a birth, the baby would rush out of its mother's womb to meet her. Without her we were unprotected. I did not understand what he meant until he died.

Word of us spread from village to village. Wherever we went, plague and death had already struck, and we followed in its wake. Uncle did his best for the people, sharing remedies, making poultices, but whispers followed in our footsteps. *Mara,* they called us. Demons.

One night Uncle roused us from sleep and told me and Sister to leave at once. We must not ask questions, just obey. We crept from our hut in darkness, and once we set foot in the jungle, we heard his scream.

A column of smoke rose in the air, carrying his cries with it. I wanted to go to him, to fix it, but Sister said that we'd promised not to, that we would suffer the same fate if we did. I had taken nothing but my doll. I would never leave it behind.

My long, tangled hair stuck to my neck and shoulders in the damp nighttime heat as Uncle's screams were replaced with the sounds of the forest, rising with the moon. We did not sleep that night, and as the sun broke through the clouds and hunger gripped my belly, I thought we would have to beg for bread, like the orphans. But we did not. Sister spoke to the trees, and they gave up their fruit for her. The ground gave up its water. The earth nourished us, sustained us, until we reached the city.

Sister took me straight to the tallest building at the port to see the man with glasses. He called himself Mr. Barbary, and Sister walked straight toward him. We were dirty and tired and looked very much like we did not belong.

"Yes?" he said when we stood before his desk. "What is it you want?"

Sister told him who she was, who her father had been. He saw us with new eyes.

"I did not recognize her. She has grown."

"Yes," I said. "I have."

I had never spoken to him before, or anyone except Sister and Uncle. I had never needed to. But I knew why we were here, and I wanted to impress him.

It worked. His eyes grew wide, and his smile spread beneath the funny bow of hair above his lip. "Why, she talks!"

I could do more than that.

He asked me questions about what had happened to us, and about other things too—what I had learned since I had last seen him, what talents I had developed, whether I had fallen ill. Then he measured how much I'd grown. After, he gave Sister a pouch, and she bowed her head in gratitude.

"I must inform her benefactor of your change in circumstances, you understand," he explained.

Sister nodded, but her face was a mask. "I understand. But her education has not yet been completed. Please inform him that I will take over for my father, if I am allowed."

Mr. Barbary nodded and then excused us, and Sister led me out of the building by my hand. I wondered at how she knew the city so well. She had never come with Uncle and me before.

Sister paid a man to find us lodging, and then she bought us clothes, fine clothes, the sort Uncle used to wear. She purchased a meal for us to eat in our room.

It was like nothing I had ever seen, with tall beds carved from trees that were dressed in linens as soft as feathers. Sister washed me and dressed me, and then we ate.

"We will leave after dark," she said, scooping up fragrant yellow rice with her bread.

As my belly filled, I began to feel pleasant and drowsy. "Why not stay?" The room was solid, empty of dust and drafts, and the beds looked so clean. I longed to bury myself in one.

"It is better to go unnoticed for as long as we can, until we find a new home."

I did not argue. I trusted Sister. She had taken care of me when I was little, as she would take care of me until she died.

It happened long after Uncle had been killed, though I don't know how long. Time held no meaning for me—it was marked only by my visits to Mr. Barbary for inspection. Uncle kept no calendars, and neither did Sister. I did not even know my age. We moved along the outskirts of villages like ghosts, until we were driven even from the fringes. Then we moved to the next.

"Why must we keep moving?" I asked her as we walked. "Why won't they let us stay?"

It was envy, Sister said. The people we lived among were not gifted like us. They were as ordinary as blades of grass, but we were like flowers, beautiful and rare. They suspected our differences and hated us for it. So we had to pretend to be what we were not, so we would not be harmed for what we were.

But they harmed us anyway. No matter how hard we tried to remain unseen, someone would always recognize or suspect us. On our third day in the most recent village, they took Sister as night fell, the way they'd taken Uncle. The way they tried to take me.

Arms pinched my flesh and I was grabbed from my mat. Sister was screaming, begging them not to hurt me, swearing to our innocence, our harmlessness, but before I was even properly awake, her words were cut short. A man had smashed a rock into her head. Just once, but it had been enough.

I went slack in the arms of my captor as the same man raised the rock again to hit me with it. I wanted him to die.

His body shuddered, and something ripped inside him, sending a torrent of blood from his nose. He dropped his rock and moaned, backing away from me.

The others backed away as well. I did not speak to them. I did not scream at them. I looked at Sister, her mouth slack, her body limp, her hair glistening with blood, and I wanted.

I wanted them to feel as she felt. I wanted them to never see another sunrise, since she would not either.

I sat beside her, cradling her crushed skull in my lap. The others formed a wide circle around us. Then someone threw a stone.

It missed me. And struck someone else.

Shouts erupted, and the air filled with fear. The village emptied that night as the men—the murderers—fled, taking their women and children with them.

I saw tools but ignored them. I began to scoop dirt with my hands, and buried Sister when I finished digging her shallow grave, right where she had fallen. I slept there until the following day. Even the insects did not disturb me. When I woke, I began walking to Calcutta alone. I passed the scattered bodies of the villagers on my way. The skin above their lips was smeared with blood, but the flies did not touch them. They did not dare.

I avoided people. I bathed in my bloody, simple shift. The forest would not give up its gifts for me, so I skirted villages and stole from them to eat. I was ignorant of everything but my loneliness. I missed Sister, and Uncle, too, in my way. But they were gone now, and all I had left of them and my life with them was ash and dust and the doll Sister had made me, and the words Uncle had given me, taught me, so that I could speak with my benefactor in England someday.

Someday had arrived.

I walked to the port, to Mr. Barbary, unaccompanied for the first time in memory. He took in my stained clothes and my matted hair. I looked like a wild thing, but I spoke as cleanly and crisply as he did, and in his own tongue at that. I told him my education was complete. He sent me to an inn nearby, and would fetch me when my passage to England had been arranged, he said.

I bathed in clean water that night, and scrubbed my body with milled, formed soap, a luxury I had learned of but not experienced. I marveled at the foam on my skin, the lather in my hair, and when I was finished, I climbed into bed naked, and let the air dry my body. I felt as though I had shed my skin like a snake, and this new skin would carry me to my new life.

The next day Mr. Barbary appeared at the door to inform me that my benefactor had died the previous week, but not to worry as he had provided for me in the event of his death. His widow had been informed of my existence and had agreed to take me in, as he would have someday. Mr. Barbary had booked my passage on the first available ship. It would leave the following week, and I was to entertain myself until then.

And I did. He left me a purse with my own coins, and I bought new clothes and food I did not have to prepare. My body softened after a week in the city, after stuffing myself whenever I wanted with glistening, steaming sweet and spicy foods.

The night before I was to leave, I laid my new things in my new small trunk with great care. I took out my doll from beneath my pillow, where I hid her during the day. I ran my fingers over her seams, touched the spot of Sister's blood that marked her wrist, and wondered what shape my new life without Sister would take.

"Why does the white man pay for me?" I had once asked Uncle, after a trip to Calcutta for my inspection. The coins jingled with his steps.

"Because he believes you are valuable. And when you go to him, you will be."

I took this in. "When will I go?"

"When you become," Uncle said.

"Become what?"

"Yourself."

But if I am not myself yet, then who am I? I thought.

5

THE FIRST THING I NOTICED WHEN I WOKE UP WAS that I was covered in blood.

The second thing I noticed was that this didn't bother me the way it should have.

I didn't feel the urge to scream or speak, to beg for help, or even to wonder where I was. Those instincts were dead, and I was calm as my wet fingers slid up the tiled wall, groping for a light switch. I found one without even having to stand. Four lights slammed on above me, one after the other, illuminating the dead body on the floor just a few feet away.

My mind processed the facts first. Male. Heavy. He was lying facedown in a wide, red puddle that spread out from beneath him. The tips of his curly black hair were wet with it. There was something in his hand.

The fluorescent lights in the white room flickered and buzzed and hummed. I moved to get a better view of the body. Its eyes were closed. It might have been only asleep, really, if it weren't for the blood. There was so much of it. And by one of the hands the blood was smeared into a weird pattern.

No. Not a pattern. Words.

PLAY ME.

My gaze flicked to the hand. The fist was curled around a small tape recorder. I moved the fingers—still warm—and pressed play. A male voice started to speak.

"Do I have your attention?" the voice asked.

I knew that voice. But I couldn't believe I was hearing it.

"Noah's alive," Jude said.

He had my attention now.

"And you don't have much time. You probably recognize the dead man on the floor as Wayne Flowers. I'm the one who killed him, in case you were wondering. The good news is that he's one of two people with access to Dr. Kells's office—the other one being Dr. Kells. The bad news is that in order for you to get that access, and get out of this room, you're going to need to cut out his left eye."

What *was* this? A trick? A trap?

"I would've done it for you but there wasn't time. I switched the syringe, the one they shot you with before your spinal tap.

That's why you had a . . . reaction . . . when they examined you, which—that was really freaky, by the way. Anyway, whatever. There's a retinal scanner above her office door, top right corner, just like there is above this one. All the doors in this place auto-lock. When you have the eye, hold it a few inches above where yours are—he was taller than you. There *is* a video camera—they're everywhere, can't help that, she'll see you, but she'll see you wherever you are. Wherever you are, except in this room. There are no records made of anything that happens in this room. That's why I dosed you before she took you in here, slipped in before Wayne could get out. I would've taken you too but you wouldn't let me near you. Anyway, once you're in Kells's office, the door will lock behind you. You can get out using Wayne's eye.

"In her office should be everything you're looking for. Your files—the real ones, not the bullshit cover-their-ass fake stuff. There's stuff about your friends; they're here too, by the way. I'm getting them out while you're listening to this. Once the tape ends, get to Kells's office, grab what you need, and get out. The map in there will show you how to get off the island. Kells will either already be gone or— I—I—had to let her go. I'm sorry. But you should have enough time to get out before she can manually set the lockdown. I'll get your friends out. Noah will be waiting for you." He coughed hard. "Also, I left my watch for you. It's in Wayne's other hand. Get it before you—before you go.

"And, I know there's no reason you should trust me. I've done— I—can't talk about it. Sick shit." He coughed again. It was deep and wet, and he was breathing hard when he spoke again. "I can't talk about it. I don't know how long I'll be like this, be me, or if this is even me anymore, but whatever. I might as well— I want to say— I'm not going to say I'm sorry—'sorry' doesn't mean anything when you can't promise not to do it again, and I can't promise. I'm just—I'm going to leave you alone now. I promise."

The tape went silent. I was silent. I stared at the recorder, my lips parted and my body still.

"Sorry about the message in blood thing, by the way."

I startled at the sound of Jude's voice on the tape again.

"There was nothing else to write with."

Then it clicked off.

Maybe I was in shock, because I wasn't panicking, or screaming, or shaking, or even scared. My mind kept repeating two words, over and over and over again.

"Noah's alive."

But Jude was the one who'd said it.

I didn't know whether I should believe him, but I did know that I wanted to. Part of me was terrified to let myself hope, but another part of me couldn't help it. My mind seized on the possibility like a shark on a seal, and then I rewound the tape and listened to Jude's words again.

"Noah will be waiting for you."

All I had to do was get out of this room.

"You're going to need to cut out his left eye."

All I had to do was cut out Wayne's left eye.

I looked over at him, a hump of bloodied flesh on the floor, his wire-rimmed glasses askew on his face. His eyes opened behind them.

"Fuck!" My heart exploded and I covered my mouth to keep from screaming. It was the first normal reaction I'd had since waking up in here. "Fuck," I said again. Wayne's small, piggy eyes followed my every movement. He was alive. Conscious.

"Are you serious," I whispered. A gurgly groan erupted from his throat.

I was rooted to the spot, but I needed to not be. I was locked in a room with not-dead Wayne, and the only way out was to use his eye to trick the retinal scanner into releasing me.

But if he was alive, maybe I wouldn't need to trick it? Maybe Wayne could just open it for me.

But for that he would need to stand. The pool of blood around him widened. The smell of it filled my nostrils, somehow metallic and animal at once. My nostrils flared.

"Wayne," I said loudly. "Can you talk?"

"Yes," he whispered.

Good. "Can you stand?"

"I—don't think— No."

Not good. "Did you hear what was on that tape?"

"What—" He wheezed. "What tape?"

The minute hand on the watch shifted. I'd heard it, somehow. Kells was somewhere in this building, and Noah was too. I couldn't wait to find him, or else she would find me first. I'd have to try to lift Wayne myself.

As I moved over him, my stomach contracted—with nausea, I think—and Wayne's eyes widened in alarm. I rolled him gently, sort of, onto his back. That was when a different smell smacked me in the face. His intestines jiggled wetly from his slashed stomach.

"Are you *serious*," I hissed through clenched teeth. I mildly wondered how I'd managed to not empty the contents of my stomach all over him as I placed my hands beneath his wet armpits and tried to lift him up.

"Stop!" He moaned. "Please."

I stopped. My eyes darted around the tiled room looking for something, anything to help me, but it was pretty bare. A plastic table and two knocked-over chairs were at one end of it, and another chair, wooden, was strewn in pieces near the wall. A few of the tiles had been smashed, presumably by the chair. But something metal gleamed in the ruins of what once must have been a neat and tidy medical-ish room.

I went over to inspect it, kicking aside jagged pieces of wood and brushing off some ceramic tile bits, and then realized what I'd found.

It was a scalpel. I picked it up, brushing it against my soiled hospital gown to wipe away the dust. Just holding it felt strange. It seemed to conform to the shape of my hand.

Wayne moaned again behind me, a miserable, desperate sound. I turned to him. He was dying. He was mostly dead, really. And the fact that his left eye was still in his skull was the only thing keeping me from getting out. From getting to Noah.

As I stared at him, I tried to imagine his eyes closing—to think about him dying from blood loss or something, why hadn't that happened yet? But Wayne's eyes didn't close. They just kept looking at me.

I told myself that in his current state, death would be a relief, a kindness. But the thing was, I didn't want to kill him. I remembered, in a clinical sort of way, that he'd played a role in trapping me here, in torturing me, and that memory carried with it the sense that he'd enjoyed it. But I remembered these things the way you remember the name of your second-grade teacher (Mrs. Fish-Robinson). I didn't really *care* that he'd done them. At that moment I didn't want him dead, and I really didn't want to be the one to kill him.

He must have seen my hesitation, because he whispered, "Good girl."

I cocked my head.

"You're not so bad, are you?"

Those were his last words before I cut his throat.

6

I FELT KIND OF BAD ABOUT IT, HONESTLY. IT WASN'T A clean cut. Too much hesitation; I could barely watch as I did it. But I did make sure he was dead before I took his eye. That was something?

And I kept the scalpel. I had a feeling I would need it again.

By then a low, whooping alarm had been set off, but when I peeked out from the examination room, the halls were empty. I couldn't remember ever seeing anyone here besides Dr. Kells and Wayne, but that didn't mean much. There was a lot I couldn't remember.

Wayne's eye squelched in my closed fist. It was larger than I'd thought it would be, and rounder, too. Part of the optic nerve was still attached to it, peeking out between my fingers. Every second that passed could bring Kells with it, so I darted to the left, to where I thought her office might be. The fluorescent lights flickered and buzzed above my head, and the white walls seemed to curve and bend around me. There was no way to know how far I'd come, no way to make sure I was going in the right direction.

I tried to unravel my tangled memories of this place so I could pick a direction, any direction, to follow. But empty hallways dead-ended with locked steel doors or doors that opened up to rooms with nothing and no one in them. And there were no windows, no statues, no artwork, nothing that even remotely resembled the blurry picture of Horizons as I remembered it.

I grew panicked, turning corners and opening doors to find nothing but whiteness and metal. None of it looked familiar. I was a rat in a maze; I might not be locked in a cell, but I was still a prisoner. I tried to believe that Jude would get Jamie and Stella out, that Noah was alive and would be waiting for me, but every dead end killed a little bit of hope, until I barely had any left.

But then, I noticed a tiny door painted white to blend in with the walls. I opened it and crawled through. I was staring at a narrow flight of metal stairs.

I climbed them, of course. They creaked beneath my feet and my heart felt like it might burst. When I opened the door at the top, the hinges squeaked and I cringed.

Behind the door, something metal clattered to the floor. I heard a whispered obscenity. I *knew* that whisper.

"Jamie?" I asked, pushing open the door.

"Mara? *Mara?* No fucking way." Jamie's voice echoed in the mostly metal room, which was in fact an industrial kitchen. I searched for him but all I saw were gleaming, distorted reflections of myself in the steel cabinets that lined the walls.

"Where are you?" I asked.

I ducked beneath a hanging pot rack and caught one reflection that didn't match the others. I tilted my head to one side as the reflection changed, distorted, as Jamie pushed open a cabinet door and crawled out of it. He nearly tripped on the cooking utensils scattered on the floor as he ran to me. He stopped just short of a hug. "Oh my God—Mara—what the fuck happened to you?"

I looked up, staring at myself in the steel backsplash behind an enormous oven. This was what I saw:

One scalpel (held)
One tape recorder (held)
One human eye (brown) (held)
One blood-soaked surgical gown (worn)
One gold Rolex (worn)

I really wished the stupid hospital gown had pockets. My reflection shrugged, even though I had not.

"Blood's not mine," I said.

"I'm afraid to ask . . ."

"Wayne," I said.

"Well, then, I have never been so happy to see you covered in blood."

And I'd never been so happy to see him. He was not a mess, and was not wearing a hospital gown either. He had on clothes that would have been normal—khaki pants, a polo shirt, no shoes, just tube socks—except they weren't normal for *him*. They didn't fit him either. The cuffs of his pants came to his ankles, and the shirt he wore hung loosely off his frame. His hair had been buzzed so short that his scalp shone beneath it.

"We have to find Stella. Any ideas?" I asked.

Jamie shook his head. "I don't even know where my room is."

"How did you get out?" I silently hoped that Jude was the answer.

"I was playing solitaire when I heard the door to my room—cell, whatever—hiss and unlock. The hallway was empty, so I made a run for it. Except I didn't know where to go, and at one point I thought I heard footsteps behind me, and I didn't really want to run into anyone, obviously, so I opened the first unlocked door I could find—this one," he said, swinging the kitchen door, "and hid. But not before I made a metric fuck ton of noise, obviously."

"And I was the footsteps."

"You were the footsteps." His expression softened. "I'm glad you were the footsteps."

"Me too."

"I really want to hug you, but you're disgusting, no offense."

A smile turned up the corner of my mouth, a real one. "Why is it that whenever anyone says something offensive, they always add 'no offense' after it?"

"Offensive or not, you're objectively covered in blood," he said, giving me a long look. His eyes landed on the watch on my wrist. "And bling. WTF?"

"Jude's." I turned away from Jamie and poked my head out into the hallway, trying to decide which way we should go.

"Did you just say what I think you said?"

"The watch belonged to Jude," I said slowly. "He left me a tape, told me how to get out of here," I said, holding out my palm and releasing my fist slowly, so as not to let Wayne's eye slip out.

"Okay. One, that is foul, Mara, and I don't understand, but that seems to be the running theme here. Two—what tape?"

I showed him the tape recorder in my other hand. "I'll play it for you but not now. But Jude's the one who let me out."

Jamie's eyes widened.

"And he's the one who let you out too, I think. Listen, I'll tell you everything, but now we need to go."

"I appreciate this, Mara. I appreciate our situation, I really do. But listen to yourself. You're talking about trusting the guy who is largely *responsible* for our current situation."

I took a deep breath. Jamie was right. But he hadn't heard what Jude had said about Noah. And now wasn't the time to tell him. "I didn't have much of a choice," was all I said. "Look, I woke up in this room, and Wayne was dead." Well, mostly dead. "The tape was in his hand, the door was locked, and on the tape Jude said the only way out was to use Wayne's eye to trick the retinal scanner, which would get me out. It also opens the door to Kells's office, which is where we have to go next. But first I thought, 'Well, Mara, your situation can't get much worse,' and so I did what Jude told me to do. And that led me to you." I started walking down the corridor, trying in vain to ignore the *squish* of Wayne's eye in my fist.

Jamie didn't have to work hard to keep up with me; he was taller than I remembered, taller than me. "And I'm happy about that, truly, but am nevertheless concerned about the veracity of our would-be savior."

I stopped short. "Do you want to go back?"

He rubbed his forehead with both hands and pulled at his face until his eyes drooped.

"Well?"

"No." He dragged out the word.

"Then kindly shut up and help me."

But, Stella found us first. She'd relied on the old hide-in-the-broom-closet trick, except that when we passed it, she reached out and grabbed Jamie by the sleeve, making him scream, which made me scream.

"What is *wrong* with you?" Jamie said, hitting her lightly on the shoulder.

"Sorry! I wanted to get your attention without calling out."

"That worked out well for all of us," he replied.

Stella looked mostly the way I remembered her, except for the clean mom jeans she wore, along with a weirdly formal silky blouse. I couldn't imagine her choosing those clothes for herself—I couldn't imagine anyone choosing them for themselves. But her face was the same—her olive skin healthy, her black hair shiny and brushed. And she wasn't covered in blood or any other bodily fluids. Of the three of us, I was the mess.

"My God, Mara. It's good to see you, but you look—"

"I know."

"No, but, like, really—"

"I know," I said. I turned a corner, then another one, trying to follow my faded, faulty memories, but there was no part of me—no conscious part, anyway—that recognized where we were. Jamie was equally clueless.

But Stella wasn't. If it weren't for her, we might never have found it.

"She brought me back here, once, for some kind of written test," she said as we stood silently in front of a nondescript door. But this one had an extra little camera thingy above the top right corner of it. A retinal scanner. Just where Jude said it would be.

"Well?" Jamie asked. "Use the eye."

I reached out to hand it to him.

He backed away, shaking his head. "Nope. I'm squeamish."

I looked at Stella.

"Not a chance."

"I need one of you to do this," I explained. "There's a map inside, and our files."

"So . . . come look with us?"

I felt a flare of anger and tried to swallow it down. "Haven't you noticed that one of us is missing?"

Stella and Jamie exchanged an uncomfortable glance.

"I can't be here. I have to find Noah."

"Mara," Stella started to say. "Noah's not . . ."

"What?"

"Alive," Jamie finished.

I ignored the word that came before it. "He's alive," I said with an intensity that shut both of them up. "Jude said he is. He said he was going to find him, and he found both of you and let you out, didn't he?" Jamie opened his mouth to speak, but I didn't wait for him to answer. "I was supposed to come here, to get our files—the real ones, so we can finally understand what the fuck is happening to us and then find the map that will lead us out of this place. But first I need to find Noah." I struggled to explain what it felt like, knowing he was alive, knowing he was here but not with me. I couldn't. "So you get the files"—I looked at Stella—"you get the map," I said to Jamie, "and I'll find you again."

Jamie put a tentative hand on my shoulder and I flinched without meaning to. "Okay," he said quietly. "Listen. I know you want to find him. But it doesn't make sense for you to try before you even know where you're going. So come in, we'll get the files, get the map, and then get out. Together. We'll do this together. Okay?"

I looked at my friend. He had always been on my side, even when he hadn't agreed with me. He didn't believe that Noah was alive, but at the moment it didn't matter. He was right. I would have a better chance of finding Noah if I had the map first.

So I handed the tape recorder to him and opened my fist. Wayne's brown eye stared at nothing. I pinched it very carefully between my thumb and forefinger and held it just above my own eyes, like Jude said.

The door unlocked. We went inside.

7

I THINK ALL OF US HALF-EXPECTED TO FIND A SWAT TEAM armed and waiting for us. Or to be felled by poison darts or something. But when I entered Dr. Kells's office, with Jamie and Stella flanking each shoulder, the room was dark and silent.

The room was also practically empty. Distressingly blank. There were no papers on the metal desk, which was really just a worktable, but there was a worn Persian rug beneath it, looking out of place in the sterile room. There were no notebooks, no file folders, not even an office chair—just a little metal stool. It looked nothing like an office, even, except for the wall-to-wall file cabinets, which I prayed weren't empty.

"Where do we start?" Stella asked. "And what are we looking for, exactly? Can someone catch me up?"

I looked at Jude's watch. Twelve thirty-six. In the morning, I assumed. We had passed no windows, and there was no way to tell whether it was night or day, but I guessed night. It seemed more appropriate.

If what Jude had said was true, Kells knew where we were, and she was probably watching us right now, so I played the tape. We listened to Jude's message together. It sounded even stranger in Kells's office, somehow, than it had in the room with Wayne, and I noticed things I'd missed the first time. Jude's voice sounded softer than I remembered it. More earnest. There was no edge to it, no hint of sarcasm or impatience. And he sounded sick. I heard him faintly wheezing between words, and his breath rattled when he coughed.

"He never told us where to find the map," Stella said when the tape ended. "It could be anywhere. And there's only one way in and out." She flicked a nervous glance at the door.

"That we know of," Jamie added.

They were both right. "But why would Jude help us escape just to trap us in her office, when we were exactly where she wanted us before?"

"Maybe he doesn't want what she wants anymore," Stella said. "Maybe . . . " Her voice drifted off. "When he took us before, I was on my way back to my room, and he just grabbed me. Stuck something into my arm, and I passed out and woke up in the Zen garden, tied up like you saw."

Jamie picked at his lips. "Same with me. And he never said *anything* to us, not until you got there. He was just—quiet. Focused."

Stella closed her eyes, and her thick eyebrows drew together. "Megan woke up, and she was begging him not to hurt her."

Who's Megan? I mouthed to Jamie.

"Megan? From Horizons? Who was afraid of everything in Group?"

It didn't register, and Jamie could tell. He looked worried.

"And then Adam—" Stella began.

"The douchecanoe who always fucked with me," Jamie added helpfully.

"—wanted to know why Jude was doing this to us, and Jude just looked at him, and then at Megan, and then at Tara, who was passed out. He slit Tara's throat while she was unconscious, just like that." Stella snapped her fingers.

"Didn't say a word till after her blood had already soaked into the sand," Jamie said. "And then he said that if we didn't stay quiet, he would do the same to the rest of us, one by one. No diabolical monologue. No explanation. Nothing." Jamie paused. "That is all to say—he is one seriously sick fuck."

"I know this." My voice was firm and clear. "I've known Jude longer than I've known either of you."

I thought about telling them about Laurelton, and the asylum, and the scars on my wrists—the things Jude had done to me, the things he'd made me do. I decided I would, but now was not the time.

"I'm not saying I trust him. I'm just saying we don't have a lot of other options. Can we just look for the map, please, and get Noah and get the fuck out of here?"

Without another word Jamie and Stella began to search. We opened drawer after drawer. They were all empty.

The minutes ticked by, stoking my frustration and my rage. I wanted to knock the file cabinets over, to lift the table and throw it into the wall. I wanted to claw the walls down to their studs. Stella grew visibly nervous, grinding her teeth, winding her fingers around her hair, until finally she said, "We have to get out of here."

"Do you hear something?" Jamie asked her.

She shook her head. "No. But I want to go." She tried to turn the door handle. It had locked behind us.

"You can't get out like that," I said as Stella let out a whimper. I was on my hands and knees on the rug, under the desk, trying to find anything that could help us. "You need to use the eye."

I'd left it on the worktable above me, but as I tried to stand back up to get it, I banged my head. *"Ow."*

Jamie poked his head under the table. "You okay?"

I shot him a glare. "Do I *look* okay?"

"Touché," he said, kneeling beside me. He patted my head a few times until I threatened to eat him.

"Hey, Mara, did you see this?" he asked.

"What?"

He was staring at a spot on the rug, and reached for it. It was a key.

Stella's face split into a smile, showing teeth. "It has to open something!"

"That is what keys generally do," I said.

"And not a drawer," she said, ignoring me. "None of them were locked."

"So maybe a safe or something?" Jamie crossed the room. He leaned one of the empty file cabinets forward, to find only solid wall behind it.

I rocked back on my heels and plucked the key from Jamie's fingers. "Where did you find it?"

"It was right there." He pointed under the table. "Maybe it was taped under the table, and when you banged your head, it fell?"

An idea crystallized as I looked at the worn, patterned rug. "Help me move this," I said, indicating the table. Stella looked unsure and cast a glance at the door before she joined me and Jamie. We lined up on one side of the table.

It was insanely heavy, solid metal, and it took everything we had, which wasn't very much, to push it off the rug. Panting, we took a moment to catch our breaths before Jamie and I reached for the rug and pulled it up at the same time.

"Well, heavens to Betsy," Jamie whispered.

A rectangle had been cut into the linoleum floor. And at the bottom of it, right in the center, was a keyhole.

Before Jamie or Stella could say another word, I stuck the key into the hole. The room was so quiet that the three of us heard the tumbler click. I hadn't noticed before that the alarm had gone silent.

I pulled back on the key, and the trapdoor lifted with it, surprisingly light. We peered down but couldn't see anything except the top rungs of a ladder.

"Jamie, you keep the eye." Never know when you might need it. I swung my leg over the first rung. Stella tugged at the shoulder of my hospital gown. "Where are you going?"

"Down." I picked her fingers off me. The ladder had raised bumps for traction, and they pricked my bare feet. "You have the tape?" I asked Jamie. He nodded. And I still had the scalpel, now tucked into the waistband of my underwear. "You guys can stay here if you want till I come back with the map."

"Yeah, no," Jamie said. "I'll be right behind you."

"Then I'll see you on the other side," I said, and disappeared into the darkness.

8

THIS WAS WHAT WE HAD BEEN LOOKING FOR.

The room we found ourselves in was massive, almost bunker-like. On the wall opposite us a global map stretched from corner to corner. It was dotted with thousands of pins in dozens of colors, connected to one another by string to form a web. By some of the dots there were pictures of people—some smiling, most not—or scribbled-on Post-its, or newspaper clippings in different languages.

"Is that it?" Stella asked as she hopped down the last rung. She landed softly on the floor in her socked feet. Jamie wasn't wearing shoes either.

"Can't be." Jamie said what I was thinking. "It's the world, not Horizons."

And then I saw something familiar. A whiteboard easel with writing on it, writing I recognized. The dark blue marker was faded but legible.

Double-Blind

S. Benicia, manifested (G1821 carri   rigin unknown).
Side effects(?): anorexia, bulimia, self-harm. Respons
administered pharmaceuticals. Contraindications suspec but
unknown.

T. Bur ows, n-carrier, deceas

M. Ca no, on-carrier, sed

M. Dyer, manifesting (G1821 carrier, original).
Side effects: co-occurring PTSD, hallucinations, self-harm,
poss. schizophr ia/paranoi subtype. Respon to midazolam.
Contraindications: suspected n.e.s.s.?
J. Roth, manifesting (G1 21 carrier, suspecte original), induced.
Side effects: poss. borderline personality disorder, poss. mood
disorder. Contrain   ations suspected but unknown.

A. Ken all: non-carrier, decease

J. L.: artificial manifested, Lenaurd protocol, early induction. Side effec : multiple personality disorder (unrespo), antisocial personality disorder (unre onsive); migraines, extreme aggression (unresponsive). No known contraindications.

C. L.: artificially manifested, Lenaurd protocol, early induction, deceased.

P. Reynard: non-carrier, deceased.

N. Shaw: manifested (G1821 carrier, original). Side effects(?): self-harm, poss. oppositiona defiant disorder (unresponsiv), conduct disorder? (unresponsive); tested: class a barbiturat s (unresponsive), class b (unresponsive), class c (un esponsive); unresponsive to all classes; ~~(test m.a.d.)~~, deceased.

Generalize side effe ts: nausea, elevated temp., insomnia, night terrors

Before I could say anything, Jamie began writing giant letters over the words with his index finger.

F-U-C-K Y-O-U.

My sentiments exactly.

I turned my attention to the stacks and piles of papers, notebooks, and files strewn around the room. Books had been haphazardly stacked on open metal kitchen shelving, rolls of paper (maps? charts?) leaned against the walls. A glass globe teetered precariously on a small table, holding what looked like a large metal grain of rice. The place was chaos. Not what I'd expected from Dr. Kells.

I had a hunch about the rolls of paper and headed for them, skirting the U-shaped desk in the center of the room. But a noise like a burst of television static snapped my head around.

A flatscreen hung from the ceiling, and with another burst of static it came to life. Dr. Kells filled the screen. She was seated at a table in front of a pea-green-and-off-white-striped wall. Her lips moved, but there was no sound. It looked like she was speaking to someone, someone offscreen. She was more animated than I'd ever seen her. The sleeves of her white lab coat were rolled up to her elbows, and her hands moved as she spoke. Then, finally, the audio turned on.

"G1821 operates in many ways like cancer," Kells said. "There are environmental and genetic factors that can trigger it, and when triggered, the gene turns on, like a switch, activating an ability in its host. But as you've witnessed, the gene also appears to turn off certain switches, like the instinct for self-preservation. Certain thoughts and behaviors can become compulsive, such as the urge to self-harm."

A burst of static distorted the image, but we heard Kells speak in fits and starts. "Jude was needed to trigger Mara, to expose her to what she was most afraid of, in order for me to know whether and when she would manifest, and in order for me to study her developed ability—its consequences and its limitations," she said, taking out a notebook. She wrote out three words, then held them up—but the camera was too far away for me to read what she'd written.

"If the ego is the organized part of her mind, and the superego plays the moralizing role, allowing her to distinguish between good and evil, then the id is just a bundle of instincts. It strives only to satisfy its own basic needs, like hunger and sex. It knows no judgments and does not distinguish between moral or amoral. In normal people, non-carriers, the ego mediates between the id—what a person wants—and reality. It satisfies a person's instincts using reason. The superego acts as the conscience; it punishes through feelings of remorse and guilt. These feelings are powerful, and in normal people the ego and the superego dominate the id. As you've seen," Kells continued, "Mara appears to have the ability to convert thought into reality, but her ability is dependent on the presence of fear or stress, as I believe it is for the other carriers. In any case, G1821 makes Mara's id reflexive; if she is afraid, or stressed, her ego and superego don't function. And the consequences, as you've seen, can be disastrous. Her ugliest, most destructive thoughts become reality."

"Well. That's not good news," Jamie said, before Stella shushed him.

"Mara doesn't even always have to be *aware* of these

thoughts, of her intent behind them. If the right mixture of fear and stress is present, her instinctual drives take over. And there's a Freudian theory that along with the creative instinct—the libido—a death instinct also exists, a destructive urge directed against the world and other organisms. The drug we've developed will, we hope, reactivate the barrier between her id and her ego and superego; it's designed to prevent any negative intent from becoming action. The dose needs to be adjusted, however, and I can't study Mara on drugs. And she's too unstable to be studied without them. High doses of another drug we've developed should bring about an almost flawless recall, so at some point, when it's safer for us, Mara should be able to recount exactly what happened at the time of any specific incident, and recount what she was feeling at that moment. Luckily, she is responsive to midazolam, which we're using to help her forget, so she needn't relive her traumas on a daily basis."

The image on-screen warped and flickered, and there was a second voice, distorted, that I couldn't make out. Then Kells came back, as sharp as before.

"Yes, I tried to study her as noninvasively as I possibly could. That's why I had her behavior recorded before I took any specific action. We installed fiber optics in her home, to observe and record her behavior before it escalated. But the fact is, I can't learn how to help her until I fully understand what's *wrong* with her. The applications—the benefits—of what we're doing here outweigh the risks. The treatments we could develop based on what you show us, the applications they could have—" Her voice grew passionate. "They're far reaching. So far reaching that I don't even know the extent of them yet. No one should have to suffer the way people have been suffering because of G1821, especially not teenagers. Listen," she said. "Anemosyne and Amylethe, they corrupt the findings. They change the outcomes of the studies we need to conduct to make sure Mara and the others can be released safely. I need to be able to study someone *without* those drugs, to map a manifested brain with an MRI and CAT scans, to study how it responds to stimuli and fear and stress. The answer isn't in the blood—it's in the brain. So blood work, test tubes—they're not going to give me what I need. I need to study patients while they're awake, and conscious."

Dr. Kells leaned forward and ran her hands through her hair. "I need to study *you*."

"What do you want me to do?" I heard Noah ask, before the screen went black.

9

I stared at the blank screen, as if just by looking at it, I could make Noah appear. But he didn't. Nothing did.

"Did you see a date stamp on that video?" Stella asked, looking at both of us. Jamie shook his head. "Mara?"

I hadn't. I was still staring at the screen. It had been Noah's voice. He *was* alive. And he was here.

"Okay," Stella said. She pressed the power button, but nothing happened. "I don't think we can turn it on or off from here, which means someone somewhere else is doing it."

"So let's figure out where somewhere else is," Jamie said.

That was where Noah would be. Everything in me knew it.

"Jude said there was a map." I looked around us, at the mess of papers and files and notebooks, and then remembered the scrolls.

I pointed at them. "Guys, some help?" We began unrolling one after another. There were maps and charts, as I'd suspected, but we didn't find what we were looking for until we were almost out of scrolls.

"Let's spread it out over there," I said, tipping my head toward the desk. Stella stacked notebooks over the corners to hold it open.

We were looking at detailed architectural plans of the Horizons Residential Treatment Center.

Except it wasn't just a treatment center. It was a compound. The treatment center was just the part we could see. Beneath it, below ground, was a sprawling, windowless structure, segmented off into different areas that together comprised the "Testing Facility."

"Holy shit," Jamie whispered.

Stella examined the map and explained what we were looking at. "So I think we're underground again, in the lowest level of the testing facility. See there?" She pointed to some small shapes within the larger shape. "It looks like these little rooms might be where they were keeping us. You found Jamie on level 2." She traced her finger to an area labeled KITCHEN, not far from where Jamie said we'd entered Kells's office—the decoy office.

"Level 3 is where we are now—not too far from where we

started, actually. And we're still on No Name Island, it looks like."

I narrowed my eyes. "Where else would we be?"

She ran her finger across a long line that ran the length of what seemed to be a tunnel. "There are three other structures. On a completely different island."

I peered over her shoulder and read the labels: MAINTENANCE, CONTAINMENT, STORAGE.

"That's a power line, I think. And there," she said, squinting at the blueprints, "that's the power grid. It's in the maintenance area. That's where Kells is, probably."

And Noah, too.

"One way in, one way out," Jamie said, pointing at the tunnel. It wasn't far from where we were now, but we'd have to go back up to the fake office to get there. I was already moving toward the ladder.

"Mara, wait—" Stella started.

"For what?" I called out over my shoulder.

"What are we going to do, just walk in there?" Jamie asked.

"Yes?"

Stella made a face. "Shouldn't we, like, have a plan or something?"

I stopped. "It doesn't matter what we plan. Kells knows we're coming. She's probably watching us right now."

I looked behind me and scanned the room for a camera. Stella followed my gaze, then stopped and pointed at a tiny little reflective globe suspended from the ceiling, in the far right corner of the room. I stared at it for a moment, then raised my hand and gave it the finger.

"I thought you were going to give it the District Twelve salute," Jamie said.

Stella snorted. "Look, maybe we should at least get a weapon?"

I lifted the hem of the hospital gown and withdrew the scalpel from my underwear. "Got one."

"You're kind of limited with that, no?"

Wayne hadn't thought so.

"She wouldn't have left anything here that we could use against her," I said.

Stella held up our files. "She left these." A few papers fluttered to the ground. She bent over, and went very quiet. "Mara," she said as she picked them up. "I think these are yours."

I took them from Stella. They were drawings, some resembling people with limbs missing, others that looked like faces, with the eyes scribbled over and blacked out. As I stared, the lines on the paper began to move, arranging themselves in a way that suggested my face. I looked away.

"She probably left them here on purpose." So I would see them. So they would upset me. "Look, you don't have to come with," I said, my voice low. "In fact, you probably shouldn't." I crumpled the drawings up and threw them at the wastebasket. I missed.

Jamie and Stella exchanged a look before Jamie rolled his

eyes. "Of course we're coming with you," he said, as Stella tucked a few files and notebooks under her arm. I offered him a small smile before climbing up the ladder.

"This doesn't look like the plans," Jamie said.

"It doesn't look like anything."

We tried to follow what Stella remembered of the blueprints, guided only by harsh auxiliary lights, which made the curving, winding, subterranean structure of the place even more disorienting. None of us could pinpoint exactly when the power had been cut off. The air felt dead and stale as we moved through it.

"I feel like any second there could be a thousand guns pointed at our heads," Stella said.

"There could be." I felt my way through the darkness. Our footsteps echoed on the metal walkway. "Well, probably not a thousand."

Eventually, the walkway parted in a fork. We could go left, right, or down a small set of stairs. I decided down. When we reached the landing, we stood opposite a metal wall; a door had been cut into it, with rounded corners and a biohazard symbol in the center. CONTAINMENT, the plans had read. Nowhere to go but in.

"Nope," Jamie said, shaking his head. "Nope."

I pressed my ear to the door.

"Is she here yet?"

I sprang back when I heard those words. *Noah* spoke them. He was behind this door. I reached for the handle, but Jamie stopped me.

"Mara," he said slowly. "Do you know what that symbol means?"

"Yes."

"Then would you kindly share why you're ignoring it?"

"Noah's in there. I just heard him."

Jamie looked skeptical.

"Listen," I told him. He pressed his ear to the door too.

"Roth's here as well, sounds like."

Jamie looked like he'd been shocked. "Jesus," he whispered. "Who's he talking to?"

"Probably Dr. Kells," Stella said it aloud as I thought it.

I looked at the both of them. Stella looked pale and frightened. Jamie looked determined. Decided.

It was time. Time to split up. I took a deep breath.

"I don't know what that video meant, or why Kells wanted us to see it. I don't know why Jude helped us get out or if he was even really helping us at all. I don't know anything, but I know that I have to open this door. I have to. And if you don't want to be here for it, you should go."

"Mara, wait—"

"There was a hatch, somewhere on the blueprints, right?" Stella nodded. "By the Maintenance Area. You should go.

Together. Get to No Name Key however you can. I'll catch up with you there or I won't."

"I think you're making a mistake," Jamie said slowly.

Stella raised her hand. "Me too, for what it's worth."

I smiled without amusement. "Noted."

Jamie ran his hand over his scalp, scratching at it. "I don't want to leave you here by yourself."

"Then don't."

Stella looked back and forth between the two of us, clearly unsure what to do. I reached for the handle again.

"Stop!" Jamie shouted.

"Jamie—"

"Mara, I love you—don't look at me like that, not in *that* way—but if you are so far gone that you are about to ignore a BIG RED BIOHAZARD symbol, me going in with you isn't going to help you. I want my innards to stay inner."

"It's okay," I said quietly. "It really is." I wasn't offended, or even hurt. I was relieved. I didn't want to feel responsible for Jamie and Stella. It was enough just being responsible for myself.

"Shit," Jamie muttered. "Shit."

"Go, Jamie."

He grabbed my face in his hands, hard, and smushed my cheeks. "If it's Ebola, you're fucked. But if not, just—try not to breathe for as long as you can, okay?"

I nodded. "Go. I'll give you a head start."

Jamie kissed me on the cheek. "Good luck," he whispered, and he and Stella began to climb the stairs. I waited until the sounds of their muted footsteps disappeared, and then I pressed my ear to the door.

"Why won't she come in?"

Noah again. I closed my eyes. Something wasn't right. He was alive, obviously, but if he was okay, why wasn't he opening the door to come to *me*?

Every instinct told me to run, but I turned the handle anyway. The door opened slowly.

The room was white and tiled, like the examination room I'd woken up in. No furniture in this one either, except for a small card table and two chairs. Dr. Kells sat on one of them. The second chair was empty.

"Where's Noah?" I asked with steel in my voice. My eyes searched the room, but there was nothing to find. "Why did you tell me he was dead?"

Dr. Kells was reaching into a cardboard box by her feet as I spoke. "Because he is."

She lifted something up, over her head. A gas mask. "I'm sorry," I heard her say before she lowered it over her face. There was a hissing sound, and by the time I noticed the vents near the ceiling, I had already fallen to the ground.

10

BEFORE

Atlantic Ocean

I rested my cheek against the ship's railing, breathing in air that smelled of salt and rain. It was night; the deck was nearly empty. Two young men jostled and joked with each other as they worked to tie ropes, arrange sails. Sailors—that was it. They paid me no mind, and I watched them out of the corner of my eye. They were familiar with each other, family perhaps. They moved and worked together the way Sister and I had when we'd used to cook. Though she and I were never sisters, which is why I was here and she was dead.

I spent every night wondering why that was, why I was here to stare out at the black sea that seemed to have no end to it, when Sister and Uncle and so many others were rotting beneath the earth half a world away. I wondered why my benefactor, as he had been called by everyone I ever knew, wanted me enough to provide for me even after his death. I wondered of what value he thought I might be to him.

It was my final night at sea, and I was too restless to spend it belowdecks. I hardly ever spent time in my quarters, preferring to watch as sailors strung the ropes from the masts into a giant web, to watch the sails breathe with wind. On past nights, when my presence had been noticed and I was chased below by a man with spectacles like Mr. Barbary's and shiny gold buttons on his coat, I would creep along the corridors, sneak behind doors, listen to conversations no one guessed I could understand.

But that morning I watched as dawn broke, crisp and clear over the horizon, before a dark cloud enveloped us as the sea narrowed into a river. Iron smoke swallowed every scrap of blue sky, and when the ship docked, I was jostled aside as it crawled with people the way the waters below it teemed with fish.

The river was clotted with other ships, the banks crowded by docks, and buildings with domes and arches and spires that scraped the sky. Pipes spit black smoke into the air, and my ears filled with the sounds of the city, with shouting and whistling and chiming and creaking and other sounds so foreign I could not even name them.

I went back to my quarters to fetch my things, only to find that someone was waiting for me.

The man wore black clothing to match his dark eyes, which crinkled at the corners. His face was kind, his voice rich and deep. "I am Mr. Grimsby," the man said. "I believe we have a mutual connection through Mr. Barbary?"

I did not answer.

"He sent word to my mistress that I should escort you to the London home. Are you ready, miss?"

I was.

He lifted my trunk from the ground, and I stiffened. He noticed. "May I take your things?"

No, I wanted to say. I nodded instead.

I followed Mr. Grimsby off the ship, watching the way my trunk bobbed with his steps. From the sounds of hooves and wheels and canes and feet, I picked out the *clop*, *clop* of my new shoes on the stone street. I counted my steps to calm myself.

The air clawed at my too-thin dress, and I huddled into it as Mr. Grimsby wound his way to a grand carriage that awaited us. The ink-black horse shied at my approach.

"Whoa, girl," the driver said, patting her neck.

I took a cautious step forward, and the horse snorted and stamped. I didn't understand. I had a way with animals; my mind was filled with hazy memories of feeding monkeys from the palm of my hand, of riding an elephant with Sister as it swam across a river.

The horse seemed to shriek, and it strained at the straps that bound its head and body to the carriage.

The driver apologized to Mr. Grimsby. "Don't know what's gotten into 'er, sir."

I reached out my hand to calm her.

Just then she reared. Her liquid black eyes rolled up into her head, showing the whites, and then without warning she bolted.

Mr. Grimsby looked in disbelief after the carriage now tearing down the crowded street, drawing shouts and screams in its wake. We heard the crash before we saw it.

Mr. Grimsby nearly forgot me and took off at a run. I was as close on his heels as my legs would allow, but then I wished I hadn't been.

The carriage had turned over, and its wheels were spinning in the air. The horse had tried to jump an iron gate tipped with spikes.

She hadn't made it.

My throat tightened with an ache that threatened to become a scream. I never cried. Not when Uncle had been burned, not when Sister had been stoned. But when I saw the once-perfect black body of the horse now mangled, her coat slick with blood, and I heard the gunshot that ended her pain and misery, my eyes stung as they filled with tears. I wiped them away before anyone could see.

11

MY EYES FLUTTERED OPEN. IT FELT LIKE I WAS being rocked, like I was swaying in the air.

"I am so, so sorry, Mara." The voice was muffled, distorted. It came from a creature with huge, dark, empty eyes and a hole-punched snout. It *whuffed* as it leaned over me, pried open my mouth. I wanted to scream, but my lips and teeth were numb.

When I opened my eyes again, the world was white and the creature was gone. My nostrils stung, invaded by chemical smells, and the ground beneath me was hard and unyielding.

Because it wasn't the ground, I realized as the room came

into view. It was a table. A gurney. I was cold, so cold, and I couldn't feel my limbs.

"I wish we could have avoided this." The voice belonged to Dr. Kells, and she appeared out of the corner of my vision. I'd never seen her without makeup before. She looked startlingly young, except for the deep lines that bracketed her mouth. Wisps of hair escaped from a loose bun at the nape of her neck. She smelled like sweat and bleach.

"I wanted to fix you. I thought I could *save* you." She shook her head, like she couldn't believe she'd been so stupid. "I thought, given regular infusions of Anemosyne and Amylethe, we would eventually be able to release you back to your family. I actually thought you might be able to go back to school!" She laughed then, the sound thin and panicked. She wasn't looking at me—I wasn't sure if she was even *talking* to me. And—was she *crying*?

"I'm sorry I made you believe Noah was alive. I am sorry for that. I know how difficult it must have been, hearing recordings of his voice. But Jude gave me no choice, you understand? He's . . . not well. I had no idea he would take things as far as he did at the Tamerlane. No idea. Sometimes even I can't predict him." She laughed again. "Claire was the only one who could. And no one can bring her back."

Kells swiped at her red-rimmed eyes with the back of her hand. "When he let you out and you . . . What happened in the examination room, with Wayne? My God, Mara. What if something like that happened again? I know you must think I'm the villain here. No doubt you've killed me a thousand times in your head since you've been conscious, and who knows how many times while you were unconscious. But think about what you've done today. Think about what you've done before. The people you've hurt? The lives you've ended?" She stared at nothing, her eyes wide and afraid. "I tried so hard, but you're just not safe."

Then she moved over to a row of steel cabinets and removed something from them. I heard the click of plastic as she fitted a cap onto a syringe.

"I'm going to give you an injection that will stop your heart. I promise you, Mara, you won't feel a thing."

But I *could* feel something. I could feel my fingers, and the way the stiff fabric of the hospital gown settled and stretched over my chest. I should have been more frightened than I was. I should have been terrified. But I just felt like I was watching all of this happen to someone else.

"I'll let your parents know, after, about what you did to Phoebe."

But I hadn't done anything to Phoebe.

"And Tara."

I hadn't done anything to Tara, either.

"You have a well-established history of violence under sedation," she said, her cheeks wet, her nose running. "And a documented diagnosis of paranoid schizophrenia. It will be extremely difficult for your family to come to terms with the loss, but with time they'll come to accept it. They'll have to accept it." She placed the syringe on a metal table by the gurney. I looked down and saw a drain in the floor. I looked back up, at the strange-looking metal cabinets behind her. It took me a few seconds to realize what they were, and where I was.

The room was a morgue.

"I've done nothing but spend years of my life trying to help teenagers like you, and you in particular. But I can't kid myself anymore." Her voice broke on the words. "You can't be fixed. You can't be saved." She rolled the sleeve of my stained gown up to my shoulder. I felt her fingers brush my skin. A wave of sensation trailed in their wake.

My body had been numb before, but the wave crested and left my arms, my hands, and parts of my back tingling. Still nothing in my legs or feet.

I felt the scalpel, tucked into the elastic waistband of my underwear, the metal warm from my body. Either Dr. Kells didn't know about it or she'd forgotten about it, because she was very surprised when I stabbed her in the neck.

I swung my arm with so much force that I fell off the table and crashed to the floor, knocking over the metal table with the syringes. Dr. Kells hadn't strapped me down. Why bother if I was paralyzed? Pain speared my left shoulder, and I fought the instinct to grab it—I needed to keep the scalpel in my right hand. Kells backed up against the wall, then sank to the floor. She held her neck with both hands, her eyes wide, blood flowing freely through her fingers.

I told my legs to move, but they wouldn't. I'd have to crawl. I glanced at the door to the morgue. I could probably reach the handle, but the door itself looked heavy. I might not be able to push it open.

Mara.

I looked up when I heard his voice, Noah's voice. And then I saw his face. Fine-boned and elegant and pale, with the sarcastic tilt to his mouth that I loved so much, and a shadow of stubble on his jaw. It was him. Just the way I remembered.

But then a gash appeared in his throat, as if someone had cut into it with a serrated knife. There was no blood, no sound as the wound formed a jagged smile at the base of his neck.

It wasn't real. I knew it wasn't real. But I was seeing it for a reason.

I rounded on Dr. Kells. She was pale but still conscious, still able to move, and she edged away from the wall. The floor was slick with her blood.

"Where's Noah?" I said. My voice was thick and flat.

"Dead," she whispered. She bunched up the corner of her lab coat, trying to use it to stanch her bleeding.

"You're lying."

"You killed him."

"Jude told me he's alive."

"Jude is *sick*," she said hoarsely.

I believed that. But I also believed that Noah was alive. I would feel it if he weren't, and I didn't feel anything.

"Tell me where he is," I said, my tongue heavy in my mouth. I tried to think what I could say or do to make her tell me, *force* her to tell me, then remembered what she had said to Jude.

She had told him I could bring Claire back. Jude had believed it. Maybe he'd been right to.

"Tell me where he is so I can bring him back."

"He's never coming back."

"You told Jude—Claire—"

"I lied."

Even I thought that was cruel. I was about to say so when I caught her reaching for the syringe. Rage threw me forward, and I managed to swat it away with my hand. Then I pushed myself up.

Dr. Kells was right. I had killed her a thousand times in my head, but she was still here. Whatever drugs she'd given me were working, making it impossible to kill her with my mind. But I could kill her with my hands.

She had dropped her coat, and the blood flowing from her neck had slowed to a trickle.

She's going to die anyway, part of me whispered.

"But she could kill you before she does."

I swung my head in the direction of my voice. I stared at

my reflection in one of the steel drawers. She—I—shrugged my shoulders as if to say, *What can you do?*

My arms trembled with the effort to hold myself up, but I would not let go until I had an answer. "How do I find Noah?" I asked.

Kells was scrabbling away from the door, away from me, but kept slipping on her own blood. I pulled at her legs, and her skin seemed to come off in my hand. No. Not her skin, her stockings. "What did you do to him? Tell me."

She didn't answer. She stared at me and then, without warning, dove for the syringe again.

I slid with her, and in a burst of strength pulled myself on top of her and pushed down on her chest, on her neck. She gasped for air as I wrestled the syringe from her curled fist.

I couldn't leave her alive. Not after everything. I couldn't take that chance. But as I held the syringe, I realized I could make death painless for her, just like she'd said she would do for me.

But was what she'd done to me painless? She'd hurt me before tonight, before today. She had tortured me. She'd said she had her reasons, but then, didn't everyone? Did reasons matter?

She was mouthing something—praying, maybe? I hadn't seen that coming.

When I'd thought about death before, it had been so abstract. I'd thought things but I'd never *felt* them. But this, this was real. My face was just inches from hers. I could hear her heart beating weakly in her chest with the effort to pump what blood still remained in her body. I could smell the sweat on her skin and almost taste her blood in my mouth, hot and metallic.

The truth was, I had known since the second I'd woken up in Horizons, since the second she'd confessed what she'd done to me, since she'd showed me the list, that if given the chance, I would kill her.

"Don't worry," I said to Dr. Kells. "This will only hurt a little."

12

I HALF-STUMBLED, HALF-CRAWLED ALONG THE METAL walkway as the feeling returned to my legs. My hands were scored from pulling myself up the grated catwalk. When I reached a fork in the walkway, I looked left, then right, and saw Jamie and Stella standing maybe a hundred feet away.

I didn't have to say a word before they began to run toward me. Stella slipped in her socked feet, and she grabbed the railing to steady herself, dropping some files she'd been carrying under her arm, but soon they were by my side. They didn't ask what had happened. They didn't say anything at all. Each of them took a shoulder, and hauled me up. They half-carried me out of the hallway that led up a brutal, narrow flight of stairs and eventually outdoors.

"We got worried you weren't coming out," Jamie finally said as the three of us collapsed, panting, against the concrete building we'd just escaped from.

"What about Ebola?" I asked breathlessly.

Jamie coughed and wheezed, then said, "What's a little hemorrhagic fever between friends?"

I smiled, despite everything.

"Guys?" Stella asked. "We should probably not stay here."

Probably not.

"We need to hide," Jamie said. "Until you can walk."

He was right of course, but we didn't have too many options. The building I practically crawled out of had to be the uppermost level of the maintenance shed. It was mostly hidden by trees, but it was nearly dawn and they weren't that thick. We could even see Horizons—part of the treatment facility, anyway—in the distance, on No Name Island. Unfortunately, that meant that someone standing on No Name Island might be able to see us, too.

I looked down at my useless legs, smeared with blood and dirt. I felt a twinge of panic. "What if I can't walk?" I swallowed thickly. "What if—what if—"

Stella knelt at eye level. "What does it feel like?" she asked gently.

"Like parts of my feet and legs are just dead, but other parts—other parts are stinging."

"I remember feeling like that once, in there," Jamie said, glancing at the closed door. "I woke up and couldn't feel my legs."

"What did she do to you?" I asked, but I was scared to hear his answer. Why would she make it so we couldn't walk? What *had* she done to us?

"It wasn't Kells, it was Wayne," Jamie said. "And he wasn't exactly forthcoming."

Not comforting. But at least Jamie could walk now. Which meant I would again, too. I hoped.

"How long did it take to wear off?"

Jamie shrugged. "There were no clocks, not that I saw anyway, so I'm not sure, but I think an hour or two maybe? I felt strange after . . . like my limbs just floated away—like they were clouds."

"A spinal block, maybe?" Stella suggested. "So you couldn't feel what they were doing to you."

"You know this how?" I asked.

"My mom's a nurse."

"Can I just take a second to say, I am *so happy* they're dead," Jamie said, running a hand over his scalp, then over his face. He peeked at me through two of his fingers. "She is dead, right?"

Oh yes. "Yes."

"What happened in there?" Jamie asked me.

"It wasn't really Noah. It was just his voice. Kells recorded it, played it, played me."

"So, 'twas a trap?"

"Yup," I said. "You were right." I felt his hand on my shoulder.

"I'm so sorry, Mara," Jamie said.

"It's okay."

"No, about—about Noah, I mean."

"He's not dead." Jamie said nothing. I pushed myself up until my spine was straight. "I don't know how I know it, but I do. He's out there, somewhere."

"Then why isn't he here?"

That was a very good question. One I would do anything to answer.

"Kells said the building collapsed," Jamie started.

"She told me that too. But that doesn't mean it's true."

There was no way to know without going back there. But even if it *had* collapsed, there was more to Horizons than just the treatment facility, we now knew. And if Jamie survived, and Stella survived, I had to believe Noah survived too. He was the only one of us who could heal. He had to be alive.

"Do you still have the tape?" I asked. Jamie's forehead creased. "The tape Jude made me?"

"Stella had it last, I think," Jamie said.

I spun around. "Where'd she go?"

Just then, a rusty hinge creaked. Our heads snapped up, but it was only Stella, emerging from the building holding three bags. One was Jamie's, another must've been Stella's, and the last one—the last one belonged to Noah.

An image of him appeared in my mind, of Noah standing with that bag over his shoulder, guitar case in hand, dripping wet from the rain, waiting to be led into the Horizons Treatment Center so he could save me. My heart leapt. "Where'd you find this one?"

"She kept our things—boxes of stuff—in a little room near the morgue," Stella said, handing the bags to me and Jamie. "I guess if we died or something, she wanted to make sure we were in our own clothes and not hospital gowns or whatever. Stage the scene."

I wondered what she'd done with my things. How she'd planned on staging *that* scene.

I gripped Noah's bag with what was probably excessive force. "How did you know this was—" No, not "was." Is. "How did you know this is his?"

"There were cubbies labeled with our names. And his guitar was next to it."

His guitar. He wouldn't have left that behind. An ache rose in my throat, but I swallowed it back down.

"Did you look *in* the morgue?" Jamie asked Stella.

"Um . . . " She shot me a nervous glance. I both did and didn't want her to answer.

"No," she finally said.

"One of us should." Jamie's voice was soft.

I shook my head. "Noah isn't in there."

"If you don't want to go, I will," Jamie said.

I thought of what he would find there if he went—the blood, Kells's body. I thought I should go with him, to explain it.

Stella decided to come with us, and the two of them helped me up and let me use them as crutches as we opened the door and began the trek back down.

Despite our lack of shoes, our footsteps echoed loudly on the metal grates, and I knew I wasn't the only one wondering if what we were doing was smart. If we weren't alone down there, someone else would easily hear us. But we kept walking (in my case, limping) anyway. We had to see what was there . . . or wasn't.

The door to the morgue was slightly ajar, and a bloody, smeared handprint wrapped around the edge, just beneath the handle. It was mine. Jamie and Stella just stared at it. I pushed the steel door open with my fingertips.

Dr. Kells was where I'd left her, her dead eyes fixed on nothing. Stella's chin wobbled as she surveyed the scene. "What happened?" she whispered. But Jamie spoke before I could answer.

"I'll look in the drawers," he said, but made no move to enter the room. I urged both of them forward, breaking the spell. We stared at the rows of large metal cabinets, wanting and not wanting to know what was inside them.

In the end it was Stella who opened the first drawer. I leaned on Jamie as she unlocked it. We collectively held our breath as she slid out the tray, and collectively sighed when it turned out to be empty. Every nerve in my body felt raw and exposed as she unlocked drawer after drawer, each of them empty, until one wasn't.

A sheet covered a shapeless mass. No, not shapeless. Body-shaped. Person-shaped.

Stella didn't reach for it, so I broke away from Jamie, using the wall to support myself. I slid the sheet off and found Adam. Dick-Adam. Whom I could have saved, maybe, but had chosen not to. And now he was here, and dead, like Kells and Wayne and everyone else I'd hated.

But not Noah. Not Noah.

13

WE SLEPT BY THE WATER. THE BEACH WAS half sand, half mud and was littered with jagged shells and tree roots, but I felt more dead than tired, so I stuffed Noah's bag under my head and crashed anyway.

The feeling came back into my legs in a trickle, not a wave. When I woke up, my muscles ached with soreness, my mouth tasted spoiled, and my stomach hurt. I was itchy and filthy and miserable, but when the sun peeked through the trees and I realized that I could stare at it, bask in it, worship it if I wanted to, my mouth curved into a smile. I was free.

Jamie and Stella were still sleeping. Mist crept up from

the gray ocean onto the beach, reaching for their feet, clinging to the tall sea grass. I stood quietly, weak-kneed but able to walk on my own. Seagulls picked over something on the shore. They scattered at my approach.

My papery hospital gown was crusted with blood and sand and dirt. I had no clothes, so I brought Noah's bag with me, figuring I'd wash myself off in the ocean and change into something of his. But my hand froze on the zipper.

I didn't know if I could keep it together if I opened his bag and smelled his scent and felt the fabric that had touched his skin. I knew he was alive—knew it—but he wasn't *here*.

I walked back just as Jamie was waking up, stretching his arms up to touch the tree branch above him.

"I feel like ass," he said.

Stella yawned loudly. "You look like it too."

"So, what's for breakfast?" Jamie asked.

Stella rolled her eyes. "Cute."

"My gastric juices are dissolving my stomach lining," Jamie said. Stella made a disgusted face. "My stomach is eating itself. And I've never been this sore in my life."

Stella propped herself up on her elbows. "Maybe there are coconuts or something?"

"We're not foraging for coconuts," I said. "We have to get off the island."

Stella agreed. "I grabbed some files from Kells's office, but I didn't really look at what I took. We could go back—she had to have a way of coming and going. Maybe we can find it."

"Then what?" Jamie asked.

"There's a resort on No Name Island," I said. "If we go back, we might be able to find a phone . . ."

But my voice trailed off as I followed that train of thought. Who would we call?

"And what would we say?" Jamie added, seeing where I was going with it.

"Kells mentioned Phoebe and Tara before—" Before I killed her. "Said that it would look like I was the one who'd killed them."

"But Jude did it," Stella said.

"Right in front of us," Jamie added.

"Dr. Kells—that was self-defense," Stella said. "We'll back you up."

I took a deep breath, steadying myself. "It won't matter. Everything is already in my file. We can't count on anyone"—even my parents—"believing any of us."

Even my brothers.

"If she told anyone about it before she died, showed anyone my file," I continued, "then, depending on what was in them, people"—my family—"will think we're crazy and still under her care, or crazy and missing, or crazy and dead. But no matter what, people"—my family—"are going to think we're"—I'm—"crazy."

"And dangerous," Jamie added, giving my bloody hospital gown a long look.

"And dangerous." I really needed to change.

"So okay," Stella said. "We don't call anyone we know to get us out of here. There's the ferry, though? What about that?"

I looked down at myself. "We look a little—"

"Suspicious," Jamie said.

"Exactly."

"Is there anything of Noah's you can wear?" Stella asked.

"I . . . haven't looked yet."

Jamie and Stella were quiet. Then, "Here," Jamie said, reaching into his bag. He handed me a black T-shirt with the word TROPE upside down in white, and a pair of baggy carpenter shorts.

Stella frowned. "I don't get it."

"Subverted trope," Jamie said.

"Wouldn't that be *in*verted?"

"You're so literal. Jesus." He marched off to let me change.

The ocean air chilled my skin as I stripped off my clothes and dipped into the water, the sand slimy between my toes. It felt like a lake, not the ocean. You couldn't see the bottom, even though the water was shallow. I rinsed my arms and legs, pulling goose bumps from my flesh. A memory of the warmth of Dr. Kells's blood came to me unbidden, drawing a spike of pleasure in its wake. I felt sick and gleeful at once.

"Oh no. No, no, no, *no*!"

It was Stella. I stumbled into the shorts Jamie had given me and rushed over to see what had happened. She and Jamie were looking out at the water.

No. Not at the water. At a massive column of smoke, rising from No Name Island into the sky.

The three of us looked at one another, thinking the exact same thing.

"All right. Let's have a vote," Jamie said. "Jude—misunderstood good guy, or bad guy with unknown motives? I vote bad guy."

"Bad guy," Stella said.

I paused before I spoke. "Undecided," I finally said. "You think he did it?"

"WTF, Mara? Of course he did it."

"He helped us get out of there."

"Yeah, but—"

"He said Noah was alive." But he also said Noah would be waiting for me and he wasn't. I shook my head to clear it. I needed to believe he was telling the truth. I didn't forgive him. Far from it. I looked down at my wrists, at the scars from where Jude had made me slit them, faded but not gone, after Noah had healed them. I would never forgive Jude for what he'd done to me, for what he'd done to Joseph, but right now I had to believe him, because I had to believe Noah was alive.

"Hey," Jamie said softly.

Stella ignored him. "Right now it doesn't matter *what* he is. How are we supposed to get out of here if we can't go back to find out how Kells did it herself?"

"Hey!" Jamie said again, snapping his fingers in Stella's face to get her attention. He pointed at the ocean. "Is that a boat?"

I followed his gaze, shading my eyes.

"That's convenient," I said.

"Too convenient," Jamie said. "What if someone's been sent to come get us? Like a Horizons person or something?"

"Like one of the counselors?" Stella asked. "Doubt it. Maybe the police?"

"Could they really take us anywhere worse than where we've just come from, though?" I asked.

Jamie pretended to think for a moment. "Um, jail?"

I shot him a glare. "Would that be worse?"

He shrugged. "I'd rather not find out. I have plans."

Stella shaded her eyes and peered out at the water. "It's a fishing boat, I think." She bit her lip, thinking. "We could ask it to take us to No Name Key, or Marathon," Stella said. "But from there?"

"Hitch a ride?" I offered. Jamie looked at me like I was crazy. "I don't know! I'm new to the fugitive thing."

Stella turned to us. "One of us is going to have to swim to it. Any volunteers?"

Jamie shook his head. "Not it. Sharks, first of all, and second of all, sharks."

Stella was already unzipping her jeans and pulling them down off her hips. "I was on the swim team, once upon a time."

"You shouldn't go by yourself," I said.

"Why? You think the fisherman could be a psychopath?"

"Everyone's a little crazy. Some people just hide it better than others." I glanced at Jamie, who was smiling, before I offered to go with Stella. Honestly, I thought we should all go. I didn't like the idea of splitting up.

She shook her head. "You've done more than enough. It's fine, I'll be okay. Just stay in the trees with Jamie, all right?" She waved at us and then stepped into the water. As she waded farther out, she yelled, "I'll be right back."

14

"I REALLY, REALLY WISH SHE HADN'T SAID THAT," JAMIE SAID.

"What?"

"'I'll be right back.' Now she definitely won't be right back."

"What are you talking about?"

"It's the rules." Jamie peeked through the mangroves as Stella swam toward the boat.

"She's fast," I said.

"Yeah," Jamie said. "But a massive shark fin is going to appear behind her any second."

"Don't say that!" I punched him not so lightly in the arm. "Asshole."

He was silent for a few minutes, and then he smacked my arm.

"Ow."

"You had a mosquito."

"No, I didn't."

"Hey, look." While we'd been talking, the boat had drawn nearer, the motor loud enough to drown out all our efforts at stealthy conversation. A grizzled, gray-haired old man was behind the wheel, or the helm, or the prow, or whatever it was. His hair hung down way past his shoulders, and a bunch of teeth from indeterminate animals dangled from a leather necklace he wore. He pulled the boat up much closer to the sand than I'd expected he would, and Stella hopped off it and into the water, wading toward the beach. Two guys in polo shirts and khaki shorts followed behind her. One of them wore a plastic visor. Both openly ogled her ass.

Stella motioned for me and Jamie. We walked out into the sun.

"Some friends you've got," Grizzly Man said to us.

"Yeah," Jamie said slowly. "Some friends, all right . . . ?"

"I told him about the practical joke," Stella said smoothly. "About Wayne and Deborah leaving us while we camped here overnight, and taking almost all of our stuff."

Ah. I got it now. "Total assholes," I said. "I'm *so* pissed."

"Can we, uh, get a move on?" Visor Guy said. "We have only, what, six hours left on the charter?"

"Hold your horses," Grizzly said to him. "I'll take y'all back out after we drop 'em off at the key."

"We're in town only until tomorrow," Visor Guy whined, looking annoyed with the whole enterprise. "We don't have time to go back out."

"I'll give you your money back," Grizzly snapped. Visor Guy visibly cheered up at this. "You kids want something to drink?"

God, yes. I nodded fiercely. Jamie was nodding too. Grizzly looked at him a bit longer than he looked at me. "You're not twenty-one, are you?"

Both of us shrugged at the same time.

"Well, beer's all we got. Don't tell no one."

I smiled. "Our secret."

Grizzly handed me a sweating can of beer. I was dying of thirst, so I popped the tab and guzzled it—then almost choked. Who would actually *want* to drink this? I looked over at Stella. I must've been making a weird face, because she was smirking at me.

It took us only about twenty minutes to get to No Name Key. Jamie chatted up Grizzly, whose actual name was Leonard, surprisingly, while the polo men tried to chat up me and Stella. She actually managed to be friendly. I couldn't get there.

The boat pulled up to a small dock, and Grizzly-Leonard hopped off with us. Stella had put her jeans and T-shirt back on, and I looked down at what I was wearing. Jamie's clothes would do for now, but not for long. They were sandy and sort of damp. And I badly needed a shower—a real one.

"Is there anywhere to get food around here?" I asked.

"No Name Pub," Grizzly-Leonard said, pointing at a little bright yellow building ahead of us, shaded by palm trees and with an old-timey sign out front. "They open at eleven. The key shrimp pizza's a winner."

"And an ATM?" Stella asked.

At this, Grizzly-Leonard laughed. "The pub is powered by a generator. There's no electricity grid on the island—the residents don't want it."

Perfect.

"You've got no cash on you at all?"

Stella shook her head. "It was in our things."

"Which your friends ran off with."

"Exactly," Jamie said.

"With friends like that, who needs enemies?" Then Grizzly-Leonard called out to a woman at the far end of the dock whom I hadn't noticed until just then. "Pizza's on me, Charlotte—"

"No," I said. "We couldn't ask you to—"

"It's no problem," he said, grinning. A few of his teeth were missing.

"We really want to get back out on the water," Visor Guy said. The other one was still staring at Stella. Gross.

"Chill your tits," Grizzly-Leonard said. "You kids gonna be okay?" he asked me.

We said yes and thanked him, and he took his useless, middle-aged cargo back out onto the water to kill some trophies. My stomach growled.

"What time is it?" Jamie asked.

I pulled Jude's Rolex out from the front pocket of Noah's bag, where I'd hidden it. "Ten-thirty."

"At least when we get to an actual city, we can pawn that thing," Stella said.

Jamie shook his head. "No pawnshops. No credit cards. No ATMs. We're going to have to figure out an alternative. But let's wait till we get inside."

The three of us basically watched the minute hand tick by as we waited for the pub to open. My stomach was downright angry. When the clock struck eleven, I practically dove into the pub, which was entirely plastered with dollar bills. They hung from the ceiling, papered the walls—every inch of every available surface was covered with them, except for the tables. The woman from the dock showed us to a table near the back.

"What can I do you for?" She handed us three menus. "Any drinks?"

"Water," Jamie and I said at once. My mouth felt spoiled after the beer. Stella ordered water too, and the waitress disappeared.

Jamie glanced at the menu. "I'm starving. I want everything."

"Co-signed," Stella said. "Maybe the key shrimp pizza?"

"Treif," Jamie said, not looking up.

Stella raised an eyebrow. "Gesundheit?"

"It's not kosher, I mean. No shrimp."

"Oh," Stella said. "The Hawaiian pizza, then?"

Jamie shook his head, still looking at the menu. "Nope. Ham."

"Pepperoni?"

"Same."

"Okay, you're impossible."

"Vegetarian and plain cheese. That's what I can have."

The waitress returned, and we placed an order for two pies with extra cheese. Before she left, Jamie asked her, "Is there, like, any way to get a cab or anything from here?"

She laughed heartily. We guess that meant no.

"Can't go back the way you came?"

"Not exactly," Jamie mumbled.

"How'd you get out here?"

"We came with . . . friends. On a . . . boat. We took a ride out to an island to . . ." He was floundering.

"Camp out under the stars," Stella said. She was good at this game. It would come in handy.

Charlotte tucked her pencil behind her ear. "That's romantic."

"It was supposed to be," I said, lying smoothly, "but then they stole away in the night with our things."

"Practical joke," Stella added.

"Some joke." Charlotte shook her head. "I've got a phone. You can call your parents to come and pick you up, and you're welcome to stay here until then, as long as you need to. Sodas on the house."

"That's the thing—we're not from here," Stella said.

"Where are you from?"

"New York," Jamie said. I raised an eyebrow at him. What was that about?

"Well, you're a long way from home," Charlotte said.

She had no idea.

The waitress left us and I thought we might eat each other in the time it took her to bring our order. The three of us reached for the pizzas at once; the slice in my hand was steaming, but I was so hungry, I didn't care. I couldn't remember the last time I'd tasted food. I had no memory of eating at all in Horizons, and I didn't know if it was because the drugs were messing with my memory or because I actually *hadn't* eaten at all.

Jamie held a slice in each hand and was looking back and forth between them. "I want to double-fist the shit out of this pizza."

Stella paused from blowing on her slice. "That's not going to work out the way you think it will."

I didn't even bother blowing on mine. I just took a huge bite, burning my tongue and throat in the process. But that wasn't what made me gag.

"Mara?" Stella looked worried.

"I'm okay," I said after I caught my breath. The aftertaste was like cement. "I can't—I can't taste it or something? It tastes weird. Doesn't it taste weird?"

Two pairs of eyes stared at me.

"It doesn't taste weird to you?"

They shook their heads.

"You should try to eat," Stella said gently.

"Yeah, you look pretty terrible," Jamie added, not at all gently.

Stella's brown eyes were warm. "You've been through a lot. More than us, probably."

Jamie took alternating bites of pizza. "I'm reserving judgment until I hear your story."

I supposed it was time to tell it.

I looked over my shoulder, eyeing the other people in the pub. There was a woman wearing a fanny pack, and her husband in a golf shirt. A man with a handlebar mustache wearing a Hawaiian shirt sat at the bar, following the fishing channel with an abnormal amount of interest. It didn't look like anyone was listening to us, but even if they were, no one in their right mind would believe what I was about to say.

15

I TOLD JAMIE AND STELLA EVERYTHING, FROM THE OUIJA board to the asylum, from Rachel to Jude and Claire. From Mabel's shitty owner to Morales. Jamie's brows drew together as the words left my mouth.

And then I told them about Noah. Why he couldn't be dead.

"Because he can heal," Jamie said.

"Himself or other people?" Stella asked.

"Both." I told them about Joseph, and how he'd been taken by Jude and rescued by Noah, and about my father, and how he'd been shot because of me but had survived because of Noah. I didn't mention the "love him to ruins" thing. That wouldn't exactly help my case. And it felt too private to share.

"But you're not saying he could survive a gun to his head, right?" Jamie asked.

Stella elbowed him sharply. *"Jamie."*

"I'm not trying to be insensitive—"

"No, you're not trying," I said.

"I'm just saying—"

I leaned forward, elbows on the table, hands flat against it. "I know what you're just saying. I know. But there's too much we *don't* know to just decide that he's—" I didn't want to say the word. "Have you guys even seen proof that Horizons collapsed?"

They shook their heads.

"But there was still the fire," Jaime said.

I clenched my jaw. "He wasn't there when it happened."

"Then where *is* he?"

That was what I was going to find out.

Stella shared her tale of woe next. Once upon a time she was a gymnast and a swimmer. Then puberty hit, and her hips and breasts grew, and when she was sixteen, she stopped eating—because of her coach and her mother, her psychologists said. But they didn't know about the voices.

To her they sounded like other people's thoughts. But that was impossible, obviously. She grew more and more panicked, and the voices grew louder and louder in response—keeping her awake at night and distracted during the day. She couldn't swim or train or eat, but then she noticed something curious. The longer she went without eating, the weaker the voices became. She was down to ninety pounds and losing her hair by the time her father finally overrode her mother (who had insisted Stella was just "watching calories") and forced Stella to get help. And she got it. After months of therapy and several stints in rehab, her doctors finally seemed to settle on a wonder drug that helped her—until it was suddenly recalled by the FDA. She backslid fast, but Dr. Kells contacted her parents just in time.

"Lucky me." Stella took a bite of pizza. "But I had a feeling there was something up with you guys the moment you walked into the program. Like when we were together for group stuff, I couldn't hear either of you, even when I could hear everyone else—but my meds make it sort of confusing. They shut out most of the voices most of the time, but when I'm stressed or anxious, it gets worse."

"Or angry?" Jamie said.

"Is that how it happens with you?" I asked him.

Jamie shrugged and avoided my eyes. "Before I was expelled and shipped off to Crazytown, I would notice sometimes that if I told people to do things, they would actually do them. But not like, 'Hey, man, would you mind handing me the keys to your Maserati?' It's more like, 'Tell me that secret' or, 'Drive me here.' It seemed so *random*, and the stuff I was telling people to do wasn't crazy. Like, it could have been a coincidence," he said, "except that it didn't always *feel* like a coincidence. Sometimes it felt real." He met my eyes, and I knew he was thinking about Anna.

Anna, our former classmate, who had bullied him since fourth grade, and whom he had told to drive off a cliff. She drove drunk off an overpass after that.

"And I felt crazy for thinking it," Jamie said.

I looked up at him. "We all have that in common."

"What in common?" Stella asked.

Jamie got it. "That what's wrong with us, the gene thing, G1821 or whatever—the symptoms make us look like we're crazy."

Or maybe it actually *made* us crazy. I thought about my reflection. About the way it talked back to me.

"That explains why no one's discovered the gene," Jamie said, refocusing my attention. "If someone appears to be hallucinating, or delusional, or is starving themselves, or hurting themselves, the most obvious explanation would be mental illness, not some bizarre genetic mutation—"

"Mutation?" I asked. "We're mutants now?"

Jamie smirked. "Don't tell Marvel. They'll sue us. But listen, though. Genes don't just appear in a few people. It just doesn't happen. Genes change over centuries. They degrade, they alter—"

"They evolve," I said.

"Exactly. So what we have—whatever we are, we've evolved into it."

"Superman or Spider-Man," I said quietly.

Stella looked back and forth between Jamie and me. "Explain?"

I remembered the conversation I'd had with my brother, when I'd told him I needed to fictionalize my problems for a fake Horizons assignment, so I could get him to help me without knowing he was helping me.

"So she could be a superhero or supervillain," my brother had said. *"Is it a Peter Parker or a Clark Kent situation?"*

"What do you mean?"

"Like, was your character born with this thing à la Superman or did she acquire it like Spider-Man?"

I didn't know the answer then, but I knew it now. "Spider-Man acquired his ability from a radioactive spider bite," I said. "Superman was born with it—"

"Because he's really Kal-El, an alien," Jamie said.

I was Superman. Just like I'd thought.

But when I'd told Noah about Daniel's theory, he'd been convinced that we had to have acquired what was wrong with us.

"How many times have you wished someone dead, Mara? Someone who cuts you off on the highway, et cetera?"

"I've probably wished a lot of people dead a lot of times," I said now, and repeated Noah's words.

"Everybody does that," Stella assured me.

"And Noah's parents would've noticed that he healed abnormally fast when they took him to the doctor for shots, right? So why is everything starting to happen *now*, if it's something we were born with?"

Jamie slapped his palm on the table. "There's a *trigger*. It's like cancer. They can screen you genetically to see if you're at risk for developing it, because there are markers. But just because you're at risk—"

"Doesn't mean you'll actually get cancer," I finished, as the missing puzzle piece clicked into place.

"Exactly. It just means that you're more at risk than someone else—and the risk factors are biological and environmental."

"Or chemical," I said, my mother's words coming back to me.

"You've been through so much, and I know we don't understand. And I want you to know that this"—she had indicated the room—*"isn't you. It might be chemical or behavioral or even genetic—"*

An image had risen up out of the dark water of my mind. A picture. Black. White. Blurry. *"What?"* I'd asked quickly.

"The way you're feeling. Everything that's been going on with you. It isn't your fault. With the PTSD and everything that's happened— What you're going through," she'd said, clearly avoiding the words "mental illness," *"can be caused by biological and genetic factors."*

"But then, what's the trigger?" I asked.

Stella looked at me. "How old are you?"

"Seventeen."

"Jamie?"

"Sixteen."

"I'm also seventeen," she said to me, "but I'll be eighteen in a few months. Do you remember what Kells said in that video? She was talking about puberty or something, and the way the teenage brain develops?"

"It makes sense, that age would be the trigger," I said. Stella first started hearing voices at sixteen. I was sixteen during the Ouija board incident. Rachel and Claire died six months later. "It makes sense that the progressions of our abilities are at different stages, because—"

"Because we're different *ages*," Jamie said. "I'm rhyming," he added unnecessarily.

So that explained something. But not everything. I told Stella and Jamie about the flashbacks I'd had, of events that I couldn't possibly have experienced. "I thought it might be genetic memory," I said, and told them about the book Noah had found on one of his transatlantic flights, the one both of us had tried and failed to read, ostensibly about genetic memory.

"What was it called?" Jamie asked.

"*New Theories in Genetics* by—holy shit."

"Is that . . . a pseudonym?"

"Armin Lenaurd," I said. "The Lenaurd protocol." I didn't have to try very hard to remember where I'd heard that before. The list was burned into my memory. We'd just seen it.

J. L.: artificially manifested, Lenaurd protocol, early induction.

"I want to kill myself," I said calmly. "Like, I actually want to die."

"I'm missing something." Stella said.

"You saw the list—with our names on it, what was wrong with us." They both nodded. "If 'J.L.' and 'C.L.' are Jude and Claire Lowe," I explained, "it means that there was some protocol, written by the author of this obscenely boring book, that basically explained what was done to them."

"'Artificially manifested,'" Jamie said quietly. "'Early induction' . . . that would mean, what? The doctors were trying to cause the effects of the thing we have—in normal people, maybe?"

"Jude is hardly normal," I said.

"Maybe that's why," Stella said quietly.

"Why what?"

"Why he is the way he is," Stella said. "But wait. If there's a whole book about this thing that's wrong with us, maybe we can stop it." Her voice rose in pitch. "There might be a cure. It might be in that book!" She rounded on me. "Mara, where is it?"

"I gave it to Daniel."

"Who?"

"My older brother."

"So if we find Daniel, we find the book, and we find the cure—"

"Whoa, whoa, whoa. Back up a second here, eager beaver," Jamie said. "*If* there even *is* a cure in that book, which is a huge, massive 'if.' I mean, the Lenaurd protocol, whatever it is, was used on Jude, right? And I'd say it's not working out so well for him. So are we sure we'd even want whatever else might be in that book? Like, Kells kept talking about how she was trying to 'cure' us and 'save' us and shit, and I don't know . . . ending up on her side doesn't feel right." Stella opened her mouth to speak, but Jamie cut her off before she could. "Also, now that I know what's actually *wrong* with me, I'm not sure I'd even want to fix it." He paused. "Is that crazy?"

No one answered.

"Anyway, whatever. There's no way to know if what we need is in that book, but there's another problem."

"Jude?" I asked.

"No. I mean, yes, he's a problem, but another one."

"How we're going to survive without money?"

"No, another one. Listen," he said, sounding exasperated. "Kells was a medical researcher. But it takes money to run the kind of facility she was running. Who was funding it? And how many people knew, or know, about it? About us? And are any of them going to be even mildly pissed that their staff was butchered and their research lost?" he went on. "And speaking of research, how many carriers are there? We can't be the only ones, which means somewhere out there, there are more of us. Do we try to find them? What if they find us?"

"That's a lot more than one problem," Stella said.

Jamie wanted answers. Stella wanted a cure. I wanted Noah. And to punish whoever had taken him from me.

Jamie bit his lip. "So. Where do we start?"

16

WE COULDN'T AGREE ON WHICH PROBLEM to solve first, so we started by identifying what each of our problems had in common: Horizons. Stella withdrew the file folders she'd culled from Kells's office and set them down on the table. This was what she'd taken:

Seven pages of patient records for someone we'd never heard of.

Twenty-three pictures of what seemed to be the insides

of our throats and other places, and lab results from samples of our hair, spit, and pee.

One drawing of me, by me, with black scribbles over my eyes.

And a too-many-pages-to-count tax return for the Horizons Group, filed by Ira Ginsberg, CPA. The address was in New York.

With what little we had (Stella kept apologizing), Jamie suggested we follow the money. Stella and I agreed. But all of us would have to visit our parents first.

We didn't know how pressing the parent problem was, which in and of itself was *part* of the problem. Where did they think we were? What did they know? All three of our families believed in Dr. Kells and had put us into her care—out of ignorance, not malice, but still. We couldn't exactly show up on their respective doorsteps and explain the situation in good news–bad news format: *Hey, Mom, I've been tortured and experimented upon, but don't worry because my tormenters are dead. Because, P.S., I killed them.* I didn't know about Stella and Jamie, but in my experience, telling the truth only led to not being believed.

But Jamie was pretty sure ("Just pretty sure?") he could manage to convince our parents of our general welfare enough to avoid statewide AMBER Alerts and enough to possibly find out where they thought we were, and with whom. Maybe they'd been contacted by someone other than Kells. Maybe one of the other Horizons employees was in on it (though Stella didn't think so). We needed to talk to them to find out.

And there was a fourth house we needed to visit, though Stella and Jamie didn't know it yet. I needed to know what Noah's parents believed. I needed to know if there'd been a funeral. Just thinking the word made me ill.

We left No Name Pub with full stomachs but not much else. Charlotte, the owner, tried to help us find a ride, but no one was heading to Miami that day. She offered to put us up for the night, but there was no guarantee that anyone would be heading to Miami the next day either, and none of us wanted to wait. So Charlotte, kind soul that she was, offered to wash our clothes and pointed us to a little tourist shop nearby that she and her husband owned, where we could change into one of half a dozen T-shirt variations on the I LOVE FLORIDA theme while our clothes dried. Jamie and Stella had shoes in their bags, but I, having no bag, had no shoes either, so Charlotte gave me a pair of flip-flops from her own closet. After everything I'd been through, I'd thought I couldn't be surprised by people anymore. But Charlotte proved that I could.

Stella was already wearing a spare T-shirt of Jamie's (the yellow one, with the text I AM A CLICHÉ), so Jamie and I were left to pick our poison, so to speak. He ended up with an I ❤ FLORIDA shirt. I picked WELCOME TO THE SUNSHINE STATE. There weren't a lot of options.

I was changing into my shirt (and matching boxers! Wasn't I lucky?) in the tourist shop bathroom when a voice said, "You look retarded."

I looked up at the mirror. My reflection looked ridiculous.

"Yeah. Well. You don't look so hot yourself," I said back.

And so it was that the three of us, dressed like tourists, started hoofing it along the highway, getting whiplash every time a car passed us, which was a lot. Between the scorching heat and the insect-thick air, I thought it couldn't get worse, but then it began to rain.

The sky opened, and we were instantly drenched; the water was warm enough that it felt like the clouds were sweating on us. Our faces mirrored expressions of misery as we ducked off to the side of the highway under a large tree that was still not quite large enough.

"My biscuits are burning," Jamie said, taking off his shoes. The skin over his toes was cracked and bleeding. "Does anyone know how to start a fire?"

Blank stares.

"So we can't start a fire," he said. "We can't fly. We can't create a force field. We are the most bullshit superheroes."

I pushed my limp, sodden hair back from my face. "Faulty premise." I knew what he meant, but still. "Though, Stella's not so bad."

She cocked an eyebrow. "That means a lot, coming from you."

I pouted. "That hurts my feelings."

"Jamie's right, though," she said. "And the list of stuff we can't do is even longer—we can't use credit cards, we can't call our parents, we can't rent a car—"

"We might be able to steal a car, though," Jamie said.

The two of us turned to him at once. "I mean, not like with hot-wiring or anything. I have no idea how to do that shit. I just meant—I might be able to talk someone into giving us their car?"

"Lending it," I added helpfully.

Jamie nodded with enthusiasm. "Lending it. Exactly. If someone comes along."

"Do you even have your license, Jamie?" Stella asked.

He feigned surprise. "Was that a short joke, Stella? Have our dire circumstances caused you to develop a sense of humor?"

"It was an age joke, actually. And an appearance joke. You have a baby face."

Our circumstances *were* dire, though. We had no car, no money, no food, and no dry clothes. The hours passed, and the rain continued its assault, and we grew wetter and hungrier and colder but had no choice but to keep walking, me in plastic flip-flops that were murdering my feet.

Thc rain finally stopped as daylight dwindled into dusk. The sun bled into the clouds, coloring them pink and orange and red. We trudged up the road, which was framed on the shoulders by dense trees and creepers. After an eternity we came upon a gas station, if you could call it that. There was one pump, and the tiny clapboard building behind it listed precariously to one side; a small junkyard squatted in shadow beside it. A plastic doll head with only one eye was impaled on the broken wooden fence.

Jamie huddled closer to me. "This is serial killer territory." He linked arms with me and Stella. "United front," he whispered. "They can smell our fear."

I would have liked to pretend that I wasn't as nervous as he was, but . . .

I dipped my hand into the waistband of the boxers to make sure my scalpel was still resting against my skin. It was. The warm steel under my fingertips made me feel better.

Finally, the three of us walked inside. It was dimly lit, naturally. We glimpsed a bar composed of ridged metal sheeting, and three rather large men sitting at it. One of them wore a black wife-beater with black sunglasses perched on his balding forehead. Another wore an improbably long-sleeved flannel shirt and a cowboy hat, of all things. The third had white hair and a tobacco-stained white beard. He had only one eye.

Someone else appeared out of the shadows, cleaning a glass with a dirty rag.

"You look a little lost," he said to us.

I expected Jamie to speak first, but Stella surprised me. She offered up our fake sob story to the men, told them about being abandoned on a camping trip, blah blah, and then said we needed a ride. I was incredibly impressed. Jamie looked like he was ready to wet himself.

"Where're you headed?" asked Cowboy.

"Miami," Stella offered.

"You're heading north. I'm heading south." He crossed his arms in opposite directions, as if we needed him to explain what that meant. The other men were silent.

Jamie nodded just once and cleared his throat. "Well. Thank you anyway, gentlemen. For your time."

Dejected, we left the gas station or bar or serial killer meet-up, whatever it was, and headed back outside. It was nearly night now. Insects buzzed around us, and on us. The air was loud with their noise as we walked down the road.

And then we heard something else—a truck spitting gravel and groaning as it left the station. It pulled up beside us.

"I felt bad for ya," Cowboy said. "Come on. Hop in."

My legs ached with relief as I sat in the front of the cab. Jamie had discreetly shaken his head when he'd been offered shotgun, and Stella had already climbed into the back.

The cowboy was doing us a favor, and a long one, so I decided to make conversation, be polite. "So where are you from?" His name, we had learned, was Mr. Ernst.

"Born and raised in Canton, Ohio. You three?"

"New York," Jamie and Stella and I said all at once, sticking to our script. Not suspicious at all.

"And your friends just abandoned you like that?" he said, shaking his head with disbelief.

Stella changed the subject. "So, what brings you to the Keys?"

"Oh, just driving the old girl here," he said, patting the dashboard with a toothy grin. "Just me and her and the road."

But as he leaned forward, I caught a glimpse of a gun in a holster on his hip. I stiffened.

Jamie had seen it too. He pretended to be interested in it, and asked Mr. Ernst about it, who happily obliged with the make and model and whatever it is people talk about when they talk about guns. I wasn't really listening. I felt wrong, off, and the feeling made me nervous.

"Never know who you might meet on the road," Mr. Ernst said. "Gotta be careful. God bless the Second Amendment." He patted the holster and winked at me.

The road stretched on into infinity, and we didn't see a single pair of headlights pass in our direction. Suddenly, after who knew how long, I felt the truck slow down.

Stella did too. She wiped her red-rimmed eyes. Jamie kept running his hand over his scalp. They were worried too.

"Where are we?" Stella asked chirpily.

"Mmm, pretty deep in the Keys," he said evasively. "Still got a couple of hours ahead of us till we reach Miami." We passed a sign that announced a rest stop in a quarter mile. "It'll be a while till we hit another bathroom," Mr. Ernst said. "Nothing around here for miles, so I thought we'd all stop and take a leak."

Jamie exhaled just a little too loudly. I glared at him.

"I should go," Stella said.

"Me too," Jamie admitted.

"Do you have a map?" I asked Mr. Ernst.

He raised his eyebrows. "Girly, I've been driving since before you were even a twinkle in your mother's eye. The only map I need is up here," he said, pointing to his temple.

"Right," Stella said, looking back at the road. But we could all feel it: Something was wrong.

17

Mr. Ernst chattered away until he pulled into a parking spot at the rest stop, if you could even call it that. The squat building was tucked off to the side of the road, almost completely obscured by a tangle of weeds that clung to the faded, rust-stained walls. There was a small unpaved clearing around it. And no other cars or trucks.

Mr. Ernst turned off the truck and pocketed the keys. "I'm gonna go take a leak myself," he said. "You coming?" he asked Jamie.

Jamie raised an eyebrow at Stella. "Yeah . . ." He didn't want to go alone, and he didn't want Stella to have to either.

Mr. Ernst winked at me. "Don't get into any trouble now," he said, then walked off toward the building.

Stella and Jamie hopped out of the cab, Stella nearly running. She must've really had to go. I felt bad for Jamie, trailing behind, so I jumped out of the truck too. As I approached the building, the unmistakable smell of raw sewage assaulted my nostrils. Stella had already gone inside, but I caught up with Jamie quickly, and we stood there just staring at it. A thick layer of grime covered the once blue stenciled sign for the ladies' room, and flies choked the entrance. Jamie swatted the air in front of his face. The men's room was on the other side of the building.

"Tough break," Jamie said to me.

"What?"

"Not having a penis."

"God, I know."

"We're stalling."

"We are."

"I don't know, Mara. I'm not sure I can do it. I don't want to walk in there and see our not so illustrious truck driver at the urinal. It could get weird. I think I'm just going to go in the bushes."

"I feel like I'm going to catch hepatitis just standing here."

"If you want to go in the bushes or something, I can watch to make sure no one's coming?"

I rubbed my nose. "I'm going to go in, I think. For Stella. Solidarity, you know?"

"You're a better man than I." Jamie held his fist out. I bumped it. His footsteps crunched on the gravel and then faded as he walked off into the bushes.

I took a few seconds to psych myself up, then held my nose and kicked the door open.

It wasn't as bad as I'd been expecting. It was worse. There were a few stalls. One of them was open, and the toilet was so backed up that it was all I could do not to gag. The mirror behind the sink was cracked and dingy. The tile floor that had probably once been white was stained in shades of brown and yellow.

No. There was no way.

I turned to leave, but as I did, I heard a noise behind me.

Stella was pressed against the wall, her body almost completely obscured by Mr. Ernst, who was covering her mouth with one hand. He saw me see him, and pointed his gun at me.

"Go on back now," he said. "Or you're next."

My veins filled with lead. I wasn't going anywhere. I was already imagining Mr. Ernst dead on the floor, his throat ripped open, his mouth a bloody hole.

"He's done this before," Stella whimpered when he uncovered her mouth. "He's going to kill us." The words barely escaped from her mouth. She could hear what he was thinking.

He shook his head. "Not the colored boy. Not my type."

Part of me was still standing there, rooted to the spot. The other part was tearing out his throat. But only in my mind. In reality nothing was happening. In the seconds that followed I imagined a hundred different ways for him to die. None of them worked.

What was wrong with me? It had been a long time since the drugs had worn off. Why couldn't I do it?

And what would happen to me and Stella if I couldn't?

"Let her go," I said with frightening calm. I don't know where it came from.

"If *you* don't go, I'll shoot the both of you right this minute."

I took a step closer. "You're making me jealous," I said in that same chilly voice that was and was not my own.

"Back up."

I didn't. I stepped closer. "This whole time I thought you were coming on to me. That's why *I* chose to sit in front."

He looked me up and down. "You'll get your turn."

"Me first," I said. "She can't do the things I can."

Those were the first words I said to him that seemed to sink in. He looked back and forth between me and Stella, then finally stepped away from her. He trained his gun on me.

"You," he said to Stella. "You stand there and watch."

Stella scooted down the wall till she was backed up against the sink. My feet carried me toward Mr. Ernst without me even having to tell them to.

"Don't scream," Mr. Ernst said. He pressed his gun into my side, spun me around, and pushed me against the wall, pinning my hands behind me in one well-practiced move. His cowboy hat fell to the ground.

I expected my heart to race, my skin to sweat. I expected to cry and scream.

I didn't.

"Don't touch me," I said instead.

He laughed. It was a little boy's laugh, a giggle really. "Don't touch you? If you didn't want to be touched, you wouldn't be wearing those shorts! Why, they're an invitation! You're advertising. Open for business."

He did something lewd with his tongue. I imagined cutting it off.

"Take them off," he said, nodding at my stupid boxers.

"I can't," I said plainly. "Not without my hands." I wriggled my arm behind me. I reached my hand into the waistband of the boxers and felt the scalpel, warm from my skin. My shoulder ached, wrenched behind my back and forced into the wall by the pressure of Mr. Ernst's body. His breath roared in my ears, rotten tobacco mingling with the stench of human waste.

Meanwhile, Mr. Ernst appeared to be having trouble with his pants. I wriggled my arm behind my back, which unfortunately arched my body toward his. He took it as encouragement.

"I knew you wanted it," he whispered into my ear. Then he licked my cheek.

"The tongue definitely has to go," someone said in my voice.

I looked up into the cracked mirror behind him and Stella. My reflection stared back. She shook her head in disgust. Neither Stella nor Mr. Ernst seemed to notice.

A small shift in movement, and the scalpel was in my hand. I tucked it against my forearm, holding it tightly against my skin. It was sharp enough to cut me.

I swallowed, then said, "I need my hands. I can't do anything without my hands."

He adjusted his gun, poking it under my ribs, then nodded once quickly.

I brought my hands in front of me, tugging the waistband of the WELCOME TO THE SUNSHINE STATE boxers down with my thumbs. Mr. Ernst was watching, but not closely enough. Stella had fled. And before he could even register the movement, I stabbed him in the eye. He screamed until I cut his throat.

I took his keys and his gun when I was finished. Before I left, I glanced up at my reflection in the dark, cracked mirror. The asinine WELCOME TO THE SUNSHINE STATE T-shirt was streaked and soaked with Mr. Ernst's blood, and so was my skin. It was under my fingernails, in my hair. It freckled my face.

I stared at my reflection, waiting for a rush of disgust or terror or regret—something. But it never came.

18

I KNEW WHAT I LOOKED LIKE AS I WALKED CALMLY BACK to the truck. Jamie and Stella were already on their way back to find me.

"Fuck," Jamie said when he saw me. That about covered it.

"I'm okay. Get into the truck."

"Is he . . ."

Yes. Yes, he is.

"I have the keys," I said. "We need to go."

Stella reached out her hand. It was shaking. "Keys?" she asked as Jamie pulled me up into the cab. I reached into my pocket and tossed them at her.

"What—what happened?" Jamie asked.

I looked out the window, catching my reflection in the side-view mirror. She shrugged. "He made a mistake," I said quietly. I began to notice the blood drying on my skin. I felt sticky. Dirty. I pulled my hair back into a knot. It was clotted with blood.

"Mr. Ernst?" Jamie asked. "Did he touch you?"

"He tried," I said under my breath.

"Mara."

I swallowed hard. "I'm okay." It was true enough. I wasn't hurt. "He thought I was someone else."

Jamie's eyebrows knitted in confusion. "Who?"

"Someone who wouldn't fight back. Listen, we need to go." I withdrew Mr. Ernst's gun from the back of my boxers and shoved it into the glove compartment. Jamie's mouth hung open, disbelieving.

"Did you shoot him?" Stella was looking at the floor of the cab. Her voice sounded hollow, like she wasn't really there.

I shook my head. "He had the gun. He was pointing it at me. I cut him while he was trying to . . . undress."

"I should have stayed with you guys," Jamie said. "Fuck. *Fuck.*"

Stella's chest rose and fell rapidly. Her face was pale and bloodless. "Mara helped me," she said, as if to herself. "And then she had to help herself. It was self-defense." She began to nod. "I saw it, most of it, before I ran to get you, Jamie. So we can call the police and tell them—"

"We can't call the police," Jamie said. His voice was muffled. He had put his head between his knees. "You know we can't."

Stella closed her eyes and squeezed them shut. "Right. Right. Okay, so, Mara wouldn't have done anything unless she had to—and she had to."

I had to.

"But now we have a problem." She looked at my hands. "His DNA is under your fingernails. Yours is probably all over his body. This isn't like Horizons. We have his *truck*. If we leave it here, we're stranded. If we take it, we'll be easy to track."

"It can be tracked anyway, even if we leave it. But Mara's right, we can't stay here," Jamie said. "I vote for ditching the truck somewhere unobvious and then we'll figure the rest of this shit out."

"We'll burn the clothes or something," Stella said, looking at my T-shirt. "Clean you up. It'll be all right." She sounded like she was trying to convince herself more than she was trying to convince me.

"Then the only way out is through," Jamie said, and Stella started the truck.

19

"THIS IS LIKE THE PERFECT STORM OF BAD DECISIONS," Jamie said as the three of us approached a bed-and-breakfast in Key Largo. It was dark out. We'd ditched the truck about seven miles before; minutes later, it had begun to rain. Not enough to wash the blood out of my T-shirt or off my skin, but more than enough to make the miserable seven-mile walk even more miserable. Stella scratched at a thousand mosquito bites, and Jamie muttered about Lembas the whole way.

"Fine. Let's get this shit show on the road," he said as we stood in front of a well-lit, charming old green Victorian with yellow plantation shutters and scalloped trim. The shingles were weather-beaten and worn, and creepers snaked up the siding from the ground to the windows. "Mara, you should probably stay outside while I—"

"What?" I looked up. I'd been picking at a flake of dried blood between my thumb and forefinger, not paying attention.

"You're not exactly inconspicuous," he said. "And I've never tried to Jedi mind-fuck anyone like this before." His voice wavered a little.

I arched an eyebrow. "Don't you mean 'mind-trick'?"

"Not when I do it," he said.

"You'll be fine," I said. "Just ask for three rooms."

But I'd never seen him so nervous. He ended up taking my hand and walking in with me, filthy and bloody though I was. Our clothes dripped water on the maroon runner that led up to the front desk. The wood had been painted a dark hunter green, and the desk itself looked like it was covered in a giant doily. A fan lazily spun above our heads, and the breeze made me shiver.

No one was actually at the desk, of course. There was a little silver bell, like an actual *bell*, with a card that said *Ring for Service* in calligraphy.

"Well?" Stella looked at Jamie.

Jamie fidgeted. "I'm not sure I can—"

"You can," I said gently.

"No, but if I can't, though . . . I mean, if I screw up, what if she calls the police?"

"Then you'd better not screw up." I smiled.

"Don't be such a dick," Jamie said, but he was smiling too. Then he rang the bell. He looked ready to bolt at any second.

"Just a moment!" The three of us heard shuffling, and then a pair of doors swung open. A bespectacled elderly woman appeared, beaming at us. Well, not all of us.

"Oh my," she said as she got a good look at me. "Oh, sweetheart, are you all right?"

I mustered up my most winning smile. It did not have the desired effect.

"Um, we'd like to book a room," Jamie said quickly as the woman held her hand to her chest. Stella nudged him. "Two rooms. Three rooms," he amended.

"Dear, what *happened* to you?" she asked me. "Do you need a doctor?"

"Um, no—We were just—Jamie," I said through gritted teeth, still smiling awkwardly. "Do something."

I could see the woman's confusion turn to nervousness and then to fear as she looked from me to the others. "Three rooms, you say?" Her voice wobbled slightly. "You know, I think I have just the ones for you. I'll just run and do a quick check and make sure they're ready. It's been a while since we've had anyone up in the suites. Won't be but a minute."

"There's no need to check," Jamie said suddenly. His voice wasn't loud, but it still felt like it was the only sound in the room. "The suites will be perfect. What floor are they on?"

"Third," the woman said, blinking at him. "Third floor, rooms 311, 312 and 313."

"Those will be perfect."

The woman nodded, looking a bit dazed. "Yes. Perfect. I'll just need your names?" She took out a guest book and a pen, and looked at Jamie expectantly.

Something came over Jamie then. He lifted his chin as he said, "Barney." I cocked my head to the side. "Rubble."

Stella put her head in her hands.

"And this," he said, a smile spreading across his lips as he sidled up to Stella, "is Betty." He put his hand on her shoulder. She smiled weakly. "And this is our daughter." Jamie placed a hand on my head. "Bamm-Bamm." I stepped on his foot.

"Ow," he said through a clenched smile.

The woman clapped her hands together, clearly pleased. "What a *lovely* family you have, Mr. Rubble." Her green eyes twinkled as she wrote our names in the guest book. "I'll just need a credit card and one form of ID?" she asked Jamie.

"We already gave it to you," Jamie replied.

"Oh yes!" she said, shaking her head. "You already gave it to me. Of course you did. Forgive me. The old brain's not what it used to be. And how long is it that you'll be staying?"

Jamie looked at me. I shrugged.

"Indefinitely," he said, flashing a dazzling smile at her.

The woman handed him three keys. He handed one to

Stella, one to me, and pocketed the last for himself.

"One last thing, Mrs.—"

"Beaufain," the woman answered.

"Mrs. Beaufain, are there any security cameras on the premises?"

"I'm afraid not," she said. "We had some once, right by the entrance, but they broke, and my son's not out here often enough to help me fix them, so I just let it go already. Life's too short."

"Truer words were never spoken," Jamie said, and thanked her.

Stella and I began to head up the stairs. "I'll catch up with you in a minute," Jamie said, looking shaky and gray.

"You okay?"

"I'm—I don't know. Mrs. Beaufain, is there a bathroom down—downstairs?"

She shook her head. "Just in the rooms, Mr. Rubble." It was a testament to Jamie's amazingness that she said it with a straight face.

Jamie nodded and turned on his heel. We watched him push open the glass door and heave into a hedge out front.

"Ugh," Stella said. "You think he's okay?"

"Should we wait for him?" I asked. As the words left my mouth, I felt a prickle of awareness, like I was being watched. I glanced at Stella.

"What?" she asked.

"Nothing." I peered behind us. My skin was still crawling; it felt tight, stretched over my bones. Even when Jamie appeared, looking normal and healthy under the circumstances, I couldn't shake the sense that something was deeply wrong.

"You look weird," Jamie said, as we headed up the stairs. "You okay?"

I shook my head but said nothing. I didn't know what to say.

We unlocked the doors to our rooms, but congregated in one for a powwow about what just happened. Jamie and Stella did most of the talking. My tongue felt thick in my head even as my thoughts raced. I couldn't focus on what had happened—I was thinking about what would have to happen next.

I crossed the room and looked at Noah's bag. My fingers unzipped it before I realized what they were doing. And then my hands settled on something familiar. The textured cover, the spiral binding—I pulled out my sketchbook. I couldn't remember the last time I'd seen it.

I heard Jamie say my name, but I ignored him as I opened it. My heart turned over when I saw the pictures of Noah that I'd drawn at Croyden. In every stroke of the pencil, every smudge of charcoal, there was a sense of cautious happiness, of restrained excitement. It felt like someone else had drawn those pictures. It felt like another life.

I moved through them quickly without knowing why, but then, when I turned the next page, I stopped.

I was staring at a picture drawn in negative space. The entire page was black, except for the figure at the center of it. It was unmistakably Noah, etched out in white; his messy hair, his sleeping face. His eyelids were closed, and I thought I'd drawn him sleeping until I looked at his chest.

His ribs were cracked and open. They pierced his skin and exposed his heart.

Time stretched and flowed around me. The world rushed by me, but I stayed still. I didn't know if I was awake or dreaming until Noah appeared and took my hand.

He led me out of the room, out of the bed-and-breakfast. When he opened the door for me and I stepped through, we were in New York. We walked hand in hand down a crowded street in the middle of the day. I was in no rush—I could walk with him forever—but Noah was. He pulled me alongside him, strong and determined and not smiling. Not today.

We wove among the people, somehow not touching a single one. The trees were green, but a few still blossomed. It was spring, almost summer. A strong wind shook a few of the steadfast flowers off the branches and into our path. We ignored them.

Noah led me into Central Park, which teemed with human life. Brightly colored picnic blankets burst across the lawn, with the pale, outstretched forms of people wriggling over them like worms in fruit. We crossed the reservoir, the gleaming sun reflecting off its surface, which was dotted with boats, and then Noah reached into his bag. He pulled out the little cloth doll, my grandmother's. The one we'd burned. He offered it to me.

I took it.

"I'm sorry," he said, as my fingers closed around it. And then he slit my throat.

I woke up gasping. And wet. Hot water splashed around me. My clothes were on and soaked, and the water was tinged a dark, deep pink. My fingers grasped the cool cast-iron lip of the antique tub, and I felt hands tighten around my wrist.

"You're all right," Stella said, kneeling by the bathtub. She was also clothed, and also soaked. I had no idea what she or I was doing there.

I whipped around, or tried to. "What's—what's happening?"

"You were—" She measured her words. "A mess." She looked down at my shirt, the one we'd gotten from the tourist shop. That much I remembered. "The blood—it seemed to be upsetting you, but you couldn't—you couldn't get to the shower."

"What are you talking about?"

Her hair was curling from the steam and the heat, and her skin was pale. "What's the last thing you remember?"

I closed my eyes. "We checked in. I remember that. We came up here to the room—and I found my sketchbook in Noah's bag."

Whatever happened next had slipped out of my mental

grasp; the harder I thought about it, the hazier it became.

Stella inhaled slowly. "One second you were fine. Then you just—went limp."

"I passed out?"

Stella shook her head. "No. Not at first. Your eyes were open but staring at nothing. And you kept trying to take off your clothes."

That, more than anything else she'd said, scared me.

"I tried to talk to you. You were *aware*, that's the thing. Your eyes followed me when I spoke. When Jamie spoke. It was like, like you were listening but you didn't respond. We coaxed you in here, and I thought maybe, if I could get the blood off, you'd come back. So we put you into the bathtub, but then you passed out."

"That's . . ." I didn't even know what to say, except, "Fucked up."

"It's okay," Stella said, squeezing my hand.

No, it wasn't. I looked down at myself. I was a mess, outside and in. "Thank you," I said to Stella. "For everything."

Her brows drew together. "Thank *you*. I know I freaked out in the truck after . . . after. But I heard what he was thinking. He would've murdered us. If you hadn't . . ."

Killed him. Butchered him.

"I wouldn't be here right now."

I wanted to tell her she didn't have to thank me, but the words tangled on my tongue.

"Can I—can I have a second?" I asked hoarsely. "I can't stand these clothes anymore."

She braced herself against the tub and quickly stood. "Of course. Do you want me to stay outside? If you need me?"

If I needed her. If I needed her to help me *bathe*. We barely knew each other, but without her help, who knows how long I would've been out?

"I think I'm all right. But thank you. Really." I heard the door close behind her.

I stared blankly at the beadboard wall, huddled in the bathtub. The water had started to cool. I pulled the plug with my toe and drained it, stripped off my clothes and took a real bath. Without help.

When I was done, I looked up at myself in the mirror shakily, wondering who would be staring back. But it was just me. My eyes looked wide and round in my pale face, and my collarbones were sharper than I'd remembered them. The heat and steam brought some color to my cheeks and lips, and I looked better than I had at Horizons, but still. I didn't really look like myself. I didn't really *feel* like myself. It hit me then that this was the first time I'd really been alone since Horizons.

Wrapped in a white towel, I stepped out of the tiled bathroom and into my room, the old wooden floorboards creaking under my feet. Noah's bag, still open, sat on the lace-covered four-poster bed. My sketchbook was next to it. Closed.

I approached his bag cautiously, staring at it like it might lash out and bite. I sat down on the bed and ran my fingers over the black nylon fabric. I needed to look inside. There might be something that could help us figure out where Noah was, why he wasn't with us, whether he was really—

I closed my eyes and bit my lip to stop myself from thinking it. I didn't open my eyes; I just let my hands wander over his things, feeling his clothes, his laptop . . .

He would've taken that with him if he could have, wouldn't he? Which meant he couldn't have, which meant maybe he—

Stop it. Stop it. I let go of the laptop, but my fingers caught on something else as I withdrew them. It was his T-shirt, the white one with the holes in it. I filled my hands with the fabric and brought it up to my face.

I caught the barest, faintest scent of him, soap and sandalwood and smoke, and in that moment I felt not loss but *need*. Noah had been there for me when I'd had no one else. He'd believed me when no one else had. He could not be gone, I thought, but my throat began to hurt and my chest began to tighten, and I curled up in bed, knees to chest, head to knees, waiting for tears that never came, and sleep that did.

20+

BEFORE

London, England

MR. GRIMSBY WAS FORCED TO HIRE A TATTERED, worn carriage driven by two old mules and an old man to match, after teams of horses refused to bear us. He huffed as he climbed in and extended his hand to help me up. When I took it, he shivered.

Neither of us spoke as the carriage wound through the streets. I bit my lip to keep it from trembling, and the smell of rot invaded my nostrils until we were far from the docks, when it was replaced by the sting of smoke. I coughed several times.

"It's the coal fires," Mr. Grimsby said. "Takes a bit of getting used to."

I peered out the window and watched my new world

unfold before me, the slow pace of the mules allowing me to take everything in. Every person we passed was white, their skin the color of fish bellies. The men dressed in tight coats and pants, while the women were swallowed by voluminous fabrics in every color. That must have been how they kept warm. I held my arms across my chest.

Soon the stink and crowds gave way to gardens dotted with trees, and rows of grand buildings that towered above our heads, made of stones and bricks. The shoddy carriage stopped before one of the grandest.

Mr. Grimsby got out and exchanged coins with the driver, who gaped and stared after us as we walked up to the gate. A uniformed man nodded at Mr. Grimsby and opened the gate for us without looking at me, and Mr. Grimsby led me up to the house.

The house was the color of stone, the front of which seemed to be held up by white columns. It towered several stories into the air. Mr. Grimsby gracefully ascended the front stairs and stopped before a gleaming wooden door. It opened immediately, as had the gate.

Mr. Grimsby held out his hand. "After you, young Miss."

I stepped in. The lamps were lit, though it was only midday. Mr. Grimsby led me down a short dark hall, then showed me into a large room.

Dark gray light filtered in through the windows, which were skirted by heavy drapes the color of cream. A magnificent fixture hung from the center of the ceiling, dripping with crystals and lit candles. Flourishes curled in the plaster around it, and a white stone fireplace so tall I could step into it anchored the center of the room.

A woman holding a candle appeared seemingly out of nowhere. She was dressed in brown, her gray hair tied loosely at her neck. A strip of black cloth encircled the upper sleeve of one arm.

"Ah, Mrs. Dover." Mr. Grimsby nodded at her.

"Mr. Grimsby," she said. "You've returned with the ship's cargo, I see."

He cleared his throat. "Is the lady in?"

"She is not yet returned from church," Mrs. Dover said, examining me. "Let me get a good look at her. Step forward, girl."

I looked at Mr. Grimsby. He nodded. I took a step toward Mrs. Dover.

"Pretty," Mrs. Dover said approvingly. "Though in dire need of new clothes and a good washing up."

"Please prepare the young miss for the lady's arrival."

"Yes, Mr. Grimsby," she said, and beckoned to me. "What's your name, girl?"

I hesitated.

"She's a bit shy," Mr. Grimsby said.

"Of course," Mrs. Dover said. "I'll have one of the maids set your things in your room. Come then. Let's get you washed up."

My shoes *thunked* on the wide-planked wooden floors. She walked me to the back of the house, where a hound of some sort stood at the foot of the stairs, baring its teeth at me.

"Dash," Mrs. Dover scolded. "Shoo." She waved her hand at the dog. The dog did not move.

Mrs. Dover looked at me queerly, then called out, "Miss Smith!" A harried-looking young girl with soot on her cheeks appeared, brushing her palms on her skirt.

"Yes, Mrs. Dover?"

"Take Dash outside, please."

"Yes, Mrs. Dover." The girl reached for the dog's collar. He snapped at her, but she didn't flinch. She just fixed a grip on the dog's thick scruff, and he yipped as she ushered him away from the stairs. Mrs. Dover went up them, and I followed behind. I glanced behind me. The dog watched me as I ascended the stairs.

At the third landing Mrs. Dover led me down a hall bracketed by carved woodwork. "Each room's named for a color—the blue room, the red room, the lavender room, the gray room, and so on. The green room belongs to the lady. The blue room is to be yours, I believe." She showed me into it. It was precisely the same color as the clothes Uncle used to always wear. I nearly gasped at the familiarity of it. A large copper basin waited for me in the corner. Steam curled from the lip.

I let Mrs. Dover undress me, let her scrub me without mercy in the scalding water. I gritted my teeth and did not make a sound, even as she tore a comb through my knotted hair.

When she finished, she dressed me and opened my trunk.

"Hmm," she said disapprovingly as she picked through the clothing I had purchased for myself in India. Then she lifted up my doll with her thumb and forefinger. "What's this?"

"It's mine," I said.

"So she speaks, does she." Mrs. Dover looked amused. "Well, we can wash it, though there might be no saving it, I'm afraid."

I snatched my doll from her hand.

"Mrs. Dover," a crisp, brittle voice said from behind me. "Is there a problem?"

A look of surprise transformed Mrs. Dover's face. "No, of course not, my lady."

I turned to face a figure draped in black. Her face was veiled by black fabric that reflected no light, the same fabric as her gown. It rustled with each tiny, delicate step she took toward me. She seemed to be floating, gliding over the floor.

"I should have a look at the girl my husband brought from across the world," the woman said, and swept the veil from her face.

My memories of her husband painted him as old and frail, but this woman was neither. She had ash blond hair that was braided in a crown around her face. Jet-black earrings dangled from her ears. The stones glittered in the dim light.

"You are older than I thought you would be," she said. "How old are you, child?"

I lowered my eyes to the floor. "I do not know, Lady."

The woman clapped her hands together. "How darling! You speak as if you were born and raised in the West End and not in the jungles of India. My husband purchased you a fine education, it seems."

I thought of Uncle and Sister. "Yes, Lady."

"If only he had lived to see it," she said queerly. "He wrote a great deal about you in his papers."

I did not know what to say to that, so I remained quiet.

"Well, you are in my care now, and I will treat you as if you were my own daughter. I would have insisted Mr. Bray draw up the paperwork to officially make you my ward, as my husband desired, except you would then be expected to mourn for him as well, and I would not mar your arrival with such darkness."

I bowed my head.

She looked at the room we stood in. "My husband instructed me very clearly to place you in the blue room, but I think a different one would be more suitable. Come, child."

I followed the woman in black, and she led me to an even larger room. The walls were painted a pale mint color, ornamented with gold candleholders in the shape of flowers. A cream-colored bed with a full canopy and skirt stood in the center of the room. No wonder I'd been scrubbed so harshly.

"Yes," she said, looking around. "This room is much more suitable for a young girl. So much lighter! Mrs. Dover, the curtains?"

Mrs. Dover busied herself about the room, throwing them open. Dozens of arched windows emerged, broken up into wavy panes of glass. The lady smiled.

"You can see the gardens from up here. Come, dear, look!"

I followed her, and peered out the windows. The gardens were brown with the season, and one of the leafless trees was choked with blackbirds.

"Before supper I shall introduce you to everyone in the household. The boys, Elliot and Simon, are with the nanny at present, but I shall have Mrs. Dover send word to the cook that they are to dine with us tonight so they might meet you."

Mrs. Dover inclined her head. "Yes, my lady," she said, and left.

The lady approached me and smiled. "And tomorrow your new tutor shall arrive, at my husband's direction. I admit that if he had not asked it of me on his deathbed, I wouldn't think of it, but I will honor his wishes, no matter how unorthodox. No one must know, however. Do you understand?"

I nodded at her.

"Good girl. Everything has been arranged, and the tutor is eager to meet you."

"Yes, Lady."

She smiled. "I should like you to address me as Aunt Sarah. We are to be family, after all."

"Yes, Aunt Sarah."

"Clever girl," she said. "And yet I find I still do not know how to address you. Strangely, my husband never mentioned your name."

Because when he knew me, I had not yet chosen one.

"And neither did Mr. Barbary," she finished. "Tell me, dear, what shall I call you?"

Before I could answer, the flock of blackbirds scattered, screaming, into the air, diverting Aunt Sarah's attention.

I took a moment to think.

"*There is power in a name,*" Sister had said. I did not want to give out the one I'd shared only with her and Uncle, so I'd given anyone else who had asked a different one instead. The name I had given to my doll, before I'd known what it meant. I decided to give Aunt Sarah the same one.

"Mara," I told her as we watched the birds disappear into the sky.

21

I WOKE UP WHILE IT WAS STILL DARK. I DRESSED IN NOAH'S clothes—his T-shirt, which hung loose over my narrow shoulders, and his jeans, which I had to roll up before I could walk. I didn't care how I looked; wearing his clothes made me feel closer to him, and I needed that for what I would have to do today.

My heart pounded against my ribs as I opened his laptop and powered it on. There might have been something on it that would give us some clue, some hint that would help me find him, and no matter what else I found on it, I needed to find *that*. I needed to know he was okay.

I was prompted for a password, and I guessed wrong once,

twice, four times, then eight. Nothing I tried worked—no variations of his name, his pets' names, his birthday, even my birthday. I slammed the laptop shut, threw it into his bag, and knocked on Stella's door before the sun rose. She answered it blearily.

"Y'okay?"

Not really. "I want to go as soon as we can."

She stood there for a minute, as if she were trying to translate what I'd said, but she finally nodded. "Ten minutes."

Jamie didn't answer the first or second time I knocked; I stood there for what felt like hours before he finally woke up.

"What?"

"Pack up. I want to go."

"Why?"

"Because we have to find Noah."

Jamie blinked, and I thought he would argue, but he said, "Five minutes." And then he shut the door on me.

We walked out of the bed-and-breakfast without breakfast, and, as Stella complained, without much bed, either, but it would be a while before we reached Miami. Stella could nap in the car. On our way out we managed to steal—sorry, "borrow"—a car belonging to an early-rising guest, thanks to Jamie. It was comfortable and roomy, but Jamie warned us not to get attached to it—we'd be ditching it as soon as we reached Miami. After that we would borrow another one, and pay a visit to Noah's parents, then ours.

Stella's mouth hung open when we crossed the bridge

that led to the gated island Noah lived on. The farther in we drove, the more extravagant the houses became. Noah's parents' house (mansion) towered over the center of a sprawling green lawn dotted with Greek fountains. Palm trees framed the driveway, which was blocked by an iron gate.

The video camera swiveled in our direction. I'd already told Jamie what to say.

"Hi," he said, as if reading from a script. "I'm here to see Noah? I'm a friend from school?"

There was a click, and then a voice on the intercom. "No visitors are to be admitted at present, I'm afraid."

I knew that voice. "Albert?" The Shaws' butler. He'd met me before. I prayed that he would remember. "It's Mara Dyer—I have something of Noah's—"

"He's . . . he's unavailable, miss."

Unavailable. Unavailable dead or unavailable alive?

"Where is he?" I asked.

There was a pause. "I'm afraid—" My heart lodged in my throat. "I'm afraid I'm not at liberty to say."

I tried to stay calm. I had to stay calm, or we would be thrown out of there with more questions and fewer answers than we'd arrived with.

"Can I give you something to give to him?"

There was no answer, but the gate swung open. I leaned my head back against the seat in relief as Jamie drove forward.

"I don't know if I can do this," Jamie said. He'd said that before. Every time, actually.

Watching him exercise his ability was sort of fascinating. He worked himself up into an anxious, nervous frenzy, wondering out loud if he could do it, mumbling to himself about the consequences. It reminded me of something I'd read once, about divers making themselves hyperventilate before they dove, to force more oxygen into their lungs or something. Since we were triggered by stress and fear and possibly pain, Jamie freaking out about whether or not he could work his magic made it more likely that he could.

Albert was waiting for us at the front door when we drove up. His hands were tucked behind his back. I fleetingly wondered how he would react to Jamie vomiting in one of the mammoth potted boxwood urns when he finished with him.

"You can do this," I whispered to Jamie. And then he did.

"Hi, Albert," Jamie said in that calm, confident, crystalline voice. "My name is Jamie Roth, though you're not actually going to remember that, or the fact that we had this conversation, once we've had it."

"Of course, sir."

"So here's how this is going to work. I'm going to ask you questions, and you're going to give me honest answers, all right?"

"All right."

"Okay, what's your middle name?"

Stella and I shared a glance.

"Eugene."

"Do you have a driver's license?"

"Yes."

"Give me your wallet, please."

Albert did so. Jamie checked it. "His middle name is in fact Eugene. Great. Okay, Albert. Now this is where it's going to get a little weird. Are you ready?"

"I'm ready for weird, sir."

"Is Noah Shaw alive?"

It took an eternal, agonizing second for Albert to answer.

"Yes, sir."

"Yes, Noah's alive?"

"Yes, he is."

I wanted to do cartwheels on the lawn. I wanted to fly. I wanted to rocket into the sun.

"Where is he?"

"At the Horizons Residential Treatment Center, sir."

No. *No.*

"Are you sure, Albert?"

"Yes, sir. I drove him there myself."

"When?"

"Three weeks ago."

That was shortly after I'd been dropped off myself.

"Do you know if he was there just for the retreat or if he'd been admitted long-term?"

"I'm not sure, sir."

"Aren't his parents worried about him?"

"Not particularly, no."

No surprise there.

"Are they home?" Jamie asked. "Can we speak to them?"

"I'm afraid they're in Europe at the moment."

"What about Katie?" I asked. Jamie repeated my question.

"Her as well," Albert answered.

Jamie looked at me and shrugged. "What next?"

I didn't know. But at least we had one more answer than we'd had when we'd arrived; there had been no funeral. Which meant his family believed he was alive. But they also thought he was at Horizons. Noah had gotten himself thrown in there for me. To be with me. And now—

Now he was nowhere. Because of me.

22

JAMIE AND STELLA TRIED TO CHEER ME UP WHEN WE got back into the car. "It's not hopeless," they said. "We'll find him." But I began to *feel* hopeless and doubt that we *would* find him. I had nothing to hold on to, so I held on to myself. My arms crossed over my stomach, pressing his clothes against my skin as I tried to think about what he would have said if he'd been there. I closed my eyes and tried to imagine him, what he would have looked like, sounded like, if he'd been in the seat next to me.

I pictured his face, careless and unworried, his hair a tousled mess as he reminded me that his parents were idiots. That they never knew where he was, even when he was home. He would tell me not to believe something unless it could be proven. Once, I would've said that just because you couldn't prove something didn't mean it wasn't real. But I wouldn't say that today. Today I needed to believe he was right.

Jamie came up with the implausible explanation we would offer to each of our respective families when we showed up on our respective doorsteps. *We're still at Horizons. Everything is fine. We're going on an extended wilderness retreat up north, where we can sing with all the voices of the mountains and paint with all the colors of the wind.* I'd seen Jamie work miracles, but this was my mother I had to convince. I did not have high hopes.

But we didn't end up visiting my house first. My mother and father would have been out working, and Joseph would have been at school. Stella's mother worked the night shift, and her dad had left when she was little, so it was just her and her mom. Jamie talked to her mother, which seemed to go well, and then he went to talk to his own parents. I have no idea how that went because he didn't invite us into his house. He walked out carrying a bigger duffel bag with "provisions." For what, I didn't ask. On his way back to the car (our third), he wiped his mouth and gave us the thumbs-up. I started the car. "Shotgun," he said to Stella.

"But I'm already sitting here."

"But I'm the one who got us the car. And the one messing

with our parents' memories. Come on," he whined. "It's hot in the backseat, and I don't feel well."

"How did it go?" I asked him.

Jamie shrugged. "Okay? They were surprised to see me at first, obviously, but I fed them the bullshit and they swallowed it." He snapped his fingers. "Like that."

"Like that," I repeated. "You're proving to be quite handy."

"Yeah, I am. And you're next."

I was, finally. The afternoon light filtered through the palm trees and oaks that dotted the cul-de-sac we lived on, and I did a quick car check when we drove by the house. Mom's, Dad's, and Daniel's cars were all there, which meant Joseph would hopefully be there too. Jamie said that would make this all easier—feed everyone the same lines at the same time, and there's less chance that an inconsistency will crop up later and conflict with what they remember.

But for this visit both Jamie and Stella would need to join me. Because it wasn't just my parent problem we needed to fix; we needed to get *New Theories in Genetics* from Daniel too. While Jamie was talking, Stella would entertain my brother, and I'd fetch the book. Lemon squeezy.

I realized when I walked up to the house that I didn't have my key, and my parents didn't keep a spare in any obvious places, like under the doormat or a decorative rock or something.

I looked at Jamie and Stella. "So what, I just knock?"

"I'd suggest it," Jamie said.

"And then?"

"And then I'll tell your family what I told my family, and Stella's mom."

Stella put a hand on my shoulder. "It'll be fine. Don't worry."

It sounded easy enough. But my hand still shook when I lifted it to knock on the door.

My mother answered it. Her eyes went wide when she saw me. "Mara! What are you doing here?"

I don't know why, but my eyes began to fill the second I saw her. I wanted to throw my arms around her and hear her tell me she loved me. That everything would be okay. But I couldn't move, and I didn't say a word.

Jamie did, though. "Everything's okay," he said smoothly as my mother ushered the three of us in. I watched her face as he spoke to her, told her the fake story of what had happened to us, why we were there, and why we'd be leaving again soon. My mother looked completely untroubled by all of it. Relaxed, even. She urged Jamie and Stella to sit at the kitchen table while she made us something to eat, and Jamie continued to talk. It all seemed so *normal*, except for the fact that it wasn't, at all. I knew why we had to do this, but I still felt the urge to take my mother by the shoulders and scream that everything was not okay, that *I* was not okay, and that I would probably never be okay again.

When Joseph and my father walked into the kitchen, Jamie went to work on them, too, repeating the story word for word. He made Horizons sound like camp. He left out the fact that I had killed the counselors.

I braced myself for my suspicious, questioning mother's reaction, but she didn't find Jamie's explanation at all strange. His words cut through any resistance my parents might have had, erasing my future absence from their future memories like it was nothing. More than anything else I'd seen, that unsettled me.

Jamie excused himself barely two minutes later. It was Stella's turn now.

"So where's Daniel?" I heard her ask. I realized I wasn't even looking at my family anymore. I'd been staring at nothing for who knew how long.

"New York," my father said.

That got my attention.

"He went to visit a few colleges," my mother added, reaching for sandwich stuff from the refrigerator. "I think he's deciding between Columbia and Princeton?"

"I thought Columbia and Yale?" my father said.

"When's he coming back?" I asked, trying not to sound too anxious.

Dad shrugged. "Next week, maybe? Or the week after?"

Mom looked like she was trying to remember. "He said he might go visit Harvard and Brown, too—"

"And Dartmouth, I think," my father said. "I remember something about Dartmouth." It wasn't like my parents to not know where all of their children were. My mother especially. Something wasn't right. Jamie returned and picked up a sandwich.

Was what he'd told them screwing with other memories? I felt a kick under the table. Jamie was trying, poorly, to indicate with his eyes that we needed to talk alone.

"Be back in a minute," I said to my parents. "Stella?"

"Still eating," she said, popping potato chips into her mouth. She'd sat down next to Joseph on the floor and was watching him play a video game. I led Jamie into my room and closed the door behind us. As soon as I did, he spoke.

"So we have a problem," he said. "I haven't done this much, but I do know that Daniel's going to notice that something's messed up when your parents tell him the bullshit about you, and why they aren't worried."

"What do you mean?"

"You think your parents would believe that you're going on a wilderness retreat, without checking on it, if I weren't here to make them believe it?"

Point. "Is there anything you can do about it?"

Jamie looked doubtful. "Doubtful. I thought about maybe trying to talk to him over the phone, but I don't know if my mind thingie works like that? Especially when I've never really talked to him before. It could get weird . . . and if he doesn't believe me, he might be able to poke holes through what I told the rest of your family too."

"So we just have to go, then, and hope he's busy, and that my parents don't mention anything strange."

"I think we do."

"Not ideal," I said.

"Not ideal."

Just then my bedroom door opened, with Stella behind it. "We have a problem."

"We know," I said. "Daniel's not here."

"Right. Daniel's not here. And neither is the book."

23

TELL ME YOU'RE KIDDING," JAMIE SAID.

"Tell me that was rhetorical?" Stella met my gaze. "I asked Joseph to give me a tour of the house, and he started with his bedroom, naturally, and then moved on to Daniel's. I looked on his bookshelves, everywhere I could think of. It isn't there."

I didn't quite trust her—she didn't know Daniel and had never been in his room before, so I went to check myself. They both tagged along after me. I looked everywhere I could think of but in the end could come to only one conclusion.

"Fuck," I said.

Jamie, looking through one of his drawers, added, "Your

brother does have quite the porn collection, though."

"Gross," I said. "Also, false."

Jamie fake laughed. "Just kidding. I'm a kidder."

I walked up to him and punched his arm.

"Ow."

"Just kidding. I'm a kidder."

"Not the same," Jamie said, rubbing it.

"Hate to break this up," Stella said, "but if the book isn't here, and Daniel isn't here, my brilliant guess is that he has it with him."

Only my brother would bring six hundred pages of nonfiction with him on a trip. Classic Daniel.

"And why would he do this?" Jamie asked me. "He doesn't know about you, does he?"

I shook my head. "And he thinks the premise of the book is crap."

"The premise being . . ."

"I was reading it—or trying to—to find out what the author said about genetic memory, because of my dreams or memories or whatever about that doll, and India. Daniel said genetic memory isn't a real thing." I paused. "Noah did too. But—"

"The name of the author turned up on that list Kells had at Horizons, and what she was doing to us was real enough." Stella said what I was thinking. "So your brother was wrong about the book."

"He *might* be wrong about it," Jamie said. "We haven't read it. We won't know until we have."

"You're not seriously saying that you think it's a coincidence?" Stella asked.

"I'm just saying—You know what? Google will resolve this," Jamie said. "Mara, computer?"

"Ask my mom for her laptop. I'm going to pack." I didn't have the energy to fight about the book now. I was too anxious—about it, about Daniel, about Noah, about everything. I needed to get out of there. Get moving.

I left Stella and Jamie to argue about the book, and went to my room to retrieve the items I might need for our quest. Jamie and Stella had packed stuff too, but stupidly I hadn't asked what they'd brought or how long they thought we'd be gone. I looked around my room, trying to figure out where to start.

My room. I wondered when I'd started thinking of it that way. We'd moved to Miami only months ago; in December I'd been in Laurelton. Rachel had been alive. Jude had been my boyfriend. God, it didn't seem possible.

I picked out enough underwear and clothes to last a couple of weeks and packed them into a gray duffel my mom had lent me once, for a school trip. She'd let me keep it even after I'd gotten home because I liked it so much. My throat tightened. I tried to tell myself that this wasn't permanent—that we would find answers, and a cure, and Noah, too, and I would come home and things would go back to normal, but I couldn't quite believe it. I couldn't even remember what normal was.

I walked down the long hallway, taking what felt like a last look at the pictures of my family that hung on the wall. I didn't linger on my grandmother's portrait. I'd seen enough of her.

Instead I tried to act casual as I hugged my father and mother and little brother before walking out the door. I could lie to them, but I couldn't lie to myself. It felt like good-bye.

It was Stella's turn to drive, but she didn't start the car right away. "We can't find the book online," she said.

"Which means it's probably out of print," Jamie said. "But there's this bookstore in Coral Gables—they have everything, and if they don't have it, they can get it for us."

"So we're going there," Stella said, and paused. "Mara? What's wrong?"

I didn't want to talk about it. "Just drive."

"Mara—"

"Drive."

She drove. After almost an hour in traffic, we parked across the street from the bookstore and walked into the courtyard. Jamie ordered a lemonade from the outdoor café before we went inside.

If I'd been in a better mood, I would have thought I was in heaven. It was beautiful, with gleaming wood floors and rooms of books neatly stacked from floor to ceiling.

"How have I not been here before?" I asked.

"Right?" Jamie said. "It's the best."

"Is there something I can help you with?" A woman stood behind us; the sleeves of her Books & Books T-shirt were rolled up, exposing colorful tattoos of illustrations from children's books on her arms. Her dark hair was knotted up in a high, loose bun.

"Why, yes," Jamie said, and sucked loudly on his straw. "Yes, you can."

He told her what we were looking for, and she ducked behind the desk to try to help us.

"What did the book look like?" Jamie asked me.

I closed my eyes and pictured it. "Black cover," I said. "Clothbound. The title was in gold."

The woman typed some things into the computer. "Author's name was Lenaurd?"

"Yup," Stella said. She was practically bouncing on her heels.

"Hmm," the woman said. She bit her thumb. "Let me try something else."

She typed and searched and typed and searched, but eventually she let out a frustrated sigh. "That's so weird," she said.

"What?" Jamie asked.

"There's literally nothing in any of the databases. I even searched for articles, thinking maybe it was published in an academic journal and then bound later, but nothing's coming up. Not for that title or for that author. I can try calling some of the rare-book dealers we know and get back to you?"

Stella visibly deflated. Jamie thanked the woman, and the three of us walked out. Jamie ordered three sandwiches to go. I left mine untouched.

"So." He put his hands on his hips. "Off to New York we go, yes?"

Yes.

Stella wanted to fly there. She was putting all of her eggs into the *New Theories* basket, and she was dying to collect them. If Daniel was in New York, she reasoned, the book would be too. Jamie wanted to get there too, for other reasons. He wanted to follow the money re: Horizons, and to do that we had to follow the accountant, and the accountant was in New York. But flying meant airport security, which meant video cameras and disgruntled TSA agents and being surrounded by a lot of people. With our semi-fugitive status, Jamie thought that would be unwise. I concurred.

So we drove. For hours. We switched cars again as we passed West Palm Beach, exchanging one not-really-but-kind-of stolen car for another, in case our absence from Horizons had been noticed by anyone who might have been looking.

The green of the trees and the gray of the sky blurred together into a humid-looking soup. At some point the air thickened with fog and rain as we followed I-95 out of the city and into the middle of Nowhere, Florida. When I woke up from a spontaneous nap, I looked up and realized

I could barely see the road in front of us. And stupidly, Stella hadn't slowed down. I snapped at her about it. She ignored me.

Jamie reached between us from the backseat to turn on the radio, but the only non-staticky stations out there broadcast evangelical preachers.

"Are we there yet?" he whined.

"Don't whine," I said to him. "It's unbecoming."

"Feeling a bit moody, are we?" Stella asked. "I'd have thought a nap would've made you less cranky."

"Die in a fire."

"Maybe she's having her period," Jamie said.

I whipped around in my seat. *"Really?"*

"You *are* acting uncharacteristically moody."

"Uncharacteristically?" Stella chimed in.

"I hate both of you," I mumbled, and rested my cheek on the cool glass. I was so hot. And I *was* actually feeling moody. And achy. Maybe I *was* getting my period.

"What day is it today?"

"The twenty-first," Stella said.

I counted. Huh. That was weird. I hadn't had a period since—since before Horizons. More than a month ago.

Or wait, I couldn't *remember* having one. That didn't mean I hadn't had one.

But what if—what if I hadn't?

The thought unsettled me. I'd never been late before. But

I also had never been experimented on before. First time for everything?

I stared ahead at the road and asked Stella, "When did you have your period last?"

Jamie crossed his arms, looking smug. "Called it." I flicked his ear.

"Um, three weeks ago? I think." She glanced at me. "When was yours?"

"A month ago," I lied. She shot me a look. "What?" I asked.

"Nothing." She turned back to the road, then swore. "I don't think I packed any tampons. Did you?"

I shook my head. "Forgot."

"As delightful as this conversation is," Jamie said, "can I ask why we're having it?"

I had no good answer to that question, but as I struggled to come up with some excuse, I realized Stella was pulling off toward an exit.

"I thought we were stopping in Savannah?" Jamie asked. "We're still an hour away."

"We have only a quarter of a tank left," she explained. "And I need a bathroom."

That liar. She thought *I* needed a bathroom, and that I was embarrassed about it, so she was covering for me so we could stop. Which was actually extremely sweet.

Thank you, I mouthed to her. And I *was* grateful. When we stopped, I could ask Stella the question I wanted to ask, just not in front of Jamie.

At the gas station Stella decided she really did have to use the restroom, thankfully, so the two of us went inside while Jamie filled the tank. I bought tampons I unfortunately didn't need and followed Stella into the bathroom. She was about to walk into a stall when I stopped her.

"Are you sure it was three weeks ago?"

"Yeah. I remember having to ask Wayne for tampons. His face turned so red, I actually thought steam might start coming out of his ears." She grinned, but it quickly faded. "Why? What's wrong?"

I bit my lip. "I'm late."

"How late?"

"I don't—I don't really know. Time is sort of screwed up for me—maybe, maybe two weeks?" Or three.

"That's pretty late," Stella said quietly.

I said nothing.

"I've never been that late."

I still said nothing. Apparently, whatever was going on with me wasn't going on with her.

Stella's expression quickly changed from curious to concerned. "Are you okay?"

"I'm fine." But I wasn't fine. I was a lot of things, but definitely not fine.

"You look weird . . . ," she said.

I looked at myself in the bathroom mirror. I looked awful, was how I looked. My face was nearly white, and my lips were gray, and the shadows under my eyes were like bruises.

Stella didn't look like this. Stella looked healthy. Normal. If she was different, like me, why didn't I look more like *her*?

"You look like you're going to pass out." She glanced back at the door. "Should I get Jamie? I'll get Jamie."

I started to protest but the room began to spin, and I couldn't speak and stand at the same time. I grabbed the sink, but my knees felt shaky, and I slid down to the floor.

24

BEFORE

London, England

AUNT SARAH KEPT HER PROMISE. SHE treated me as if I were her own child. Better, perhaps. She had always secretly wanted a daughter, she said, a girl who would be docile and gentle, unlike Elliot and Simon, rough young boys, always tumbling in the dirt and battling each other with sticks.

I dined with her at nearly every meal. She would brush and braid my hair, though I had a lady's maid to do it for me. I was her Indian princess, she said, a gift her husband didn't even know he had given her, to keep her company after his death. I spent nearly every moment with her as she taught me every rule.

Rules about what to eat and when and how. What to wear and how to dress. How to behave. How to address women, how to address men, how to address men of title, the differences among the servants, among the butler and valet and the different types of maids. She taught me whom I could be seen with, and what I could be seen doing.

We dined together in the morning, took calls together in the afternoon, and she taught me to dance and play cards in the evening before she retired for bed. I could never have imagined a life like this. I became accustomed to the tastes of rich foods prepared painstakingly, of clean linens that I did not myself have to clean. I took long walks with Aunt Sarah. I spent time with the little boys. And three times per week, in secret, the professor came to me during the day.

The first time I met him, I was startled by how familiar he seemed. He was dark and handsome, and I could have sworn I had seen his face before, but he made no mention of it, and it would have been rude if I had.

Mr. Grimsby ushered him into the house without ceremony, and he bowed when I arrived. I bobbed a curtsy, and he smiled. We were to study in the library, Mr. Grimsby said, and showed the professor the way.

It was my favorite room in the house. I loved the smell, and the quiet, and the way shafts of light trapped little motes of dust. It felt like another world.

We sat down. "Well, Mara," he said to me in English with

just the faintest trace of a foreign accent. "Tell me everything you know."

"How do you know my name?"

"Ask the wrong questions, and you will get the wrong answers. I will let you ask three of them before we begin our lessons."

I had never been challenged so directly, not since arriving in London, at least, and I was perturbed by it. "Who are you?" I asked warily.

The professor smiled, exposing all of his white teeth. "I am a person. A human. A man. I have been a father and a son, a husband and a brother, and now I am your teacher. Is that really what you want to ask me?"

Frustrated, I blurted out, "Why do you look familiar?"

"Because we have met before. That is three. Now—"

"Wait! You never answered my first question," I said as I crossed my arms over my chest.

The professor smiled again. "I know your name," he said, "because Mr. Grimsby announced you before you walked in."

I narrowed my eyes at him. "What's your name?"

"There is power in a name. That is four questions, and three was our agreement, but for practical purposes, I shall answer. You may call me Professor. Now, let us begin."

Most days the professor taught me about the world and its people. Which countries were at rest and which cities were at war. He taught me the history of the world and of the universe, about mathematics and science. But every now and then we would do something different. He would play cards with me, and not the way Aunt Sarah did. I never understood the rules of the game. He would have me cut the deck, and then he would lay out his cards, with strange numbers and pictures on them. Sometimes he would give me objects, like bird feathers or stones or, one time, even a sword, which he withdrew from his cane, and he would tell me to write stories about them. Other times he would give me pretend problems and ask how I would solve them. He never answered my questions, about the objects or cards or their purposes. He said I had asked my three questions, and had wasted them. In the future I would be more careful. On those days I hated him.

Every other day I was Aunt Sarah's doll, to be dressed and played with and entertained. My own doll lay buried but not quite forgotten in the trunk I still kept beneath the skirts of my bed. I scarcely remembered the *befores*—my days spent with Sister beneath the hot sun, or nights with Uncle as he'd showed me the stars. I became an indoor creature, like Dash, the late Master Shaw's foxhound, who had been relegated to the servants' quarters since he'd taken an immediate disliking to me.

I watched my reflection change in the mirror above the marble fireplace as the seasons changed outside. The garden bloomed with roses, and I bloomed into womanhood. After Aunt Sarah's year of full mourning ended, she began to talk of presenting me at court, so that she might begin her search for a suitable match for me.

She would not hear that I might not be considered by the greatest families in London because of my skin, or my lack of family and property. "You are fair enough, and your face is so lovely! With your full lips, your raven hair—and your eyes, so exotic! You are a rare beauty, Mara, and I will ensure that you have the grandest dowry—any man would be lucky to have you." She fingered the locket of her husband's hair that hung around her neck.

But the professor discouraged this idea. In fact he discouraged any mention or proposal of my being brought out into society. Aunt Sarah was not a meek woman, but he was persuasive, and he persuaded her for a time. But he could not talk her out of marriage.

I told him I did not mind. I saw ladies and gentlemen paired off together, sitting sweetly in Hyde Park. Why not me? I dared not say it to the professor, of course. He was not married himself. He did not believe it natural to have one partner for an entire lifetime. *"Animals do not mate for life, and we are animals, no matter what anyone pretends,"* he told me more than once.

But I was presented at court anyway, and engaged six months later. My fiancé was sweet and shy, and he loved me. Our engagement lasted three months. He died on our wedding night, just before dawn.

25

JAMIE'S EYES WIDENED AS HE SAW ME AND STELLA approach. I was too shaky to stand on my own. Stella cut him off before he could ask any questions.

"Mara's sick," she said, "and you're driving." She tossed Jamie the keys and helped me into the backseat.

I was grateful for the help, but I hated it. I couldn't even muster up a proper amount of self-loathing about it, though. I was too tired and too scared and too sick to do anything but lean back in the seat and close my eyes as Jamie drove.

It was early in the afternoon when we reached Savannah an hour later. We pulled into a hotel parking lot not far from the highway.

After we got our keys, Stella said to Jamie, "I need to talk to Mara. You go ahead."

"Can it wait?" I asked. "I have to go to the bathroom." I didn't need to, actually, but I wasn't up to talking about what she would want to talk about. I just wanted to sleep. Really sleep. In a real bed.

"Didn't you just go?" Jamie asked.

I threw him a look, and he handed me a key to my room.

Stella followed me in, but I escaped into the bathroom immediately and turned on the faucet to hide the fact that I wasn't peeing. But I soon heard voices outside—Jamie was in our room too, for some reason. Damn it.

After I could no longer justify hiding, I washed my face, took a few deep breaths, and opened the door.

"My key's not working," Jamie said. He looked from me to Stella. "Um, am I interrupting something?"

"Yes," Stella said as I said, "No."

"We have to talk about this, Mara," Stella said.

Now I was just angry. "There's nothing to talk about."

"Mara's period is three weeks late," Stella said to Jamie.

"Awkward," Jamie mumbled as he backed up toward the door. "I'm, uh, going—elsewhere."

"We can't ignore this, especially not if—"

"I'm not pregnant," I said to her, answering the question she was going to ask eventually.

She raised her eyebrows. "You've been feeling dizzy.

Emotional." She ticked off each word with a finger. "Nauseous—"

"Jamie's nauseous. We're all fucking nauseous. And we're all fucking emotional."

"Not like you," Stella said. "When I was first—when I first noticed what was happening to me, when I first started hearing voices, I thought I was crazy. I didn't know what was going on but I knew something wasn't right. I was confused all the time, my body felt weird, like it belonged to someone else. I stopped eating because it was the only thing that helped. But then I started taking drugs. And the drugs *helped*. I stopped hearing voices. I started eating again. And even at my worst—and my worst was pretty bad—I wasn't like you."

She didn't say it, but I knew she was thinking about what I'd done to Dr. Kells. To Wayne. To Mr. Ernst.

I had nothing to say to that, so all I said was, "I'm not pregnant, Stella. I'm a virgin! Jesus."

"As far as you know," she muttered.

"What was that, Stella?" I asked sharply.

"As far as you know," she said, louder this time. "You were out of it at Horizons. We all were. They did all kinds of tests in that place. What if—"

No. "No, Stella."

"But *what if*—"

"Noah wasn't there," Jamie cut in.

"He was at one point," Stella said. "But what if—"

No.

Stella swallowed hard before she spoke. "What if it's not Noah's?"

It felt like her words had sucked all of the oxygen out of the room. One look at Jamie told me he felt exactly the same way.

I couldn't speak, but I could shake my head.

"You won't know unless you take a test," Stella said.

I couldn't believe this conversation was even happening. How did I get here? I racked my broken brain, desperately searching for a memory, any memory, that could help me answer that question. I forced myself to think about Horizons. They'd done things to me there. But what things?

Stella couldn't be right. I felt sick. I was going to *be* sick. I covered my mouth with my hand and rushed to the bathroom, barely making it to the toilet before I threw up.

I crouched on the tile floor, shaking and sweating. I felt the pressure of her hands on my head as she swept my damp hair back.

"It's still early," Stella said gently. "You could terminate it."

I threw up again.

"You need to know, Mara. One way or the other."

"Oh, God," I moaned.

When there was nothing left in my stomach, I stood up and washed my face. I brushed my teeth. I said good night to Jamie and Stella. My voice sounded robotic. Alien. It didn't sound like it even came from me, but that wasn't really surprising anymore. My body didn't feel like *mine* anymore. Sometimes I did things I didn't want to do, or said things I didn't want to say. Sometimes I felt like crying for no reason, or snapped at the people I cared about for less. I'd been so worried for so long that I was losing my mind, but now it felt like I was losing my body. I felt like a stranger.

What if I was carrying one?

26

OUR NEXT STOP SHOULD'VE BEEN DC, BUT I MADE that difficult.

I couldn't stand being in the car. I was sweating through my clothes, even though Jamie had made the air as cold as it would go. Every hour or so I got sick, and I didn't always have control over it. Stella and Jamie took turns at the wheel so one of them could sit with me in the backseat.

It was a quiet drive—no one said anything about the night before, least of all me, but by some tacit agreement, Jamie stopped in the middle of the eight-hour drive to switch cars and hole up at another hotel, for my sake, no doubt.

Jamie persuaded the owner of a convertible to lend it to us, thinking the air might make me feel less nauseous. After the owner tossed him the keys, Jamie threw up himself behind a bush.

He was getting more and more confident about using his ability, but I still caught him digging his nails into his palms sometimes, or biting his lip until it bled. Perversely, it made me feel better to see him struggle too. Like I was less of a freak among freaks. Maybe what we had *was* an illness, like Kells had said. Sometimes I caught Stella watching me nervously, like I might be contagious.

But Jamie never acted that way. We talked about it later that night, in my room in one of the motels we'd found clustered by the highway exit, while Stella went off in search of something more palatable than fast food.

"I think Stella's a little scared of you," he said, while I changed for bed in the bathroom.

"And you're not?" I called out.

"Of you? You have the soul of a kitten."

I popped my head out of the bathroom. "A kitten."

"An assassin kitten."

I laughed for the first time in I couldn't remember how long. The thing about Jamie was that he didn't seem disturbed enough, sometimes, by the things I'd done. He'd say they were fucked up the way he would point out that the sky was blue. Just a fact, like anything else. But the things I did never seemed to really bother him. *I* never seemed to bother him. In some ways it made him easier to talk to than even Noah.

"So, what are we going to do with you?" Jamie asked.

"In what sense?"

"In the sense that you go from zero to homicidal in sixty seconds."

"I'm passionate."

"You're manic," Jamie said.

"Promise to put me out of my misery before an alien erupts from my stomach?"

"No lie, I think Stella thinks that's a thing that could actually happen. You scare the filling out of her doughnut."

"I'm *not* pregnant. Not with an alien or anything else."

Jamie quickly changed the subject. "You know, I've been thinking—"

"How novel."

"About your ability," he said, ignoring me. "Have you ever tried to, like, make good shit happen?"

"Of course."

"And?"

"Nothing." I paused, wondering if I should ask something I'd been thinking about for a while. Oh, why not. "Do you ever think about Anna?"

"Nope," Jamie said without hesitation, which is how I knew he was lying. But I understood why. Sometimes lies are easier to believe.

Jamie changed the subject. "It's too bad you can't just, like, will yourself to win the presidency."

"At seventeen?"

"Whatever. I just mean—if the stuff you imagine could actually happen, you could change the world."

"I don't think I'd want to be president."

"Really?" Jamie looked incredulous. "God, I'd love it."

"Why?"

"Someone has to be leader of the free world. It might as well be me."

"And what would you do with your great power? It comes with great responsibility, you know."

"New world order," he said, grinning. "The freaks shall inherit the earth."

"I don't think that's how democracy works."

"Democracy is overrated."

"Spoken like a true dictator. If only we could trade abilities."

"I have an inappropriate amount of enthusiasm for that idea."

"This whole conversation is inappropriate." Which was probably why I was enjoying it.

Jamie frowned. "We need some music up in this joint." He looked around. "Is that Noah's laptop?"

I had opened his bag, as well as mine, and the computer was sticking out. "Yeah."

"Have you . . . looked at it?"

I shook my head. "Password protected."

"You can't crack it?"

"Nope."

"Can I try?"

I shrugged. If I hadn't had any luck, he probably wouldn't either.

Less than five minutes later his eyes closed and his face fell. As I predicted.

"No luck?"

"No, I got it," he said. His voice was weird.

"Really?" I felt a nervous thrill in my stomach. "What was it?"

Jamie hesitated before he spoke. Then he said, "Marashaw."

I couldn't breathe. I dropped my head between my knees, but when Jamie put his arm around me I flinched.

I had not seen that coming. It was sweet, too sweet for Noah. If he were there, I'd make fun of him for it, tease him about doodling my would-be married name on his binder.

But he wasn't there. I couldn't tease him. Suddenly it was just too much. I reached for the laptop.

"Should I go?" Jamie asked. I nodded, not looking at him. I heard him leave the room.

My fingers trembled as I poked around in Noah's files, looking for something, anything that might tell me where to find him, but nothing stood out. Finally I just started opening things at random. What I found made me wish I hadn't.

It was in a folder labeled *MAD*:

Gather my leaves,
Twist them into crowns
Let me be the king of your forest
Climb on my branches,
I will seek out your hide
As you sleep beneath the shade
Of my giving tree

I held my breath as I read poem after poem that Noah had written for me—the old *Velveteen Rabbit* one, a new *Lolita* one, and even the terribly filthy Dr. Seuss one. My hands shook and my throat ached but I didn't cry. I couldn't. I felt angry instead. If he could have been with me, he would have been, which meant he couldn't. I would make whoever kept him from me pay.

I turned on the bathtub faucet and closed the door, breathing in the steam as the tub filled with water, trying to calm myself down. I let myself imagine Noah in there with me as I undressed.

I thought about him lifting his shirt over his head, the way his muscles would tense beneath his skin. How he would climb into the tub first, wearing nothing but a smirk as he waited for me to join him. I closed my eyes and smiled, but when I opened them, I bit back a scream.

Noah was there, in the tub. The water was red with his blood. His veins were slashed open at the wrists.

I bolted from the bathroom, threw on clothes. I snatched Noah's laptop from the bed and carried it with me to Jamie's room. I pounded on the door.

"Put on some music," I said the second he opened it, thrusting the laptop into his hands.

"Mara—"

"Just do it, Jamie." Thoughts roared in my brain, none of them good. I had to drown them out.

"You don't think he'd mind?"

I shook my head without looking up.

I heard Jamie scroll through his music. "What are you in the mood for?"

I closed my eyes. "Something we can dance to."

Five minutes later I heard the intro for "Sympathy for the Devil." Jamie stepped up onto the bed and held out his hand. I took it and plastered a smile on my face, but it didn't reach my eyes. He kicked off his shoes, and I kicked off mine.

When the door opened, we didn't even hear it—we were screaming along with Mick Jagger at the top of our lungs. It felt good.

"Hate to interrupt," Stella said, eyeing us both, "but dinner has arrived."

"Oh, thank God." Jamie jumped off the bed. "I'm starving."

The smell of whatever was in the plastic bags she'd brought made my stomach growl. "Me too." I peered into the bag Stella was holding. "What did you get?"

"Mexican," she said.

"Perfect." I plucked a foil-covered burrito out of the bag. We ate together with Noah's playlist still playing. We talked and laughed about nothing, because if we didn't, we would give up. Before she and I left Jamie's room, Stella handed me a plastic bag. "I bought this for you," she said as she opened the door.

"Um, thanks?"

She was already walking away, and waved at me without turning around. I looked into the bag.

It was a pregnancy test.

27

I LOOKED AT IT, CRADLED IN THE PLASTIC BAG TELLING me to HAVE A NICE DAY!, but I couldn't even seem to take it out to read the instructions. I saw the scene unfold in my mind: me in the bathroom, fumbling to open the package and dropping the instructions on the sodden tile floor. Picking them up and trying to read the blurred letters. Sitting on the toilet, practically forcing myself to pee on the stick. And then, after, waiting for fate to hand down my sentence. I just couldn't do it.

Stella and Jamie knew I hadn't taken the test, and the atmosphere in the thousandth stolen/borrowed car was dark and uncomfortable. Every time I gagged, Stella and Jamie exchanged a knowing glance, which made me want to kill them, which made me feel even sicker. I caught my reflection in the mirrored entry to the Georgetown hotel Jamie checked us into. I looked undead. I was mildly surprised no one had tried to behead me.

"Just wait," the girl in the mirror said back.

"Shut up."

Jamie and Stella both turned to look at me. Guess I'd said that out loud.

As soon as I'd dropped my things in my room, Jamie knocked on my door. He brushed past me and then flung himself onto my bed. "Mara, dear, hand me that menu?"

"Make yourself comfortable," I said, tossing it to him.

"I'm ordering room service," Jamie said.

I dropped into an armchair. "It's not even six."

"I'm a growing boy. Leave me alone." Jamie changed the TV channel. "Oh, a Tarantino marathon!"

I eyed the television. "*Pulp Fiction*? Not my favorite."

"Blasphemy."

"I prefer *Kill Bill*."

"Hmm. Acceptable," Jamie said with a nod. "Ugh, I can't order what I want until seven. Bastards." He punted the remote, and it bounced off the mattress.

"Temper, temper."

"Pot, meet kettle. Where's the minibar?"

I pointed to the other side of the room.

"Fetch me something?"

"Fetch yourself."

Samuel L. Jackson was reciting the last bit of his Ezekiel 25:17 monologue on the flatscreen TV: "And I will strike down upon thee with great vengeance and furious anger, those who attempt to poison and destroy my brothers."

Jamie blocked my view. "You didn't take it, I'm guessing?"

"Take what?" I asked, watching John Travolta and Sammy empty their clips into that sad guy.

"The, uh, test."

"The—oh." The pregnancy test. Before I could even answer, Jamie's focus was diverted.

"Oh, *hello* there." Jamie tossed a little black cardboard box at me just as Samuel was saying, "And you will know my name is the Lord when I lay my vengeance upon thee."

I caught it even though I wasn't looking, and turned the box over. "What is this?"

"It's, like, a sex kit." Jamie ripped open a bag of Skittles and tossed a handful into his mouth.

I threw the box back at him. "You're more likely to need this than me."

"Since you're incubating an alien fetus, you mean?"

"There. Is. No. Fetus. And I'm a virgin. Still. Which I believe I've told you already. Several times."

"I don't think Stella believes you," Jamie said. "And I can't entirely blame her. It strains credulity to imagine Noah could avoid such temptation."

"You're not funny."

"Yes I am. You just have a crappy sense of humor. God, only *you* could manage to get pregnant without even getting to have sex first."

"My life does seem to be uniquely shitty lately."

"I'll give you that," Jamie said. "But really, though—why *haven't* you done it yet?"

The best defense is a good offense. "Why haven't *you* done it yet?"

"I'm saving myself for marriage," Jamie said, chewing openmouthed.

"Really?"

"Yes. Probably. Maybe. I don't know. We're not talking about me. Did you— I mean, do you want to? Have sex with Noah? Current predicament aside?"

I noticed Jamie's switch from past tense to present, but ignored it. "Of course," I said quietly.

"So what stopped you? Current predicament aside."

I wondered how to explain what had kept me and Noah apart even before Horizons. What I was afraid I might have done to him. What the fortune-teller had told me and what part of me still believed.

"I was afraid . . . I'd hurt him."

Jamie quirked an eyebrow. "I'm pretty sure that's not how it works."

"Ha-ha, hilarious."

"Seriously, though. You can tell me."

I was embarrassed, putting the kissing conundrum into words, worrying Jamie might think I was crazier than I actually was, which, given the circumstances. But he listened intently, and didn't mock me when I was finished.

"You think it's just kissing?"

"I don't know. I mean, I've kissed Noah before, obviously—"

"*Obviously*. He could never be *that* much of a saint."

I ignored him. "And we did notice that something—happened. I think maybe it's connected to my emotional state or whatever—like, I don't know if it would happen with just a peck on the cheek, because—"

"Because there's no intensity."

"Right."

"So you could probably kiss me or Stella and nothing would happen."

"Stella would think I was trying to bite her. She'd mace me."

Jamie cracked a grin. "God, that's so accurate. It makes sense, though, the kissing thing? Like, if you stray out of your stable emotional range, something changes with your ability. Excess energy or something."

"So a peck on the cheek wouldn't do anything," I said.

"Probably not."

I planted a kamikaze kiss on Jamie's cheek.

"FUCK," he shouted, wiping it off. "What if you killed me!" He threw a Skittle at my face. It hit my forehead.

"Ow!"

"Taste the rainbow, bitch."

"Don't be a baby."

"I am going to be a baby. I am going to lock myself in the bathroom and cry now, in fact." Jamie did go into the bathroom, and he did lock the door. Whether he cried, who knows.

I heard the toilet flush and the water run, and when he opened the door, he said, "I left something on the counter for you."

"I'm . . . afraid to ask."

"You really should take it."

"Are we talking about the pregnancy test again? Because, no."

"Whatever the result is, you have to know. We'll figure it out, but we can't pretend this isn't happening."

"I will admit to deriving a positive psychological benefit from your using the word 'we.'"

"Positive psychological benefit intended."

I wanted to argue with him, but I couldn't really. Jamie was right. If it was negative, I was like this for some other reason, and nothing changed. But if it was positive . . .

If it was positive, everything changed.

"Don't even think about it," Jamie said, popping another Skittle into his mouth. "If you think about it, you'll change your mind. Like you said, you're probably not . . . you know. But won't it be a relief to know?"

Yes. It would be.

He turned around and not so gently pushed me into the bathroom. "Like ripping off a Band-Aid," he said, closing the door behind me. "Just pee."

I looked at the box. Jamie had already opened it, and the instructions were lying next to it, by the sink. I read them. Plus sign for positive, minus for negative. Easy enough. I ripped open the package and sat on the toilet. I could practically hear him outside the door, breathing.

I felt like a defendant, waiting for the jury to hand down its verdict. Seconds passed, or maybe minutes, before someone knocked on the bathroom door.

"I don't hear peeing," Jamie said mockingly.

"Eat me," I muttered.

"What's that?"

"Leave me," I said louder. My voice was hoarse, and my bladder was shy. Or something. I couldn't do it, not with him listening. I said so and told Jamie to leave. To my surprise, he did.

And then I did. I quickly put the test on the edge of the vanity. I felt sick just looking at it, felt the urge to run. I *could* run. I could run out of the room, run out of the hotel, lie to Stella and Jamie and myself, never mention it again.

But my mother always said that the truth will catch up with you eventually. It always does.

So I forced my eyes shut and reached for it. On the count of three, I swore to myself that I would look.

One.

Two.

I opened my eyes.

It was negative.

28

I TOLD THEM ON THE WAY TO THE TRAIN STATION IN DC. Stella, who had been ignoring me for nearly the entire cab ride, actually broke into a grin. "Don't you feel so much better?"

I did and didn't. My mind could now finally let go of the ugliest, scariest possibility, that something had been done to me while I'd been at Horizons that could have gotten me pregnant. My mind shied away from the word "rape," but I didn't know what else it could've been. But it didn't matter now. I could finally let myself feel relief.

It was short lived, however. I got sick in the cab, opening the door at a red light to throw up in the street. The driver freaked out.

I might not have been pregnant, but I *was* sick. With what, I didn't know. Or maybe I did know—maybe this was just the gene. Maybe something made me different from Stella and Jamie, and it would just have to run its course.

It wasn't a pleasant thought, and I felt shaky as we followed Jamie up to the ticket counter. Whatever was happening to me was happening quickly, and we needed to get to New York faster than we could drive there.

"Three tickets to New York," he said. "One way."

The train was clotted with people, and we had to walk through a thousand cars before we could find seats even remotely close to one another. I stumbled twice. Jamie caught me both times.

When we finally found seats, I practically collapsed into mine. I was shaking. I crossed my arms to make it less obvious. It didn't work.

"Cold?" Jamie asked from across the aisle.

I wasn't, but I said I was anyway, because that made more sense than the truth. "Be right back," he said as he stood up. "Watch my stuff?" I nodded, then leaned my head against the glass. People swarmed the platform, trying to make it on board before the train pulled away. I watched them, hypnotized, letting my vision blur out of focus, until something snapped it back.

No. Not something. Someone.

A man stood out in the crowd. Not because of what he

looked like, or what he wore, but because I knew him.

Abel Lukumi watched the train pull out of the station, wearing the same dark suit he had worn when I'd seen him at the hospital, after Jude had made me slit my wrists. The same suit he'd worn in Little Havana, when he'd slaughtered a chicken and had me drink its blood. My lips parted to speak or scream, but by the time Jamie came back, he was gone.

I stared out the window for seconds, or hours maybe, as people stood up, sat down, moved around the car. What did he *want*? Why was he following me?

I didn't know what to do or say to Jamie and Stella. They didn't really know about Lukumi; they wouldn't understand. Noah would, but he wasn't there.

"You're sweating," Stella said as she slipped into the seat beside me.

I was. I was shivering, too.

"Do you have a fever?"

I shrugged.

Her expression softened. "Try to rest, if you can?"

I couldn't. "I'm scared," I said, though I didn't mean to say it out loud.

"I know," Stella said.

I wanted to scream that she didn't know, that she would never know, because this wasn't happening to her, it was happening to me. I wanted to scream that it wasn't all right, and that it never would be again, because I'd killed people and that wasn't the kind of thing that you could ever fix. Even if they'd deserved it. But I was tired and my friends were tired, and even if they didn't fully get it, they understood what it was doing to me. They could lie to my face and pretend it was going to be all right, but I saw the truth in the fear in their eyes. I was getting worse. Much worse. And time was running out.

I was drenched in sweat when I woke up an hour later. I lifted my head from the seat, and the movement shook images loose from my dreams. Lukumi standing on one side of the platform, a black feather in his hand. Me standing on the other, a human heart in mine. The train tracks between us were filled with bodies without a scratch on them, except for a smear of blood beneath each of their noses. Bile rose in my throat. I stood up, grabbing the seat for support. Stella didn't wake up, but Jamie turned as I crossed into the aisle. He pulled out his earbuds.

"Where're you going?"

"Bathroom," I said. I didn't know if I would be sick, but better safe than sorry, and anyway, I needed to change my shirt, which was plastered to my skin. I haltingly made my way down the aisle, grabbing my bag on the way to the tiny train bathroom.

But I'd grabbed Noah's bag, I realized, once I was locked inside. His was black and mine was gray. I blinked. My vision was filmy, so *everything* looked gray. I put the lid of the toilet seat down and sat on it, holding my head between my hands, blinking again. My T-shirt clung to my skin, making me itch.

Whatever. It didn't matter about the bag. I'd change into one of Noah's shirts. He wouldn't mind.

I rummaged through it, but I could barely tell one piece of clothing from another. I bit my lip, clenched my jaw to keep myself from losing it, to keep myself here. As I did, my fingers curled around something in his bag that wasn't clothes. I pulled it out.

My hand shifted into focus, and so did the thing in it. A straight razor. Noah's razor. I remembered asking him once why he used it. He'd said it was the sharpest kind.

It gleamed under the fluorescent light. The weight of it was solid and reassuring, somehow, in my hand. I wasn't shaking anymore. I could stand up.

I looked at it, and then at myself, in the mirror. Pain shot through my stomach—in an arc, it felt like. Left to right.

No one else felt like this. No one else was acting like this. Not Stella, not Jamie. Something inside me was different.

Something inside me.

Something *inside* me.

I looked at my face in the mirror.

"Something inside you *is* different," my reflection said.

The razor hovered just an inch above my lower belly. A rushing sound filled my ears, like the sound of a thousand voices breathing, *Yes*. There was so much pressure, but my fingers didn't shake. I looked at myself again.

"Get them out," my reflection said.

Time skipped forward. One second I stood there, facing my reflection, listening to it. The next, my hand had already drawn the razor against my stomach.

It was just a tiny line. An inch long, no bigger. Little beads of blood welled from the cut, jewel-like and shimmering. Vivid. Everything was, actually. Whatever haze had clouded my vision had now lifted. I didn't feel sick or hot. The only strange thing was the pressure in my fingers, drawing the razor to my stomach again.

A knock on the bathroom door startled me before I could trace the line again.

"Mara?" Jamie's voice was muffled through the door. "We're here."

Mechanically I wiped the blade off with the hem of my shirt and put it back into Noah's bag. I dabbed at my skin with tissues and exchanged the T-shirt I was wearing for a clean black one. I walked out of the bathroom on steady feet, feeling impossibly light. Almost giddy.

"Feel better?" he asked.

"Yes," I said brightly as a trickle of blood ran down my stomach. "Much."

29

I HADN'T BEEN TO NEW YORK SINCE I WAS LITTLE, AND I didn't remember it like this.

We were practically the only non-suited people on the train, but when we stepped onto the track and climbed up the stairs, we blended right in. Penn Station swarmed with people—a man with dreadlocks down to his waist bumped my hip with his briefcase and apologized, but as I stepped aside, I was hit by a stroller being pushed by a mother with glazed, dead eyes. We got out of there as fast as we could.

The taxi line wasn't much of an improvement. We were sandwiched between a preteen couple with matching acne, loudly making out, and an old couple wearing matching tennis shoes, arguing loudly over a map in a language I didn't know.

"Ouch," Jamie said.

"You okay?" Stella asked him.

"Oh, I am," he said quietly. "But that dude's wife just told him, 'If they had to put your brain in a chicken, it would run straight to the butcher.'"

"You understand them?"

"Hebrew," Jamie explained, and then it was our turn in line. "Where to first, ladies?"

"I need a shower," Stella said.

"Hotel?" I asked.

Stella tugged at a strand of hair. "I guess. If we have to. But I don't like using you for that stuff, Jamie."

"Pish tosh. But my aunt has a place on the Upper West Side. We could go there."

"Except wouldn't she maybe wonder why her nephew and his two female friends have turned up on her doorstep on a random school night?"

"She's not there. She's at her condo in Florida right now till the summer."

"How would we get in?" Stella asked.

"I'm sure we could figure it out," Jamie said. "And she's not even my real aunt. She's my mother's BFF. Even if we're being looked for, no one would tie us together."

Good enough for me. Stella agreed, and so Jamie gave the driver directions to his aunt's house. I didn't pay much attention. My gaze kept wandering to my stomach. It was still bleeding a little—there was a small wet spot on the T-shirt, but luckily the shirt was black. No one would notice.

My thumb kept running over the tiny line, and I realized I was picking at the seams of the cut. I couldn't seem to stop. I kept thinking about the train, and the edge of Noah's razor, and the relief—the release—when I'd pressed it against my skin. A voice whispered in my mind.

Something inside us.

Get them out.

I glanced at Stella nervously. She didn't see me; she was staring out the window on the left, and Jamie was looking out the one on the right. I ran my fingertips against my belly, pressing into it. I didn't feel anything—no, wait. I slid my hand left, toward the inside of my left hip, pressing down. Something seemed to—to *shift*, like a tight muscle being kneaded out of place, but small. What *was* that?

"Stomachache?" Stella asked.

Caught. "Mmm-hmm." I crossed my arms and folded myself slightly over them.

"We'll be there in a few," Jamie said.

Shame warred with need. I couldn't let them see that I'd cut myself. I had to figure out a way to get ten, maybe twenty minutes alone.

The cab pulled over to the curb, and Jamie said in that voice of his, "You never saw us."

"I never saw you," the driver repeated, sounding dazed.

"You drove this astonishingly hot underwear model from south Texas. You wanted to lick his abs."

"I wanted to lick his abs."

"You're such an asshole," Stella muttered as she climbed out of the cab.

"I get my kicks where I can."

As we waited for the traffic to stop and the light to change, Jamie took the opportunity to throw up into a garbage can.

"Ugh, *gross*," a high-heeled, miniskirted girl squealed as she walked by.

Head still bent, Jamie raised his middle finger at her, then spat into the garbage can and wiped his mouth with his sleeve.

"Ugh. Gross," he said. "I'm never going to get used to that."

"You're not supposed to get used to it," Stella said. "You're supposed to not do it."

Jamie's aunt's house turned out to be a brownstone on a relatively quiet tree-lined street. We walked up the front steps, and he peered in through the glass door. It was dark.

"How are we supposed to get in, again?" Stella asked.

"My cousin once told me a story about breaking in post-curfew using a spare key from under a fake rock or some such. Maybe . . ."

Jamie hopped back down the steps and ducked behind a small gate in front of the garden apartment. There were some wilted plants there, and a package with the word "perishable" on the side of it, and—

"Fake rock!" Jamie said, bending down. "Score." He held up the key, hopped back up the steps, and unlocked the front door. Stella and I followed him inside.

The house was gorgeous. The parlor still had most of its original details—an ornate plaster medallion in the center of the ceiling, carved woodwork between the parlor and the kitchen, and a massive fireplace with a mirror as the overmantel. Stella whistled.

"I know, right?" Jamie said. "Bedrooms and bathrooms are upstairs. Take whichever ones you want. There's a package outside for my aunt. I'm gonna bring it in. Shall we convene in an hour for food plans?"

Stella nodded. I did too, even though I wasn't hungry. I was already on my way up the stairs.

"How do you feel?" Stella asked. She was following behind me.

"A little better," I lied. Then crinkled my nose. "You smell ripe." I needed to get rid of her.

"Yeah, I feel gross," she said. "I desperately need a shower."

"I hate to say it," I lied, "but you really do."

We each claimed a bedroom, but just as I'd hoped, Stella did not pass go or collect two-hundred before she ducked into the bathroom, duffel bag in hand. When curls of steam began to filter out from the beneath the door, I set Noah's bag on the bed in the room I'd chosen. I had his razor in my back pocket still, but I wasn't sure that was what I wanted. What I needed.

After a minute or two my hand closed around a tightly rolled T-shirt I'd buried near the bottom of his things. I took it out and unrolled it, finding the scalpel I'd hidden there. *That* was what I needed.

My fingertips seemed to tingle as I held the metal up. I knew, objectively, that what I was about to do was crazy, but somehow my feet carried me toward the guest room door, and my fingers turned the lock so no one would be able to stop me. And then I lifted up my shirt and began to cut.

30

"OH GOD, OH GOD. STELLA, GET IN HERE!"

My eyes fluttered open, just enough to see a blurred outline of Jamie leaning over me.

"What's wrong?" Stella's voice, from a distance away.

"It's— Mara did something!"

He grabbed a towel, and I felt pressure on my stomach.

Did I get them out did I get them?

"Don't you dare even try to talk, you idiot," Jamie said to me. He propped my limp hands over my stomach, over the towel, then sprang up to get the door.

"What happened?" Stella said as she appeared in my frame of vision. "Oh. Oh my—"

"I wanted to use Noah's laptop for something," Jamie said, "and I knocked on the door to get it from her, but she didn't answer. So I knocked again, louder, and still nothing. And I just had this bad feeling, so I used a needle from the sewing kit to pick the lock, and I opened the door, and she was like—"

"Oh, God," Stella whispered.

"Like this."

"Oh my God, Mara, what did you do?"

There's something inside me, I tried to say.

"There's nothing inside you, Mara." Tears filled her eyes. "It's in your mind. It's in your mind." More pressure on my stomach. My vision darkened.

"Call 911, Jamie."

Get them out

"But what about—" Jamie said.

"I can't tell how deep the cut is. She keeps moving her hands to cover it, but there's a lot of blood and she's pale and shaking."

"Believe me," I whispered.

"What did you— Oh my God." Jamie's eyes went wide.

"Don't talk, Mara." A hand on the back of my neck, cradling my head. "Jamie?" Stella asked.

"There's something in the house," he said, backing away.

"What? Jamie, I need you. She looks really . . ."

"It was just sitting by the door to the garden apartment,"

he said. "It said 'perishable' on it, and so I opened it, but it was just this leather bag inside with a note."

"What are you *talking* about?" Stella's voice was shrill.

"I thought it was for my aunt, but the note said—the note said—"

"What?"

"'Believe her.'"

Stella looked at me, then at Jamie. "What are you—"

"Someone knows we're here. That note—that bag—it's for us."

"Did you look in it?"

"I thought it was for my aunt. I'm going to get it."

"No, Jamie. I need you to stay—*shit*."

Some of the weight lifted from my stomach. My eyelids fluttered, and I heard footsteps recede. Then they came back. Something thumped on the floor.

Get them out

"She keeps saying—she keeps saying that," Jamie said.

"She doesn't know what she's saying."

"The note, though. It says believe her, Stella. What does that mean?"

"I don't know! I don't fucking know. I'm just as lost as you."

"What if—what if there *is* something inside her?" I heard something unclasp, and then, "Oh my God. Stella. Stella, look."

"What—"

"It's a bunch of—doctor shit. Gloves, thread, gauze, scalpels. Jesus, who *left* this?"

"Any drugs?" I felt pressure on my stomach again. Stella was trying to pry my hands away.

"No. Wait, maybe—yes."

"Can you get another towel? She's bleeding through this one."

A few seconds passed before Jamie said, "Got them."

"Switch with me so I can look in the bag?"

The pressure lifted on my stomach for a second, and I gasped.

"Press down hard," Stella said.

"I am."

"Harder."

"Are you going to call 911?" Jamie asked.

Stella paused before answering. "We might not need to."

"Meaning?"

"Let me see for a second."

The pressure lifted. "She's still bleeding but not as much, and it's not superdeep. I could maybe close it on my own, but—"

"She's saying that there's something in there."

There is there is

"Can you—can you hold her hands down so I can really look?" Stella asked.

There was pressure around my wrists, radiating through my arms and shoulders.

"Mara." Jamie's voice. "You've gotta let us look, okay?"

Jamie held me, pinned me down, as Stella prodded me with something sharp. My entire body winced.

"What—?"

"She's right. She's fucking right," Stella said.

"How did she know?"

"How *did* she know?"

Another stab of pain. I screamed, I think, because one of them moved to cover my mouth with something.

"Mara, you have to be quiet. Jamie, what's in the bag, drug-wise?"

"I can't look while I'm holding her down."

Stella's shadow lifted, and I heard the sound of metal against metal as she rummaged. "I'm going to give her this so she stops moving."

"No hospital?"

"She really didn't cut that deep. I can do this, I think. Okay, Mara—Mara? Can you hear me?"

Yes

"I'm going to close your—uh, incision. It might feel like you can't breathe, but you can breathe, okay? And you're going to be fine."

Get them out

"We will," she said, and I felt the bite of a needle in my shoulder as she plunged a syringe into my arm.

31

BEFORE

London, England

THE FIRST THING I NOTICED WHEN I WOKE WAS that our marriage bed was soaked with blood.

I lit a tallow candle, and the smoke and sulfur filled my nostrils as a tiny flicker of light showed me Charles, my husband. He was painted in shadow; the line of his back, exposed to the waist, was smooth and still. It did not rise and fall with his breath, because he was not breathing. He lay on his stomach, his head tilted to the side, a pool of blood puddled beneath his face. His eyes were open, but they did not see.

I heard nothing but the rush of blood in my ears, the harshness of my own ragged breath in the air. I threw off the blankets that covered him, and he did not move. I watched a bead of blood drip from his nose, and he did not wipe it away. I choked on a sob, covered his body back up, wound my fingers in my hair, and pulled it to try to wake myself. It did not work, because I was not sleeping.

But it did bring me back to myself enough so that I heard a new sound—the crack of something against the bedroom window. My head snapped up, but my eyes saw nothing.

With trembling fingers I reached for the brass candle-holder by the bedside. A spill of hot tallow hit my fingers, and I flinched at the pain, then welcomed it. It shoved aside the horror for a moment, allowed me to think of something else. I crept numbly toward the window and peered out of it, the candle reflecting in the distorted glass.

The professor stood below Charles's house—below *our* house—silhouetted by light from the gas lamp across the street. He raised one arm and pointed at me, accusing.

What a mad thing to think! A shrill giggle escaped from my throat, and my laughter blew the candle out. I had not seen the professor in six months, since I had become engaged, and his presence here, now, was as senseless to me as the events that had transpired.

Something small hit the window again. I tilted my head at the professor, and saw that he had been pointing not at me but at the east side of the house, to the entrance that led to the mews behind it. He wanted me to open the gate.

But the servants—oh, God, the servants. What would I tell them? How would I explain?

Pulling at my hair again, I tried to think. I could avoid the servants' quarters if I took the main staircase, exited through the front door instead of the rear. The gate key was kept in the kitchen. If I was careful, and quiet, I could get it without disturbing anyone.

I nearly left the room in my dressing gown stained with my husband's blood, but I stepped on the hem, drenching me in horror anew. I felt sick but dizzily managed to find a clean dressing gown and clumsily slipped it on. It had been so long since I had dressed myself, and I had nearly forgotten how.

I descended the main staircase in bare feet, my long, undone hair veiling my face, my gown billowing at my ankles. All thoughts of propriety were banished by the memory of my husband's blood pooling beneath his face. Quivering with panic, I cringed at every creak of the floorboards, held my breath at every sound. My fingers trailed the wall to help me find my way in the dark.

Finally I reached the kitchen and the key, silently slipped out of the house's side entrance, and unlocked the gate that led to the mews. The professor was waiting for me.

The coal-colored sky had swallowed all the stars but had bitten only a slice out of the moon, leaving just enough light to see him by. He stood there dressed in a black waistcoat with black shirtsleeves beneath. He led me quietly into the empty stables. Since Charles had begun courting me, he had been unable to keep horses here. They kept injuring themselves, kicking the stall doors in fear or fury to escape some unnamed fate, and had to be moved to a stable nearby.

Ghosts of cobwebs hung in corners of the quiet stalls, and a light breeze tossed leaves at the cobbled steps. They danced at the professor's feet, and I shivered from the chill.

"We must leave tonight," the professor said.

I opened my mouth, but the only words that came out were, "My husband—my husband—"

"Where is he?"

But I could say nothing else but those two words. I kept repeating them as if it would make him reappear.

The professor took me by the shoulders—I never remembered him touching me before. I recoiled as he said, "Your husband is dead."

He knew. He *knew*.

"Your husband is dead," he repeated. "You must leave this house, and London."

I could not speak, so the professor continued, "The life you lived is no longer available to you. Everything you once had will vanish. You will be shunned, cast out. If you are not treated like a criminal, you will be facing destitution, poverty. A woman with no property, no husband, the curse of a husband's death looming over her—"

His words brought me back to myself. "But my family—"

"They are not your family. Have you forgotten where you come from?"

The question frightened me. "How do you know where I come from?" He didn't answer, but he hadn't been wrong to ask. I *had* forgotten. Between the dinners and the balls and the courting and the wedding, I had forgotten many things. It had been so long since I had done anything for myself; I'd spent years learning how to let others dress me, feed me, teach me, all under Aunt Sarah's careful tutelage, and now, now I was helpless.

"I cannot—I cannot leave."

He spoke firmly. "You can and you shall." Then his head tilted, as if he had heard something. "We must—"

"We?" I asked sharply. His words had opened a vein of anger I hadn't realized was even there. "Where have you been? You left without a word, and now—"

"I left because I had done all I could for you then, and I am doing all I can for you now. You are not my only student," he said a bit snappishly. "I was assisting another at Christ's College in Cambridge, and I came here as swiftly as I could. Now gather yourself. We have a long night ahead of us."

"This is *madness*," I said. "My husband—"

"Your husband is dead because you killed him," the professor said, stunning me into silence. "You are not what Simon Shaw thought you were," he added softly.

My eyes brimmed with tears. "And what was that?"

"A cure."

"So, what am I?"

His gaze dropped. "A disease." He hesitated, and looked around us at the empty stable. "The horses knew."

The rough hardware of a stall door pressed into the curve of my spine. I had backed myself up against it without realizing. "How do you know?"

"I have seen it."

"Where?"

"In your future."

His words chilled my heart. "Who are you?"

"You know who I am."

I swallowed. "*What* are you?"

"Your teacher," he said simply. "Now obey me. Get dressed, in dark colors preferably. Take nothing from this house. Nothing from this life." He looked at the sky, which threatened to lighten. "We must begin before dawn."

"Begin what?" I whispered.

"Your real education." He reached into his waistcoat then, and withdrew something I could not see. He stepped out into the dim moonlight, and I followed him as he opened his palm. Something silver glimmered in his hand. A pendant, half of it hammered into the shape of a feather, the other half a sword.

32

"OKAY, SHE'S OUT."

I'm not

"What did you give her?"

"Morphine, I think."

"You think?"

"I don't know! Whatever was in that vial."

"How do you even know how to do this?"

"YouTube videos."

"Ha."

"Okay, um, there's like, tissue around it—"

Around what

"I think I'm going to throw up."

"Hand me a scalpel first?

"Which one?"

"I don't know. No, not that one, a different one. Yeah, that one I guess."

"You guess? What if you cut, like, an artery or something?"

"Stop making me nervous."

"Sorry!"

"Should we just take her to the hospital?"

"I think . . . I don't know. I think maybe. Yeah."

Something smashed against the wall. "Okay. Okay. Go call."

No no no get them out

"Oh, shit, Jamie. She's moving. Hold her—"

"I can't!"

"She's digging. Oh, God. She's, like, *digging* . . ."

"Give her more morphine or something. Christ!"

"I don't want her to OD!"

"Well, she's tearing out her intestines!"

"She is not. Don't be so dramatic."

Their voices blurred to silence, and my hands disappeared into warmth. I saw red and felt pain, but my hands kept moving, pushing, pressing, until I felt—

"Is that— What the fuck are those?"

What are they what are they

"There are two of them. Oh my God."

"She was right. She was right."

"Is that—maybe that's what's been making her sick?"

"I don't know. I think—I think I can stitch this up."

"How can you even see?"

"Here, give me that towel."

It hurts it hurts stop please

"Stella, her lips are white."

"Put some pressure here, maybe?"

"Should she be shaking like this?"

"Oh, no. She's *seizing*—"

"What should I do?"

"Mara? Mara, look at us, okay? Just keep looking at us."

But I couldn't. Their words faded into darkness, and I did too.

33

BEFORE

London, England

I DISOBEYED THE PROFESSOR IN ONE THING WHEN WE FLED London before dawn. I carried in my trembling hands the doll Sister had made me. Nothing more. Nothing less. I stared warily with tear-blurred eyes at the hansom cab the professor hired. The horses were uneasy, but he gave them something to calm them, he said, before he noticed what was in my hand.

"Mara—"

"That is not my real name," I said hoarsely. I wanted to change the subject, so he would not force me to leave the doll behind.

He considered me. "Did you choose it for yourself?"

I nodded.

"Then that is what I shall call you."

"What is *your* name?" I asked as the carriage rolled over the stone streets, toward the smoky sunrise.

The professor lifted an eyebrow. "I have had many."

"What is the one you've chosen for yourself?"

At this he smiled. "I have chosen many. Abraham, Alexander, Alim, Abel, Arthur, Armin, Abdul, Aldis, Alton, Alonzo, Aloysius—"

"All beginning with *A*? Why?"

"You are just as inquisitive as when I left. When you live the way I have, you must find ways to amuse yourself."

I didn't see how it was amusing at all, but I said nothing. There was too much else on my mind. What would happen at dawn, when the servants woke and found my husband—what Aunt Sarah would say, do, when she learned I was gone. My throat tightened, and I gripped the doll until my knuckles were white.

"How did you find me?"

"In England, or in India?"

My eyes widened in shock. "India?"

"By the well," he said casually. "You were younger then."

I reached back, searched my mind for some glimmer of recognition. I remembered a woman pointing at me, whispering something. A man was with her, but I could not remember his face.

"That was you?" And then, before he could answer, "How did you know where to find me?"

"I was paid by Simon Shaw to unlock what he believed would be the secret to immortality." The professor smiled just slightly.

"He thought I was—"

A slight nod. "I knew the man you called Uncle, and suggested that Mr. Shaw contract with him to care for you until you grew up, as no one could be sure what you would become until you were older."

"But I thought you saw my future?"

"I can see shades of it, under . . . particular circumstances. But many things are hidden, even to me."

"How did you know Uncle?"

The professor pursed his lips. "There are not many of us, and we are . . ." He searched for a word. "Attracted to each other." The carriage slowed to a stop. He stepped out of the carriage and held out his hand to me. I took it, clutching my doll with the other.

"Professor?"

"Yes?"

"What am I?"

The look he gave me was tinged with sadness, but also hope. I would never forget it. "You are a girl, Mara. A girl blessed and cursed."

34

THE LIGHT CHANGED FROM BLACK TO BRIGHT RED. I squinted against it.

"She's moving. Look."

"Hey, you."

Jamie's voice. I tried to answer him, to swallow, but my throat was filled with sand. I forced my eyes open—the light in the room was blinding. A backlit shadow shifted beside me.

"Stella—some water, maybe?"

In seconds another shadow joined Jamie's, handing him something. He held something cold and hard to my lips—a glass. I was weak and couldn't take it from him, but I sipped from it greedily. Freezing water ran down my chin, and as it did, I noticed that I was freezing too.

"Cold," I said between gulps. My voice was still hoarse, but at least I had one. The room was coming into focus too. The more aware I became of everything around me, the more aware I became of myself. I was freezing, and nauseous, but somehow I didn't feel sick.

"What happened?" I asked.

Jamie and Stella exchanged a glance.

"What do you remember?" she asked cautiously.

I thought back, rooting through hazy memories of the past few days—the road trip, the sickness, the train, the razor—

Oh, God. "I—I cut myself," I admitted. My cheeks burned with shame.

But then Jamie said, "We got them out."

I blinked.

"There was totally something inside you, Mara. You were right."

Horror. "Oh, God. What *was* it?"

"Like, capsules, they looked like?" Stella said.

"Do you still have them?" I asked.

"Yeah. Jamie?"

"They're in my room. Hold on." Jamie left, and when he came back, he held out his hand.

There were two of them, slightly larger than grains of rice, and transparent. Something copper and black was inside one, copper and red in the other.

"How did you know they were there?" Stella asked.

I thought back, remembered my face in the mirror, and the whispers:

Get them out.

Please stop.

I opened my mouth to tell them, but then swallowed the words back. "I had a feeling," was all I said as I shivered. Stella wrapped a blanket around my shoulders.

"You scared the shit out of us, you know."

I knew. But I'd had no choice. Or at least it felt like I'd had no choice. I remembered the feeling I'd had on the train, the feeling that had been with me since I'd woken up in Horizons, on the island. It was gone now. I felt like—like *me*.

"You look better," Jamie said, studying me. "How do you feel?"

"Better." I was thirsty, and tired, and nauseous and hungry at the same time. But I felt normal. Normal for me, anyway.

"Listen," he started. "There's something you need to know."

I raised my eyebrows.

"When you—when we found you like we found you, we found something else."

Jamie looked at Stella, who reached into her pocket. "Someone left a note at the door." She handed it to me.

Believe her.

I didn't recognize the handwriting. "I'm 'her'?"

Jamie nodded. "It came with a medical kit or something. A big bag of surgical shit."

I felt cold again. "Someone knew what was inside me."

"And knows that we're here."

"Which means we have to leave," Stella said. "Like, yesterday."

"But whoever it was, whoever left it, they told you to believe me. And they were right."

"But this person knows what's wrong with us, and why wouldn't they just say something if they wanted to help?"

My mind seized on the image of the man I knew as Abel Lukumi. If Noah had been there, he would have said that I was grasping at coincidences and trying to force them into facts. But Noah wasn't there. It was just me, and Stella, and Jamie, and a trail of breadcrumbs that led to no one and nothing but the priest.

So I told them. About the botanica in Little Havana, where he had seen me, recognized me, and tried to kick me out before giving me some weird concoction to drink that had made me finally remember what I had done to Rachel and Claire. I told them about trying to find him again, after I'd killed everything in the insect house at the Miami zoo. I explained how it had been his face I'd seen in the hospital after Jude had slit my wrists, him on the platform as the train had pulled out of DC. By the time I'd finished, Jamie had backed up onto the bed, his head in his hands.

"So, what you're telling me is"—he held out his hand—"some Santeria voodoo guy from south Florida followed you—followed *us*—all the way to DC, and he knows we're in New York, and he knows where we are, but won't show himself?"

"Yes," I said.

"Why, though? What would he stand to gain?"

I remembered words that had once belonged to Noah, but that now belonged to me. "You never know what a person stands to gain or lose by anything."

"I don't get it, though," Stella said. "Why would he just leave the bag? If he wants to help us, then he should just fucking help us."

"Maybe he can't," Jamie said.

"Or maybe he doesn't want to," I said, the thought forming as the words left my mouth. "Maybe he's . . . responsible for it."

"Responsible how?" Jamie asked.

"Responsible like, maybe he's the one behind it. All of it," I said. "If this—if *we're* some kind of experiment or whatever, him following us could be part of it. Watching what we do, how we react, what happens to us when we *do* react." I thought of the things we had seen in Horizons, the things Kells had said to us. "Maybe he's the one—maybe he's the one who funded Dr. Kells."

"But then why bring us the bag? Why would he want to help get those—whatever they were—out of you?" Stella asked.

"Maybe she put them in without permission," Jamie suggested. "Speaking of which." He looked at me. "Do you think the rest of us have them too?"

"I don't feel any different," Stella said. "You?"

Jamie swallowed. "I don't really know what 'different' means anymore. I woke up one day on the island and couldn't walk, just like you," he said, staring at me. "But then why aren't I sick?"

"You are sick," Stella said carefully. "But you're a year younger than us. Maybe you're just in the first stage of whatever's happening . . ."

I remembered the words written on the whiteboard when I'd first woken up in Horizons.

J. Roth, manifesting.

"Manifestation," I said out loud. "That list, remember it? It said Stella and Noah, they've manifested already. Kells wrote that, in her notes."

"What does that even mean, though?" Jamie asked.

"It means that you're going to get sicker," Stella said. "When it was happening to me—I got worse before I got better."

"What, you mean when you were—"

"Manifesting, or whatever. The voices, they weren't always loud. In the beginning I could kind of ignore them. Sometimes I even listened to them," she said quietly. "I heard things I shouldn't have, and sometimes I—did things," she said. "I used what I knew, even though part of me knew it was wrong. I cheated on a test. This girl who was bullying me, I exposed her secrets to everyone. And each time I did something, the voices got louder. Stronger. There were more of them. It got so I couldn't tell which thoughts were mine and which belonged to someone else. I felt like I was going crazy. I *was* going crazy." She rounded on Jamie. "Using your ability—it's not free, even if it seems that way now. It's working pretty nicely for you right now, and for that you're lucky—but it's going to eventually bite you in the ass."

Jamie seemingly had no reaction to this.

"And if there is something inside of you," Stella went on, "like whatever was inside Mara? It's going to activate at some point, just like it did with her, and you're going to go through the same shit."

Jamie rolled his eyes, but he was unsettled. I could tell. "So fine," he said. "What do we do now?"

I interrupted the both of them. "I almost died tonight," I said. "Tomorrow we're going to find out who almost killed me."

35

IT WAS ELEVEN-ISH WHEN WE FINALLY DRAGGED OURselves out of bed the next morning. I could walk on my own, but it hurt. A lot. So I was slow. But our only real lead was the tax stuff Stella had taken from Kells's office with the address of the accountant on them, and he wasn't going anywhere. Probably.

The cab burped us up in the bowels of Midtown. The three of us stared up at a squat, ugly building sandwiched between a Laundromat and a FedEx, a building that bore the address where Ira Ginsberg, CPA, purportedly filed taxes for evil corporations such as Horizons LLC.

"So, what's the plan exactly?" Stella asked.

"We're going to ask him who he works for," I said.

Stella scratched her nose. "And what if he doesn't just . . . volunteer that information?"

"Then Jamie will encourage him to volunteer it." And if that failed, I would encourage him myself. I felt strangely well and strangely confident. Whatever Dr. Kells had tried to do to me, she had failed. I was still here, and those things that had been inside me, whatever they were, were gone. We had the address of the man who'd made it possible for her to do what she'd done. We were getting closer to everything. Closer to Noah. I could feel it.

Jamie cleared his throat. "Shall we?"

We shall. A doorman handed us visitors' badges, which we slapped on (my chest, Stella's hip, Jamie's left ass cheek). Then we rode the elevator up to the stated suite. The waiting area looked like a doctor's office, complete with a gum-chewing, ponytailed receptionist. Stella looked at Jamie and gestured at Chewy.

"You owe me so much, I can't even count how much you owe me," he muttered.

"Names?" the receptionist asked us.

"Jesus," Jamie answered.

"Mary," said Stella.

"Satan," I said as I walked past her and pushed open the door to Ira Ginsberg's office.

The room was painfully unremarkable, and so was Ira. He

had a slightly doughy face that emerged from the collar of his slightly too tight dress shirt and tie. He rose the instant we walked in, followed by the receptionist.

"It's all right, Jeanine," he said. "Tell my client on line one that I'll have to call him back."

"Yes, Mr. Ginsberg," she said, glancing at us on her way out.

"How can I help you?" Mr. Ginsberg said to us.

Jamie slid into a seat opposite his desk. "I'm so glad you asked." He handed Mr. Ginsberg the tax thing Stella had stolen from Kells's office. "Who hired you to prepare this?"

"I'm afraid I can't divulge client information, Mr. . . ."

"Jesus," Jamie said. I snorted.

"Mr. Jesus," Ira said, without humor.

Jamie nodded thoughtfully. "I understand. I'll rephrase. Who hired you to prepare this?" This time when Jamie spoke, his voice was sharp and compelling, and Mr. Ginsberg looked at the paper for only a second before answering. The interrogation had begun.

"Horizons LLC is a wholly owned subsidiary; a representative of its parent company contacted me and asked if I could incorporate them in New York and handle their finances. Why?"

"Do you know what they do?"

"No," Mr. Ginsberg said cheerfully.

"Someone from the company, Horizons, must have had to sign these, right?"

"I believe there was an appointed agent of record, yes."

"Who?"

Mr. Ginsberg rubbed his chin. "I don't recall the name. It was very generic."

"But it's on the documents you prepared for them?"

"Indeed."

"Then give us the documents," Jamie said, his voice cutting the air like glass.

"Oh, I would, I would, except I don't have them. Everything that relates to EIC—the parent company—is kept in the archives, not in the office."

"The archives?"

"A repository of documents relating to the corporation and its subsidiaries. But the files are all coded. You're going to have a hell of a time finding anything in there without the access key."

Jamie gave Mr. Ginsberg a hard look with a raised eyebrow. "Then give us the access key."

Mr. Ginsberg's eyes looked unfocused. "I can't. I no longer have it."

I locked eyes with Stella.

"What did you do with it?" Jamie asked him.

"Those particular documents were requested just a few days ago, along with the key. I was instructed to send the key to a box at New York University."

"By whom?" Jamie asked.

"I don't know," Mr. Ginsberg said. "You have to understand, these are the corporation's operating procedures. One authorized person provides the access *code* to me, and I provide him or her with the access *key*, to facilitate the location of documents in the archives. Very useful for litigation."

Jamie leaned forward in the chair. "Explain?"

"Without the access key the corporation could provide discovery and bury its opponents in paper, and they would have no clue what any of it meant," Mr. Ginsberg said with a sly smile. "It would take years to sort it all out, and they'd have to pay their lawyers by the hour while they did."

I couldn't accept that we'd come all this way and been through everything we'd been through to face yet another dead end. "Tell us who you sent the documents to, then," I said, my patience dwindling. "And give us the address for the archives."

Mr. Ginsberg acted like he hadn't heard me. Jamie repeated my questions.

Mr. Ginsberg sighed. "There was no name to go with the address at New York University, only a department.

"Which one?" Jamie asked.

"Comparative Literature."

I was already walking out the door.

36

WE LEFT THE OFFICE WITH TWO addresses in hand—one, the archives; the other, the Comparative Literature Department at New York University.

"So where to?" Jamie asked as we stood outside. "Archives first, right?" he asked, at the same time Stella said, "NYU first."

She shook her head. "If we figure out who received the access key at the university, that could give us at least a name to go on more quickly than sifting through millions of pages of possibly crap documents."

"But there's no name with that address," Jamie said. "Whoever gave the code to Ginsberg could have just had him mail the key there to pick it up, and I just want to find out something, *anything*, already, even if all we find are crap documents in a mammoth warehouse somewhere. What say you, M?"

"Actually, I'm with Stella." I shrugged. "NYU is going to be easier, simpler, than finding our needle in the archives haystack."

Jamie held up his hands in defeat, and the three of us took a train to the Village. Jamie had to persuade the security guard to let the three of us in without ID. Then we headed to the floor where literatures were compared, and asked the blank-stared intern at the front desk where and how the incoming mail was routed. She pointed us to a milk crate piled high with envelopes.

"I distribute mail to the professors during their office hours. Everything without a professor's name goes to the head of the department, Peter McCarthy."

Stella and I raised our eyebrows. "And where is Professor McCarthy's office?"

"Last door on the left."

When we reached it, it was locked.

"Of course it's locked," Stella said after she'd tried it. "Of course."

"Wait," Jamie said, and withdrew something from his pocket. He stuck what looked like a bobby pin into the keyhole and jiggled it around purposefully. We practically held our breath until we heard the mechanism click.

"After you," he said, pushing the door open. I went in first.

Rows of overflowing bookcases lined the room, littered with papers and notebooks and random objects on every available surface, and many unavailable ones too. A damp-looking plant hung from a planter attached to the ceiling. Jamie ducked beneath it and began exploring.

"What are we looking for, exactly?" he asked.

"The access key, I guess," Stella said, carefully lifting up some papers on the desk.

Jamie squinted. "You realize that could be a code, not an actual key?"

I made a beeline for a half-buried inbox perched precariously on a shelf, and started looking through his mail. "Ginsberg said he'd sent the access code here, though. Which means he mailed it." I lifted an armful of envelopes and doled them out to Jamie and Stella. "Happy hunting."

"I'm pretty sure opening someone else's mail is a crime," Stella said.

"I'm pretty sure so is accessory to murder," Jamie said. "And yet here we are." He held up a manila envelope and raised his eyebrows. "No return address . . ."

"Open it," I told him.

He carefully slid a finger beneath the flap and peeked inside, then withdrew a thick, glossy IKEA catalogue.

Next. The three of us worked in silence. I flipped through my pile, looking out for anything with Ginsberg's name on it, or even just an address. But nothing stood out.

"This can't be another dead end," Stella groaned.

I knew how she felt. Frustration and anger bubbled up inside me, and I found myself abandoning the pile of hastily-checked-through mail and dropping to the floor to sort through the papers, notebooks, and file folders stacked up in piles all over the cramped, stuffy office. Any hope I'd originally had was thinning out by the second. The archives would be a thousand times worse than this. How could we find what we were looking for if we didn't even know where to look?

Stella and Jamie had each abandoned their stacks of mail and were now following my lead, looking through the papers on the floor. "These papers are at, like, a fourth-grade reading level. What does this guy even teach?"

"'Pacific Islander Gender Studies from 1750 to 1825,'" Jamie said, reading from a paper and not looking up.

"This is useless," I said as I rose from my crouch. "If the key was mailed here, whoever told Ginsberg to mail it here could have picked it up already. We might be looking for something that isn't even here."

"So, what, we just leave?" Stella asked.

"We have a better chance of finding what we're looking for in the archives," Jamie said. "As I told you before, FYI. Look, there's going to be a ton of stuff there, obviously, but we're bound to stumble onto something we can use to find out who's behind all of this. Eventually," he added.

I hated to admit it, but this was in fact turning out to be another dead end. "Let's just put everything back where we found it before someone finds us rifling through his shit."

Stella looked stricken. Jamie was eager to leave, and started putting things away as fast as his hot little hands could move. I rearranged the pile of notebooks I was holding on the corner of the desk and turned around, but as I did, I tripped over a small wooden carved statue I'd moved to the floor earlier. I threw my hands out against the bookcase to break my fall, which worked, but the movement sent something tumbling down from the top of it, right onto my head.

I swore and held both hands against the crown of my skull as I mimed kicking the stupid bookcase. Jamie picked up the thing that had fallen on me.

"I would've thought your head would be hard enough to break the glass," he said, holding the picture frame.

"You're going to feel crappy about making fun of me if I have a concussion."

"You don't have a concussion," Jamie said. He turned the picture over. "Does anyone remember where this was?"

I said, "I think it was on top of the bookcase?"

Jamie reached up to put it back. The picture was facing forward—it was of someone speaking at what looked like a graduation ceremony. McCarthy, I think, was the grizzled man at the podium. But that wasn't what caught my eye. In the background, standing off to the left of the stage in front of dozens of robed graduates and in a cluster of suited academics, was someone I thought I recognized. I snatched the frame from Jamie's hand.

"What is it?" he asked.

"Not what," I said. "Who." I was pointing at Abel Lukumi.

37

STELLA STEPPED OVER A PILE OF ACADEMIC JOURNALS on the floor and stood next to us. "What are we looking at?"

"The person responsible for all of this," I said without hesitating. There was no other explanation. "That's Lukumi."

"Wait—the guy from Miami? From Little Havana?"

"As opposed to the one from Sweden?"

"Shut up." Stella punched Jamie's arm.

Jamie snapped a picture of the photo of Lukumi and McCarthy immediately, and then we hastily rearranged the professor's office to look the way we'd found it. Mostly.

"What are the odds, though?" Jamie asked as we walked.

I shrugged. "One in who cares? He was in the picture with that professor—the head of the department where Ginsberg mailed the key. And he was on the train platform in DC. And he was in the hospital after Jude slit my wrists. He's been following us the whole time."

"Not us," Jamie said quietly.

Jamie had it exactly right. "Me. He's been following me. Ever since I met him." My thoughts raced faster than I could speak. "He has to have been the one who sent the note, with the doctor's bag, when I got sick. Which means he has to have known what was happening to me, what was inside me, which means—"

He would know where Noah was too. Maybe he was the one keeping him.

"But then why would he need the access key?" Jamie scratched his nose. "If he's the man behind the man or whatever, if he orchestrated all of this, funded all of it, and is following us to, I don't know, monitor what's happening to us, wouldn't he have access to the archives already? Why would he need the key?"

"Maybe that's not how this works," I said. "Maybe, to stay anonymous, he organized the corporation that funds Horizons so that only one person at a time can access the archives—so he needed to get the key before he could check whatever he wanted to check, and because even the people who work for him don't know who he is, he had the key sent here to his friend."

"Far-fetched," Jamie said.

Stella wound her hair around her finger. "I've heard worse theories. But wait . . . does that mean he has the key now? If one person at a time can access it, maybe—"

"Maybe he's there," I said, finishing her sentence. "Maybe he's there right now."

We all looked at one another. It was more than past time to end this. "Let's go."

We caught the train just before the doors closed, and Stella and I squished in between an older lady with purple hair clutching a Bloomingdale's bag to her chest and a Hasidic teenager slouched over a copy of *The Catcher in the Rye*. Jamie mocked a man in a business suit jamming audibly to something on his headphones, but otherwise we were silent until we got off. When we emerged from the subway, the sun was setting. Whatever neighborhood we were in looked pretty industrial. There were hardly any people walking around at all. It almost looked deserted.

"Okay," Jamie said. "Two blocks east, three north, and we should be there."

The sun slipped behind the jagged city horizon as we walked. It was almost dark when we arrived.

"This is it," Jamie said, looking up at a mammoth shuttered

warehouse. There were dozens of windows reaching up several stories high. Most were boarded shut with wood, and others were just dark. Adrenaline surged through my veins. *This* was where we were supposed to be. I could feel it.

"How are we supposed to get in?" Stella kicked the huge metal shutter enclosing what must have been the entrance.

"Fool of a Took!" Jamie hissed through his teeth. "If someone's in there, they probably heard that," he said, and stooped down to the ground. "Look. Padlock's off."

"So someone *is* in there," Stella said. "Lukumi?"

"Maybe," I said. Or maybe Noah.

Jamie looked at me. "Are you sure we should do this?"

"No," I said honestly, staring up at the building. "Lukumi has been leagues ahead of us this entire time. He's known everything we're about to do before we've done it. He's probably expecting us."

Stella tugged at her hair. "I don't really like the idea of that."

"I don't either, but the alternative is turning around and going home," I said. "And I can't do that."

Jamie looked at me and then crouched and lifted the shutter with both arms. You could probably have heard the metal groan all the way in Miami. We stood in front of a dark brown, or maybe rusted red door with a window covered in newspaper in it.

"Well," Stella said, "if he didn't know we were here before, he definitely does now."

I put my hand on the doorknob. It turned without effort, and I led the three of us in. The darkness outside was nothing compared to the darkness inside. It seemed solid, almost. Like if you reached out your hand, you would feel it.

"Should we look for a light?" Stella whispered.

"Are you afraid of the dark?" Jamie asked.

"I'd rather not break my neck tripping over you."

"And I'm pretty sure we already announced ourselves unintentionally," I said. "I vote for light." In no small part because I suddenly felt *very* afraid of the dark.

Jamie turned and scanned the wall behind us for a switch. It took a while, but soon—

"Bingo," he said, and flicked it on.

Rows and rows of lights slammed on, illuminating the vast space, which was lined with shelves that nearly scraped the ceiling. We heard something crash to the floor.

"Ow!"

Jamie and Stella looked at each other. Neither of them had spoken.

I didn't look at either of them. I just stared straight ahead, my mouth hanging open. I *knew* that Ow.

"Daniel?"

38

WHAT—*MARA*?" DANIEL SAID AT FULL VOLume. And then he poked his head out from behind a shelf at waist height.

I couldn't run fast enough. My brother was kneeling on the floor, rubbing one knee, and I dropped down and gave him the hug of his life.

"What are you *doing* here?" I asked, my voice muffled by his shoulder. I closed my eyes. I couldn't believe how good it felt to be hugged by my big brother. Or hugged period, really.

"I heard the shutter opening and flipped off the lights and hid, sort of, behind the stacks. And then you turned the lights on, and I tripped over a footstool."

"You *are* a genius," I said, smiling.

"What are *you* doing here?"

I pulled back, and the words just came pouring out of me—what had happened to me at Horizons, what had happened to me *before* Horizons, all of it. The dam had burst, and there was no putting it back together. Daniel's expression morphed from confusion to shock to horror to resignation and back to confusion as I spoke, breathless and flushed by the time I finished.

"So you're telling me . . . ," Daniel started. "You're telling me it was all real." A nervous laugh escaped from his throat. "Everything you—everything you said you were writing, for that Horizons assignment, that fiction thing? It wasn't fiction. There was no protagonist. You were talking about you."

I smiled, thinking of what Noah would have said if he were there. He'd thought I was being too obvious about my little problem, by telling Daniel it was an "assignment." I wished he were there, so I could say, *I told you so.*

Instead I said to my brother, "I knew you wouldn't believe me."

"Because it's— How is it possible?"

"We don't know," Jamie said. "We're here to try to figure it out."

Daniel closed his eyes. "I need a minute." He rubbed his eyes with the heels of his palms. "You're not telling me—you can't fly or anything."

"Nope," I said.

"And you can't, like, scale tall buildings and shoot webs out of your fingers."

I shook my head.

"Okay," Daniel said. "Okay." He looked around, his eyebrows drawn together, and he seemed to notice Jamie and Stella for the first time then. "I don't know you," he said to Stella. "But I know you." His eyes were on Jamie. "The Ebola kid, right?"

"Daniel."

"Right," Jamie said, a smile turning up the corner of his lips. "Jamie Roth," he said, holding out his hand. Daniel shook it slowly, still dazed.

"Stella Benicia," she said next, introducing herself. "And now that you know who we are, and we know who you are, mind telling us what you're doing here?"

Daniel looked a bit taken aback.

I sighed. "We were expecting—"

"A Santeria priest," Jamie interrupted. "You didn't happen to see anyone else here when you arrived?"

Daniel shook his head, looking even more confused, if that were possible. "It was just me."

"How did you get in?" Jamie asked.

"That's kind of a long story," Daniel said.

"Lucky for us," I said, "we have a bit of time."

Daniel narrowed his eyes at me. "I bet you do. Follow me, Little Sister."

⁂

Daniel led us up a winding, rickety metal staircase and then down a narrow passageway that led to the back of the building. He pushed open a door to an exposed-brick room with a bare bulb and a drafting table. Several books and files were neatly organized on and around it.

"I think this was a garment factory once," he said, pulling up a stool. There were a few dusty old sewing tables and crates leaning against the walls of the small room. We each pulled one up and sat on them as Daniel began to talk.

"I first figured out something was wrong after the Horizons retreat," Daniel said, looking at me. "When Noah didn't come back."

My heart skipped a beat when my brother said his name. Everyone at school knew about the Lolita incident, Daniel said. And the fact that Noah had been shipped off to a residential treatment facility for pushing a man into a killer whale tank had been big news. Daniel had suspected that Noah had been sent to Horizons—I'd been there, for one thing—but Daniel hadn't been able to confirm it; patient privacy laws had prevented the Horizons staff from telling him. So he'd tried the next best thing—Noah's parents. He had driven up to the house and been let in by Mr. Shaw.

"Wait, you met Noah's father?" I asked, leaning forward, elbows on knees.

Daniel nodded. "He said Noah would be at Horizons until he was 'sorted out,' and then he asked me very politely to leave. Why isn't Noah with you, by the way?"

My mouth opened, but I didn't know what to say, or where to begin.

"He was in Horizons with us," Jamie said. "And then the whole thing with Jude happened, and I wasn't there, for the end of it—I was helping Stella because he'd hurt her, and Noah told us to run. I never saw him again after that," Jamie said.

"Kells told us he died," Stella said. "In the Horizons collapse."

"But she's a liar," I cut in. "She lied all the time, about everything."

"So where is he?" Daniel looked at each of us.

"We don't know," I said. "But we're going to find out."

Daniel's eyes narrowed. "I got a weird feeling from his dad. Like, I know Noah doesn't get along with him, but shipping him off for the Lolita thing seemed extreme."

"Our parents shipped me there," I said.

"I know. But, Mara, you have . . ."

"What?"

"A history," Daniel said carefully.

So does Noah.

"Anyway, I started looking into Mr. Shaw."

"And?" Jamie asked.

"Every publicly filed document seemed legit. And there

was no connection to Horizons at all, obvious or otherwise. So anyway, I decided to go out there, to Horizons—"

"Wait, you were there?" I blurted out. "When?"

"A couple of weeks after you left. I grilled Mom and Dad about Horizons, and your being there, but they were so sensitive about it—Mom especially. She could barely talk about what you—about what she thought you did to yourself," Daniel amended, glancing at my wrists. "So in the end I just told her me and Sophie were going to go out on Sophie's dad's boat for the day, and I went to Horizons instead."

Daniel told us how he arrived at the island and security wouldn't let him in to see me, which frustrated him so much that he began skipping his independent study in the afternoons and digging through the last five years of the corporate filings for Horizons LLC.

"And that was my first clue," Daniel said. "I remembered Mom saying that Horizons had been open for only a year, but there were years of records to sort through—tax filings, annual reports, money coming in, money going out. And one of them led me to this accountant in New York—"

"Yeah, we met him too," Jamie said. "So, what did you do?"

"I called him."

"You just called him?"

"I gave him the name of one of Kells's employees and said I'd been ordered to acquire documents relating to one of the 'programs.'"

My eyes widened. "And that actually worked?"

"No."

Oh.

"He told me I needed to give him some access code and follow the appropriate procedure, whatever that was, even if I was calling on Kells's behalf. I knew I'd have to get to New York to find anything else out, but I didn't want to go before I knew I'd be able to get what I needed, and at that point I obviously had no idea. So I kept digging through whatever documents I could get at that were publicly available, but there was nothing that told me anything. And then one day I came home exhausted and went to my room to play piano, and this was sitting on top of it."

Daniel lifted something from one of the crates behind him. A copy of *New Theories in Genetics*.

"I'd forgotten about it after you left, and when I saw it there, I opened it and started reading. The premise was screwy, but it was so well researched that I couldn't put it down."

I made a face. "Only you would find that book captivating."

"Well, it's a good thing I did, because this baby is how I got in."

Daniel told us about his hunch that a series of numbers that kept appearing in the book might be the access key the accountant had told him about. His hunch turned out to be right. He started to tell us more, rattling off incomprehensible jargon, and I had to fight to stay awake, but then I heard him say, ". . . eighteen twenty-one."

I snapped to attention. "What did you just say?"

Daniel looked at me with a curious expression. "Those numbers I was talking about? The sequence? Lenaurd, the author, kept referring to them as genetic markers—the numbers of the genes that carry the anomaly that makes the subjects different. One of the studies he self-published determined that subjects with the anomaly see those numbers everywhere. The sequences stand out to them. Whenever they see a cluster—any pairing of one, eight, two, or three—they notice. It's like an obsessive thought, or a form of OCD counting. They start seeing patterns where there are none, but they may not even realize they're doing it. It's one of the earliest symptoms."

I wondered if I'd done it. If so, I hadn't noticed.

"He talks about the degradation and evolution of these particular markers, claiming to have traced the lineage of some subjects back to before gene sequencing technology even existed. It's junk science, like the stuff about genetic memory—"

"Like what stuff?" Stella asked.

"Sometimes an additional protein will bind to the gene. He called subjects who had it G1821-3 and claimed the third protein allowed them to retain memories from genetic ancestors, which is ridiculous."

"It's not ridiculous," I said softly. "It's true."

"What?"

I told Daniel about the dreams, the memories, whatever

they were—about India, and our grandmother's doll.

"I don't know what that means," Daniel said when I was finished.

"It means that whatever Lenaurd wrote about in there is accurate," I said. Stella's eyes lit up with hope.

"He also said subjects with the anomaly had 'additional greater abilities,'" Daniel said, looking at each of us. "Like, superheroish stuff."

We were silent, until Jamie said, "Not superheroish, exactly." I kicked his crate.

"But you can . . ." Daniel let his voice trail off, waiting for the rest of us to speak. No one did. "Do things?"

Jamie nodded slowly. "Yup."

"Just—correct me if I'm wrong, here—so what you're saying is, you can—"

"Hear your thoughts," Stella said.

"Make you do what I want you to do," Jamie said.

"And Noah can heal," I said, watching the gears turn in Daniel's mind. I knew what he would ask next, and I wasn't ready for it. But I didn't have a choice.

"What about you?" he asked me.

My gaze flicked to Jamie, then Stella. They avoided my eyes.

"I can do things," I said lamely. "With my mind."

Daniel tilted his head. "Things? Like . . . *Carrie* things?"

In a sense. "Do you know what Jude did to me, the night the Tamerlane collapsed?"

Daniel nodded. His Adam's apple bobbed in his throat. "Yeah."

"That's why I did it," I said quietly, as Daniel's eyebrows drew together. "I was scared. And angry. The asylum collapsed because I wanted it to."

Daniel shook his head in confusion. "You're saying—"

"I killed Rachel and Claire." Daniel was opening his mouth to argue, but I spoke before he could. "And Mrs. Morales? She died because I was angry at her for failing me."

"Mara, she died of anaphylactic shock."

"Because I wanted her to choke on her tongue."

My brother had no response to that. There was nothing to say.

It was Stella who finally rescued me from the awkward, painful silence that followed my confession. "Did you read anything in there about how to fix us? Like a cure?"

Daniel shook his head. "It's not like that—the anomalous gene is more like, like an X or Y chromosome." He met my eyes. "It's just . . . part of you."

"You're not broken," Noah had said to me when I'd asked him to fix me a lifetime ago.

Maybe he was right.

39

STELLA HAD A HARD TIME SWALLOWING WHAT Daniel had said, and she asked him if she could look at the book.

"You should all read it," Daniel said as he handed it to her. "Maybe you'll think of something I missed."

Jamie unfolded his legs and rose from his crate. "What else have you found so far?"

"Not much to confirm what's in the book," Daniel said, "but a whole lot about one Deborah Susan Kells." Daniel lifted up a stack of files from behind one of the crates. It was one stack of many. "I didn't know anything about anything till I got in here, so I had no idea where to even start. Kells's name was the only thing I had to go on, so I used the access code to figure out the archiving system and found her file."

"How long have you been here?" I asked him, looking around the small room at the little piles of knowledge Daniel had acquired and assembled in painstaking order.

"*Here* here? Or in New York?"

"Both."

"When I got to the city, I had the accountant mail the access code to a professor I've corresponded with at NYU."

"But wait," Jamie said, holding out his hand. "So you're saying it was a coincidence that Lukumi was in that picture?"

I shook my head. "There are no coincidences."

Daniel eyed Jamie and me. "Back the truck up—who's Lukumi?"

"We'll explain later," I said. "Keep going."

"Okay . . . Well, so anyway, I made an appointment with him so he could show off his department and try to recruit me, but managed to filch it from his inbox with him none the wiser."

"How naughty and daring of you. All that and you lied to our parents about the reason for your New York visit? I'm impressed."

"Well, I *did* visit a college here." Daniel grinned. "So, it's not completely false."

Jamie looked up. "A half-truth is a whole lie, my mother says."

"He's right, you know," I chimed in.

"Guess I'm a rebel, then."

"But wait," Stella said. "What if the access code changes?"

"Then I'm screwed."

"*We're* screwed," I said. "We can't leave here without this stuff. There might be something here that will help us find Noah."

Daniel nodded. "We should go through what I've found so far, and then one of us should start making a list of what we still need. We won't be able to go through everything, but if we're asking the right questions, maybe eventually we'll hit on the right answers."

"You can be our Gandalf," I said, remembering our conversation from weeks ago, and smiling.

"I'm only a year older than you. But I'll take it as a compliment, if you let me be Dumbledore instead."

"If you insist." I shrugged. "But Dumbledore is more dead."

"Point," Daniel acknowledged.

"You're neither, actually." Jamie looked up from a file he was reading. "You're a muggle—"

"Hey, now."

"Which makes you Giles."

Daniel considered it for a moment. "I'll take it."

"Good. Now, Mara?" Jamie batted his eyelashes and handed me a stack of files. "Get reading."

Stella and Daniel roamed the stacks and made their list, coming back periodically to dump file folders bursting with paper onto the drafting table. Jamie and I sat in that dim room, crouched and hunched over hundreds, thousands of pages of records, emails, transcripts, everything. I sucked down the information until I was saturated with it, until my fingers were sore from paper cuts and my brain sloshed with mostly irrelevant details. I seemed to have gotten the pile of crap containing the most mundane bits of Kells's early life—notes from her kindergarten teacher, her fourth-grade science project, et cetera. I idly wondered why they—whoever they were—bothered collecting this shit, but the truth was, I didn't really care. I was hungry for answers, starving for them, and they were here, somewhere under this roof, and I would find them.

"Mara," Jamie said quietly. "Come look at this."

Or they would find me.

Jamie handed me a thick file folder, already opened. "Don't lose my place."

I glanced down at the pages. Medical records, they looked like. There were hospital admissions, discharges, prescriptions, and more records of visits to—

"The Obstetrics and Gynecology Department," I said aloud, and rechecked the name at the top of the page.

Kells, Deborah S.

"'Patient conceived intrauterine pregnancy. Patient experienced miscarriage. Required termination.'"

"I counted six miscarriages in there so far," Jamie said. "Then I skipped ahead. She was diagnosed with idiopathic infertility—they didn't know what was causing it."

"So . . ."

Jamie shrugged. "I don't know what it means exactly. We need more."

I looked at the dates of the records—1991, 1992, 1993. And that was just in this folder.

"Should we skip ahead?" Jamie asked.

"To when?"

"I want to know how she ended up working at Horizons."

Jamie was right. Without fully realizing it, we'd been reading her file to find the answer to just one question: Why? Why had she brought us there? Why had she tortured us? If there was a reason, it wouldn't be in her kindergarten records. We needed to find out how she'd found out about Horizons in the first place. And who had recruited her.

Jamie rifled through some of the other folders and picked up small little envelopes with discs in them. "CDs?" He turned them over. "No. DVDs," he said. "'DSK Interviews 11-3-1999, 10-2-1999, 09-2-1999 . . . What the . . . ?"

"DSK," I said. "Deborah Susan Kells."

Jamie raised an eyebrow. "Right. How far do you think these go back?"

I dipped my hands into the file folder Jamie had found them in. There were dozens. "To '98, I think."

Jamie stood and looked in another folder. "There's '96 and '97 in here."

We kept looking through folder after folder and eventually realized that the earliest DVDs were from 1994, beginning not long after the medical records ended.

"I'm kind of dying to watch these," I said.

"Me too."

"They're set at around the same time every month—some kind of experiment, maybe?" That would fit with what we knew about her. Maybe Dr. Kells's first test subject had been herself.

"Maybe."

"We should bring them with us."

"All of them?"

I gestured to the room. "Well, we can't watch them here."

Jamie stood and opened the door, then turned to me. "Should we go look for more?"

We should. "I want to see how many there are. And if there are any from this year." She might have talked about us. She might have talked about me.

Just as we gathered up some of the files and left the stuffy little room, we ran into Daniel and Stella.

Daniel took a dramatic step back. "What's up?"

"We found something," I said, and then Jamie began to talk.

40

"WOW," DANIEL SAID AS HE WALKED INTO THE brownstone. "What does your aunt do?"

"Teacher," Jamie said. "She made intelligent real estate decisions."

"That she did."

"I'm hungry," Stella announced. "Anyone else?"

"Starving," I said, realizing it just then. We hadn't eaten anything the whole day.

"Should we order in?" she asked.

Daniel shook his head. "The less attention we attract, the better."

He was right, so we managed to scrounge together a meal out

of the junk we'd bought at the bodega down the street. Daniel divvied up the file folders between us and, taskmaster that he was, told us to get reading. But I wanted to watch the videos first.

Daniel dug his heels in. "We'll get more done if we split up the work."

"Split it up however you want," I told him. "But I'm calling the interviews."

"I want to watch too," Jamie said.

Daniel looked at Stella, who held up her hands in defeat. "We bought popcorn," she said. "Should I make popcorn?"

"This isn't movie night," Daniel grumbled.

I couldn't help my smile. "Yes," I told Stella. And then, to complete the picture, Jamie fetched blankets and tossed them at us. "Where do you want to start?" Jamie asked me as Stella walked in with a bowl of popcorn.

"What's the first one we've got?"

Jamie shuffled the little DVD envelopes and announced, "January eighth, 1994."

"That one, then."

Jamie dutifully popped the DVD into his aunt's Xbox (I very much wanted to meet this aunt), turned out the lights, and plopped down in an armchair.

There was static at first, and then it cleared to reveal a very young-looking Dr. Kells sitting at a small card table in front of a pea-green-and-off-white-striped wall. It looked familiar. After a moment I realized why.

It was the room from the video of her I'd seen in the Horizons Testing Facility, the one she'd used to trick me into searching for her, so she could lure me into the containment room. It had been there since 1994.

"State your name for the record," a male voice said. I didn't recognize it.

"Is this a deposition?" Daniel asked. I shushed him.

"Deborah Susan Kells."

"Have you ever gone by any other name?"

"My maiden name," Dr. Kells said.

"And what is that?"

"Lowe."

"Holy shit," I whispered.

"No fucking way," Jamie said.

It wasn't possible. I'd met Jude and Claire's parents. I'd seen them at the funeral and memorial service. I'd—

"What is your date of birth?"

"Wait, someone pause this, we *must* discuss," Jamie said as Dr. Kells started to recite what sounded like addresses.

"Where's the remote? Fuck!"

"Degrees conferred?"

"I was awarded a PhD in genetics from Harvard, and my first postdoc appointment was at—"

Dr. Kells paused midword. Jamie left his hand extended while pointing at the television. "So okay," he said. "Deborah Susan Lowe. As in—"

"Jude Lowe," Daniel said.

"What the fuck, guys," I said. "What. The. Fuck."

Jamie looked taken aback. "Who would marry that bitch?"

"I've met Jude and Claire's mother, though," I said thinly. "I've met her and their dad. And I went to their house." Then I remembered something—something Noah had said. "But . . . it *wasn't* their house."

Daniel cocked his head. "What are you talking about?"

"Noah went there before Horizons," I said. "Before . . ." I held up my wrists. Daniel flinched as if I'd hit him.

"To Laurelton? Seriously?"

I nodded. "To try to find Jude's parents, to see if they knew anything, when we thought he was hunting me. But they weren't there," I said. "Jude's parents, I mean. The people who answered the door said they'd owned the house for the past eighteen years. Noah thought I'd given him the wrong address."

"So okay." Stella held up a finger. "If the people you thought were his parents weren't really his parents," Stella said, "who were they?"

"Jesus, how far does this go back?" Jamie looked nervous.

"Jude and Claire moved to Laurelton a year before they died," I said. "Claire was in my grade, but Jude—"

"Was in mine," Daniel said.

"Did you know him?" Stella asked.

"Not well," my brother said uncomfortably. "I should have. Maybe if I'd known him better, I could've—"

"No," I said quickly. "Even you wouldn't have guessed this."

"*What*, though?" Jamie asked. "I mean, we were just looking at pages of records of miscarried pregnancies. You think she's his mother?"

I thought back to every interaction I'd had with Dr. Kells, rifling through my memories for a clue, a hint, anything. But every time I'd talked to her, she'd been dispassionate. Clinical.

Except for the last time, anyway.

"Lowe isn't really an uncommon name," Jamie said.

We all looked at him.

"Maybe it's a coincidence?" he asked meekly.

I leaned forward. "You're not serious."

"I don't know!" he admitted. "Maybe they're related but she's not their mother? We've barely even watched five minutes of this."

He had a point. "We're going to have to marathon them."

"There are hundreds," Stella said.

Jamie rubbed his forehead. "And they're not exactly *The Lord of the Rings*."

"Well, we're not exactly the fucking Fellowship," I said. "Unless anyone here can think of a shortcut, you should probably press play."

"Wait." Daniel stood up. He disappeared into the kitchen and returned with five spiral notebooks, which he must have bought at the bodega. He tossed one to each of us.

"No pens?" I asked.

Daniel threw a box of pens at me, and then the five of us got to work.

By five a.m., we'd barely scratched the surface of Dr. Kells: The Early Years. We broke to sleep—or nap, really, since Daniel had us up by ten to begin again. We were afraid to divide the work—what if one of us noticed something that the rest of us didn't? So we watched them all together, Stella and Daniel skimming through files that seemed to correspond with the months and times Kells was interviewed, though each file wasn't properly labeled or dated. The sequence 18213 was a cipher, and we needed to use it to find the files we wanted. Jamie was inordinately good at it, so he did the code-breaking. Daniel and Stella hunted for the files in the stacks, and they brought them back to me to read. This is what we learned:

Dr. Kells was a carrier of G1821. She never manifested, though. That's a thing that can happen, apparently, an interesting little factoid that Daniel made much of. Manifestation was like cancer, kind of. There's a gene involved, but there are also environmental triggers, so even if you have the marker for the condition, you might still be safe if nothing switches the gene on.

Which brought us to the second thing we learned, though we kind of already knew it—Kells was obsessed with finding a way to correct "the anomaly," having blamed it for her infertility. As we watched her interviews, we heard her mention working with a man—a pharmacologist, Daniel guessed—to develop different drugs to counteract the effects of the gene, to switch off its effects, whether a carrier had manifested or not. But nothing worked . . . on her, at least. So she wanted to see if drugs worked on anyone else. But she couldn't jump through the appropriate hoops to be able to do human trials on women who were trying to become pregnant who might have been carriers too. Couples undergoing infertility treatment tended to be wealthy, which meant Congress cared about them.

No one cared about foster kids, though, so Kells became a foster parent. Once I realized what I was looking for, I began to find records for A. and B. Lowe, C. and D. Lowe, E. and F. Lowe, and G. and H. Lowe. All identical twins. All boys. All dead.

And they'd all been under her care. They died at different ages, with different symptoms, but all culminating in a fever and "death arising from natural causes," according to the medical examiners' reports in each of their files. My heart hurt as I looked at the pictures of them; Abraham at eight months old, teething on a green plastic stegosaurus he held with two hands up to his mouth; Benjamin, who lived a year longer than his twin, squatting on two chubby legs as he pushed a toy fire truck; Christopher, dead at two, shirtless in his picture as he stuck his tongue out at the camera; David, his twin, three at his time of death, wearing a little suit, surrounded by ducks in a park; Ethan, four when he was placed into foster care, four and a half when he died; and his twin, Frederick, five when he died, four in the picture with Ethan, their little arms around each other's shoulders; Garrett, six, legs splayed out over the back of a shaggy, bored-looking pony, with his twin, Henry, holding the halter. Garrett almost made it to seven. Henry died on his seventh birthday.

And then a picture of a little eight-year-old boy with a too-wide grin and a missing front tooth, a spray of freckles across his nose and a dimple in his cheek as he smiled beneath a too-big Patriots cap tilted haphazardly on his nearly white-blond head.

Subject nine: Jude Lowe.

41

JUDE AND CLAIRE LOWE, PAIR FIVE. FRATERNAL TWINS. "Artificially induced at age eight," according to their files, their *real* files, which meant that was when they were injected with whatever version of whatever drug Kells was working on then to cause the symptoms of G1821.

"Wait a second," Jamie said, looking up from the files. ""What happened to I. Lowe?"

"There is no I."

Jamie snapped his fingers. "Exactly."

Stella just shrugged. "Maybe she didn't like any boys' names that started with *I*?"

"Like 'Ignatius'?" Daniel chimed in.

"Or 'Ira,'" I said.

"Which brings up another point," Jamie said, and bit his thumbnail. "These weren't the kids' real names. They couldn't have been. They would have all had names on their birth certificates."

"I didn't see any birth certificates in the files," I said. Only death certificates. "Their medical records use the aliases or whatever, though."

"So Kells must have renamed them—but how do you get a six- or seven-year-old to accept a new name?"

"And lie to doctors and nurses about it?" I asked. I thought about the files I'd thumbed through, but no hospital names stood out. "Give me that," I said to Jamie, and he handed me one of the files. F. Lowe. Frederick.

"These records are from Mount Tom Hospital. Someone Google it."

Daniel did. "Doesn't exist." He paused. "So are these records even real?"

"I think they are," Stella said. "I mean, why fabricate someone's entire medical history? Especially if you're not even using that person's real name?"

A thought dawned on me. "It's another layer of protection," I said. "The names were changed, the places and dates—none of it's real. If it were, it would make the children, and what happened to them, too easy to actually find. But I think

Stella's right, that what's actually *reported* there is real. The symptoms, the treatment, the consequences. I mean, we *saw* the archives. The *real* files, with the kids' real names, might be in there somewhere, but without knowing what they are, no one would ever find them."

Daniel nodded slowly. "So none of this can be used as evidence," he said quietly. "Kells was a real person with a real identity, and once you have an identity, it's not easy to shake. If anyone traced *her* history and found the archives, like we did, and tried to report this stuff, like *I* want to, these would just look like the fictional records from fictional kids that never existed."

"Smart," Jamie said.

Very.

"But how would she be allowed to foster so many kids? Especially when they kept dying on her?" Stella asked.

"The same way she had the resources to find us," I said. "And to experiment on us, and to do all of this research—"

"Plus," Jamie said, "bad shit happens to kids in foster care all the time."

I looked at Kells's frozen image on the screen, and pressed play.

"J. woke up two days after induction complaining of sickness. The thermometer showed a fever of 99.6. I'm hopeful that this is just a normal cold, or flu, since the others presented with temperatures above 101 before they expired."

"Expired? Damn, that's cold," Jamie said.

"Claire seems fine, anyway," Kells continued, looking perfectly calm, not worried at all.

"Fast forward," Jamie said, and I did.

Kells looked tense and worried now. "J. has developed the fever. Same symptoms as the others, mostly, but with a few key differences. He seems disoriented. I've caught him speaking in the third person, to himself, and occasionally to me. He has asked to see Claire, but I don't want to frighten her. I need her amenable and willing to endure future testing, particularly if Jude expires like the rest."

I stopped the DVD. "Claire was in my grade," I said to no one in particular.

"And Jude was in mine," Daniel said.

Stella picked up the pile of papers on the table. "But it says they were fraternal twins. Pair five."

I nodded.

"Why lie?" I asked.

I pressed play, but Dr. Kells had switched the focus of her interview, or recording, or whatever this was, to a discussion of the properties of Amylethe. Daniel and Stella kept watching as Jamie and I picked out the DVDs with the months and dates that corresponded to medical events in Jude's file. When this DVD finished, we put the next one in.

Kells sat down at the little table in the green and white room, practically beaming. "My name is Deborah Susan Kells," she said to the camera. "Today is Monday, March fifth, two months after the induction of subject J.L. according to the Lenaurd protocol, which appears to have been a success."

The four of us looked at one another.

"After the injection series, he began developing at a magnificent rate," Kells said, leaning forward in her chair. "Beyond what I could have hoped." She kept talking, about Jude's advancement, his development, physical and otherwise. He was becoming "gifted," to use Kells's words, and she was proud of him, proud of what she'd done to him. But it was also changing him—subtly at first. And then not. When he was ten years old, she began to worry.

"He is moody, depressive—aggressive, even. I've noticed the development of secondary sex characteristics—deepening voice, the beginnings of facial and chest hair. He appears to be undergoing puberty, despite his age. I've ordered an evaluation and intervention, and I will report back with the results next month." She turned the camera off.

We put the next DVD in, riveted.

"The psychiatrist has returned with a diagnosis of conduct disorder," she said, clearly shaken. "And the behavior of Subject J continues to deteriorate. He has become antisocial and extremely aggressive. Claire reported that she caught her brother pulling the feathers off a sparrow fledgling that had fallen out of its nest. We've been administering Amylethe to try to arrest the . . . side effects . . . of the manifestation."

"That's why," Daniel said quietly.

"Why what?"

"Why they lied about his age. If he started undergoing puberty at ten, he would have looked too old to pass for seventeen." Daniel picked up a handful of paper and spoke while reading it. "She kept testing all kinds of drugs on him, not just the typical antipsychotics—hormones, experimental stuff." And then Daniel looked at each of us. "This is why you guys look older than you are. There was something about rapid maturation in *New Theories*. It started at age eighteen in subjects, and continued to twenty-one."

"Except none of us are eighteen," Stella said aloud.

Jamie looked skeptical. "And people always think I'm younger than I am. Maybe it's like that thing where growth hormones in milk make you go through puberty earlier?"

I wished Noah could have been there to hear that. "She gave me Amylethe too," I said to Daniel, remembering Kells's words in Horizons. "She said it would make me better."

Daniel looked at me then. "Did it work? Do you feel better?"

I did feel better, but it wasn't because of the drugs, or the implants. How could I describe what I'd gone through just to get here? How I'd felt beyond sick and not myself every day since waking up in Horizons? Until I'd gotten those things inside me out?

"No," I said. "I don't think it worked."

"What about your, um . . . power?"

Jamie cringed. "It sounds cheesy when you put it like that."

I didn't answer my brother, because the truth was, I didn't know if it still worked or didn't. I hadn't tried it, not since—

"Wait right here," I said, and threw off my blanket. I took the stairs two at a time and pushed open the door to the bedroom I would sleep in for as long as we were here. I spotted what I was looking for on a chair in the corner.

I looked through the small gray duffel bag until I found them. The implants, the capsules or whatever, that had been inside me until Stella cut them out. I closed my fist around them and brought them downstairs. Daniel examined one of them under the light.

"These were inside you?"

"Yup."

"Where?"

"In my stomach, I think."

"They couldn't have actually been in your stomach, or you would have died taking them out."

"Fine," I said. "They were forty-two degrees south of my right fibia and seventh metatarsal."

"You don't have a fibia. That's not a real bone."

I gave my brother the finger.

"No need to get snippy," Daniel said prissily. "Okay, so, these were inside you when you left Horizons, right?"

"Right."

"And your ability didn't work after you left there, right?"

"Correct."

"You tried?"

I thought about Mr. Ernst. About what I'd done to him after what he'd tried to do to Stella and me. "Yes." I did try.

"What happened?" Daniel prodded. "Who did you try to . . ." His voice trailed off. "Who hurt you?"

Jamie almost literally began to whistle and twiddle his thumbs. Stella looked at the floor.

"It was nothing," I said, falsely calm. "It was fine in the end."

Daniel handed me back the implants and then looked down at the mess of papers. "All right. We know the anomaly is triggered by fear and stress. So, what if anytime your nervous system was flooded with adrenaline, or cortisol, those things reacted, negating your ability? Like a fail-safe to make you safer, better, in case you ever left Horizons."

But they hadn't made me safer, I thought. My mind conjured an image of Mr. Ernst, what I did to him, and I blinked, hoping it would disappear.

Daniel chose his words carefully. "But you *were* actually safer in the sense that you couldn't *accidentally* . . . hurt someone. You couldn't protect yourself, but you were safer for other people to be around."

I wondered if that were true.

"Anyway, Dr. Kells thought of herself as a scientist, a researcher. She had plans to send you back home, right?"

"That's what she said."

"So those implants must have been part of her plan to do it. She thought she'd have time to tweak the effects, figure out how to counteract the anomaly, before you guys escaped."

Before I killed her. But Daniel had a point. Everything Kells had done to us, done to me, had been in pursuit of a cure. If at first you don't succeed, try, try again. And when she hadn't succeeded, and Jude had let me out, she'd decided to put me down like an animal before I could be set loose and hurt anyone else.

As we watched the interviews, we realized Daniel had been right. Jude got worse, no matter what Kells did to try to fix him. She attempted to hide her distress as he grew older, more dangerous, but the drugs she pumped into him didn't always mitigate his behavior. Sometimes he didn't seem to know who he was; he was diagnosed with multiple personality disorder, and when someone "else" emerged, Claire was the only one who could get him, the *real* him, to break through, which Daniel guessed was why Kells had been willing to foster her, gender notwithstanding.

Hearing and watching Kells talk about Jude made the hair rise on my skin. You could tell she was losing control but she couldn't admit it. Jude was her success story after years and years of failure. She couldn't accept that in trying to cure the anomaly, she had actually done something worse. Her only true success had been managing to keep Claire and Jude alive after induction. Claire was completely normal, actually, despite Kells's efforts to make her otherwise. Kells guessed

Claire wasn't a carrier. If she had been, Kells could've triggered the mutation the way she had with Jude.

"That explains why Jude survived after the asylum but Claire didn't," Daniel said. But then again, almost to himself, "But what about his hands?"

Jude's hands. The hands he supposedly didn't have anymore, after the patient room door at the Tamerlane had slammed shut on him, separating him from me, and his wrists from his hands.

"It doesn't make any *sense*," Daniel mumbled.

"Doesn't it, though?" Stella looked from Daniel to me to Jamie. "Jude has a healing factor."

"So did Noah," Jamie said. I shot him a look. "Does. So *does* Noah."

Which is why he *had* to be alive. "Which is why he's still out there," I said.

"But Jude can't heal without hurting someone else," Stella said. "When the door slammed shut on him in the asylum, you wouldn't have been affected, because you're . . . different."

"Oh my God," Daniel said.

"What?" I looked at him.

"Rachel and Claire," Daniel said. "They were normal, not carriers. They were at the Tamerlane with you and Jude. Jude healed because of *them*. *He* killed them, not . . ."

Me. Not me.

I swallowed. There was no way to really ever know what

had happened, or who was more responsible. I'd wished that the building would collapse. I'd wished for Jude to die. It had collapsed and he *hadn't* died, but if Rachel and Claire had been killed because of Jude's ability, because his body had needed to heal itself, it still wouldn't have happened if I hadn't been the one to hurt him. So who was responsible for that? Him or me? Did it matter?

"A question, though," Stella said, interrupting the silence. "Something I don't get. Maybe one of you can help me out. Why no girls? Why did Kells foster only boys till Claire? I mean, if I'm a carrier, and Mara's a carrier, and we've manifested, then why—"

Daniel cut in. "Why were most of the twins boys?"

Stella nodded.

"There was something in *New Theories* about the Y chromosome and a healing factor," Daniel said, getting up to search for the book. "Most greater abilities were of different subtypes that could bind to an X or Y chromosome, but not that one. It had to be a Y."

I thought about the children Kells had experimented on. Eight little boys, once healthy and now dead. She'd been trying to solve a problem, she'd said, to fix the anomaly, to create someone who could heal himself and, by extension, others—and her, too.

She had been trying to create Noah, but she'd made Jude instead.

42

I TOLD EVERYONE WHAT I THOUGHT. THEY WERE silent, but they knew I was right. *I* knew I was right. In trying to develop a cure for what was making people sick, she'd just made them sicker. If she'd been alive, she'd still be trying.

And as we watched deeper and deeper into the night, we found out that once she'd tracked down my grandmother as being a known carrier (by methods she never specified), she'd started watching my family. Everything had been arranged, planned—Jude and Claire's move to Rhode Island, enrolling them in my school so Jude and Claire could get close to me—all of it. Daniel even found records that showed a subsidiary of

Horizons LLC, paying for 1281 Live Oak Court, the address that I'd once thought was Jude's. Whoever Noah had met there weren't his parents, but they *were* liars.

"She couldn't have done all of this on her own," Daniel said. "We know she didn't—she was recording these interviews for someone, using research she didn't come up with herself. Someone was supporting her, funding her, making everything she did possible."

"Lukumi," I said.

"We think," Jamie added.

Daniel rubbed his eyes like a little kid. "This is much, much bigger than just us," Daniel said. "I mean, look at the archives. There are millions, maybe billions of pages in there. And what Kells said before, about tracing the gene back to our grandmother? There are other carriers out there. Like you," he said, looking at me. "But what doesn't make any sense is, if that's true, why hasn't anyone else discovered you guys by now?"

No one understood the answer to this better than I did. "Because if we tell anyone the truth, people just think we're crazy."

"Okay, well, at this point you're right, Mara. All roads are leading to Lukumi," Daniel said. "He's the only person whose name keeps coming up."

"Actually, that's not his real name," I said.

"Uh, what?" Stella had been reading something, but looked up.

"Noah and I looked for him," I explained. "We went

back to Little Havana, we did the requisite Google search. 'Lukumi' is the name of some Santeria case that went to the Supreme Court."

Jamie nodded. "Of course it is. That doesn't make this harder at all."

"Whoever he is," Daniel started, "he's the only one who can actually prove that you're innocent."

Well, not innocent exactly.

"He's the only one who knows about you."

The only person alive, anyway.

"Which means that if I were a betting man, I'd bet he knows about Noah, too."

I was betting on that too.

We watched interviews and read papers and worked all night, combing through everything we'd brought with us from the archives. Property records, the deed to my parents' house, the bar admissions certificate of the man who'd referred my father to the Lassiter case, medical records from the sixties, medical records from the nineties, pictures of scarring on the inside of Jamie's throat. ("What in fresh hell?" Jamie said.) But there were still so many pieces of the puzzle missing.

My thoughts hung like loose threads, frayed and tangled. It didn't help that I was exhausted. I leaned my head in my hands, staring at the documents in front of me. The words on the page arranged themselves into an incomprehensible shape as I fought to stay awake, and lost.

43

BEFORE

Cambridge, England

IT HAD BEEN OVER A CENTURY SINCE I FLED LONDON WITH the professor, and yet he still treated me like a child.

Tonight he was in a particularly sulky mood. The weather was customarily dreary, and his office was cold and damp and in ruins. He warmed himself with a bottle of whiskey, his preferred poison, and scribbled furiously in one of his books. Torn paper and worn books littered the scarred wooden floor. I watched him in silence.

Something had caught his attention recently, focused him in a way I had never before seen. A coming shift, he called it. He thought he might have discovered a way to trigger it. But he refused to share his thoughts with me.

He had cared for me during the fevers as my Gift blossomed inside of me, as my body changed to accommodate it. He forced me to eat when food lost all its taste. He comforted me during my night terrors and caught me, stopped me, the first time I tried to do myself harm.

But I didn't need him for those things now—I hadn't in many, many years. I had shed the girl who had fled London in darkness, the one who cried over her husband of one night. I was strong, bold, and I could control myself perfectly. If I wanted to.

I did not want to anymore.

I'd grown tired of pretending to be someone else just so I could be safe for others. I wanted to be who I was. The professor knew me the way no one else did, which was why I wanted to be with him. But no matter how I broached the subject, he dismissed it. Dismissed *me*. He still wouldn't even tell me his name.

The sound of shattering glass snapped me to attention. The professor sat stick straight at his desk, staring at nothing.

No. Not nothing. I followed his gaze to a painting of himself that hung on the opposite wall. It had been given to him by a student, he'd said, and though he would not tell me which, I had my suspicions—the style was familiar and distinctive. But the picture glistened with the remains of his drink, making his skin and hair look wet. The fiery scent of spilled whiskey mingled with that of his old books.

"What is it?" I asked gently.

He didn't answer, so I stepped between his desk and the portrait. He looked right through me, as if I were invisible.

But I would be seen tonight. I would be felt.

I skirted the edge of his desk, until I came to his chair. "What is your name?" I asked him, not gently at all. "Tell me."

He smiled a little. I'd been asking that question for a very long time. Each time I asked, he would give me a different answer.

But this time, tonight, he reached for a scrap of paper, a torn-out map. My heartbeat quickened. He wrote something on it in a language I'd never learned to read, and showed it to me.

I smoothed my finger over the words. "I am in love with you," I said.

"I raised you," he replied, and did not meet my eyes.

"You did not raise me. Sarah Shaw raised me—"

"Until you were eighteen. Then I took you, I taught you—"

I moved over to him, pressed my hand to his cheek. He flinched. I didn't move. "I know you watched me when I was young. I know you feel responsible for me. But you are not my parent and I am no longer young."

"This is wrong." His voice was blank and empty.

I climbed onto his lap. "It doesn't feel wrong," I said. There was no sound except for our breath, and the slither of a belt being pulled through its loop. I kissed him below his jaw. He shuddered a breath, and I kissed his lips, just once.

It was enough.

The professor was gone when I woke the following morning. I bore a daughter nine months later. I did not see the professor again for twenty-one years.

Laurelton, Rhode Island
Twenty-one years later

The Professor knocked on the door of my cottage on the morning of Indira's graduation from Brown. I did not want to open the door for him, but I knew I had no choice. He didn't look a day older than he had when I'd last seen him. Then again, neither did I.

"I found him," he said to me, his eyes lit with a childish excitement that was incongruous with the dark, serious suit he wore. He looked like an undertaker.

"What are you doing here?"

"I found the one."

"Please leave," I said flatly.

"Mara—"

"Don't you dare say my name. You have no right to say anything to me."

He closed his eyes. "May I come in?"

"No."

"Please."

I wanted to close the door in his face, but I knew him well

enough to know he wouldn't leave even if I did. He would stand there, sleep there, turn up everywhere I went, until he gave me the message he wanted me to hear.

"You left me," I said, as I let him in. I didn't have to make it easy.

The professor's gaze fell to his feet. "I saw what would happen to her if I'd been there. It was for your, and her, protection."

"That's so convenient, isn't it? You can excuse anything that way, can't you? By saying it couldn't be otherwise, that you had no choice. So why are you here now? What do you want from me? I want you gone before Indi finds you here."

"There's a girl. I need you to befriend her. She's passionate, hyperintelligent, but skeptical." His words were rushed—I'd never seen him so excited. "She won't listen to me. You're the only one who will be able to persuade her to do what's necessary to have the child."

"Why would I do that?"

"Because your daughter is pregnant."

I blinked, stunned. "What?"

"She didn't want to tell you until after she'd graduated. She's going to marry her boyfriend. She thought you'd disapprove."

I sat down, rested my elbows on my knees, my head in my hands.

"It's recessive, Mara—Her child might be a—"

My head snapped up. "Have you seen anything?"

"The child's fate is too tightly wound with mine, so I can't distinguish the threads. But I know that we need the boy Naomi will have. We need a Hero. Just in case Indira's turns out to be a—"

Shadow. Like me. He didn't need to say it.

"Your ability will fade as Indira's child begins to manifest. But if the boy is born of the girl, Naomi, there might be a way—if you die by his hand, you might be able to reverse it. End the cycle completely."

"Might."

"There are no guarantees," he said. "You know that."

"And the girl? What will happen to her?"

"She makes the choice. She consents. She dies."

It was a risk. But I would take it for my daughter's sake. I flew to London with the professor the next day.

44

HE'S HERE!" DANIEL SHOUTED. "HE'S IN NEW YORK!"

I lifted my head up from the kitchen table, wincing at the stiffness in my neck. Had I fallen asleep?

"What time is it?" I asked hoarsely.

"Wake-up time," my brother said cheerily. He was neatly dressed in jeans and a henley shirt, standing next to Stella. She was also annoyingly alert, and freshly clothed.

"I thought about waking you to go to bed," Stella said, then sipped from a glass of orange juice. "But Daniel said not to."

"You looked pretty pitiful," my brother added.

I couldn't muster up an equally irritating response, but I

didn't have to because Jamie appeared in the kitchen, rubbing the sleep from his eyes. "Who's in New York?" he asked.

"Lukumi! Whoever! He's giving a lecture at Columbia." Daniel flipped around his laptop to show me an online announcement for the Columbia Department of Comparative Literature, and he read it aloud as I read it silently: *The Final Girl: Jungian Archetypes in Pop Culture, a lecture presented by Dr. A. Lukumi, MD, PhD. Contact the Columbia Student Affairs office for tickets.*

Jamie stood in front of the fridge. "Are you finished speaking?"

Daniel narrowed his eyes. "Yes."

"Can someone tell me why there's no cream cheese in the house?"

Daniel ignored him. "It's today," Daniel said. "I'm leaving at four."

I looked at the clock. That was in two hours. I felt a jolt of energy and stood up. I had time to change, maybe even shower. I wasn't going to miss this.

"What are you doing?" my brother asked.

"I am going to get less gross," I said, "And then I am going to go with you, obviously."

Daniel shook his head. "That's what he'll be expecting. He knows who you are, Mara—he was in your hospital room, on the train platform. He's been following you, right?"

"Right . . ."

"Then he'll know if you show up."

"He'll know who *you* are too," I said to my brother. "Haven't you been paying attention? He's calling us out. He knows *everything*, about *all* of us, about our whole family. He definitely knows what you look like."

"Maybe, but I don't plan on being seen. And if I am seen, so what? I'm visiting colleges, after all. It's only natural that I'd be—"

"Auditing a lecture?" Jamie snorted. "I wouldn't describe that as natural."

"Natural for Daniel," I said as I took a bagel from a bag on the counter. "Is there any peanut butter?" I asked Jamie.

Jamie made a face. "Peanut butter on a bagel?"

"Yes?"

"Who are you, Mara Dyer?"

I ignored him. "And what exactly is your big plan, then?" I said to my brother before taking a too-big bite of my peanut buttered bagel. "Are you going to bum-rush him at the podium?"

"I'm going to go to the lecture and then follow him. I want to know where he's staying, where he lives, everything about him."

"And then, after your Scooby-Doo mission is complete?"

"Then I'll force him to tell me how to fix you," Daniel said.

His words brought me up short. I'd wanted that, once upon a time. To be fixed. To be saved. I'd begged Noah to do it. He couldn't, he'd said, because I wasn't broken.

I turned to Stella, who had been noticeably quiet during this entire conversation. "Stella? What say you?"

"I want to see him," she said firmly. "I want him to fix me, too."

Hmm. Back to Daniel. "How do you think you're going to be able to force Lukumi to do anything? He holds all the cards."

"If he's really behind all of this, then he has gone to great lengths to keep his identity a secret. We'll threaten to splash his face, his name—"

"His fake name," I corrected him.

"Everywhere," Daniel continued. "We'll publish all of this." He swept his arm around the kitchen island, where stacks of files and notebooks were piled high. "What happened to you, what was done to you, what he was responsible for—and then he won't be able to hide anymore. I'll need to snap a picture of him at the podium and match it up to something else. I haven't been able to find any of him online anywhere."

"There's that photo from McCarthy's office," Jamie said, whipping out his phone.

Daniel looked confused. "Let me see?"

Jamie handed him the phone.

"Wait, that's him?" Daniel asked. "He looks familiar."

Goose bumps rose on my arms.

"I can't place him, but I feel like I've seen him before."

Maybe you have, I almost said.

Daniel shook his head as if to clear it. "It doesn't matter," he said. "What matters is that we have to follow him, find out as much as we can about him so we can find out who he really is—his real name, his real identity, so we can connect him to all of this, so you can have a normal life," Daniel said to me.

In fact, almost *everything* he had said was to me. *For* me. *I* was the one who needed Lukumi more than anyone else in that room. I was the only one of us who wasn't innocent.

"What do you think he's hiding from?" Jamie asked quietly, but no one answered. None of us could guess.

"We're going to have to talk to a lawyer," my brother said, head cocked to the side. "You know that, right?"

I hadn't thought about it, but he *was* right.

"The things you've—" He stopped himself before continuing. "The things that have happened to you, and what happened at Horizons—we need to get them out in the open, deal with them, make sure we can establish that you were tortured, that it was self-defense—"

Not always. But I bit my tongue.

"And then, once he tells us how to fix you guys, we'll go public anyway."

"Stop saying that," Jamie said.

The three of us turned to him.

"Stop saying that we have to be fixed. I like who I am. I don't think I need to fix anything. I'm not broken." Jamie left the room.

Daniel leaned his elbows on the table and rubbed his face. "You knew what I meant, right, Mara?"

I did. But Jamie had voiced what I hadn't been able to put into words until then, what the slight sting of shame kept me from saying out loud.

I didn't think I needed to be fixed either. I liked who I was becoming too.

45

TO DIFFUSE THE TENSION, DANIEL SUGGESTED WE take a break before the lecture. We were tired and cranky and confused, and we'd been trapped in the house for too long. Daniel wanted to keep reading, though, so he stayed home, leaving Stella, Jamie, and me to our own devices. Which to Jamie meant buying food.

Without a car, and with our agreement not to order out, we ended up having to take the train to a Whole Foods (Jamie insisted), which meant lugging bags of groceries with us on the way back. The platform was weirdly empty, except for a couple of preppily dressed guys urinating on a heap of what looked like rags. Stella and I were debating the artistic merits of graffiti (my opinion, art; hers, vandalism), but I digressed for a moment to loudly inform the guys of their disgustingness. They didn't say anything back. Not even when Jamie called out to them. It was only then that I noticed that the heap was actually a person.

Jamie spoke first. "What in the ever-loving fuck do you think you're doing?" He was already marching toward them.

I was close at his heels, and Stella brought up the rear. We could see the person, the woman, huddled against the wall, her small, pathetic collection of things strewn around her like trash. She was older and her face was dirty, and she was awake. Part of me hoped she'd be unconscious so she wouldn't ever have to know what was being done to her, but one look at her face told me she did know. And she was ashamed.

I vibrated with rage, just as one of the assholes flashed a shit-eating grin at Jamie and said, "When you gotta go, you gotta—"

He never finished his sentence, because I punched him in his freckled face. The other one, Blondie, raised his arm to swing back at me, but Jamie yelled "Stop!" in that voice of his. Both of them froze, completely, but they could still hear. They could definitely hear.

My hands were balled into fists so tight that my nails dug into my skin. "She's a person," I said. "How could you do this to a person?"

"Answer her," Jamie said flatly. "And tell the fucking truth."

"The homeless are a plague," Freckles said, then swallowed hard, as if by doing so he could take the words back. Blondie just smirked. He wasn't ashamed at all.

Stella had knelt down near the woman, and I heard her ask if she was hungry. I took a step toward the assholes, who were farther from the woman, and closer to the platform.

"She's more of a person than you are," I said. I could hear the woman sobbing softly. "Stella, help her?"

I didn't look to see if she nodded, but I assumed she did, because I heard plastic crunch as the woman stood.

"Give her something to eat?" Jamie said to her.

Stella glanced at our groceries and nodded. She offered the woman her arm. "What's your name?"

"Maria," the woman said.

Stella helped her up and said, "Guys, let's go?"

"No," I said slowly, looking back at the boys. "I'm going to stay, I think."

"Mara." Stella said my name through gritted teeth. "Come on."

Jamie edged closer to me. "I'm going to stay too, actually."

Freckles burst out laughing. "You're not seriously suggesting that you're going to punish us?"

Little did they know. I flicked a glance at Stella. "Do you need something?"

"No," she dragged out the word.

I looked at Freckles and Blondie as I said to her, "Then go. Now."

But she didn't. Instead, she unlooped her arm from Maria's. "What are you going to do to them?"

"I kind of want to see Mara Crucio their asses," Jamie said.

The boys snickered.

"Avada kedavra, more like," I said.

Stella looked back and forth between the two of us. "You're not serious."

"They deserve it," I said quietly.

Blondie chuckled. "Two girls and a child?" He looked Jamie up and down. "How old are you?

"Old enough to kick your ass."

Freckles doubled over.

"I would cut out your eye just to see what it looks like in my hand," I said to him to absolutely no effect.

Which was fine. He didn't have to believe me yet.

"You're not really . . . You're not going to . . . ," Stella said, but from the tone of her voice, I knew she wasn't sure.

I shrugged. "It would be fair."

Stella turned to Jamie. "Jamie."

He didn't answer her.

"Make them sit still and then piss on *them*," Stella said. "*That* would be fair."

Jamie shook his head. "Look, if you peed on me—"

"I would never piss on you, Jamie." Stella had relaxed a bit. She thought Jamie was playing with her. Maybe he was.

"I appreciate that, but let's say you did. Then according to Kant, I could pee on you. That's retributive justice right there."

Jamie turned back to the boys, who were frozen in place, presumably because Jamie had told them to stop. They watched us warily. "Peeing on a homeless person, that's different. It's worse. There are levels of awful, and that's near the top."

It was. I hadn't felt this angry in so long, and there was so much pleasure in it. My nerves were electrified. New synapses were firing. I felt different, and wondered if I looked it. I craned my neck to see my reflection in a mirrored tile and waited for it to say something, to tell me what to do the way she used to. But she was silent. Hmm.

Meanwhile, Jamie continued to explain to Stella why the assholes deserved more than what she thought they did. "There's a power differential," he said. "They're taking advantage of someone weak, and it's horrible and disgusting and amoral, and anyone who does something like that needs to be taught a lesson. Peeing on them back isn't enough."

No. It wasn't. A hot breeze made its way through the tunnel, giving me an idea. "There's a train coming," I said to Jamie.

He met my eyes. He understood. "Listen carefully," he said to the boys, and they did, because they had no choice. "Climb down off the subway platform. Don't step on the third rail, but stand on the tracks."

Stella's eyes widened. "No," she said, staring at Jamie. *"No."*

But he ignored her, and the boys walked over to the yellow line, which warned them in huge block letters to stay away. They jumped down off the platform and onto the tracks, avoiding the third rail like Jamie said. Two rats scurried over a discarded chip bag and a stray purple ribbon before disappearing into the tunnel.

"Follow them," Jamie said to the boys, as he pointed at the rats. "Walk into the tunnel."

"You can't do this," Stella said. "Jamie. *Jamie*."

I answered for him. "What they did was wrong."

"But they don't deserve *this*."

"How do you know?" I said. "What are they thinking?"

Stella went very still. I watched her focus, watched her face change, darken as she listened to the words in their minds.

"It doesn't matter what they're thinking," Stella said quietly and from the tone of her voice, I knew she hadn't liked what she'd heard. "Thoughts are just thoughts."

But now that I had asked, I very much wanted to know. "Jamie, can you make them say what they're thinking out loud?"

"I can try," he said, and walked to the edge of the platform. "Let's hear it, assholes. Tell me every thought running through your tiny minds."

Another hot breeze ruffled their hair, and Freckles glanced over his shoulder before shouting at Jamie, *"Fuck you!"* Blondie added an unspeakable word.

I watched Jamie's expression harden. "Oh, don't stop," he said, softly. "Tell me how you really feel."

"You people are parasites," Blondie went on. "Lazy and useless and worthless. You should be my *slaves*."

Stella's face was wiped blank. Her voice shook when she spoke again. "They're just ignorant, Jamie. Ignorant and stupid."

Jamie was quiet. "Killing them is going to hurt you more than it hurts them," Stella continued. "And what about their families?"

I felt the telltale subway rumble beneath my feet. Stella said something to Jamie, but I didn't pay attention. I was looking at the woman, Maria.

"Stop," she said quietly, so quietly I wasn't sure I'd heard it. Then she said it again. "Let them up," Maria told Jamie.

That was when Jamie's facade cracked. He was still angry, but it was a different kind of anger. Cold. Resigned. I knew what he was going to say before he said it. "Get out of here. Climb up." He looked sick when he said it. "She's a better person than either of you."

She was, and so was Jamie. But I wasn't.

Jamie was never going to let them die, I knew. He just wanted to scare them. I wanted to kill them. Their brand of cruelty wasn't illegal but it *was* poisonous. They would do worse, someday, and hurt other people, people who didn't deserve it. I wanted to stop them before they had the chance. I wondered if I was really capable of it.

And as I wondered, Freckles offered his hand to Blondie to help him up. The train was approaching—I could see the light in the distance. But Blondie would be off the tracks by the time it got there. I wasn't sure what to wish for, what to think, and that made me even more angry. They couldn't just walk out of here. I wouldn't let them.

I heard Freckles swear. He was looking at Blondie, whose face was contorted in pain. His nose was bleeding.

"What the fuck!" Freckles shouted, as blood streamed over his lips. He looked up with wild, unfocused eyes as he pinched his nostrils to cut off the flow.

Stella looked at me in horror. "Mara." Jamie looked at me too. They knew.

When Freckles finally heaved Blondie up the rest of the way, he collapsed. Then he began to bleed, too.

Stella tugged on Jamie's arm. "Jamie, tell her to—make her stop. Make her stop!"

Maria covered her mouth and looked like she might be sick.

The train rushed into the station, bringing a horde of people with it. A cluster formed around Freckles and Blondie, and I felt a twinge of surprise to see Maria in it. She'd broken away from Stella, from us, and she was gesturing to someone authoritative, trying to help the same people who had made her their victim. I was moved by it. I decided to let the boys live.

For today.

46

JAMIE WAS TUGGING MY ARM OUT OF ITS SOCKET AS he rushed me up the stairs. My heart was pounding in my chest. When we were finally outside, I closed my eyes and took a deep breath. I needed to calm down. But then I realized something.

"We have to go back," I said.

He shook his head vehemently. "No, Mara."

"We left the food."

He looked at me like I was crazy. Then he hailed a cab, threw me in, and actually paid for the ride with cash he'd gotten from who knew where. Once back on the Upper West Side, he unlocked the door to his aunt's house and we walked in just as Stella was ascending the stairs. Her face was tear-streaked and pale. She took a step back down, toward us.

"How could you do that?" she asked me.

She didn't need to be specific. I knew what she meant. "They deserved it."

She walked calmly down the rest of the steps until she stood at the bottom of the stairs facing me. I didn't see the slap coming before I felt it across my face.

"Fuck! Jesus, Stella, what is *wrong* with you?" I asked her.

"What's wrong with *you*?"

"The world would be a better place without them," I said, holding my cheek.

"You don't know that," Stella said. "People change."

I shook my head slowly. "No. No, they don't. We are what we are."

"Why all the shouting?" Daniel said, as he descended the stairs. He looked back and forth between me and Stella. "What happened?"

"There was . . . an incident," Jamie said.

"You don't feel guilty at all, do you?" Stella shouted, her hands balled into fists at her sides.

"For scaring them?"

"For torturing them," she said.

No. I didn't feel guilty. I was tired of feeling ashamed for the things I thought and wanted. "I've evolved," I said.

Her jaw tightened, and she brushed past my brother on

the stairs, bumping his shoulder as she climbed them. Then, halfway up, she turned to the three of us and said, "I thought we were better than this. I thought we were the good guys."

Everyone was silent, until Jamie said quietly, "None of us ever claimed to be the good guys."

Daniel's brow furrowed. "*I'm* a good guy," my brother said.

But you're not one of us, I thought.

Daniel followed Stella back up the stairs, probably to find out what had actually happened this afternoon. I wasn't entirely sure what she'd say, but I was entirely sure that I didn't want to hear it. And I didn't want to think about Daniel hearing it.

I sat down in the living room, toed off my shoes, and I looked at my reflection in the flatscreen TV. My face was blank like an empty plate. I caught a flash of movement behind me and turned. Jamie leaned against the door frame. He didn't speak.

"Are you mad at me too?" My voice sounded dead.

"Mad at you?" He seemed surprised by the question. "No," he finally said. "I'm not mad at you."

But he was still standing there, looking at me in a way I couldn't describe but didn't like. "Then what?"

"I'm scared of you," he said, and left the room.

47

I'LL NEVER FORGET THE WAY STELLA LOOKED THAT afternoon, standing at the foot of the stairs with her things.

Her black hair hung in limp waves over her shoulders, and her eyes—there was something wrong with them. I'd seen her worried, and scared, and horrified, but she was none of those things today.

The four of us had been planning to head out for the lecture, but when I descended the stairs behind my brother and saw Stella's red-rimmed eyes, I knew that it would not be the four of us after all.

"I'm leaving," Stella said. She sniffed, but there was steel in her voice, not tears.

"Us too," Daniel said. "Come with—"

"No, I'm *leaving*," she said, cutting my brother off.

Daniel looked stunned for a second. "But we're so close—"

"We aren't," she said sharply. "I just couldn't see it till now." My brother looked like he was about to speak again, but Stella wouldn't let him. "You haven't been here. You haven't seen—" She stopped, and flicked a glance in my direction. "Whatever I was hoping for, it's too late." She bit her lip, and without looking at him said Jamie's name.

I hadn't been expecting that. "You too?" My voice shook.

His eyes bounced between me and Stella, and after what seemed like forever, he said, "I want to figure this shit out more than anyone, but maybe—Mara—"

"Mara's sick," Daniel said, and I didn't correct him, even though I didn't agree. "We need you to help her. To help us."

Jamie didn't answer him. He just stood there as Stella waited for him by the door.

I couldn't believe it. Didn't want to believe it.

"Take care of yourselves," Stella said, in a voice so quiet I almost didn't hear her. The anger had gone out of her, and she looked tired as she said to my brother, "It was nice to meet you."

"You too," he said. "Where are you going to go?"

Stella lifted her shoulders in a shrug and smiled sadly. "Home."

I didn't want to watch her and Jamie leave. I slipped past

my brother, who didn't stop me, and ducked into the den, closing the door behind me. Mostly.

"She's not herself," I heard my brother say.

"That is an understatement," Jamie said back.

So he was still there.

Then he said, "She's getting really scary, man."

"I know," Daniel said.

"I don't think you actually do. That was some cold shit."

"Look, all we have to do is find the guy responsible for what's happening to her. This is a problem that has a solution, but we need you to get it."

To anyone else, my brother probably sounded exasperated. Condescending, even. But I could hear the nervousness in his voice.

"I think we need to at least entertain the possibility that—" Jamie stopped and took a deep breath. "What's plan B?"

Daniel spoke after what seemed like an eternity. "There is no plan B."

Jamie stayed, in the end. We were silent as we soldiered on to Columbia as a threesome. Stella's departure had made everyone uncomfortable, though none of us admitted it. Jamie was particularly shaken. Since fleeing Horizons we had never split up. It was part of his strategy—splitting up gets you killed. But now I kept wondering if he wished he had split with her.

Other than that I had no feelings at all. I blindly searched inside myself for some reaction to what had happened on the subway and I found nothing. Or no, not quite nothing. Before I'd cut myself, before Stella cut the implants out, I could have thought and wished and wanted anything, and nothing would have happened. Dr. Kells had made sure of it.

But after? Now?

I was myself again. Thinking something *can* make it true. Wanting something *can* make it real. And I didn't regret it anymore. I'd wasted so much time wishing I could be different, wishing I could change things, change myself. If given the chance, I would've shed myself and become a different girl. Slipped on a name like Clara or Mary, docile and gentle and smiling and kind. I thought it would be easier to be someone else than to be who I was becoming, but I didn't think that anymore. The girl who wanted those things had died with Rachel, buried under the asylum I brought down. And I realized now, for the first time, really, that I didn't miss her.

It didn't matter that I was different. I didn't need to understand why. I didn't need a cure or even answers anymore, though we were so close to getting them. There was only one thing I needed.

I knew Noah wasn't dead, because that was something I wouldn't just feel—that was something I would *know*. So I would turn everything and everyone inside out until I found him, and I would start with Abel Lukumi today.

Daniel linked his arm in mine as we descended the rain-slick stairs to the train. When you have no one else, you still have your family.

The unmistakable perfume of the subway—a mixture of coffee, bodies, cigarettes, and fish—greeted us as we swiped MetroCards through the turnstiles. It was half past four, and the platform was packed with people: a shy teenage boy holding a cello case that looked like it might topple him, a girl with platinum blond hair woven into a braid crown, wearing patent-leather pants. A lost-looking bird hopped near the information desk or whatever it was, picking at the remains of a grimy sandwich. As soon as I noticed it, I was swept beneath a wave of overwhelming, indefinable sadness. I stopped where I stood, jerking Daniel back.

"What's up?"

I didn't know how to answer him because I didn't know myself. I pointed at a little kiosk, and my brother nodded, unshackling me from his side. I bought a sandwich and dropped it for the bird.

A muggy breeze announced the arrival of an oncoming train, and we shoved our way in behind the braid-crown girl and before a man with dreadlocks down to his waist, who held the hand of a little girl who kept shouting, "I am Spider-Man!" A businessman with a purple birthmark on his face sat with his leg squashed against a pole, eating from a greasy bag of sweet roasted nuts.

Jamie was quiet as we sped through the veins of the city, until a space large enough for the three of us opened up and we slid into it. The Spider-Man girl was still broadcasting her identity when Jamie spoke.

"What if someone had lice on the subway?"

A preteen couple with matching sprays of acne who had been kissing half a second before looked at him with disgust.

"Uh, what?" Daniel asked.

"What if there's a kid on the train with lice? And you're sitting next to him and then you get it."

"That's disgusting," I said.

Jamie ran his hand over his scalp. "I bet it happens."

"Stop!" I yanked at his hand. Just the thought was enough to make me itch.

"Don't worry, Mara," he said as he ruffled my head. "Your hair looks luminous."

We both burst out laughing at the same time. Relief was not a big enough word to explain what I felt. Jamie was my friend still. I might be different now, but I still needed as many of those as I could get.

Feeling lighter, I let my thoughts drift as I watched my reflection blur in and out of the darkened train window across from me. My reflection was obedient and silent, and I felt weirdly peaceful. I was just about to fall asleep when the lights flickered and the train screeched to a jarring stop. The next stop was ours, but we never made it.

48

"Hi, folks," a tinny voice announced from the speaker. "There seems to be some sort of service interruption." He began to say something else, but the words dissolved into static before we heard, "We'll get you folks moving as soon as we can."

New Yorkers are pretty unflappable as a group, and the motley crew in our car was no exception. An elderly Asian woman held the hand of an adorable little boy in a blue peacoat, who spoke to her calmly in English, though she spoke to him in something else, maybe Chinese? Next to her a frazzled-looking mother was trying to keep her two children from breaking off in opposite directions after her bag of groceries had fallen to the floor. Her apples scattered across the car like billiard balls. But no one cried. No one panicked. Not until the lights went out.

There was silence at first, then noise. People talking, a child crying. The car wasn't completely dark—the emergency lights were on in the adjacent cars, just not in ours.

"This stuff happens all the time," Jamie said. His face was painted in a faint, eerie glow. "They'll figure it out."

A burst of static startled Daniel—I felt him jump against my shoulder. Someone's cell phone buzzed with a text. And then a stranger said my name.

"Mara Dyer?"

The owner of the voice was a twentysomething girl with gauges in her ears, a hoop in her nose, and a bushel of wild, curly hair. She held a book with a leafy green tree on the cover, title obscured, and a cell phone in the other. "Who is Mara Dyer?"

I felt Daniel's and Jamie's eyes boring into each side of my face. The stale air seemed to press in on me, slowing my thoughts. "Uh, me?" I said, before Jamie shushed me.

Everyone in the car stared as Curly Girl walked over to me and handed me her phone. "Someone's texting you."

"I don't know you," I said, pointing out the obvious.

"And I don't know you. But the person texting me doesn't seem to care." She gestured with the phone. "See for yourself."

I tried to, but realized that my arms were in the iron grips of my brother and Jamie.

"This is bad news," Daniel said. "Bad news."

I shook them off and took the phone from the girl.

I HAVE WHAT YOU WANT.

Below that was a picture of Noah. I couldn't see where he was and didn't know what he was doing; it was just a close-up of his face. But it was Noah to the life. And there was a newspaper next to him with today's date.

"Can I have my phone back now?" Curly Girl asked. I ignored her.

"Ask who it is," Jamie said.

"Like he's going to answer?" Daniel replied.

"How do you know it's a he?" Jamie asked.

Daniel rolled his eyes. "It's a he."

Who is this, I texted back. A few seconds later, the girl's phone pinged again.

DOES IT MATTER? OPEN THE DOOR BETWEEN CARS AND GET OUT. LEAVE YOUR BROTHER AND FRIEND BEHIND SO THEY DON'T GET HURT.

"Trap," Daniel and Jamie said simultaneously.

"Hey," Curly Girl said, clearly annoyed now. "My phone?"

Jamie looked at her and said, "This isn't your phone." Her

forehead creased and her eyes glazed over. "You dropped your phone on the tracks."

"I dropped it?" Her voice wavered as she looked back and forth between Jamie and the phone in my hands.

"Yes. Run along now." Jamie gestured at her. "Shoo."

When she walked away, I stood up.

"Oh, come on, Mara," Jamie said.

Daniel was shaking his head as he spoke. "You're not going out there."

"Of course I'm going out there." More static from the speaker, but no lights and no movement still. Daniel and Jamie were right. Obviously right. And I was in no frame of mind to process the picture other than to seize it as proof that Noah was, in fact, alive. I had to make sure he stayed that way. I had to make sure Daniel and Jamie stayed that way too.

"Sister, I love you, and I would do anything for you, but I really do not want to creep around in the bowels of the New York City transit system for you. Please do not make me."

"Not only am I not making you," I said as I reached for the handle of the door between the cars. "I'm not going to let you."

"You're not going to stop me," Daniel said.

Jamie bent over. If he'd had hair, he'd have been pulling it. "Damn it, Mara. We've been here before."

I opened the door and stepped out into the darkness. "True," I said. "And I was fine before."

"I suppose that depends on your definition of 'fine.'"

"Look," I said to Daniel and Jamie, "what's the most terrifying thing you can think of in these tunnels? Rats? Mole people?"

"Evil mastermind hell bent on killing you?" Jamie suggested.

"Wrong. The most terrifying thing in these tunnels is me." I shut the door on both of them and jumped onto the tracks.

The girl's cell phone buzzed in my hand.

WALK TOWARD THE END OF THE TRAIN UNTIL YOU PASS IT. GO TO THE THIRD NICHE WITH A DOOR.

The curved walls seemed to stretch into infinity, but I started walking, following a miniature creek between the tracks that was choked with garbage. Air ruffled papers taped to the graffitied, wet-looking walls. My pulse began to race as I neared the end of the train, but not from fear. I believed what I'd told my brother and Jamie. I believed in myself. I would find Noah, and I would punish whoever had taken him from me.

I passed the first niche, and then the second. But before I came to the third, I heard my name shouted behind me.

"Mara?" Daniel's voice echoed in the tunnel. Panic seized me.

"Wherefore art thou, Mara Dyer?" Jamie's voice this time.

"That means 'why', not 'where,'" I heard my brother say. "Just saying."

"Go back!" I yelled automatically, then cursed myself. Not for giving away my position to my mystery texter but for giving it away to my brother. Marco Polo used to be his favorite game.

Daniel yelled, "No chance! I'm your big brother. It's my job to protect you."

And then a shadow peeled itself from the wall, forming the outline of someone I knew, of the person I'd expected ever since I'd seen that first text. Ever since I'd heard the girl on the subway say my name, really.

"Don't hurt them," I said to Jude, and I meant it. "Please."

"I didn't want to," he replied, and punched me in the face.

49

BEFORE

Cambridge, England

THERE WAS NO KNOCK ON THE PROFESSOR'S DOOR before it opened, throwing a shaft of dim, gray light into the room.

A girl stood in the doorway, but did not enter. She was half in shadow, but I did not need to see her to know who she was.

The professor lifted a glass of amber liquid to his lips and sipped as he wrote in his notebook. "Come in, Naomi."

Naomi Tate hurried in, bringing the scents of rain and nervousness with her. She shut the door forcefully, rattling the shutters, and a few leaves that had clung to her coat scattered to the scratched wooden floor.

"Bit early to be drinking, Professor?" she said casually, as she shrugged off her coat.

"Perhaps it's a bit late." He continued to write without looking up.

Naomi's hair was damp and wild, and she tied what she could into a messy knot at the nape of her neck as she moved in front of the professor's desk. Fine blond wisps curled around her forehead and temples, framing her face.

That face. With high cheekbones and a long, elegant nose, Naomi was beautiful in a rare, peculiar way, in a way that demands attention. I'd known her for a year and still, I could never quite get used to looking at her.

But there was something different about her today. I shifted in the tufted, battered leather armchair I always sat in, my island amid the chaos that was the professor's Cambridge office, and sniffed the air. The scents in the room were all familiar: old paper mingling with leather and mold; the coriander and musk that was the professor; the paperwhites and cedar that was Naomi. And something else, something—

"What can I do for you, Mrs. Shaw?" he asked. He took another slow sip of whiskey.

Mrs. *Shaw*. She was Mrs. Shaw, now. I kept forgetting. She'd married the grandson of Elliot, whom I last saw at eight years old, throwing books and toys about his room, because he couldn't find the one he wanted. I did not know her husband well, but my impression was that David Shaw was not terribly different.

Naomi refused to answer the professor; she would not fight for his attention. She would make him fight for hers. I loved that about her.

After several seconds, he finally abandoned his notebook and looked up at her. His lips pulled back into a smile. "You're pregnant," he finally said.

A sharp intake of breath. Mine. "How far along?"

I hadn't heard the professor rise from his desk, but he was standing when he spoke. "Early," he said, approaching Naomi with slow, graceful steps. "About two weeks?"

Naomi didn't speak, but she nodded. She rubbed at a knot in the ancient desk with her finger—she was nervous, but grinning madly anyway.

I let out the breath I hadn't realized I was holding. "It's too early," I said to the professor. "She might not be—"

"I am," she said, in a tone that left no room for argument. "I am."

The professor ran a hand over his chin and mouth. Then said, "May I?" He indicated her flat stomach. Naomi nodded.

The professor drew nearer, until he was close enough to touch her. I noticed the way her muscles tightened in apprehension, the way her aqua eyes dropped to the floor as he reached out to her. When he placed his hand low on her belly, Naomi flinched. A tiny movement, one she tried to disguise. If it bothered him, he didn't show it.

"Three fifteen," he said, and withdrew his hand. Naomi relaxed. "What does it mean to you?"

Her cheeks flushed, and she began rubbing at the pock-marked desk again. "The day I conceived, I think. March fifteenth."

"Does David know?" I asked quickly.

Naomi shook her head. "Not yet," she said, and swallowed. She glanced up at the professor. "I wanted to tell you first."

"Thank you." The professor inclined his head. He leaned over his desk and began to write. "For now, I'd prefer you didn't mention it to him. Can you do that, Naomi?"

"Of course," she said, rolling her eyes.

"You'll be having a boy, you know."

All traces of her earlier irritation vanished. A smile lifted the corner of her mouth. "A boy," she repeated, as if saying the word for the first time. "You've seen him?"

The professor hesitated for a moment, then said, "Yes."

"Tell me everything," she said, her face lit with excitement.

"I don't know everything," the professor said, "but I do know he has your smile."

Her hands drifted down to her lower belly. "I can't believe this is really happening."

"It is happening." The professor had counted on this, on her, and I had too. "The boy is destined for greatness. Because of you, he will change the world."

And because of him, Naomi would die. It was a sacrifice

she was willing to make. It cost the professor nothing; but I was the one who had convinced her to make it. I needed her child too, and her death was easy to accept when Naomi was just an abstraction, a stranger. But now I knew her, and I was haunted by guilt. I had befriended her, persuaded her, knowing that there was no time line in which she would have this child and live, and over the months, the specter of her someday-death haunted me. I dreamed of her hanging by a rope from the rafters in a stable, her feet bare, her body swinging after the tension in the rope snapped her spine. I dreamed that a shard of glass pierced her chest after in a car accident, and she died choking on her own blood. I dreamed of her murder, her drowning, her being buried alive beneath a collapsing building. I didn't know when it would happen, but I knew that it would.

Before her wedding, I couldn't help but warn her again. She would be a martyr for this child, I told her.

Every gift has its cost, she had said back.

I could see the beginnings of that cost today. There was none of a new mother's emotion in her expression, no awe or wonder, or even love. Instead she looked like a child who'd been told she'd be setting off on a great adventure soon, and she couldn't wait to begin.

She nearly bounced on her heels. "I wish I didn't have to wait nine months to meet him," she said.

"He will be born in a good hour. Be patient."

"When should I tell David?"

"I'll let you know the next time we meet."

"And when will that be?"

"Next Thursday. You, Mara and I shall meet at the lab, and we'll see how everything is progressing. All right, then?"

"If you say so."

"Very good. Then I shall see you then. Good day, Mrs. Shaw," he said, as Naomi turned to leave. "And congratulations."

She looked over her shoulder at him. "Don't call me Mrs. Shaw," she added petulantly. "Makes me feel ancient."

A hint of a smile touched the professor's mouth, and then the door closed behind her.

"This pregnancy will be difficult for her," the professor said, staring after her.

"The child will live, yes?"

"Yes. Of course."

I paused for a moment. Then asked, "And Naomi?"

"She will not die in childbirth."

But that wasn't what I asked, and we both knew it.

50

I OPENED MY EYES TO DARKNESS. I SAW NOTHING BUT felt like a small thing alone in a wide, cavernous space. And high—I felt high up, which made me want to tuck my limbs in, tight and close to my body. I tried to but couldn't. My arms and legs were bound. But I wasn't afraid; I felt removed, distant. Where I should have felt frightened and terrified, I just felt clinical and calculating.

Until I remembered my brother, calling for me in the dark.

I could see only what was above me and on either side of my head, and not well at that. I was in some kind of warehouse; there was a source of light somewhere, but I couldn't find it. I blinked and blinked again. A crumbling, pockmarked concrete ceiling materialized above me, framed by casement windows fogged with grime. And to my left and right were the shadows of hundreds, maybe thousands, of people.

No. Not people. Mannequins. Or parts of them, anyway. An army of headless torsos standing at attention, extending farther back than I could see. Dingy resin hands and arms, cloth torsos and plastic eyes, were heaped and scattered on the ground.

But Daniel wasn't there, not that I could see. I knew I wasn't alone, but maybe I was the only one Jude had taken. I prayed to a God I did not believe in that I was right.

"You're wondering where we are," a voice said. A strangely familiar voice, resonant and compelling, even though I'd never heard it before. My ears were ringing and my head was cloudy, and everything, including my thoughts, seemed distorted.

"You're wondering why we're here." I heard the sound of slow, purposeful footsteps but didn't see anyone at first. Then, slowly, my eyes detected movement. A figure moved between the bodies, as tall and narrow as they were. I discerned the outline of a black suit among them, and as the footsteps grew nearer, the outline became a person.

He had Noah's blue-gray eyes, but he wasn't Noah. And behind him stood Jude.

"I'm afraid we've never been formally introduced," the man said to me. His eyes crinkled at the corners when he smiled, the slight curve of his mouth emphasizing the hollows beneath his sculpted cheekbones. "My name is David Shaw."

My tongue was thick in my mouth, and my thoughts dissolved before they could reach it. I had heard about Noah's father but had never met him, and now, now he was here. He was here, and I had been *brought* here by him.

By *him*.

He stood there looking at me kindly, sympathetically, as if Jude, my tormenter, were not standing beside him. As if he hadn't been the orchestrator of my torment, using Horizons and Wayne and Kells as tools.

Struck dumb by shock or drugs, all I could do was stare at him and Jude, who scarcely resembled the creature I remembered. Gone was the smooth conviction he'd displayed at the dock when he'd forced me to cut my own wrists. I saw none of the anger he'd shown in the garden at Horizons, when he'd tortured my friends and Noah and me. He was whispering to himself. Mumbling. I couldn't make out the words.

"You're afraid," David Shaw said to me.

I wasn't. Not anymore.

"I am truly sorry for this. I wish things could be different."

They would be. I wasn't going to kill him like I'd killed everyone else. I would torture him, the way he had tortured me.

I didn't need him to tell me why he had done it. I didn't care. I only cared about only one thing, but my mouth wouldn't form the words until David Shaw gave it permission to. I recognized the sensation. I was on Anemosyne, Kells's drug of choice.

"Did Noah know?" My voice was scratchy and hoarse, and I wasn't sure he heard me, until his eyebrows lifted in surprise.

"You're wondering if he betrayed you?" David's eyes narrowed a bit. "How little you trust him." His sentence was punctuated by the ringing metallic clang of metal on metal and the sound of approaching footsteps. "Speak of the devil," David said, and then Noah appeared behind him.

51

NOAH

I DULLY STALK BEHIND MY FATHER, BRIEFLY NOTING the fiberglass army of armless, headless mannequins that surround us. They seem to stiffen at my arrival, to cringe at my too loud steps. So sinister. Lovely touch.

Walking feels like an effort, as does thinking, unfortunately. My vision is oddly tunneled; we appear to be in a large, probably condemned warehouse of standard decrepitude; the plaster is peeling off of the dingy once-white walls, the casement windows are thick with grime, et cetera. I notice a sign just outside one of the windows with the words STORAGE WAREHOUSE: FIREPROOF painted on it, except someone had blackened out the letters so that it read,

RAGE WAREHOUSE: IREPROOF. Mara would love that so much.

Thinking her name cuts through something in my brain, steals the laughter from my throat. And then I see her.

But it isn't Mara—or at least it isn't the Mara I remember. The one with quick, smudged fingers, lips that couldn't decide whether to swear or smile, with eyes that told me nothing about her and everything about me.

The last time I saw that Mara, she stood held against Jude's body, his blade at her naked throat. Or no, no, that wasn't the last time. A split-second frame flickers in my mind, a quick and blurred picture of her pressing Jude against a wall, almost into it, with *her* hands at *his* throat, digging into his bare skin. And I remembered what preceded it. Mara began as his victim, and then she made him hers.

But it wasn't just us fucked up teens that last night in Horizons. A scentless something invaded the air, made it shimmer and wave. I remembered my voice as I called out to her, the way it competed with the sound of blood rushing beneath my skin, with the sound of my ragged breath roaring in my ears, before my world went black.

God knew how many minutes, hours, days I'd spent in darkness after that, waking up to be forced to eat by a person, or people, with blurred, blank faces and gloved hands, only to be swallowed back into unconsciousness as a dark, wet tongue pushed me to the back of its throat. I remembered practically nothing until today, when my father's face appeared at the door.

"You're safe now," he said, and miracle of miracles, led me out into the world. I felt bliss for a moment when I saw the sky, until I realized it was the color of spoiled milk. My father seemed to be talking to me, reassuring me or something, but I had trouble translating the words. I did try to find some sliver of gratitude for him, some rejoicing at my freedom, but I felt absolutely nothing at all.

Until he mentioned her name.

My father had found her the way he'd found me, he said. She needed help that only I could give her, and would I go with him?

I would go anywhere, with anyone, to see the girl I loved again. Obviously.

The girl before me now doesn't quite look like her. She is different in a way I can't name, in a way that goes beyond her thinness, her new shape. If she were naked beneath the faded black T-shirt she wears (one of mine—the hem is half-torn), her ribs would show, her spine would protrude, her collarbones would cut glass. But she doesn't look ill, not the way she had begun to before Horizons. Color blooms in her cheeks, and her eyes are lit with an emotion I can't name. And there's something more, more than the change in her features and in her body. Looking at her is like walking into a home you once lived in to find it changed by new, alien owners. She is bound, prone, and Jude, that absolute horror of a human being, looms over her, but she looks nothing like a damsel in distress. She looks like a dragon instead. I am struck dumb and thoughtless with the sense that I don't know a thing about this person until she speaks my name.

The sound of her voice thaws my mind and my blood; it pulses hotly through my veins. I ignore Jude's presence—she and I can butcher him together later. My feet carry me to my girl and I kneel and reach for her. Something stops me—not Jude. Not my father. My hand curls into a fist and falls by my side, and a strange, unfamiliar voice inside me whispers, *Don't.*

I look to Mara for an answer to the question I haven't asked. She says instead, "You're here." But what I hear in her tone is, *Where were you?*

My heart would break if it weren't filled with happiness. Her voice is the same. It's home.

My father pollutes the air with his, however. "Mara was told that Horizons collapsed."

I look up in confusion. "Why?"

"To keep you safe," he says to me.

"From what exactly?"

"From her."

Mara is silent for a moment, and blinks her dark lashes that frame her too-wide eyes. They would look innocent on anyone else. "I would never hurt him."

My father looks at her with no expression. "You already have."

52

BUT NOAH WASN'T HURT. HE WAS ALIVE. WHOLE.

Here.

I nearly choked on my own breath when I saw him, and when I heard him speak, I thought I would dissolve. If I had been standing, I would have fallen to my knees.

He wore unfaded jeans and a T-shirt, too new-looking to be his, and they hung loosely on his already lean frame. He knelt beside the table and examined my hands.

"Do you have something I can cut these with?" he asked his father. I blinked, confused, as his father withdrew something from a nylon briefcase beside him. My neck hurt trying to see what it was.

A knife.

"Yes," Jude mumbled. "Yes."

Whatever warmth I'd felt at Noah's timely reappearance vanished. Something was happening here, but I didn't understand *what*.

Noah didn't either, clearly. He cut the zip-ties on my wrists, on my ankles, with no protests from David or Jude. What were they playing at? What *was* this?

My limbs were shaky and weak, and I knew I wouldn't be able to stand or run. But I could sit up. Noah helped me.

"What happened to you?" he asked as his hands gripped my shoulders, propping me up against the wall.

I laughed. I couldn't help it; it just bubbled up from my throat. How could I even begin to answer that question?

Noah looked away from me, his jaw tense now. "Who did this to her?" He focused on Jude. His voice was flat when he asked his father, "Why is he here?"

David plucked a manila folder from his bag. "I told you today that I needed you to help her," he said, and I wanted to spit in his face. "This is why."

He laid out several sheets of paper. Or no, not paper. Pictures. Photographs. Full color. Graphic.

"Wayne Flowers, age forty-seven. Mara cut his throat and took his eye as a souvenir."

Noah's face was impassive, his eyes flat.

"Deborah Susan Kells, age forty-two, died of several dozen stab wounds, inflicted by Mara with nothing but a scalpel.

Robert Ernst, age fifty-three, father of two. Mara stabbed him with a scalpel as well. His body could barely be identified by the police when they found it, rotting in a rest stop in the Keys."

Noah didn't look at me for confirmation, but he lifted the picture of Dr. Kells from the table. Then looked at his father.

"Did you know her?" he asked. "Do you know what she's done to Mara? To me?"

It hit me then, how little Noah knew. It scared me.

"I do," David answered.

Because he hired her, I wanted to say. I wished I could stand up, grab his shirt, make Noah listen, make him understand. But the drugs, David's drugs, made sure I couldn't.

"Do you know about—me?" Noah asked coldly.

"Your mother hid it as long as she could, but I found out when she died. It's why she and I were chosen."

"For?"

"To be your parents."

David closed his eyes, and when he opened them, a quiet fury had settled in his face. "The man you call Lukumi, whom I knew as Lenaurd, manipulated your mother, recruited her, then introduced her and me so we could *breed*. You were *planned*, Noah. *Engineered.*"

Noah practically radiated frustration. "For what?"

"To be the hero," David said, looking at Noah like he was his greatest disappointment. "To slay the dragon. But you fell in love with it instead."

53

NOAH

Had my father been driven mad by the loss of my mother? By perpetual disappointment in his son, perhaps? I may never know.

"I hear electroshock therapy has come a long way in the last century," I say to him. My wit falls on deaf ears.

"All I ever wanted for you, Noah—all most parents ever want for their children—was for you to be healthy, to be normal. But I'm part of the reason that never happened for you," he says. "Your mother and I, we are both carriers, both unmanifested, of the original gene, the one that makes you abnormal."

I nearly laugh out loud at the word. "All right. Fine. How long have you known?"

"Your mother left papers, letters," he says flatly. "I didn't believe them until you were eight years old."

I search my memory for a hint and find none.

"You managed to climb up onto your dresser while your nanny was in the bathroom, and dove off it. You cracked your head open. I was terrified." A brief, flickering smile appears on his lined face, and in that moment an image of my old bedroom materializes in my mind, high-ceilinged with dark wood trim. The floor had an inlaid pattern to it. I climbed my tall dresser to get a better look, and when I did, the floor seemed to take on dimension, to recede, as if I could jump into it. So I tried.

"I rushed you to the hospital, but by the time we arrived, your wound was nearly closed. I ordered a private doctor to attend to you, to take you for CAT scans, MRIs, blood work—nothing turned up. You were perfectly healthy," my father says with a bitter smile. "Except for the fact that you kept getting hurt. No, not *getting* hurt—you were hurting yourself," he adds nastily.

I want to hit him so badly.

"There was the fractured leg at nine."

When I jumped off the roof at our country house, hoping I would fly.

"The adder bite on the Australia trip when you were ten."

When I uncovered a snake beneath a pile of leaves, and decided I had to hold it.

"The broken hand at twelve."

After a fight with my father, when I punched the wall.

"The burns at thirteen."

When I set fire to the garden my mother had planted years earlier, which my father loved more than he loved me.

"And the first time you cut yourself, when you were fifteen."

When I had had enough.

"And in between, there was the smoking, the drinking, the drugs—exercises in contempt for the life your mother and I had given you."

A refrain I have heard so many, many times before. Boring.

"Psychologists and psychiatrists insisted you were traumatized by your mother's murder. At five you were too old to forget it—"

True.

"But too young to talk about it."

False. No one tried.

"So you lashed out at the world, at me, at yourself. Your mother gave up her own life to have you, and you kept spitting on her memory." My father's eyes are thankfully missing that telltale maniacal glint, but still. I don't think I've ever seen him so furious. It's oddly riveting.

This might be the longest conversation we've ever had.

He pauses to regain his composure and withdraws a kerchief from his pocket. Good God. He dabs it at the corner of his mouth. "I couldn't look at her things after she died. I could barely look at you, you looked so much like her. But in time, I managed to force myself. She wrote about what she had done, what you were, what you would become. No wonder the psychiatrists and doctors were useless." He shakes his head in disgust. "They couldn't begin to comprehend your affliction. So I hired Deborah Kells."

I realize, as my father confesses his involvement in the plot that has ruined the life of the girl I love, and my life by proxy, that I should feel a profound sense of betrayal. Righteous anger, perhaps. Shock, disgust, wrath—any of these would be perfectly normal.

That he hired Kells to experiment on the others and Mara, that he let Jude torment Mara, torture her—*that* much I could actually believe, monstrous and psychopathic though it was. If there were any profit to be had in it, my father would make it. That is a thing that makes sense. And the Lukumi bit is an interesting touch, I admit.

But the dragon business, this hero shit? Complete madness. My father is unhinged.

And yet he looks so *normal*. Particularly next to Jude, who is twitching, possibly drooling a bit, I can't quite tell.

My father confirms my assessment with every word he speaks. "Deborah had theories about how to find others like you, and theories about how to cure them. I had her record her monthly progress and send the videos to me so I could keep up, but nothing in them promised to help you. Not until she found your Mara."

I am repulsed by the sound of her name in his mouth.

"Deborah wasn't sure Mara was the one. In Providence, Deborah thought it might be the older brother, actually. But after some birthday party, her foster daughter convinced her it was Mara. The asylum was chosen as a staging area, in the hope that the fear of spending the night there would trigger the beginning of Mara's manifestation. And it did."

It sinks in slowly, what he is saying. He is talking about Claire, Jude's sister. He is talking about the asylum, the place where Jude nearly raped her. He is telling me how it was staged, planned, and my bemusement morphs into loathing. I don't know how I'm still standing.

"Mara ended up teaching me as much about you as you taught me about her. More perhaps. I had no idea how your ability worked. How you heard things, what you saw. But it was hubris," my father says. "If there is a way to arrest the anomaly, we haven't found it. You might be the key to it, Noah, but we'll never know as long as she's alive. And you can't stay away from her, and she can't help what she is."

I almost can't wait to hear his answer. "And what is that?"

"Every generation someone along the affected bloodline develops an ability that parallels an archetype—"

Fucking hell. Time to go.

My father smiles, as if he can hear my thoughts. "My son, the skeptic. I was once too. But tell me, haven't you ever wondered why she can't wish for anything good?"

His words erase the snide comments that were on the tip of my tongue, and replace them with a memory. I wondered exactly that. And I wrote about it in the journal I kept for Mara.

My theory: that Mara can manipulate events the way I can manipulate cells. I have no idea how either of us can do either thing, but nevertheless.

I try to get her to envision something benign, but she stares and concentrates while her sound never changes. Is her ability linked to desire? Does she not want anything good?

"She is the embodiment of the Shadow archetype—destructive, harmful to herself and others. She embodies Freud's death drive."

"How dramatic." I glance at Mara but she doesn't meet my eyes.

"Mara *can* will what she wants," my father continues, "and her desires become reality. But the nature of her affliction is that she will never create anything good."

Even if what he says is true, I am simply out of fucks to give. I had few to spare to begin with. But I watch Mara as he speaks these nonsense words—"carrier," "anomaly," "manifestation," et cetera. What they mean doesn't matter to me, but what they mean to her does matter. I haven't seen one flicker of hate or fear in her eyes—if I had, we would be gone already. Instead I see something else. Understanding.

"Reluctant though you may be, Noah, you are the embodiment of the Hero. You don't have to learn to become good at anything. You simply *are* the best at everything. Your telomeres don't stop replicating. If you aren't killed, you might actually live forever. You have every gift, Noah."

I don't want them.

"But once she has fully manifested, if you are near her, you'll be powerless. Vulnerable. Weak. She can't help what she does to you. She is your weakness, as you are hers."

54

I HADN'T REALLY BEEN WORRIED UNTIL I HEARD those words. Noah's father wasn't going to kill him. He most likely couldn't kill me, or I wouldn't be alive. So I simply sat back and enjoyed watching Noah arrogantly swat away his father's grave warnings, his dire predictions. He was the boy I loved, still. He couldn't have cared less. But then.

She is your weakness.

Contraindication: Mara Amitra Dyer

As you are hers.

Contraindication: Noah Elliot Simon Shaw.

"When she evolves fully, you will be at risk every day you spend with her. Your cells will not regenerate. Your telomeres will not replicate. If she exceeds her threshold—if she is in pain, or afraid, or under severe stress, and you are close? You will not be able to heal yourself. Her ability is dominant; it negates yours. Which is why I made sure she was told you had died. Your propensity for self-harm, a side effect of the gene that makes you different, makes Mara irresistible to you. It isn't your fault, but being with her isn't your choice." And then David Shaw gave me this look, a mixture of pity and contempt. "He wouldn't love you if you weren't what you are."

I remembered kissing Noah in his bedroom during a thunderstorm, watching his lips turn blue. I remembered facing him in a midnight-colored dress on a silent beach after I'd read something I shouldn't have, and thought I understood what it meant.

"I won't be what you want," I'd said to Noah then.

"And what do you think that is?"

"Your weapon of self-destruction."

Noah had said that I wasn't, that I couldn't be, and I'd wanted so badly to believe it. But hearing those words issue from his father's mouth sliced me open with the truth.

"I don't want to be here," Noah's father said. "Whatever you think of me, I loved your mother. She was my life. She was my reason for existing. And I promised her that I would keep you safe. I may have failed her in every other way, but I cannot fail at that. Look at Jude," he said, gesturing to him. "A project of Deborah's, one that has not paid off."

If Jude minded being spoken about as if he were a thing, as if he weren't there, he didn't show it. His expression was flat, his eyes empty.

"He is unpredictable and unstable, despite Deborah's efforts to control him. It could be said that he is responsible for her death, since he is the one who let Mara out."

"It was a mistake," Jude said then, in a firm, alien voice.

David regarded him warily. "Yes. It was." Then he refocused on me. "What is happening to Jude will happen to you, too, Mara. You hallucinate. You are violent in response to pain. You show signs of dissociative personality disorder. You are on your way."

Maybe I was already there.

"I knew your grandmother, once upon a time. Not well, not well enough at all, but she haunted my wife in the guise of a friend, a confidant. She was unpredictable. She was unstable. She was a liar, like you, and a murderer, like you. She led my wife to her death, and you would lead my son to his."

Noah interrupted his father. "You think I care if I'm powerless? That's what I *want*."

"So you can finally kill yourself?"

I held my breath, waiting for Noah to answer. He never did.

"You are sick, Noah. The consequences of your affliction could destroy you, the way they have destroyed other sick children, and I will die before I let that happen," David said.

Maybe I could help him with that.

"The more time passes, the stronger she'll become, until she fully manifests, and I can't predict when that will happen." David turned to me. "After that stunt you pulled on the subway platform, I figured you must be close."

So he knew about that. Hmm.

"We can't afford to wait any longer," David said to Noah. "Do you understand what I'm saying? There's a bomb ticking inside of her, waiting to go off. With one thought, *one* wrong thought, she could end millions of lives." He took a cautious step forward.

"If you don't stop it, your mother will have died for nothing. You would exist for *nothing*," David said, his voice cracking. "I loved your mother, and she died to save you so you could be the answer to illness, to aging, possibly even to death. I couldn't have cared less—all I wanted was her. But I wasn't given a choice. However, I will give you one."

David Shaw drew in a shaky breath composing himself. Then he lifted the leather bag and opened it. He withdrew a gun and a syringe and set them on a table in front of me next to the knife.

Jude wasn't here to hurt me, and Noah wasn't here to save me. I knew that now.

"I didn't know how you and she would prefer to do it."

"Do *what*?" Noah shouted.

I waited until the echo faded before I answered for his father. "Kill me."

An obscene laugh bubbled up from Noah's throat. "If you could think that there is anything in the world that could possibly make me do this," he said to his father, "you have no idea who I am."

"I don't need to know who you are. I know her."

David withdrew something else from his bag. A laptop. He typed something, and then propped the laptop up on an empty cardboard box, positioning it so I could see.

My brother lay in a bed, in a room, hooked up to a thousand machines. Jamie sat next to him in a chair. He was tied to it, and conscious. My brother was not.

55

NOAH

"IT ISN'T REAL," I SAY. I TRY TO SOUND CERTAIN, AND FAIL.

"It is very real," my father replies. "Daniel has been given a variant of a venom that will cause him to go into shock, and then his organs will fail in an hour or two unless he receives the antivenin. He's being monitored very carefully right now, but I will need to make a phone call to make sure he gets it, once Mara has expired."

"Mara?" Jamie says, squinting through the laptop screen. A bruise shadows the left side of his face.

"Jamie," she whispers. Then, "Jamie, is Daniel—"

"He's alive," Jamie says. "We got whacked in the subway tunnel or something, woke up here. He's sick, though." Jamie flicks a glance at Mara's brother, wincing at the movement. "He's—he was foaming at the mouth before. These people, they came in and used a crash cart on him. I saw everything. I tried to make them listen to me, but . . ." He shakes his head. "It was like they couldn't hear me. Like I was on mute."

Mara is silent. I used to be able to read her thoughts on her face, but now, nothing.

"Where are you?" she asks him. Clever girl.

Jamie tips his face to the ceiling. "Generically bland room, as always. I woke up with a hood over my face. I don't know." Jamie's eyebrows furrow, and he tries to lean forward in the chair. "Wait—is that fucking—is that *Jude* with you? And Noah?"

Jude doesn't respond. I do.

"We'll find you," I say to him.

Jamie looks over at Daniel, whose lips are pale and chapped. Daniel has a cannula beneath his nose, and there are IVs attached to the backs of both wrists. Then Jamie says, "Whatever you guys are being told to do, you should do it."

My father watches me. Jude watches me. Jamie watches me. Mara does not.

She watches her brother. Her eyes never leave him, even as I reach for the gun.

56

I COULDN'T TEAR MY EYES AWAY FROM MY BROTHER, and so I didn't notice at first when Noah pointed the gun at his father.

"You could kill me," David said. His words drew my eyes up. "That is certainly an option."

"It certainly is," Noah said. The gun looked familiar, like one I'd held before.

"I've been expecting to die because of you someday. I wouldn't have revealed myself if I weren't expecting that. Though I did assume she would be the one to do it." His father smiled slightly, and met my eyes. He didn't once look at the gun.

"Maybe I'll save her the trouble," Noah said.

"Well then, I should warn you that you would be ending four lives with one bullet."

"How do you figure?"

"Your death will not prevent Mara's. If you don't take responsibility and end her, then Jude will." He caught Jude's eye. "For Claire, yes?"

"For Claire," Jude repeated robotically.

David sighed. "If an original carrier is killed by anyone besides its foil, the anomaly will manifest again along the affected bloodline. In this case, Joseph Dyer; he is a carrier as well. And then he would eventually either kill himself or be killed by someone else. That's the pattern of the afflicted."

"And of course Daniel would die, because I would not be able to make the call to save his life. So, four."

Noah was silent, and I was stunned.

"And I should probably mention that if you miss, and I don't die instantly, you could trigger Jude's ability, which seems to make him rather . . . unpredictable. I honestly don't know what he might do if that happens. Noah, please listen to me." His father met Noah's stare head-on, unflinchingly. "Whether it happens today or tomorrow or some other day, like the archetypes you parallel, you will play out your roles whether you want to or not. You don't have a choice."

"You always have a choice," Noah said, and clicked the safety back.

David turned his blue-gray eyes on me. "Are you willing to let him bet Daniel's life on it?"

I tore my gaze away from them and looked at the laptop. At my brother in the bed, at Jamie in the chair. "Don't," I said to Noah. "Please."

"You're not a murderer, Noah," his father said. "The only person you've ever really wanted to hurt is yourself."

Noah let out a small chuckle. "You're right," he said, then turned the gun on himself.

57

NOAH

I PRESS THE GUN TO MY TEMPLE. I ALMOST LITERALLY can't wait to do it.

There's this damned push and pull with my father. I feel complete disdain for the man standing before me, who looks nothing like me and is nothing like me and is disgusting to me. Yet at the same time I feel the senseless obedience of a child toward him. I want him to admire me, to be proud of me. To find me worthy. It is truly pathetic.

Mara sits on the table, her legs askew, her body trembling slightly, from the drugs or something else, I don't know. Something about her, a restrained physicality, carries an implicit threat, like a cobra the second before it strikes. She looks tigerish, a wild animal trapped and cornered. I want to unleash her, and I think this is how. Maybe she'll be able to save her brother then.

"I would rather die for her than live without her," I say to my father.

A smile twists his face. "You just love to play the martyr, don't you. You can lie to her but not to me. You would do it to spare yourself the sight of watching her die, the burden of guilt that her death and her brother's would bring you. Let's not pretend."

"Oh, I'm not pretending."

"Good. Then let me tell you, as clearly and precisely as I can, what you will be doing if you pull that trigger. You will unleash a Shadow upon the world. She will trail sickness and death behind her, wherever she goes, and it will start today, with her brother. She will burn like wildfire through her family, through everyone she cares about, leaving nothing but darkness and ashes in her wake. And you will be denying the world the answer to diseases that torment children and adults alike. If you choose to live, however, you could save millions. Billions, perhaps. You could usher in a new era of humanity. All it will cost you is one life."

Mara's life. The price is too high.

Fuck it. I press the barrel harder against my skull. The metal is warm from my skin, and the pressure is shamefully satisfying.

"Do it then, if you're that selfish," my father says.

"Don't you *dare*," Mara hisses, but I barely hear her.

"If I am, it's because you made me that way."

"Spoken like a true spoiled brat." The disgust is evident in my father's voice. "No, Noah, I think the shitty childhood excuse is played out. You don't want to be protected like a child anymore? Because you're seventeen? Then take responsibility for your own decisions. Own your own choices. It's more than past time for you to grow the fuck up, Son."

"I'm not your son," I say, cringing immediately thereafter. What a babyish thing to say. Idiotic.

My father replies, "I wish that were true."

The words break something inside me that I didn't even know existed.

"If you weren't my son, your mother would still be alive. She believed in you. I'm glad she isn't here to see this."

My mind refuses to seize on his words, so it focuses on Mara instead. She has been mostly quiet—eerily so. She says nothing in her own defense, so I speak for her. "If anyone is responsible for the things Mara's done, it's you."

"You know that isn't true. The original owner of that dog of yours? I had nothing to do with that. Nor did I have anything to do with that teacher, who paid with her life because Mara was simply having a bad day."

God, why doesn't she speak? "She didn't know what she was doing."

"Oh, she would have killed your dog's owner anyway. Ask her. She'll tell you."

"I would have killed him too," I say, and I mean it.

My father smiles again, his eyes crinkling at the corners. "But you can't kill anyone, Noah. Not even yourself."

"What about her family?" I ask, hating the desperation in my voice. "They don't deserve this."

"No. They don't. They're good people who got saddled with a bad problem."

Mara inhales sharply.

"You can't choose your children. No one knows that better than me. But you can help her family. And so many more at that."

"I love her." My father thinks I'm speaking to him, but I look at Mara as I say it. There is defeat in her eyes.

"You love her the way you would love a horse no one but you could ride. Like that Arab mare I bought years ago; I thought she'd breed good hunters, but not even the stallions would go near her. Do you remember what happened?"

I wish I didn't.

"One night Ruth couldn't find you. It was after your bedtime, which you rarely obeyed. We searched everywhere and found nothing, until we reached the stable. The mare's stall door was open. You'd mounted her bareback, at nine years old. We found you lying by her side near the back gate. She'd thrown you, trying to go over it, and you'd cracked your head open. You survived with no damage, thanks to what you are. The mare broke three legs and had to be put down. Do you remember?"

"Stop," Mara says.

"I've never heard screaming like that from an animal. It was a terrible death. And it wasn't her fault. It was yours."

"Stop!" The sound of Mara's voice is frightening. "Noah," she says with perfect calm. "Put the gun down."

I ignore her, of course, and so does my father. "Mara is what she is. She isn't safe, but she is capable of love, and she loves her family, and needs you to save them for her. She would give you a reason to do it someday. She knows it. You know it. The least you could do for her is save the younger brother before that happens." My father's eyes narrow. "But I'm beginning to see the futility in hoping you would be brave and selfless enough to do something for someone else, for once in your short life. Part of me wishes I could let the both of you go, just to watch you come crawling back to me on your knees someday, begging me to fix her, once you finally see what she's capable of. Once you have to start burying her bodies yourself."

He takes a step closer to me, but not close enough to matter.

"I thought you were ready to be the man your mother hoped you would be, but I see you're just a child, who would burn all his gifts because he can't have the one he wants."

"Put it down." Mara's tone has changed. She is begging me now. Desperate. But my hand doesn't move.

“The syringe contains sodium pentobarbital, which will stop Mara’s heart. The knife is the one method you’ve always . . . preferred. And that gun you’re holding to your head has only one bullet.”

He’s so sure I won’t do it. Doesn’t care whether I do.

“Please,” Mara says. *“Please.”*

I barely hear her. All I can think is that I am nothing more than a tool to him. But a tool can’t work if it’s broken.

I pull the trigger.

58

BEFORE

London, England

THE PROFESSOR PICKED UP ON THE FIRST RING.

"Get here *now*," I said. "David keeps threatening to call an ambulance."

"Don't let him—if anything changes, I can't predict the outcome anymore. The ambulance might crash before the child is born. It could die while still in the womb."

"She's bleeding," I said to him. My clothes were damp from the evening drizzle, and I hugged myself to stave off the chill. "It's bad."

"She'll survive." The professor's calm was maddening. It always has been. "He'll come when he's ready," he added.

That's what Naomi said. "Look, I'd feel a bit more comfortable if I had some assistance? Unless you're busy with something more important than the potential future of the human race, or whatever it is you're fucking around with here?"

The professor refused to be baited. "She lives. He lives. It has to be this way, Mara." But before I could argue, I heard Naomi scream.

"Come," I ordered him. "Come now." I hung up the phone and rushed back into the room.

Naomi was still in bed, propped up against several pillows. Wisps of her blond hair were matted to her forehead and her pale cheeks. She looked at me with glassy eyes but managed a wry smile.

"I think my water finally broke."

I looked down. A red stain blossomed beneath her.

"I'm calling the ambulance," David said, his expression a mixture of wrath and terror. He'd wanted to call one from the beginning. He'd wanted Naomi in the hospital, a controlled environment. Protected. He rushed to the door and shot a dark look at me over his shoulder. "Stay with her."

As if I would leave now, after everything. But of course David didn't *know* everything. He barely knew *anything*.

"This." She paused to breathe. "Sucks." She tossed her tired head back against the pillow. "How come no one told me how much this would suck?"

"I believe I did, actually," I said.

"It feels like he's trying to chew his way out."

I managed a small smile. "You're so weird."

"I'm fascinating. There's a difference." She breathed shakily and opened her eyes. The humor had left them. "I'm really scared, Mara."

"I know. But he's seen this," I said to her in a low voice, one David could not hear. "I know it feels like you can't do this, but you can. I believe in you." The words were bitter in my mouth. I felt like a farmer leading an animal to its slaughter, holding out a sweet to tempt it to its death. That Naomi knew what she was doing, that she chose this, didn't make me feel less guilty.

The sound of the doorbell echoed through the house just then, and I both hoped and feared that the ambulance had arrived. It hadn't. It was the professor instead.

He followed David into the room, carrying a doctor's bag that I recognized from half a century before. He settled in beside the bed. "May I?" he said, gesturing to the sheets. Not even so much as a hello. Bastard.

"Make it stop," Naomi whispered as he checked her.

"Not much longer, my girl. You are doing well."

"What about the blood?" David said angrily, trying to mask his fear. It didn't work.

The professor did not look up. "The placenta may have detached."

David seethed. "May have?"

The professor ignored him. "But the contractions are strong enough now that even if there were time to take her to a hospital, I wouldn't. But Mara," he said, turning to me.

"When the baby comes, I want you to be ready to call one if we need to."

"Is he going to die?" Naomi asked between gasps.

"He is not going to die."

"Am I going to die?"

The professor smiled. "Not today."

I could kill him. Sometimes I wish I had.

"Just promise he's going to be okay," Naomi said through gritted teeth.

The professor obliged. "I promise."

"Swear it."

"I swear."

Naomi twisted in the sweat-soaked, blood-soaked sheets and screamed. David's face was ashen. He looked so young. My heart ached for him.

"Brave girl," the professor said to Naomi. "You know how to do this. Now I want you to start pushing."

"Fuck. It hurts."

"It was no different for me," I said to her, hating the sound of my own voice, hating my false smile. "Or the millions of women before us."

David looked shocked for a moment. "You have children?"

I have a grandchild, I almost said, which would've shocked him even more.

It was barely a few minutes later when the professor said, "He's ready, Naomi. Are you?"

She nodded.

"All right, then. Give it everything."

She did. I held one hand and David held the other.

"Good," the professor said. "He's almost—he's here."

Naomi made a sound, somewhere between a sigh and a whimper, and fell back against the pillows. David's face was ashen, but his eyes were full of awe.

"I want to hold him," Naomi said weakly. Then, a beat later, "Toss him here."

"Is it—is it a boy?" David asked.

"Yes," the professor said in the eerily silent room.

"Why isn't he crying?" David asked, and then saw the baby. He was blue.

"Oh God," David whispered.

"What?" Naomi said, with an animal fear in her eyes. "What is it?"

The professor worked quickly. He was afraid, too, but no one would ever be able to tell but me. I held Naomi's hand as she asked, "Is he—is he—?"

The cord was around the baby's neck, but the professor cut it, and a second later, the baby turned from blue to pink. He was still silent, but the professor no longer looked alarmed. "There," he said with satisfaction. "Good boy. He's fine," he said to Naomi.

"Why isn't he crying?" David asked warily.

The professor cleaned him off a bit with a towel, looking relaxed. "What reason does he have to cry?"

"I thought that was normal? That babies cry when they're born," David said.

"Some do, yes," he said, and handed the child to Naomi, who watched him raptly. "He's scrappy," she said with a smile on her lips as she cradled him in her arms. The infant's eyes were open and eerily alert. "My little hero."

She was a fierce girl, ferocious, even, but at that moment, she looked completely at peace.

But David was still unsettled. "Is there something wrong with him?" He looked at the baby with suspicion.

"No," the professor said. "Everything is right."

"What's his name?" I asked Naomi.

She looked at the baby, then at David. "Noah," she said, her eyebrows raised as if daring her husband to challenge her. Wisely, he didn't.

I looked at the little shell of the newborn's ear, the soft, perfect skin on his cheeks, the tiny fingers on the hand that would one day extinguish my life, and I said, "Good choice."

59

I DIDN'T EVEN HAVE TIME TO SCREAM BEFORE I NOTICED that Noah was still standing. The gun had jammed, or something. I didn't know and did not care.

Noah was staring at nothing. He was blank, expressionless, stunned, motionless. The gun was still at his head. His father didn't even react.

I was going to have to fix this. I was the only one who could. I said Noah's name and he looked at me as if I'd spoken to him for the first time in history, as if he had no idea who I was.

"Give me the gun."

He didn't. But he did lower his hand, and then he spoke as if we were alone.

"Let's go look for your brother." He took my hand in his free one.

"There's no time," I said calmly.

"We can torture my father until he tells us." I thought I caught David rolling his eyes in disgust. He was clearly not threatened.

"Uh, guys?" Jamie's voice. We both blinked, confused, until we remembered the laptop. Jamie had seen everything. "As much as I'd like to watch that, I think—I think you should be quick," he said diplomatically. But I knew what he was thinking.

Noah acted as if he hadn't heard him. "We should start looking." He tugged at my limp arm. My fingers were dead weight in his. I wasn't going to follow him. There was no point. And parts of my legs were still numb anyway. I wouldn't get very far, even if David and Jude let me.

"I can't walk," I said.

"Then I'll carry you."

Noah still didn't get it. "We're never going to find him before—before—" I couldn't say the word.

"Not if we don't try."

I forced myself to remember that for Noah, Horizons seemed like yesterday. He didn't know what had happened since.

I'd woken up strapped to the table like an animal, but I wasn't one. I'd done things—things I regretted and things I didn't. I was too old to blame them on being young. My family had been too good to me for me to blame it on them. I'd made my choices by myself. Some of them had been wrong, but they were my choices. I owned them. No one else.

Noah's father knew he would never be able to convince Noah to kill me. This display was for me, so that *I* could prove to Noah why I should die. No one else could do that for me.

I didn't want to die, but maybe I should. Maybe the world *would* be a better place if I did.

"No," Noah said, in response to the question I hadn't asked out loud. I wondered for a moment if he could somehow hear my thoughts, but then I realized that he didn't have to; he could read my face.

"I can't let Daniel go," I said, fighting vainly to stay calm. "I can't let what happened to me happen to Joseph. They've done nothing, *nothing* wrong. I've done everything wrong."

"Not everything."

"You haven't *been* here." I could tell that my words stung him. "You haven't seen—" I tipped my head in the direction of the pictures of Dr. Kells and Wayne and Mr. Ernst. "Your father isn't lying. I did those things. All of them."

"I'm sure they deserved it," Noah said, a tiny smile lifting the corner of his mouth. I couldn't smile back.

David Shaw was sick and awful, but he was right about me too. Nothing good would ever come from me. Nothing ever did. But Daniel, Joseph—they were different. They would do good. They *were* good. And I could save them.

All I had to give was my life. My life for my brother's. It would be worth it. It could never not be worth it.

Leaving Miami with Jamie and Stella had felt like good-bye. It felt like good-bye because it *was* good-bye. Something in me had always known it.

I pulled myself up onto my elbows—my feet still felt numb—and reached for Noah's hand, the one with the gun in it. It had jammed once, for Noah, but I knew it wouldn't for me.

A shiver rolled through him when my skin met his. He looked like he might be sick.

"Please," I whispered. "Please."

"You don't know what you're asking me."

"Yes, I do. Come closer."

He held the gun limply, so I lifted the barrel of it for him and pressed it against my forehead. We were beaten, and I was decided.

"Do it," I said softly.

He was tortured, and I hated to be the one to torture him. I hated that it had to be him, that he had to watch me die and live with the guilt for the rest of his life. I hated that just as my hope of finding him had been rewarded, I was being forced to throw it into the fire, and myself along with it. I hated leaving my family. I hated leaving him.

"Mara," he whispered. His finger was on the trigger. He was shaking.

"I'm begging you. I don't want to be this person." It wasn't true, but that didn't matter. What mattered was what Noah needed to hear. "This is my choice. Help me."

His eyebrows drew together, and for a fraction of a second, I thought he would do it.

"I *can't*." His arm went slack, his face twisted with disgust. Then immediately he raised his arm again, but not at me. He shot a mannequin instead.

No more bullets. I looked at David; there was no surprise in his expression, no shock. He'd been expecting it.

"We're going to figure this out," Noah went on, his voice firm, strong, determined. "I'll call the police. We'll find Daniel. I'll heal him. You'll get better—"

"Stop it!" My words battered the walls of the factory. They seemed to echo forever. "This is not something you can fix." And I couldn't risk letting him try.

"You always think the worst of yourself," he said with bitterness.

"And you always think the best." It was true, which made me smile. "You can't see me objectively because you love me. But I've done things. How am I any different from him?" I flicked my eyes to Jude, who lowered his to the floor. If I hadn't known any better, I'd have said he looked guilty.

Jude was sicker than me and crazier than me and crueler than me, but he'd loved his sister, his only family. Deborah and David had used that love to control him. I didn't forgive him for the things he'd done—I would never do that. But I understood them.

"It doesn't matter what you've done. It only matters why," Noah said. "He uses his ability to hurt people. You use yours to protect people."

Not always, I thought, and said so. "The villain is the hero of her own story. No one thinks they're a bad person. Everyone has reasons for doing what they do. Jude and I are not as different as you think."

Those words did something to him, lit a spark in him. He looked alive, really alive, for the first time since he'd been back. His hands cupped my face as he said, "Never say that again. You've been lied to. Manipulated. Tortured. It's not your fault."

I shuddered, from his words or the contact, I didn't know.

"It's not your fault, Mara. Say it."

"Noah," David said. There was a note of urgency in his voice and I began to panic.

"There's no *time*, Noah."

"Say it and I'll—I'll give you the shot."

"What?" I wasn't sure I'd heard what I thought I'd heard.

"I can't with the—the knife. I'll see it forever," Noah said. His voice sounded different. Like something had broken inside of him. I wanted to smooth the crease between his brows, take his face in my hands, kiss him, make it better. But I was the one hurting him.

I swallowed my sadness, for him, for myself.

"It'll just look like I'm going to sleep." I glanced at the laptop. Jamie's eyes were wide with horror. My brother's were closed. I realized I'd never see them open again, and that was the moment I started to cry.

"Jamie," I said, catching my breath, "Tell my brother—tell him I love him."

Jamie nodded silently. Tears streamed down his face.

"Tell him I'm sorry."

"Mara," my friend said.

"Tell him he's my hero. And, Jamie?"

He sniffed. "Yeah?"

"Make him forget what he knows about me. Make him forget all of this. Can you do that?"

"I don't know."

"Can you try?"

His chin trembled. "God, you're so demanding."

A laugh escaped from my mouth.

"I'll try," he said. "You know I'll try."

"You're a good friend."

"I know," he said back. "You're not so bad yourself."

"Yes I am."

"Mara," David said. "You should hurry." He didn't say it unkindly.

I hated him, but it was a cold, distant kind of hate. I would see him in hell, someday, and punish him there. But right now

I just wanted to love Noah. I wanted to leave the world feeling that.

I looked at the boy I loved, the one who saved me, every day. He was so hurt. I didn't know what to say to him, but he seemed to know what I needed.

He scooped me up from the table and carried me, the way a groom would carry a bride. We walked a little bit, but not far; I needed to be able to see my brother. I wasn't ready to leave him yet.

David and Jude gave us space. They knew we weren't going anywhere. There was nowhere else to go.

Noah unfolded me into his half-kneeling lap. He wrapped one hand around my stomach and the other over my chest. My soft cheek was against his rougher one, his mouth pressed against my shoulder. Once upon a time his lips on my skin would have made me forget myself. I could laugh and joke and pretend with him, and his voice would drown out the thoughts inside me that no one should ever hear. But he couldn't change me. No one could. I was still poison, and even Noah couldn't make me forget it anymore.

My chin trembled as I said what Noah needed to hear. "It's not—it's not my fault," I whispered.

"Again."

"It's not my fault," I lied, louder this time.

Noah uncapped the syringe, his face ashen, and I held out my arm.

I think that was when I knew, for real, that there would be no SWAT team barging in to save us. No epic battles would be fought in some cinematic climax. There would be no screaming, no explosions. It was just us. Two people and a choice.

"I won't even feel it," I said, trying not to imagine all of the conversations we would never have. That was what I would miss most, I realized. Just being able to tell him things. There was still so much to say.

"I love you," I whispered against his neck. Noah held me tighter, not saying it back—I knew he couldn't speak. Then, without warning, I felt a tiny prick in my arm, which deepened into a burning sting. I managed a crappy smile as Noah plunged the contents of the syringe into my veins. "Thank you," I said when he was done. He held his fingers over the puncture wound. His breath caught, trapping a silent sob. He was so brave.

"If Daniel's still—" My chest felt tight, and I opened my mouth, trying to swallow more air. "If he's still sick when I'm—and your father doesn't—"

"I will," Noah said hoarsely. He looked so fierce and beautiful. I would miss that face.

"Find him," I said. My words slurred, and my eyelids drooped. My breath was too shallow. "Fix him," I said with my last one, and then the world went dark.

60

BEFORE

Laurelton, Rhode Island

Naomi gave birth to a healthy baby boy that day. You have just been born.

When your mother was pregnant with Daniel, I spent countless nights wondering if he would be Afflicted, like me. But within hours of his birth, the professor declared him safe and healthy. The second I saw you, I knew you would not be so blessed.

The professor told me about the Shaw child, what he would become, but not the consequences of it—that you would become something too.

I've discovered what actually happened on that night when I believed I seduced the professor.

He had known it would happen. He knew that your

mother would be born, that you would someday as well. I'd thought I was his partner, but I was only a tool.

I raged at him for what he had allowed to happen. For what would someday happen to you. He lied, said he couldn't have changed it. Said, "She cannot become other than what she is."

He is right about that.

You will make a difference in this world, child, whether you want to or not. Most people are like sand, the impact of their lives washed away by years. They cause no lasting damage, no lasting benefit.

You are not most people.

You are like fire; you will burn wherever you go. If contained, channeled, you can bring light, but you will also always cast a shadow. You can choose to end life or choose to give it, but punishment will follow every reward. And if your fire is unchecked, you will burn through lives and history. The closer anyone gets to you, the more at risk they are of falling under your shadow, or being consumed by your flame. You will have to pretend to be other than what you are. You must wear enough armor so that no one can see or touch you. It isn't your fault. It's nothing you did. You cannot change who you are, any more than you can change black eyes to blue. You can only accept it. If you fight yourself, you will lose, and fighting leaves scars. But you will survive them. I have survived many. You will do good things you will regret, and bad things you won't, but you must keep going, for my daughter's sake if not your own. She loves you so much already.

I want you to know that I would have wished for a different life for you, and for my beloved daughter, who will never know about any of this if I can prevent it. Sometimes I wonder, if I had chosen a different name for myself, might I have grown into a different person? Might I have become someone else? There were days when I felt that a dragon slept inside me, and exhaled poison with every breath. I flirted with suicide more times than I can count. But I know now why I never did it. I was saving that day for you.

There is a chance, however slim, that if I die before you manifest, the cycle for my bloodline might end with my sacrifice. I don't know what the odds are, but I'm willing to take them for my daughter; I can't change the past, but I can choose my future.

I should warn you, though, that the professor will find you someday, as your fate is tied to the boy's. He might ask you to help him, to join him, to make a difference. He picks at history like a child at a scab, and might offer you the same opportunity. But know this: He has more knowledge than anyone else alive, but it has not brought him happiness. It hasn't brought me much, either. I've known many people over many lifetimes, and the ignorant ones seem more content.

But you must decide for yourself. If you wear this, he will know of your choice.

I don't know where to leave this for you so that you'll find it, when you're ready, without your mother seeing. If I shared the professor's Affliction, perhaps I'd have some idea. But I will make the best choice I can with the knowledge that I have, and hope.

Letter in one hand, doll in the other, I made my way to the kitchen for a knife. I slit Sister's doll open from groin to chin, then slipped my letter inside. I stuffed the doll back up, and began to sew before I remembered the necklace. I carried it back to the doll in my closed fist, then pushed it inside with one finger. I sewed it closed.

There. Done. I would wait three days, and then I would leave the world as I'd entered it—alone.

61

NOAH

I HOLD MARA IN MY SHAKING ARMS AS HER PULSE FADES to nothing. My father doesn't even wait until she's dead before he soils the air with words.

"You did the right thing, Noah. I'm proud of you."

For as long as I can remember, I've had trouble with feelings. Other people get scared, or nervous, or shy, or excited, or happy, or sad. I seem to have only two settings: blank or empty.

I feel neither of those things now.

The pain of losing her is physical. Every breath of oxygen tastes like poison. Every beat of my heart feels like a hammer to my chest. How could she possibly have expected me to bear this?

"I'm going to take care of her brother," my father says as he types something into his phone. "Her whole family. They'll never want for anything." He holds the phone up to his ear, and I hear a ring echo from somewhere inside the building.

Inside the building.

Daniel has been here the whole time.

It's a double blow, one I can barely process as I stare at her unnaturally still body. I've spent too many nights with her to be able to pretend, even to myself, that she's only sleeping.

"Noah?"

Jamie's voice cuts through the static in my brain. I look over at the laptop.

His tear-streaked face is anxious, afraid. "Something's happening. The machines sound weird."

My father puts his hand on my shoulder. I can't muster the energy to tell him not to touch me.

"I'll go find out what's happening," he says. "He will be all right, Noah. I promise."

As if his promises mean anything to me. But if he's wrong, I will make him suffer every day for the rest of his worthless, pointless life.

He entreats Jude to watch me—so I won't do anything crazy?—and when Jude agrees, my father leaves me to choke on my grief alone. Or almost. I am aware of Jude's presence, the way his eyes have been hungrily staring at the knife my idiot father left here. I know Jude will reach for it. I'm not sure what he'll do next, but I am sure that I don't care.

"What are you waiting for?" I say.

He turns to make sure my father is gone, and then, as predicted, he reaches for it. Jude looks at me, his eyes filled not with hate but with hope.

Freak. "Go on, then. Do it."

"Put her down," he says. "And I will."

I do. He does.

62

LIGHT STAINED THE BACKS OF MY EYELIDS RED. I bolted upright as if someone had plunged a syringe of adrenaline straight into my heart.

I remembered hands that weren't mine sewing a letter into a doll. I remembered what the letter said. I remembered deaths I hadn't wished for, families that weren't mine, trees and beasts, ships and dust, feathers and hearts.

I remembered everything. Every feeling, every scent, touch, sight. I brimmed with echoes of my grandmother's memories, her knowledge, my inheritance. They rose at the back of my throat, and I was bursting with the urge to tell Noah everything. But it wasn't Noah's face I saw when I opened my eyes.

Jude grinned, showing both dimples and looking like a child on Christmas. He held a syringe. "I knew you'd come back once you'd manifested. Doctor guessed you would, when you were finished changing."

I didn't care enough to ask him what he was talking about, or to think much about what he was saying and how creepily he was saying it. I had only one question, but my heart knew the answer before my eyes could confirm it.

I turned around to see Noah's body stretched out behind me. The knife was still in his chest.

63

NOAH

I HEAR THAT VOICE BEFORE I SEE THAT FACE.

"You are not going to die," Mara says. Her distinctive alto has an edge to it now. Angry. Hopeless. She's a terrible liar. Always has been, at least compared to me.

I manage to open my eyes. I watch hers travel my body, and revel in the weight of her fingers on my chest. She looks so determined, so furious.

For some reason I think of the first time I saw her, kicking the shit out of the vending machine that refused to release her candy. Before that day, every hour of my life had been exactly like the one before it. Relentlessly boring. Painfully monotonous. But then she walked out of my waking nightmare and into my life, a complete mystery from Second One. Her presence was a problem I needed to solve, a problem that finally interested me. And then, somehow, she made me interested in myself.

Mara began as a question I needed to answer, but the longer I'd known her, the less I felt I actually knew. She was constantly surprising, infinitely complex. Unknowable. Unpredictable. I had never met anyone more fascinating in my life, and all the time in the world wouldn't be enough to ever know her.

But now I want that time. My mind closes around memories of her, the feel of her hands in my hair, her cheek on my chest, her voice in my ear, her breath in my mouth. It's so classic. I've spent most of my life waiting to die and now that I am, I don't want to anymore. I manage a small, wry smile. Be careful what you wish for, I guess.

64

THERE IS NOTHING LIKE HOLDING THE BODY OF THE person you love and knowing those heartbeats are numbered.

Noah was still breathing, but shallowly. His eyes didn't open when I said his name. I cradled him in my arms, and looked up at Jude with hate in my eyes.

"Why?" I barely recognized the sound of my own voice.

"I needed to trigger you. Doctor said. She said if you manifested, you could kill me. And I want that. It's the only way I can die. I knew if I killed him, you'd be mad enough to do it."

But I didn't feel mad. I felt empty.

"Mara?" Jamie's voice. The laptop was still on the stack of

boxes. I craned my neck to look at it. "Jesus Christ," he said, "I thought you died."

"Is Daniel—my brother—"

"They took him," Jamie said. "Fuckers took him and left me here."

"Is he—"

"He was alive, yeah. They put something in his drip. Mara, I'm here—somewhere in the building. Come get me?"

I looked down at Noah's face. His pulse fluttered in his throat. I glanced at the knife in his chest. Maybe—if I pulled it out . . .

I didn't know what to do. I didn't know.

"Do it before he gets back," Jude said.

"Who?" Noah's father? I didn't care about him. He would get what he deserved. I would make sure of it.

"The one inside me," Jude said, sending a ripple of revulsion through me. "Doctor was working on something, a cure. I gave myself a shot, but it pushes the other one away for only a little while. You've gotta do it, Mara. Please. There's no one else who can. You couldn't do it before you manifested, but now, now you're done. You came back. You healed yourself. You can do it now. Please."

Jude was asking me to kill him. And I would. He couldn't live, not after what he'd done. But what he was saying, how he was saying it, peeled the skin off of a memory.

I remembered him standing in the torture garden at

Horizons, telling me I had to be afraid, afraid enough to bring Claire back. Which was impossible.

The moment I thought this was the moment Noah stopped breathing.

I watched as the pulse died in his throat, and a breath, his last one, escaped from his lips like a sigh.

"Oh, God," I whispered. One tear fell, then another. I looked at the knife through blurred vision.

Jamie said, "Mara, do you hear that?"

But I heard nothing. Saw nothing. Felt nothing but Noah. I pulled the knife from his chest, hoping, desperately, that it might not be too late, that somehow he could heal, *would* heal, despite the things his father had said, despite the fortune-teller's words.

"You will love him to ruins."

I thought about all of the choices that had led us here, how each one could have gone a different way. How Noah might never have met me. How he would have been whole and unbroken and alive now if he hadn't.

"Sirens," Jamie said with hope in his voice. "Is he—is Noah—"

But it was too late. The life I'd almost had died in my arms.

"He's gone," I said, holding his body, and the knife that had killed him.

"Please," Jude said again. "Please, please."

I looked at the knife in my hands, the blade wet with Noah's warm blood. There was so much of it, on his chest, beneath him. Even in his hair.

The knife didn't kill him. Jude did.

But maybe I could bring him back.

I let Jude's pleading voice fade into the background with Jamie's, with the sirens, with everything else. I closed my eyes and pictured it.

Noah, alive, tying my shoelaces in front of my house before he drove me to school.

Noah, alive, looking at the picture I'd drawn of him, folding it and putting it into his pocket to keep.

Noah, alive, looking down at me with his messy hair and sleepy eyes, his arms wrapped around me as we lay in my bed.

I opened my eyes.

Noah was still gone.

I was doing something wrong. I flipped through memories, mine and not mine, searching desperately for a way to fix this. Noah's father and Dr. Kells had given Jude an ability but hadn't been able to control him. They'd tried to take mine away, and I'd lost the ability to control myself. Until now.

I wiped Noah's blood from the knife, looked at the sliver of my reflection in it, hoping it would speak to me, tell me how to fix this. But it was silent.

Jude was begging now, shivering. I got that he wanted me to kill him for his sake, so he wouldn't have to become the thing he was ever again. But I didn't care. I wanted him to suffer. He *should* suffer every day for what he'd done. *That* was what he deserved.

But I knew I wouldn't make him.

Noah's body was warm in my hands. The weight of him filled my lap. I didn't want to think about Jude. But unless I wished him gone, he wouldn't go.

So I thought about his corrupted heart stopping, his blunted nerves dying, his pointless lungs drowning in fluid. I thought those things and more, but he was still alive. He was hunched over himself. I thought I saw a drop of blood drip from his nose, but I wasn't sure.

"Please," he whispered again. "Please."

I could kill him without touching him, but I didn't know when he would actually, finally die. That was always the part I couldn't seem to predict, couldn't control. Or if I did, I didn't know how yet.

So I said to him, "Come here."

Jude looked at me. Something hateful and sly flashed behind his eyes. How had I missed it, all those months ago? How could I have looked at that blond head and those dimples and missed what an empty, nothing, shell of a thing he was? How had I ever let him get close enough to hurt me?

Whatever. I wouldn't make that mistake again.

It physically hurt to rest Noah's head on the floor, to empty my arms of him and stand up to face his murderer. Jude was kneeling, but he was straining to do it. He was at war with himself; his muscles were corded and the veins stood out on his forehead and neck.

Maybe I should have taken the opportunity to make him recount his sins before he died, to force some grand confession of regret from his lips, to make him own all of the pain he was responsible for. But that felt like more than he deserved. Jude was no better than an animal really, so in the end, I slaughtered him like one. I slashed the knife across his throat and he fell to his side. I watched as he bled out.

I was vaguely aware of bodies, living ones, rushing into the room, shouting things as red and blue lights flashed through the grime-clouded windows. I glanced briefly at the laptop, watched as police broke into the room where Jamie was being held. Something moved at the corner of my vision.

"Drop the weapon," a female voice shouted. I hadn't realized I was still holding the knife. I opened my fist. It clattered to the dusty floor.

"Put your arms above your head and turn around slowly."

I did. About a dozen NYPD officers stood among the mannequins, holding guns, pointing them at me.

I looked down at Jude's body, and at Noah's. Then back up, at the female officer. I wondered what she saw when she looked at me. A grieving girl? A murderer?

I realized I didn't care. I'd told Noah he wasn't going to die. The last words I ever spoke to him were lies. I was a liar. He did die, and even though I'd tried, I hadn't brought him back.

I wasn't crying anymore. Instead there was just the sob that wouldn't come, the sting of tears that wouldn't fall, the ache in my throat that was dying to become a scream. Crying would have been a relief, but I wasn't filled with sadness. I was filled with rage.

Rage because he'd died, for no reason, for bullshit, while everyone else got to live. If people heard about what had happened, their faces would turn into masks of horror for a moment, but then it would become just a story to them. They would go on living, and laughing, and I would be alone with my grief.

"He tried to kill her," Jamie shouted from the crappy laptop speakers as an officer on screen untied him. It drew the attention of one of the cops in the room with me, but the other pairs of eyes didn't waver in their focus.

If they'd known me, what I'd been through, what I'd lost, they might have said they were sorry for me, sorry for my loss. They might even have meant it. But beneath that would have been relief—that death hadn't happened to them.

All I wanted in the world right then was for Noah to live. That was what he deserved. But thinking something does not make it true. Wanting something does not make it real.

Except that when I want it, it should. That was supposed to be my gift. My affliction.

I closed my eyes, squeezed them shut. Saw writing in my mind, in handwriting that wasn't mine.

You can choose to end life or choose to give it, but punishment will follow every reward.

Punishment. Reward.

I wanted to give Noah life. To reward him with it. But it wouldn't be free. Nothing was. If I wanted something, I would have to trade for it.

I wanted Noah. What would I trade for him?

Who would I trade for him, was the question I needed to be asking.

"The people we care about are always worth more to us than the people we don't. No matter what anyone pretends."

They'd been Noah's words once. But they were mine now. Who wouldn't I trade for him? I would not trade my family. Never them.

But there were other people. The world was full of them. How many would have to be punished so I could reward? What was Noah's life worth?

His father, David, needed to be punished for what he'd done, no question. But a million of him wouldn't equal one Noah. He was worthless. Less than.

But not all people were worthless. I looked around me, at the men and women who filled the room, rushing into danger in the hope of saving someone's life. They were good people. Brave. Selfless. Heroes, really.

Would I trade one of them to have Noah back?

Would I trade all of them to have him back?

I was stripped of all illusions, about this and myself. I knew without thinking that the answer was yes.

65

I KNEW WHAT WOULD HAPPEN NEXT. AS THE POLICE approached, the woman said, "Are you holding anything that could hurt me?"

Ask the wrong questions, get the wrong answers. I shook my head as she reached for my hands and cuffed me.

"What happened here?"

I didn't respond. How could I?

Besides, I had the right to remain silent, so that was what I did.

The paramedics had arrived, and they were setting up gurneys, checking the bodies, as if there were any point.

The female officer tilted her head and asked. "Are you all right?"

The question was almost funny. I shook my head.

"I think she's in shock," she said to an EMT. "Do a quick check, and we'll take her to the hospital."

"We've got another one here," a voice said. I followed the source of it and saw Jamie, flanked by two cops.

"I told them," he said loudly, too loudly, as he passed. "About your crazy ex."

Clever boy.

"Your ex-boyfriend?" the female officer asked me. "Which one?"

I looked at Jude.

"This your boyfriend?" She tipped her head at Noah, at his body, as he was being lifted onto a gurney without urgency. I nodded numbly, dumbly. They were going to take him away. I didn't know how I would bear it.

"I think I know what happened here," the female officer said in a low voice to another, who had joined her. "We'll track down the parents once we get to the hospital." She put her hand on my elbow as they began to wheel Noah's body away. My limbs felt like lead. I couldn't move. I could barely see. My vision blurred with tears. I blinked furiously, but they just kept coming.

The female officer tugged me in the direction of the exit

just as one of the paramedics lifted a sheet to cover Noah's face. I saw him blink.

Face covered, wheels squeaking. Noah was almost gone when I finally managed to say, "Wait."

No one heard me the first time, so the second time I screamed it.

The action stopped. The paramedic who had done the face covering must have seen something in my expression, though, because he looked at me and then back down at Noah, and then lifted the sheet.

"Holy shit," he murmured. "He's breathing."

A second ago, the air had been dead, practically silent, but now it buzzed with frenzy. Paramedics swarmed around Noah, blocking him from view. I caught a glimpse of an oxygen mask being placed over his face as I was pulled away from him by more than one pair of hands. I watched his eyes open, and beneath the clear mask I thought I caught a hint of that half smile that I loved and missed so much.

I'd seen a lot of things since all of this had started though. And not all of them had been real.

But as Noah passed me, he slipped his hand off the gurney. His skin brushed mine. Electrified it.

He was alive. He was real.

66

A MACHINE BEEPED TO THE LEFT OF NOAH'S hospital bed as another on his right hissed. I could see them, hear them, as I was escorted past his open door. Two police officers flanked it, and when they noticed me trying to peer in, one of them moved to close it. Detective Howard—that was the female officer's name—led me to a makeshift interrogation room. Number 1213, I noticed.

"The doctor says your boyfriend is recovering remarkably well. Astonishingly well," she added. "That chest wound of his—it looked pretty bad, like his aorta might've been punctured, even. The paramedics thought he was dead. . . . They don't usually make mistakes like that."

She stared, waiting for me to speak, but what could I say? That I wanted him alive, so he lived?

What a crazy thing to think.

"Your friend—Jamal, right?—told me what happened to you. He gave us your parents' number, and we've called your mother and left a voice mail. Hopefully she'll be here soon."

Not likely.

"But I'd like to hear what happened from you, in your own words, before she gets here, if you can tell me."

I could, but I wouldn't. I was a lawyer's daughter, after all. I tilted my head forward, veiling my face with my hair. I was a psychologist's daughter too. I knew what I needed to do.

"You were all in some kind of, what, treatment center together?"

You could say that. I looked at the table and blinked as if I hadn't heard her.

"This must be very difficult for you," she said gently, trying a different tactic.

I bit my lip, hard, so I wouldn't laugh. She thought I was trying not to cry, and put a comforting hand on my shoulder.

"If it was self-defense, you didn't do anything wrong."

Little did she know.

"Just a few more questions, and then the doctors will come in to talk to you, okay?"

No response.

"Someone reported a homicide at that abandoned

warehouse. Any idea who that might've been?"

I had my suspicions; David Shaw topped the list. He thought I was dead, of course, and someone would have to answer for killing me, wouldn't they? He was going to blame it on Jude, I bet.

"And the hospital admitted a boy not much older than you, not far from the warehouse, only a half hour before we got there. Any idea who *that* might've been?"

Daniel.

My heart seized on the idea, but I couldn't ask. I couldn't say anything. I looked out the window instead. We were on the twelfth floor, and New York City stretched out below us. It looked like a doll world from up here, with pieces I could move or play with or break.

The door squeaked on its hinges, and a doctor gestured from the doorway to Detective Howard. "Psych's on the way," he said in a low voice. "Someone's here to see her, though."

A person stood behind him, but I couldn't see who it was.

"Are you the mother?" the detective asked.

But the woman who stepped into the room was not my mother. She was young, in her twenties, and wore tortoiseshell glasses on her pale, round, freckled face. She was outfitted in skinny jeans and Chucks, and for the life of me, I had no idea who she was.

She extended her hand to the detective. "I'm Rochelle Hoffman. I'm the lawyer."

67

SHE WAS JAMIE'S COUSIN, IT TURNED OUT. HE'D called her as soon as he'd dispatched his police escort. Then he'd given the cops her number and told them it belonged to my parents. They believed him, of course. They had no choice.

When I was finally alone with her, I cut the catatonic act and told her I wanted to talk to Jamie. She made it happen, probably with Jamie's help, and left us alone. He pulled up a chair and sat in it backward.

"So. Here's the deal."

He could not talk fast enough to satisfy me.

"Daniel's in the hospital too." I opened my mouth to ask

about him, but Jamie said quickly, "He's okay. We'll have to Wormtongue our way in after dark or something, stage a hospital break for him and Noah. Maybe during the shift change."

"What about us?"

"Well, you would be a murder suspect, if I hadn't managed to painstakingly, painfully, at great cost to my physical and mental well-being, persuade the police otherwise."

"I'm grateful."

"You sound it."

"Does this mean we can just go?"

"Sort of. Rochelle's taking care of it."

"What did your cousin say we should do? About everything?"

"Well . . ." He drew out the word slowly. "I sort of described the situation hypothetically."

"Elaborate."

"As in, 'Let's say this billionaire was funding these messed-up genetic experiments on teenagers . . ."

"Right . . ."

"Let's say these teens have superpowers . . ."

"Uh-huh . . ."

"Let's say one of them ended up killing some people with her thoughts sometimes and also with her bare hands. Hypothetically."

I buried my face in my hands.

"Let's say there was physical evidence tying her to some of the deaths . . ."

Kells. Wayne. Ernst. "Christ, Jamie."

"And other evidence had been planted to make it look like she was guilty of murders she didn't commit."

Phoebe. Tara.

"Oh, and, just for fun, to make it interesting, let's say all of these teens have documented histories of mental illness. What do you think our chances would be if we went up against said billionaire in court?"

"I'm guessing you mentioned the stuff we have? The videos? Documents?"

"Yup."

"I'm guessing her response was not encouraging."

"Shocking, isn't it? She said—hypothetically, of course—that the documents couldn't be authenticated. Chain of custody problems, not admissible, blah, blah. I don't know, do I look like a lawyer?"

I inhaled slowly, trying to stay calm.

"I even left out the parts where you and Noah died and came back to life, but for some reason she still seems to think I'm fucking with her. She was kind of huffy about it, actually. But she's trustworthy. And smart. With her brains and my awesome power, we'll be able to leave whenever we want."

"Good news."

"P.S., you were right about Noah. I am willing to acknowledge that now."

"About what? About him being alive?"

"Yes, but also about him. Like, generally."

"I'm not following . . ."

"When I met you, I thought he was going to use you."

"This is a shock to no one, Jamie."

"Can you shut up for a second so I can admit my wrongness?" He cleared his throat. "As I was saying. He could never use you. You own him. You should've seen the way he was looking at you while you were out."

I smiled a little. "How?"

"Like you're the ocean and he's desperate to drown."

His words wiped the smile off my face. Noah had drowned. With my help.

I shook my head as if to clear it. Jamie must've thought I was disagreeing with him because he went on.

"You don't get what you do for him. You're like his manic pixie dream girl or something." Jamie thought for a second. "Actually, more like his psychotic demon nightmare thing, but whatever. You get my point."

I refused to acknowledge it.

"Speaking of demon nightmare things," he segued gracefully, "you dying and coming back to life? That was a neat trick. How'd you manage that?"

"Jude said it's because I manifested finally, or something. That I healed myself."

"Huh. And Noah?"

I stayed quiet.

"He looked pretty dead when you were sitting there rocking back and forth, holding his seemingly lifeless body, I have to say."

"Do you? Have to say?"

"Why do I get the feeling you're not being entirely truthful, Mara?"

"You're imagining things. You're under a lot of stress."

He looked like he was about to hit me, when someone knocked on the door. Rochelle peeked inside and motioned for us to follow her out into the hallway.

"You owe me, Cousin," she said to Jamie as we passed Detective Howard and some nurses.

"You love me and you know it."

"You're lucky I do."

We passed Noah's closed door on our way to the elevator. The cops were still there, still guarding him. I recognized one of them; he'd been at the factory. The one distracted by Jamie shouting from the computer.

Jamie stopped walking. "You okay?" Jamie asked the officer. I stopped to listen.

"Yeah," the cop said slowly. "Why?"

Jamie motioned to his own nose. "You have . . . something."

The cop's eyebrows drew together and he sniffed, then rubbed his nose. His fingers came away red. They left a bloody smear above his lip.

He nodded at Jamie. "Thanks."

We resumed our exit. When we neared the elevator, though, something caught my eye.

A scalpel rested on a little cart outside a patient room. I glanced around to see if anyone was watching me.

No one was.

I slipped it into my back pocket and followed Jamie and Rochelle into the elevator. The officer was dabbing a bloody tissue to his nose when the doors closed.

68

NOAH

MARA IS WAITING FOR US WHEN JAMIE SPRINGS Daniel and me that night. She stands beneath a streetlight on an empty sidewalk, looking very gorgeous in a very bad way.

"Subway?" Jamie suggests.

Daniel sticks his hand up in the air. "Cab. Definitely."

A minute later one pulls up to the curb. The cabbie turns around once we're in. "Where are we going?"

Mara grins at me. "Wherever we want."

Almost as soon as Jamie unlocks the front door to his aunt's house, he ducks into the bathroom, and Daniel passes out on the couch in the parlor.

I look around. "Nice place," I say as Mara leads me farther in.

"Upstairs or downstairs?" she asks.

"Bed," I answer. Her smile widens as she leads me up the steps. I follow her into a bedroom and we collapse together in each other's arms.

I wake up the next afternoon. Mara is beside me, dead, her limbs tangled in the sheets.

No. Not dead. Sleeping.

But the panic stays with me. I extract my arm from beneath her as guilt rises in my throat. It's so thick I could choke.

There's a bathroom in here, thank God, and I escape into it and bolt the door behind me. I look at my reflection in the medicine cabinet mirror, at my empty eyes, my blank face. Then they disappear and I see other things. The pale blue veins in Mara's arm before I stuck the needle in it. Her closed eyelids, unnaturally still.

I want to cut myself into pieces no one can reassemble. Instead I take off my shirt, knowing, fearing what I'll see.

There are stitches in my chest, as expected, and the wound is almost completely healed, as I'd feared.

I steal scissors from the medicine cabinet and cut the stitches out, wondering without much curiosity at all if I'll have a scar. Hope so.

"Knock, knock." Daniel's voice, muffled, accompanied by tapping on the door. I step out of the bathroom as he says, "Everyone decent?"

Mara opens her eyes blearily, looking up at me from the bed. Her hair is a wild, tangled mess. I want to fill my hands with it.

"Who is it?" she asks.

"Your brother," I say.

She's up in an instant and launches herself out of bed, stubbing her toe in the process, swearing creatively as a result. She flings the door open and attacks him with a hug. Daniel staggers back, but his arms wrap around her just as tightly.

"I'm so sorry," she says, her voice muffled. "So sorry."

He backs up and holds her shoulders. "It's not your fault."

She'll never believe you, I almost say. But this is not my moment.

Daniel looks at me anyway, as if he knows what I'm thinking. "Noah. Thank you."

The words make me sick.

"For saving me and my sister."

Except I didn't save him, or his sister. If it weren't for me, Daniel would never have been in danger. His father never would have moved their family to Florida. Mara never would have been at the asylum. Jude never would have hurt her—she'd never have met him. Everything that happened to them was because my father *made* it happen. I think about the times I promised to keep her and her family safe, when all the while she was in danger because of me. Just thinking about it makes me want to swallow a bullet.

I can't say any of this to Daniel, obviously, for fear of sounding like a little bitch.

"So this is where the party is," Jamie says as he sweeps into the room. "Guess what?"

Mara raises an eyebrow.

"We've got mail."

He tosses something at me, and I catch it, wincing slightly. My full name is on the cream-colored envelope, otherwise unmarked. Jamie hands one to Mara, too.

"From?" she asks.

"Lukumi. Lenaurd. Whoever that dude is. There's one for Stella, too, but . . ." He holds up his hands as if to say, *What can you do?*

"How do you know they're from him?" Daniel asks.

Jamie holds up a larger manila envelope in his other hand. "It was addressed to 'The Temporary Residents of 313 West End Avenue.' That's us," he adds superfluously.

Mara pouts. "You opened it without me?"

"I thought you might be having sex."

"You would have heard it."

Their banter is intimate in a way. I'm not jealous, exactly, but I feel like a stranger, watching them play together. Left out. Cue violins.

"Who knows, you could've been at it for hours," Jamie continues. "I wasn't going to wait."

All right, enough. "Please refrain from being a tool," I say. "What's in them?"

"I dunno." Jamie shrugs. "I was supposed to wait to read mine till you had yours. Now you have them." Jamie rips his open with a dramatic flourish. Mara begins to open hers.

Daniel frowns. "I feel so left out."

"Count your blessings," Mara says to him, with unusual seriousness.

"You can have mine, if you like," I offer. Mara looks at me queerly. "What? I don't care what it says."

Her eyes narrow. "Can I read it, then?"

I hand it over. She opens it carefully and begins to read, but stops almost immediately. I can't tell if she's afraid or angry or upset; her expression is flat. Blank.

Christ. She looks like me.

She holds the letter out. "It's for you."

"Yes, I'm aware. I'm trying, vainly it seems, to communicate that I don't want it."

"Take it," she says softly. "Please."

Bloody hell. I feel Daniel's eyes bounce back and forth between us.

"I'm . . . going to go make something to eat," he says, backing slowly out of the room. "Come down if you're hungry?"

Jamie waves at him without looking up. Mara says yes.

I finally, reluctantly take the letter from her. I owe her at least that.

There's another envelope inside it, addressed to no one. Sealed. I unfold the note and begin to read.

Noah,

Enclosed is a letter from your mother. I managed to find it before your father did. She left it in an old jewelry box she never used, along with her necklace, which you now wear. If you take it off, I will know of your decision.

A.L.

I want to be strong enough not to read it, but I'm not. Of course I'm not.

Noah, my son,

I'm practically crying already. Jesus.

Most parents, when asked why they want to have children, say that they want to raise a child to be happy. To be healthy. To be wanted. To be loved.

That is not why I had you. I want more for you than that.

I want you to topple dictatorships. To end world hunger. To save the whales. To make sure that your great-grandchildren will know what gorillas look like, not because they have seen them behind a moat, playing with dog toys in a zoo, but because they have tracked them in the mountains of Uganda with sweat bees in their eyes and leeches in their socks. You will see children with bellies fat with worms instead of food. You will sit down to meals, only to find that endangered animals are on the menu. Happiness will elude you, and there will be no rest—you will have to fight every day because there is so much injustice and horror to fight against.

But if you don't fight, you will grow lazy and discontent under the guise of wanting peace. You will acquire money to acquire toys, but the biggest ones will never be big enough. You will fill your mind with trash because the truth is too ugly to look at. And maybe, if you were another child, someone else's child, maybe that would be all right. But you aren't. You are mine. You are strong enough and smart enough and you are destined for greatness. You can change the world. So I leave you with these words:

Do not find peace. Find passion. Find something you want to die for more than something you want to live for. If it is your children, then fight not just for your own but for orphans who have no one else. If it is for medicine, then do not just seek out a cure for cancer but search for a cure for AIDS as well. Fight for those who cannot fight for themselves. Speak for them. Scream for them. Live and die for them. Your life will not always be a happy one, but it will have meaning.

I love you. I believe in you. More than you will ever, ever know.

P.S. when you find someone to fight with, give her or him this.

69

I WATCHED NOAH WALK OUT OF THE ROOM AS HE READ his letters. I didn't stop him. He deserved privacy. I owed him that.

I opened my letter instead. As I began to read, I pictured the professor in his office, my mind filling in details from memories that weren't mine.

Mara,

When I first caught sight of you in Miami, I did not know who you were. I was expecting someone Gifted to walk into the botanica that day, but you? You were quite a surprise.

You have been wondering who I am and what I want from you, but you should have been wondering who you *are. I had hoped you would discover yourself on your own; knowledge acquired on your own means that you are responsible for it, no one else. What you know determines what you do and I cannot afford to change you. It has taken me centuries to learn it, but I have no power to change anything.*

You do, though, and you have. Your will has cleansed the world of some people it is better off without, and others who have harmed no one, not even you. I will not patronize you by absolving you of responsibility—we are responsible for everything we do and do not do. But I will say that you belong to a legacy of others who have faced similar challenges.

Euhemerus wrote that the gods of ancient myths were simply people with greater abilities than most, deified by those around them. Then came Jung, and we, the Gifted, became archetypes. Normal men became gods. Plain women, monsters. We are none of those things. We are simply people, blessed and cursed.

Our abilities could not be explained by science. But these abilities weren't without a cost. We harm ourselves. Ignore wisdom. Throw ourselves into danger. Attempt and commit suicide. We have no greater enemies than ourselves. For most of our history we did not know what was wrong with us, or right—why some of us manifested painfully, others without consequence, why some were ignorant of their origins while others relived moments we had never personally experienced. I have spent more than one lifetime trying to answer these questions and many others, and I am not sure whether my answers have done more harm than good. Without my work the boy you call Jude would never have been polluted. But the boy you love, Noah, would also never have been born.

I believe that every person has a responsibility to leave the world a better place than he found it. My particular Gift allows me to draft a vision for that better world—but my curse is that I lack the tools to build it. I have tried and failed to alter the course of history myself, and have learned that my Gift is useless on its own. And so I have found others to help me, your grandmother among them.

Noah was destined for greatness, until you were born. I had hoped that the manner of his birth would prevent the cycle from perpetuating—the eternal conflict between Hero and Shadow, the curses attendant to Tricksters, Mothers, Wise Women and Men. I had hoped that with my knowledge, I *could end our madness. You are never too old to be susceptible to pride. The universe demands balance, and three months after Noah was conceived, you were conceived as well.*

Noah's Gift is that he could live forever and help others

to as well, but his curse is that he only wants to die. You, Mara, are Gifted with the ability to protect those you love, but only in a way that hurts them and others. You can reward with life, but you must punish to do it.

It has been said that there must be a villain for every hero, a demon for every angel, a monster for every god. Despite what we are, I do not believe this. I have seen the villainous act heroic, and men called heroes act villainous. The ability to heal does not make one good any more than the ability to kill makes one evil. Kill the right people, and you become a hero. Heal the wrong ones, and you become a villain. It is our choices that define us, not our abilities.

Do you know why it is that, even today, women are counseled to scream "fire" instead of "rape"? Because the fundamental truth about humanity is that most people would rather look away.

Whatever your faults—and you have many, Mara, challenges no one else will ever face—you have never looked away. When evil smiles at you, you smile back.

The pendant your grandmother left you represents two symbols of justice—the feather and the sword. Those of us who choose to make a difference in the world have adopted it as a way to recognize one another. Your grandmother wore it. Noah's mother wore it. Whatever you decide will not be the end for you but a new beginning. I encourage you to think carefully; you need not decide today. But do know that it is an irrevocable choice, and it can lead to a lonely life.

Whatever you choose, as time passes, you will grow in strength and conviction, and apart from you, Noah will as well. My hope for him, his mother's hope for him, was that he would help create a better world. Without you, he can.

So even though I already know what your choice will be, I cannot help but implore you one last time. You will love Noah Shaw to ruins, unless you let him go. Whether it is fate or chance, coincidence or destiny, I have seen his death a thousand ways in a thousand dreams over a thousand nights, and the only one who can prevent it is you.

Should you choose to wear your grandmother's pendant, I will know of your decision. But no matter what, we will see each other again.

A.L.

I looked up as soon as I'd finished reading. Jamie was staring at me.

"What did yours say?"

My hope for him, his mother's hope for him, was that he would help create a better world. Without you, he can.

"Stuff," I said slowly. "About me. Yours?"

"Me too. Stuff." He paused. "Do you believe him?"

Without you, he can.

"I don't know," I lied. My mind was crowded with words

I hadn't written, thoughts I didn't think, memories I'd never experienced, and I couldn't untangle them yet. "Do you?"

"I want to," Jamie said. And then he bowed his head and clasped his necklace around his neck before I could say another word. He half-smiled and shrugged one shoulder. "The freaks shall inherit the earth."

70

I WAITED EXACTLY ONE HOUR BEFORE HUNTING NOAH down. I wanted to give him space, but I also wanted to tell him about what I'd read. What I remembered. I wanted to ask him what he thought we should do.

I knew what *I* thought I should do, but I needed to work up the nerve to do it.

I was not the girl I'd been when Noah had met me. I was not even the girl I'd been before Horizons. I've been remade by what happened to me, by the things I've done. I've become someone new; I feel something, I do it. I want something, I take it. Maybe I haven't changed to Noah but I *have* changed. He'd seen pictures, heard words, detailing my crimes, but he didn't watch me commit them. Part of me was glad. There are some things the people you love should never see you do.

And I did love him. Whatever parts of me had been burned away by what I'd been through, what I'd done, that wasn't one of them.

But Noah was like the Velveteen Rabbit. I would love his whiskers off, love him until he turned gray, until he lost shape. I would love him to death. And he would let me. Gladly.

I found him hiding out in a different guest bedroom. He had his duffel bag with him, the one Stella had rescued from Horizons after we left the morgue. He'd finished reading the letter from his mother, but he hadn't come to find me. I wondered what she'd said to him, but I couldn't bring myself to ask.

I stood in the doorway, unacknowledged. "Can I come in?" He was reading something, and he nodded over the edge of his book.

"What are you reading?" I asked, then sat on the bed. Whatever it was, he was almost done with it.

"*The Private Memoirs and Confessions of a Justified Sinner.*"

My book. He must have taken it with him to Horizons. I hadn't even noticed it in his bag.

"Did you like it?"

"No."

"No?"

"The editor never tells you whether the protagonist is mad

or was pursued by the devil. He didn't resolve anything." Noah set the book down on the nightstand. I moved closer, until I could feel his heat.

We'd been exhausted the night before and had passed out without talking, and when I'd woken up this afternoon, Daniel and Jamie had been there with the Lukumi letters. We needed to talk about what had happened yesterday, last night, and what would happen tomorrow, but the words I needed to say to him wouldn't come. All I wanted to think about was today. Tonight.

I was not sure I ever really believed that Noah was dead, but I wasn't sure I really believed he was alive either. I still couldn't quite adjust to the reality of him. There were shadows beneath his eyes, and his cheeks were rough with stubble. The fading afternoon light from the window behind the bed shone through his hair, turning the strands gold. I never wanted to stop looking at him. I wished I wouldn't have to.

Maybe I don't have to yet, I thought. There was so much to say, but maybe I didn't have to say it now. Noah was alive. *Here.* Neither of us was in mortal danger. We were sitting next to each other in a bed. I wanted to reach out to him, but my hands stayed knotted in the sheets.

"I let you die," Noah said casually. "In case you were wondering."

I wasn't wondering. "Because I begged you to."

Noah hesitated before he asked, "Do you want to die?"

"No." It was the truth. I would have, for my brothers, but

I didn't want that for myself. "Do *you* want to die?"

I knew the answer, but I asked the question anyway, because he'd asked me. Maybe he wanted to talk about it. Maybe we needed to.

"Yes," he said.

"Tell me why."

"I don't have the words." His voice was smooth, his expression unreadable, but I knew it masked how worthless he felt, how screwed up and damaged and wrong he thought he was. How he felt responsible for everyone, for me, and how it broke him that he hadn't saved me.

I didn't know what to say to him, so I asked, "Are you thinking about your father?"

His jaw tightened; it was the only sign that he'd heard me. After what seemed like forever, he said, "I'm never going back there."

"To Miami?"

"Wherever he is, I won't be. He's dead to me."

I wondered if that were really true. I hoped, selfishly, that it was.

I remembered the way his father had spoken to him. David Shaw was guilty of many crimes, and the way he'd treated Noah was one of them. I would make sure he suffered for all of them someday. He would be punished, somehow, the way he deserved, before he could hurt anyone else.

But one look at Noah told me this was not the time to

mention it. "What about your sister?" I asked. "And Ruth?"

He stared blankly at the opposite wall. "I'll figure something out, I suppose."

"What will you do? If you don't go home?"

He didn't say anything, just shrugged. I had a bad feeling about where this conversation was going, and changed the subject in fear.

"What do you think about the letter?" I asked him, but he didn't respond except to say, "I'm tired."

He had shut down. I couldn't blame him—he'd had less time to process things than the rest of us, and in a way he had even more to process.

We used to process things together. Before yesterday. Before Horizons.

It was like the life we'd lived before was in some alternate time line. There was something missing in both of us, and when we first met there, we found it in each other. But now, after, everything was different. We'd slipped out of that time line, and that life was lost to us. We were strangers to each other now. We weren't even a foot apart, but it felt like a thousand miles.

Noah stood up, pulled back the covers and held them until I crawled under. I expected to feel him slide back into the bed behind me, to feel his arms wrap around my chest, my waist, to feel his legs tangle with mine. But he didn't. He just gently tucked me in.

"Stay," I said. He hesitated for a moment, but then stretched out next to me.

"I dreamed about you, while you were gone," I said.

That smile appeared again on his lips, just for a moment. "Was it good?"

"Yes," I lied. "Yes, it was good."

He closed his eyes, but I didn't close mine.

"Noah?"

"Mara?" he asked, without opening them.

"Can I ask you something?"

"Anything."

"Anything?"

"There's nothing I wouldn't tell you. No secrets," he said. His eyes opened, and he looked at me, finally. "I hope you know that."

I hadn't known that. I had never before asked what I was about to, because I'd never felt like I needed to hear his answer. But I needed to hear it now. "Do you love me?"

There was a pause before Noah spoke. He shifted in the bed and rested his hand on my cheek.

"Madly," he said, and I felt the truth of it in the pressure of his hand.

But when he took it away, the feeling went with it.

"Do you love me?" he asked.

Hopelessly, I thought. "Madly," I said.

He leaned over me, his long lashes casting shadows on his

cheeks, and kissed my forehead. The words "I need you" left my mouth as soon as his lips touched my skin.

I had never said those words to anyone before, and I'd never imagined I would say them now, even—or especially—to him. But it was the truth, and I wanted him to know it, no matter what happened next. No one else would or could do what Noah had done for me. What he did for me even now.

"You have me," he said back.

But then why did he feel so far away?

71

NOAH

THERE IS SOMETHING DIVINE ABOUT SEEING MY mother's faded words incarnated in the girl beside me. Even while sleeping, she looks like a deadly goddess, an iron queen. Mara is anything but peaceful—even in repose she is a silky gray cloud, bright with the promise of lightning. I will not find peace with her. But there will be no greater passion.

She sleeps with her cheek on my chest as my fingers trace the blades of her shoulders below the sheets. I imagine wings cutting through her skin and unfolding around us, blanketing me in velvet darkness before I close my eyes.

But I startle in my sleep, as if I'd dreamed I was falling over and over and over again. I wake up remembering fragments of dreams; Mara bending to smell a flower, watching it die under her breath. Her stepping barefoot into the snow and watching it bleed red beneath her feet.

Her sleep seems untroubled, her breathing deep and even. Peaceful. How could everyone be so wrong about us? It is impossible that she could make me weak. Next to her, I feel invincible.

I don't know what day it is, or what time; I left the hospital feeling like I could sleep forever, but now I'm restless, so I leave Mara in bed. I descend the stairs. Jamie and Daniel are nowhere to be found. The view beyond the windows is dark, though the sky is edged with gray. They must still be asleep.

I wander the house and end up in what appears to be an apartment converted to a music room. There's a drum set, a keyboard, and a few guitars lying about, as well as a piano at the opposite end of the room, by the garden doors. I head for the piano and sit at the bench. I want to play, but I can't think of any music.

"Is there anything you don't play?"

Mara's standing at the foot of the stairs. Blocking my exit, I notice.

"The triangle," I respond.

She manages a smile. "We have to talk."

"Do we," I say. *I'm caught,* I think.

She holds something in her hand. I think it's my letter, the one from my mother, and I tense, until I realize its hers.

"I don't care about that," I say, and mean it.

She shoves it into my face anyway. "Read it," she says. "Please."

I know the second I begin what it will say, and what will happen when I finish, and with every word my body slackens and I dissociate. We're going to have the same fight again, but this time, for the first time, I feel like I deserve to lose.

I look up when I finish. "What do you want me to say?"

"You heard what your father said about us."

"I'm not deaf."

"And you read what the professor said."

I narrow my eyes. "The professor?"

She blinks and gives an almost dreamy shake of that dark, curly head. "Lukumi, I mean."

I hand the letter back to her. "I'm not illiterate." I want to provoke her, to taunt her, to distract her so she doesn't say what I know she'll say next.

She says my name. It sounds like good-bye.

I want to tear up her letter, pull the words my father spoke, the words Lukumi wrote, out of her brain. Instead I get up from the bench and open the garden doors. It's drizzling outside. I don't care.

She would be right to leave me, after everything. But I'm a coward and can't bear to hear it. She follows me out anyway, of course.

"I'll love you to ruins," she says, and my eyes close. "I get what it means now."

"It doesn't mean anything," I say stupidly, because I can't think of anything else.

"My ability negates yours. With me you're—"

"Powerless, weak, et cetera. I know."

She's quiet for a moment. "It's real, Noah. That you'll die if we stay together."

I don't respond.

"You died already, once."

So did you. "And yet, here I am."

"I need you safe."

"From what?" I ask.

She takes the bait. "Me."

I face her then, armed with my argument. I have no defense for what I allowed to happen to her, what I did to her, so like the asshole I am, I go on offense instead. "You mean you want to protect me from yourself."

"Yes."

"The way my father was trying to protect me?"

A shadow passes over her face. "Fuck you."

A thrill travels down my spine. She's never said that to me before. "Good," I say, and take a step toward her. "Get angry. It's better than listening to you talk in that voice from hell about doing what's best for me as if I'm a child. As if I don't have a choice." I should be screaming. I want to. But the voice that comes out of my mouth is dead and flat. "How could you treat me that way?" I ask, sensing an advantage. "Like him?"

Her nostrils flare. "You have no idea what I've been through."

"Tell me."

But she doesn't, so I speak instead. "I have a choice. I can walk away from you anytime I want," I lie.

"Can you?" she asks. "Can you really?"

That's when I know I've lost.

"Your father said—"

"Don't ever begin a sentence with 'Your father said.' He's nothing."

Mara ignores me. "He said you can't help but want me. That it's like a side effect. I'm not a choice for you. I'm a—a compulsion."

I shrug, as if the thought doesn't wound me the way it wounds her. I don't want to believe it. I can't believe it. "I don't believe anyone can help who they love."

"What if you could?"

"I wouldn't want to."

She pauses, unsure. "Would you risk it, if you were me?"

I already did. "I trust you enough to let you make your decisions for yourself. I wouldn't make them for you."

"I don't believe you," she says plainly.

"You keep hearing and believing that I'm going to die if we stay together. But when? Has your fortune-teller told you that?"

She is silent.

"Maybe I will and maybe I won't, but if I do, it isn't because of destiny or fate—it's because everyone dies someday. We get one life, Mara. You might live forever and I might die tomorrow, but right now we're both here. And I want to spend the time I have with you."

She looks up at me, and I can tell she's going to say something mean. "You didn't want to last night."

"Wrong. I did want to. But considering I gave you a lethal injection not twenty-four hours ago, I thought you might not be in the mood."

A smile flickers on her lips. I move closer. "I don't know how to make you understand what you do to me. Just thinking about kissing you is enough. Feeling your tongue against mine. The way you taste. The sounds you make. Everything. I've wanted you so much, for so long, but in the way you want things you'll never, ever have. Like no matter what I do, you'll always be just out of reach. But when you kiss me? It's like I'm on fire."

Her breath catches, but I'm not quite sure why. Her face is unreadable.

"I want to touch every part of you," I go on, because if I flinch now, it's over. "I want to touch you now," I say, and close the distance between us. I wrap a curl of her hair around my finger and give it a little tug. She shivers. "Maybe I didn't have a choice in the beginning because I didn't understand what I was choosing. But I do now. I *know* now. You are what happiness means to me. And I would rather have today with you than forever with anyone else."

I can tell she wants to believe it, and I pray that she does, because I don't think I can stand to lose her. I can't let her go. Not yet. I take her face in my hands. "We will do this while we can, and when we can't anymore, I will remember the feel of your mouth on me and the taste of your tongue and the weight of your hands on mine, and I will be happy." I whisper against her skin, "If you choose me."

72

THE CHOICES YOU MAKE WILL CHANGE YOU.

The words appeared in my mind, unbidden. I'd chosen Noah before, and I wanted to again, now that we both knew who and what we were. I didn't care if it changed me. I did care about how it might change him.

"You make me happier than I deserve," I said thickly. His touch, his scent, his everything was distracting me.

Noah smiled. "Then why do you look so sad?"

My hope for him, his mother's hope for him, was that he would help create a better world. Without you, he can.

"I have no right to want you," I said, unable to hide my bitterness.

"You have every right. It's your choice. It's ours. We don't have to be what they want."

But we were.

"We can live the lives *we* want."

Could we?

Noah took off his necklace and held it out in his palm. He'd chosen. I closed my eyes and tried to remember his mother's face, my grandmother's words, but it was useless. All I could see was him.

I shook my head. "I tried so hard not to love you."

"Well, you're a failure, I'm sorry to say." He kissed me on one cheek.

"No, you're not."

"No. I'm not." He kissed the other.

"You know, when I met you, I thought you had everything. A perfect life."

"Mmm." My neck.

"I thought you were pretty perfect too."

He stopped, went still. "And now what do you think?"

I didn't answer at first. "You didn't have what I thought you had. I think part of you must have always known how fragile your life really was, if you were willing to risk it for me."

He shook his head. "You don't get what you give me."

I wanted him to say it. Needed him to say it. "Tell me."

"It's like you're a mirror, and you show me who I want to be, instead of who I am."

I closed my eyes.

"When I look at myself, I see nothing," he said. "When you look at me? You see everything." I felt his fingers in my hair, on my neck. "I need to be the person I am with you."

"You're that person all the time."

Noah's expression was uncharacteristically open. Earnest. He meant what he was saying. Believed it. "Maybe sometimes we can only see the truth about ourselves if someone shows us where to look."

I didn't need Noah to see the truth about myself—I found it on my own. But he needed me to see the truth about him.

"Maybe we are codependent," he went on. "Maybe we are fucked up. Maybe I'm stupid and you're trouble and both of us would be better off alone."

"Maybe?"

He ignored me. "I don't care. Do you?"

The list of what he would lose with me was longer than what I could give him. But no. I didn't care.

Noah had seen me scarred and broken, dirty and limp, covered in blood and wearing someone else's smile. He didn't cringe or flinch or hide. He knew who I was, he'd seen what I'd done, and he knew what I would do to *him* someday too. But he was still here. I would be a fool to let him go, and I was many things—a liar, a criminal, a murderer—but I was not a fool.

You can be seen and not loved, or loved and not seen. Noah

loved me, and saw me. But more than that, he chose me. I couldn't give him forever, even though he deserved it. I couldn't keep him safe, even though I wanted to. But I could give him today. Tonight. And I would try to give him tomorrow, and every day after, for as long as I possibly could. It wasn't enough for me, but it was enough for him.

I tilted my head up and asked, "What would you do if I kissed you right now?"

He pretended to think about it for an obnoxious amount of time before saying, "I would kiss you back."

I'd been surviving on crumbs for so long—thoughts of him, memories of us. But now, with him here and close and willing, I realized I'd been starving.

I wrapped my hands around his neck and kissed him softly. His hand grazed the hem of my shirt, and when I felt his skin on mine it was like a storm beneath his fingertips, the rolling of clouds, the snapping of lightning. All at once it was too much and not enough, and I arched against him and kissed him harder, roughly.

You think it can't get worse than wanting someone and not having them, but it can. You can want someone, have them, and want them more. Still. Always. You can never get enough.

We broke apart to breathe, our foreheads still touching. He didn't say he loved me. He didn't need to. I could feel it in the way he pressed my palm against his neck. His eyes were closed, and my heart turned over. He needed me too.

What had happened would always be part of us, but we'd survived it. We were still here. The curtain would fall on us eventually, but I would fight to keep it up as long as I could. For now it was just us, together, and there was nothing in our way.

Still, I heard David's words replay themselves in my mind, in his voice, as I led Noah back into the house and up the stairs.

"He wouldn't love you if you weren't what you are."

But I am what I am. And he does.

73

NOAH

I KNOW WHAT I CAN DO TO A GIRL WITH A WORD, A LOOK, A touch. And I want to do them all to her.

MARA

I PRESSED MY LIPS TO HIS THROAT, AND HE TILTED MY chin up, my face aside. He whispered wicked things against my ear.

I grinned, and unbuttoned his shirt.

NOAH

I KISS HER SOFTLY, TWICE. THEN HER HEAD TILTS, DIPS, and her mouth closes over my heart. As she kisses my burning skin, a shock shudders through me.

Mara is the one I never knew I was waiting for, and as long as she'll have me, I will never let her go.

MARA

I SHRUGGED HIS SHIRT FROM HIS SHOULDERS, AND HE lifted mine from my chest. We shed everything until skin met skin.

And then Noah Shaw showed me why he had the reputation he had.

I shivered at the delicious sting of his jaw as he trailed kisses down the dip in my navel, at his fox smile as he painted me in feeling. Soft, muted, dreamy colors first—ochre and umber and rose with his tongue. My breath caught, and I needed—I needed—

"Hurry," I pleaded.

"Slowly," he said.

NOAH

I THRILL AT HER RISING, ACHING, SWELLING SOUND AS I draw out every torturous kiss. Her muscles tighten and tremble and she grasps the sheets and I glance up, needing to see her face.

She is wild. And I have never seen anything more outrageously beautiful in my life.

But then she threads her hands into my hair and pulls.

MARA

As I drew him up against me, into me, there was a pinch of scarlet.

"Are you all right?" he asked, his voice gentle in a way I'd never heard.

I breathed "Yes" as the color softened and faded. I pulled him closer.

NOAH

I SLIDE MY HANDS UP HER BACK, AND HER ANKLES LOCK around my waist and she takes me in with those fathomless eyes. We are connected: hands, limbs, mouths, bodies, souls. I have never known this.

Mara kisses me and it is sugar on my tongue and champagne in my blood; I want to drown in her taste and scent and sound. Hers is the body electric; she is the high I'd been chasing but never caught until now.

MARA

NIPPING. PULLING. TEASING. TASTING. HIS STROKES were slow, intricate, as they blended and feathered and blushed me into something radiant. The colors glossed and glazed into something bold and bright.

NOAH

EVERY TOUCH COMPOSES A NEW, UNHEARD MEASURE; I am hypnotized by the texture and timbre of her notes as they trill and turn and beat and slide. The sheets are our world, and in them she is finite and infinite, beautiful and sublime, bound in my arms and boundless at once.

I move and her scale lengthens, stretches, rhapsodic and gorgeously violent as her eyes grow dark and threaten to close.

"Stay with me," I nearly growl, trying to bite back my desperation, my fear that she'll slip away. I never want to stop looking at her from here. "Stay."

They flutter open—she's still here, still her. "I need to hear you," she begs in that voice, and I can't refuse her, not anything, not now, not ever. But the words that come aren't enough for this. For her. So I speak in a language she doesn't know.

Je t'aime. Aujourd'hui. Ce soir. Demain. Pour toujours. Si je vivais mille ans, je t'appartiendrais pour tous. Si je vivais mille vies, je te ferais mienne dans chacune d'elles.

I love you. Today. Tonight. Tomorrow. Forever. If I were to live a thousand years, I would belong to you for all of them. If I were to live a thousand lives, I would want to make you mine in each one.

MARA

THE WORLD DISTILLED TO ONLY THE SOUND OF US as we both stretched out on the edge of the world.

The colors shone, burned through. Sienna and crimson and gold, and I swallowed my name from his mouth and he kissed his from my lips, and I was incandescent as I tripped into—

NOAH

BLISS.

The echo of her pleasure hits my blood and takes me with her. Mara is unstrung, unbound, unleashed in my arms.

Finally.

MARA

AFTER, I LAY AGAINST HIM. OUR HEARTBEATS synchronized, and I twined around him like moss on a limb. I was soft in his grasp and he was so solid and warm and *real* against my cheek. My smile wouldn't fade, but the colors began to. Violet to cobalt, then indigo, then black.

NOAH

THERE IS NO SILENCE, BUT THE TIMBRE OF HER sound does change. Grace notes, sweet and blue, sweeping, sliding, falling. I know what they mean.

"Stay," I whisper into her damp, curling hair, as if it's the only word I know. "Stay with me."

But her eyes flutter and shut.

I can't close mine. Mara falls asleep to "Hallelujah."

EPILOGUE

DAWN CREEPS IN THROUGH THE CURTAINS, staining the backs of my eyelids red. I blink once, twice in the near darkness, then stretch. I inhale the scent of Noah's shampoo and smile as I reach over in bed to pull him closer. My hand closes around a piece of paper, though, not his hair.

I prop myself up on my elbow and yawn, scanning the room for evidence of Noah. When I don't find any, I turn on the bedside lamp. His bag is here, and his clothes are in them—not strewn around like mine. We were supposed to be leaving New York today, and it looked like he'd already packed. That wasn't unusual. But not waking up to him beside me was.

I bite my lower lip, remembering his mouth on it last night, and draw back the sheets to look for my clothes. The note flutters to the ground beside me. I pick it up.

Couldn't sleep, went for a run. Back soon. Prepare yourself.
xxxxxx
N

A smile spreads across my lips, so wide it hurts. I'm overpowered by love for him, for this boy who knows exactly what I am, exactly who I am, and loves me anyway, despite it. Because of it. I couldn't wait for him to get back so I could tell him. Show him. A week had passed, but it could have been a year—I would never get enough.

And I don't have to. We have all the time in the world.

I glance at the clock—9:30 a.m.—and shower and dress before heading down to the kitchen. My brother is banging cabinets around, loudly, to announce his presence; a charm of protection against any stray public displays of affection, no doubt. Luckily for him, I was just as embarrassed by our loud colonization of the town house as he was—more, probably. Unluckily for both of us, Noah didn't care. God knew what Daniel heard.

A ferocious blush rises in my cheeks, and I vainly try to hide it with my hair. "Morning!" I chirp. I'm so obvious. "Is there coffee?" I rummage through the pantry, making a ton of unnecessary noise myself.

"In the pot . . . that you just passed."

Right. "Right! Thanks!" I snag a mug from the cupboard.

Daniel shot me a look. "You okay?"

"Yes! You?"

"I'm slowly adjusting to a new reality that includes superpowered teenagers and the entities that try to control them. Are you packed yet?"

Nope. "Mmhmm."

"Car's picking us up at four."

"I know."

He then says what I'm thinking. "It's going to be weird for you at home, isn't it."

I nod.

"But you'll be back soon? That still the plan?"

It was. Once we returned to our respective homes, Jamie would present our proposal to skip our senior years and head directly to college without passing go. It was a real thing, early admissions or something, and it would get us out of Florida faster and with fewer loose ends than anything else we could come up with. And we needed to get out. None of us could imagine finishing out our senior year of high school. It would be hard enough performing for our parents, pretending for them, but I knew I needed the summer. Joseph would be losing not one but two siblings in the fall—it would be hard for him. I wanted him to have the time with us. With me.

Daniel takes a swig of orange juice and then slips his arms

into the sleeves of a long button-down shirt. "I'm going to meet my friend Josh over at Juilliard before we go. Don't forget, car at four."

"I won't forget."

"Oh, also." Daniel spins around on his heels and heads for the hall closet. "You need to start prepping if you're going to test in June." He reaches for something on the top shelf, which is stacked with board games. They topple to the floor.

"Not how I planned that." We start picking up game pieces: Risk, Monopoly, Scrabble. "Oh. Hello there."

I look up to see my brother holding a wooden, heart-shaped piece in one hand; a planchette. From a Ouija board. I look around and sure enough, there it is behind him, lying between Sorry! and The Game of Life. My brother peers at me from the little plastic circle in the middle.

"Wanna play?"

I glare at him, goose bumps notwithstanding.

"Kidding, kidding." He drops the piece back in its box. "This is what I actually wanted to give you." He rummages through the games and then picks up a book: *One Thousand Obscure Words on the SAT.*

I roll my eyes. "What would I do without you?"

"You won't ever have to find out."

I wonder if Daniel knows that I will do anything I can, everything I can, to make sure that stays true.

"Having a little post-breakfast séance, are we?" I turn at

the sound of Jamie's voice. He's staring at the unfolded Ouija board. Not kindly.

"Accident," Daniel says, and tosses the book to me. I stuff it in my new messenger bag as my brother puts the games back in the closet where they belong. "See you kids later," he said with a wave. "Car's coming at four, J."

I look at Jamie once the door closes behind Daniel. "J?"

He lifts his chin. "We've become fast friends. While you and Noah were . . . *busy*."

I walk backward toward the door, slinging my bag over my shoulder. Blushing too. "I'm going out for a walk."

"You? A walk? Since when do you need food, sunshine, fresh air?" Jamie looks around dramatically. "Oh. Noah isn't here. That explains it."

"Shut up."

"Come. Let us find him together," Jamie says, and offers his arm, which I take. We wander a bit before heading to the park. I do not fail to notice the pendant around Jamie's neck; he's developed a habit in the past week of hooking his finger around it while he talks. Mine rests in my pocket, nestled next to Noah's. I haven't made my decision yet.

"So what college am I going to lie to your parents about for you?" Jamie asks, bumping my shoulder.

"Not sure." We walk past a street cart selling roasting nuts; the smell mingles with the scents of dust and metal from the construction being done on the street. "But I like New York."

"Same. I was thinking about Columbia, or NYU maybe. Not sure I'll get in, but I'm black, queer, and Jewish so I got three brochures."

I smirk and catch a glimpse of our reflections in the dark glass of an office window. Not that long ago, I probably would've died laughing at the things Jamie said. But what we've been through has thrown us forward a decade, at least. People who didn't know us would think we looked like teenagers still, and if they saw pictures of us Before and After they might not even be able to tell the difference. But I can tell. Our smiles for cameras are jaded now, our grins at jokes a bit bitter. That's what separated us from the multitudes of Them. We lived harder. Knew better. But we laughed anyway. Laughed because there was nothing else to do but give up.

And I would never give up. I've done terrible things I regret and terrible things I don't. But I don't need to be fixed. I don't need to be saved. I just have to keep going.

We cross the street into the park, and blossoms fall like snow as we walk beneath the trees. The sky is blue and cloudless—a perfect spring day. It's like a dream, light and beautiful and happy, the kind I never have.

"Fancy meeting you here," says Noah. He's right behind us, in slim, dark jeans and a faded black T-shirt. His hair is carelessly tousled and noticeably clean. He's carrying a shopping bag, which dangles lightly from his fingers.

I look him over with narrowed eyes. "How long have you been following us?"

"Forever."

I touch a finger to my lips. "Funny, you don't look like you've been running."

Jamie claps his hands once. "That would be my cue!" He kisses me on the cheek. "I'm going to bid farewell to my illustrious cousin, your illustrious attorney."

"Say hi to her for me."

"Shall do."

"Me as well," Noah chimes in, but Jamie's already walking away. He raises his hand to give him the finger from over his shoulder. Noah's mouth spreads into a grin.

"So where were you?"

He moves the shopping bag farther behind him. "Oh, hookers, blow, the usual."

"Why do I even love you?"

"Because I come bearing gifts," Noah says, and withdraws the thing from the bag with a flourish. A sketchbook.

My cold heart melts a little. "Noah."

"The old one was a bit morbid," he says, the corner of his mouth turning up with a smile. "Thought you could use a fresh start."

I rise on my toes to kiss him.

"Wait," he murmurs against my lips. "You haven't seen the best part."

"There's another part?" I ask as he takes my hand and tugs me toward a bench. He slips the sketchbook under his arm and sits me down by my shoulders.

"Close your eyes," he says, and I do. I hear him turning the pages of the sketchbook. "All right. Open."

I'm looking at a drawing, if you could call it that. But of what, I have no idea.

"I thought I'd christen it for you, so I drew your portrait."

"Oh!" Oh, hell. "It's . . . really special, Noah. Thank you."

He bites his lip. "Mmm."

"But wait." I turn it horizontally. "Why do I have a tail?"

He tilts his head to look at it. "That's not a tail, that's your arm."

"Why is it coming out of my ass?"

He closes the sketchbook. "Behave."

"Or what, you'll spank me?"

He leans toward me. His mouth makes contact with my earlobe, his rough jaw with my cheek, and he says, "That would be a reward, darling. Not a punishment."

My heart is already racing. Gets me every time. "Speaking of," I say softly. "I missed you this morning."

"I'll have to find a way to make it up to you. Have you packed?"

"We have time still," I say, because I'm not ready to go.

Noah knows what I'm thinking. He laces his fingers between mine. "We'll be back."

We would be. I could feel it. I stretch out next to Noah, my head in his lap, my feet on the rail. People weave around us, but it feels like we're alone in a sea of beating hearts and breathing lungs. I watch smoke rise from a manhole across the street, and can almost see it form words in the air: *welcome home.* We could be anonymous here. Just a normal couple, young and in love and holding hands in New York.

I lean down and withdraw a book from my own bag as Noah plays with my hair. It's the SAT book. Wrong one. I drop it back in and finally find the one I'm looking for—a novel, freshly bought, about superpowered teens. Call it research.

"What book?"

I show Noah the cover, then flip to the last page.

"Wait—are you—Mara Dyer, are you reading the ending first?"

"I am."

"You are fascinating."

"I'm weird," I say, without looking up. "There's a difference."

"Really though, how did I not know this about you? This changes everything."

I glare at him and snap the book shut.

"Oh, don't stop on my account."

"I am. I am stopping on your account."

"I'm sorry."

"No you're not."

"No, I'm not. Besides, we should probably be reading . . ." My neck crunches as Noah leans over to rummage in my bag.

He pulls out the SAT book. "This. A Daniel purchase?"

"How'd you ever guess?"

"Here, I'll quiz you."

"Noah—"

"No, no, I insist." He flips through it. "All right, first word: quintessence."

"I do not want to play this game."

He ignores me. "Nom de plume."

"That's not obscure."

"And it's not really a word, is it? More like a phrase. Who wrote this book anyway?"

"Who cares?" I pluck the book from his hands, drop it into my bag, and slip out a notebook instead. And earphones.

"What are you doing?"

I take a deep breath. "I am running away to join the circus. What does it look like I'm doing?"

"The circus would never have you. You're not flexible enough. We're going to have to work on that."

I hit him. Hard.

"Are you going to draw?"

"Nope."

"Shame. I was going to ask you to do me like one of your French girls."

"You're quoting it wrong."

"Am I?" He pretends to look thoughtful. "Freudian slip, I suppose. So what *are* you doing?"

"I decided I need a new hobby."

"Writing?"

"Trying to," I say, annoyed.

"Your memoir?"

Earlier this week, I'd signed a retainer agreement with Rochelle. She is a criminal defense attorney, I'm a criminal—it's a perfect match. We thought Jamie would be able to damage-control most of what had happened to us, in terms of exposure, but I actually want to go public. Rochelle warned me against it, as any good lawyer would, citing the lack of evidence, the possibility of countersuits—all solid arguments. But I couldn't pretend that this last year hadn't happened. People needed to know about it. I needed to share it.

It was Daniel's idea to publish our story as fiction that wasn't really fiction. I swore to Rochelle that I'd change names and redact dates and adopt a pseudonym. She was skeptical, but she knew she couldn't stop me, so she agreed to help instead.

Daniel thought the whole thing was hilarious. *Like a meta-narrative! Oh my God that's priceless.* Jamie wasn't impressed. Noah, as usual, was entertained by the prospect, and even said he'd help.

"Sort of like hiding in plain sight," he'd said when I'd told him my idea. "I like it."

"I'll need your help," I'd said. "There's a lot I don't remember."

"I'll fill it in for you."

"You have to tell the truth, though."

"When have you ever known me to lie?"

"Are you seriously asking me that question?"

"You're hurting my feelings. I've never been anything less than excruciatingly honest. Painfully reliable. Don't you trust me?"

"Yes," I'd said honestly. "I do."

Now I just have to write the thing. How hard could it be?

Noah winds a strand of my hair around his finger and tugs on it, just as I'm about to put one of my earbuds in.

"No one's going to believe it, you know."

I do know, but I don't care. If we had learned anything concrete by now, we had learned this: we weren't alone. There are others like us out there. People that think they're just strange or different or troubled or depressed or sick. They might just be. But they might also be something more. They could become one of us. And they should know it before it's too late.

"The truth should be told, even if no one believes it," I say. I tilt my head to look up at Noah. "The people who don't can love it or hate it or not care and forget they've ever read it. But maybe someone like us will read it and they'll know they're not alone. Or maybe someone not like us will read it but they'll believe and be warned about people who are."

Noah indulges me, as always. "So what kind of story will it be?"

A good question. It isn't horror, even though parts of it are horrifying. It isn't science fiction because the science and the story are real.

I look at Noah, grinning at me with my head in his lap, his hands in my hair, and I think about him and Jamie and my brothers and my parents. People who would do anything in their power to help me, even if they didn't always understand me. People I would do anything for, no matter who I had to hurt or what it would cost. I look back at the blank page, then, and know.

This is a love story. Twisted and messy. Flawed and screwed up. But it's ours. It's us. I don't know how our story will end, but I know how it will start. I pick up my pen and begin to write.

My name is not Mara Dyer, but my lawyer told me I had to choose something.

ACKNOWLEDGMENTS

IT ISN'T EASY TO THANK EVERY SINGLE PERSON WHO HAD a hand in helping with the creation and support of one book, let alone three. This trilogy has been five years in the making, and there are more people who have helped me make it than I could possibly name. Also, I probably thanked a lot of them in previous books, so I'm going to keep this one short and semi-sweet.

Thanks are first due to my editor, Christian Trimmer—I feel so lucky to have your brilliant mind on my side, and Mara's. And to everyone at Simon & Schuster who made this book happen, schedule be damned, I can't thank you enough.

To my agent, Barry Goldblatt—you helped me choose

right when I was tempted to choose wrong. This book is so much better for it, and I am so much happier for it.

My forever-thanks to my family, for their patience with/tolerance of me while this book took shape. It wasn't easy, I know, but I am so grateful.

There are two people I could not have written this book without, and I know this because I tried. Several times. Without you, Lev, this book would not feel right or true. Because of you, it is both. And without you, Kat, I would still be writing it. Forever. Both of you saved me, again and again. I can't ever repay you.

And finally, thanks to those who inspired elements of this story. I tried to do you justice. You deserve it.